'This is truly incredible! My implants have immediately synchronized with every part of this ship and we have become as one in mind and body. It's completely micro robotic and also has a nervous system of its own. I am now in a virtual world and can scan through every galaxy in the known universe almost immediately,' Lady Roseanne said.

'They are also much faster than any other ships built by the federation. Speed is only limited by space-time variations in this continuum, and our minds can function over a thousand times faster than in real time.

Because of its unique InterDrive, we can get to any galaxy within the known universe in minutes. I think our Lordorian friends have excelled once again in yet another clever design,' Lord Malory said.

Chronicles of Galaxy Osmaron series

Chronicles of galaxy Osmaron - I am Shadite

Chronicles of Galaxy Osmaron - The power of One

Chronicles of Galaxy Osmaron - Escape from Andromeda

Chronicles of Galaxy Osmaron - The Solarian Empire

Chronicles of Galaxy Osmaron - Fertilates

Chronicles of Galaxy Osmaron - Infilates

Chronicles of Galaxy Osmaron - Son of destiny

Chronicles of Galaxy Osmaron - Jull, The Supreme Patriarch

Chronicles of Galaxy Osmaron - Battle for Andromeda

Chronicles of Galaxy Osmaron - Battle for Osmaron

First Edition

Chronicles of Galaxy Osmaron

Battle for Osmaron

The wars against the evil Nano-bot Javols will end with this final battle, But this series may continue.

By
Adrian Graye

Nutralian Publishing
http://nutralianpublishing.com

nutralia
An imprint of Nutralia Publishing
5 Brayford Square, London E1 0SG
http://nutralianpublishing.com

This paperback edition 2014
B00005555

First published in Great Britain by
Amazon KDP 2024

ISBN 978-1-0687902-9-4

Printed and bound in Great Britain by Amazon KDP Publishing.

A CIP catalogue record for this title
is available from the British Library.

*To all those that believe in Universal Existence
and respect the lowliest of life; for like babes, -
they are the beginning.*

TABLE OF CONTENTS

Book 3
The fight back

'My love of nature will outlast even the memories of those I truly love.'

God lives in the hearts of all forever,
Evolution itself is beyond nature.
The stream of life does flow.
Invisibly it flows its spirits to and fro.

By Prince Seno of Mond.

Prologue

In the past, the Cosmos had always been a most turbulent place, where the struggle between good and evil had always been played out in diverse ways. Because of certain natural laws of mutual coexistence, the balance between order and chaos had to prevail for evolution and life to exist, and that balance must be in the nature of all things to eternity.

Incidentally our universe is one of many and as a rough minimal estimate there will be as many universes as there are galaxies. Of course with over 1000 billion galaxies in our universe this works out to be an enormous figure.

This hierarchical structure forms a pyramid with the apex of the Cosmos at the very top, then generic Universal Planes that contain universes that are of the same types, with similar laws for matter and causation. Below that we have the Universes themselves, then the Galaxies and finally their Stellar Systems. Stellar Systems contain Planets. Many of these planets contain life-forms, then those electromagnetic based life-forms contain matter which in turn contains other parts, etc. The constituents towards the top of the pyramid are fewer.

Those at the base of the pyramid are numerous. Electromagnetic type matter is a very small part of our universe. It is less than 5 percent of all matter and the only type of active matter that can create our type of living organism that live on stable planets like Earth. However, because of its nature we are unable to easily travel to other stellar systems due to light speed limitation. Other types of matter may travel at any speeds, unaffected by the vacuum of space, which is itself a composite of numerous substances including those that are electromagnetic in nature.

Primitive self-indulgent species should not be allowed to visit other living worlds. Such species would destroy the original occupants for their resources like gold and precious gems. Therefore, light speed limitation would be necessary for those reasons.

In the early days of our universe, from around 2 billion years ago, there were many predator species with advanced technologies that visited worlds and corrupted them for their own evil purpose.

However, there were also the Patriarchs, who although not numerous in number, were even more advanced than the Predators. Those special few constantly waged war against the Predators until a balance was met, then they left our universe never to be seen again, at least not until our present times.

There were just a family of **thirteen** Patriarchs that existed in this universe about 2 billion years ago. They were most likely demonic in nature. But fought on the side of life. They existed for a very long time.

The **eight males** were; **Aron, the father and Bella his wife, Jull, his eldest son, Melka, his youngest Son, Bohemoth, Spasmotim, Tellor and wife Carrol, Roth and Demos.**

The **five female daughters** were; **Corra, the eldest, Kali, the youngest, Isimoth, Carrol, ItiKa.**

The females were just as fierce as the males, but a lot more clever and cunning. God help anyone who would dear face them in battle. Such species were what we would call Demonic Warriors today.

They had evolved within a young universe with many more elements, energies and forces that is present today. As our universe grew old, many of the strange aspects of its nature had been lost due to evolution. Like any living body, as it grows and ages, it irreversibly changes and its once youthful energies soon become spent. Hence, these once great demons could only exist in our present universe with permanent changes to their form and substance.

The Grand Lord of the Seven Universes, Grand Lord Gerra, had decided to bring them back into our universe, with his brand of Class Ten technologies. Their main purpose were to help us fight the evil Javols. They would be the new Titans with the most powerful bodies.

Of all the Patriarchs, Jull was the first to appear, in the form of George Peterson, The Son of Destiny.

Aron, was now Michael with Bella, his future wife Joan. She was his real wife in ancient times. Then there was Corra as Clair. She was priestess of her cult, with the ability of all knowledge. Finally there was Melka as David. They all carried the surname of Longhurst, which was also the surnames of their parents of adoption.

The other eight Patriarchs would enter our universe at a later time as need arose. Although, they had knowledge of their past existence, the Grand Lord had constructed them in such a manner that their bodies and souls were renewed.

The war in Andromeda against the Javols began just after the patriarchs arrival on Earth, now called Solaria. At the initial stage of the war the Javols' population had grown to enormous levels, whereby it was impossible to destroy them by any technological means available, before they absorbed the complete galaxy. The Javols required the blood supply of primal life-forms for their own sustenance and procreation. Soon almost all life within the galaxy of Andromeda had been either absorbed, used for their morbid pleasures or frozen for food.

The Javols were a microid life-form with the ability to change into different forms and were controlled by their MasterMind close to the galactic centre. Their main goal was to multiply and conquer all the local systems within Andromeda, destroying all threatening intelligent species in their wake. Then they would turn their attention towards the local galaxies.

One of the most advanced civilizations at that time realized their time was limited and decided to build a large underworld city beneath the existing city of Cantor on planet Caefon in Andromeda. They were called the Ancients and were also responsible for the creation of the Javols, in a failed experiment.

With the assistance of many advanced minds from our galaxy, The Milky Way or Osmaron, they had engineered a complex plan for the Javols' destruction 3000 years later. That plan had begun with the young surrogate Andromedan humans in New Cantor. They appeared on the scene about 3000 years later. The city of New Cantor had been built over the ruins of the original Cantor many decades after its destruction.

By a universal law, the original six Ancients who had set the plan in motion, had to somehow live to see the downfall of the Javols, but they could only live a limited number of years. Therefore, they stored their specially re-engineered genetic material, which could be used after their death. Those embryonic structures were subsequently used to fertilize unsuspecting females at the appropriate time.

The young six Andromedans were completely different to their ancient parents, who had six fingers and two thumbs with golden hair and piercing sea-blue eyes. While the young had brown hair, brown eyes, with eight fingers and two thumbs. However, behind all their intricately laid plans were the Grand Lord Gerra of the Seventh Universe, who was incredibly clever and had made them create the young six for a completely different purpose.

First of all, they were sent to Osmaron in a special ship, which exploded on route killing all its crew along with several hundred thousand Javols. Therefore, as far as the Javols were concerned no one had left Andromeda to warn the other galaxies. However, during the explosion they were transferred into another dimension, called Gohenna or Goh, where they would miraculously meet the previously dead Ancients. A small part of the surviving ship was able to recreate the complete ship and extend its dimensions for the extra passengers. Nevertheless, the reformed ship and its new crew were still on schedule to Galaxy Osmaron (our Milky Way Galaxy), without even the knowledge of the Javols' MasterMind.

The time of their arrival on Earth was in the latter part of AD2041.

The Ancient Andromedans, on that trip, were; Meron, his wife Lucia and son Tomas, Merian, Sintra and Hamil. They had fewer fingers, with golden hair and piercing sea-blue eyes.

The six young Andromedans on the same trip, who were the surrogate children of the above ancients, were; Jon, Lira, Merol, Julia, Petra and Ecrol, taken in order of seniority. Although they were usually referred to as the children of the Ancients, they were their genetic copies, although not identical and resembled

Caucasian Italians, with eight fingers, brown hair and brown eyes.

Grand Lord Gerra, A supreme being responsible for our part of the Seventh Universe had created a complex plan of plans within plans within plans, that no one other than himself could ever unravel. Its strategies would be enacted over a period of 3200 years. The most important part of that plan had been initiated with the Andromedans arrival on Earth. However, with the escape of the Javols overlords, Dracma and Lupher, from galaxy Andromeda to galaxy Triangulum, a new plan had to be devised to take those changing circumstances into account. Nevertheless, his initial plans were precise and had led to the defeat of the Javols in Andromeda.

He had sent his **Shadite Lumak** two years before to clear the way for their arrival. Lumak's home world was situated in one of the larger globular clusters orbiting the Galaxy of Osmaron. His world was run by large intelligent bee-like creatures called Semonites of which Lumak was a sexless worker. However, for that special mission, he was transformed into a human male before landing on Earth. Lumak was a most brilliant scientist and mathematician, who had soon found a cure for all kinds of cancer and was getting prepared for the conversion of planet Earth by introducing **Class Five** technologies. Those advances included **LPD(Linear Progressive Drive) or interstellar drives, micro-robotics(microids or nanites), advanced bio-engineering and a range of rejuvenation drugs**. The microids were robots no larger than a human cell. They linked together to form complex organisms that could transform into virtually any form and could complete any given task twenty times faster than any normal human.

Around that time the two great space ships Martia and Venusa was made by the people of Polok and Lodor for the Federation. They were composed of microids and were almost two kilometres long and just under one kilometre high. They utilized the most advanced drives that could transfer almost a million passengers across the galaxy in under fifteen minutes. Their presence was symbolized by their beautiful female near human selves also called Martia and Venusa.

Lumak had married, Sarah, from the remote hills in Turkey and both worked together for the enhancement and benefit of all life. Due to the intervention of the Grand Lord, her mind became very powerful. Soon thereafter, she had become president of Solarian Banking and all their ventures on Earth. Later, she became the Empress of Solaria. Solaria was the name given to the arm of the galaxy that contained Earth. But later Earth was also given that name.

At that time the American President was Gerald Fraser, known to his close friends as Jerry. There was also the Andromedan Shadite, Plato, and many Turkish students that assisted Lumak in his experiments while in the USA.

After the evacuation of the remaining Andromedans from planet Caefon in Andromeda, Sarah, Lumak and the other Andromedans left Earth and now reside on a most beautiful world call Eden.

Earth Time... AD 2072

During that time the population of Earth was close to eleven billion and rising without end. Many of the larger rain forest were gone and so were many important species along with their habitats. To prevent the real disasters ahead, it was decided to bio-engineer a specific type of virus that would invade human reproductive organs and stop further children from being born. That disease was christened the Terminal Virus.

Once infected, it could not be removed from the system. Neither could the infected be cured. Just five-hundred million humans were selected for the antidote, which were given as a type of vaccination or through foodstuffs on a regular basis. Nevertheless,, the infected had no symptoms and would live out their normal lifetimes, until the planet's population had gradually decreased to just under the five-hundred million.

During the time of the Antidote distribution, Mallory, his wife Roseanne and his six Amazonian warrior women were in charge, with further assistance from Professor Khan, Sarah's father.

Mallory had formed the global army of Specials, whose main purpose were to secure the Fertilates and their children from violent Infilates. They had also put a halt to most of the paedo smugglers, child kidnappers and other criminal organizations during a period of gross unrest. Once his plans on Earth was secure, he faked a boating accident, where he and most of his family were killed, but had instead left to take control of the stellar system called Polion.

His organization included the following;
Mallory and his wife, Roseanne. Oscar, his famous Roadstar. Carl Marsden, his business partner. Chad Collingsworth, in charge of Specials training in Warland.
The Amazonians, Clara Boden, nicknamed Ebony Blade. Tracy Cummings, nicknamed White Dragon. Joan Kennedy, nicknamed Black Arrow. Nadia Wechsler, nicknamed Wild Falcon. Anne Astor, nicknamed Cold Fury. Joeanne Sampson, nicknamed Still Warrior and of course his loyal Specials. They fought vigorously to maintain order within those chaotic cities at that time.

Earth Time... AD2094

George Peterson, the Son of Destiny, takes charge of his Gang and begin to find answers to discrepancies in the past history of Earth. He soon realizes that the Ancients were really aliens from another galaxy that had made irreversible changes to Earth's technologies and its human population. They also learnt about the existence of the Planet Eden and the Empire of Solaria. They realized that during the period of time since the arrival of Lumak and the Andromedans to Earth, only a few people knew of their true nature and purpose. Those included the past Presidents of the USA and a few scientists.
Nevertheless, George was chosen by the Grand Lord and was soon fulfilling his purpose in the greater scheme of things. The Greater Purpose as it was called. He was also known as Jull the Percussor, with powers to move or transform stellar systems by concentration. Even at the age of twenty-one he had no idea who

his real parents were.

Their organization included the following;
George Peterson, Son of Destiny and his wife Catherine Keenan or Cathy. Incidently George Peterson was the firstborn of Lumak(Professor Jeffery Longhurst) and his wife, Empress Sarah Khan. There was Gerald Fraser Junior, the grandson of President Gerald Fraser of the USA. Donald Fraser was the current president of the USA and the father of Gerald Fraser Junior. At that time he had no knowledge of the existence of Lumak or the Andromedans.

The other members of the gang were; Miranda Fernandez the girlfriend of Gerald Fraser Junior. Barry Stenburg, Tim Chiang and Carol Freeman. Andy Coleman, the Son of Mallory Coleman and his wife Ann Coleman joined the group later. There was also the Roadstar, Oscar, used by George Peterson and their space ship Vogan.

During the period of unrest on Earth, they moved to their newly built city on Mars. It was called Terminus City. From there they began the lengthy war of attrition against the Javols in Andromeda. That was only possible with the existence of the great Omegron Portal. It linked both galaxies as one and was used to transfer many soldiers in an instant to the underground city of Lower Cantor on Caefon in Andromeda.

Earth Time... AD2194 (100 years later)

The war against the Javols still rages in Andromeda. However, the intelligence of the Javols' masters were grossly underestimated. The new Javols' creations or Muts now pose a much greater threat to civilization. They are a lot more cunning and intelligent than their predecessors, without the usually craving for flesh and blood, and can change their bodily shapes more precisely into several forms, including humans.

The return of the ancient Patriarchs in the form of our new Headrons had recently come into existence. They are not of flesh and blood, but of a type of matter that cannot be affected by the natural order, although they could affect the natural order. With virtually indestructible bodies they are given super intelligence and life eternal. They are truly the new Grand Lords of the Universe. With supreme powers at their finger tips they are expected to seal the faith of the Javols and their Overlords.

BOOK 1

THE FIRST JAVOLS DEFEAT

CHAPTER 1

A world apart

Earth time ... 2072 CE

Place ... Tantorian System within the Setti Cluster

With one week before the Javols arrival to destroy him and his world, a worried Karot viewed the still waters of the tranquil bay for a while. Then transferred his attention to the red horizon as the sun dipped below the terminator.

'I sense a change. I don't know what it is?' He said, while Kriss his girlfriend held his waist from behind. The image of the large galaxy Andromeda with its numerous stars, becoming visible again and looming large above them.

'Darling, the view at this time of day is always so spectacular. These days you are always worried for some reason or another. You changed a lot since your last encounter with the Gaean. I wonder what they really are?' she said and he was perplexed by her strange mood.

'You know what they are!' he said looking quite worried. He could not understand the current changes to his world. It was as if a catastrophe was to befall them.

'Ancient folklore says they were once like us and chose a simpler life by modifying their form to the tiniest creatures. What bothers me is they never eat anything and I swear I saw one change into a Scrote beatle before my very eyes. That beatle became three times its original size,' She said.

'That's ridiculous! No creature can do that,' he responded. Then he pulled her towards himself and they kissed passionately. She removed his green Robin Hood felt hat and placed it on her head. Then she ran towards the cabin.

'Catch me if you can!' she shouted.

'I will get you for that!' he shouted back while chasing her towards the cabin. Without even a word, the couple walked towards the lake and began to remove their clothes. They stripped naked and dived into the lake together. At barely eighteen they were fully grown and considered a couple by family and friends.

'I love our current way of life. It's so much better being a simple farmer caring for animals and crops,' he said.

'And family!' she replied. She grabbed him by his legs pulling him under water. He struggled for a while pretending to be at her mercy. Then he got hold of her and did likewise. Then once again they embraced and kissed. Then she left the water and took his clothes, leaving him stranded.

'Please, my love! Have mercy on a poor farmer's boy!' he pleaded.

She didn't show any compassion and ran with his clothes towards the cabin. His only option was to run after her in the nude. She was a fast runner and could not be caught until she opened the cabin's door.

As they entered the cabin the door closed behind them and a light came on to reveal swarms of strange Gaean beatles. Slowly they moved to form letters over the fireplace. Then they fluttered their wings in such a way as to form audible words.

'My god! We are doomed! They will consume us for sure!' she cried. For some reason Karot did not worry about the strange creatures and held her at close range for protection.

'Come on! You creatures!' he shouted, taking a large shovel in hand to repel and squat them.

'Karot and Kriss we are not here to harm you. We are here to warn you of impending disaster. Our world is to be invaded by an alien life. They will kill and eat every single one of you. You have been chosen to collect your people and warn them. These alien monsters will be here in just 20 days. Traps and baits must be laid before we can destroy them and the time left is so short. From this moment you and Kriss have been chosen to be a link between your people and us,' the beatles said. Although petrified where they stood, they were amazed.

Then a few beatles climbed up his body and in a short time the complete shovel had disappeared, as if consumed by a myriad of those creatures. Then they began building something. It resembled a strange weapon they had never seen before. It was a most powerful plasma weapon that was fabricated from materials the could find around the cabin. The two humans observed the situation and could little believe in what they saw.

Then a map appeared on the floor before them.

'This is a safe location for your people. You are to visit this ancient city and open the main doorway. It will lead you and your people into the safety of our underworld. Now go quickly and inform everyone on your world. All large animals must be evacuated within 20 days,' They said. In a blinding flash they disappeared, leaving behind the strange weapon to remind them that the beatles and their warning was real.

My god! They are not glow beatles at all, are they? They are a more superior life-form. Even more superior than us,' Kriss said, still trembling from fear. Karot did not utter a word but bent over to retrieve the weapon.

'You heard the Masters. We have to prepare for war. This is a large world with many races. Everyone should be informed before the arrival of our enemies,' he said and she agreed.

'Perhaps more of these weapons exist within the underworld of which they spoke. We have been a peaceful people since ancient times and have never fought for any purpose. Not even the most disgusting Bane tribes in southern regions,' he said.

'When it comes to saving our family and friends we have little choice, or else everything will be lost. But how do we convince them of the invasion?' She said.

'With this weapon, of course!' he replied. Then he pointed it to an old tree, pressed the trigger and the complete tree became a ball of flames and then dust.

'Is that enough convincing!' he replied.

CHAPTER 2

Beneath the ancient cemetery

'Where have you been? Dad was looking everywhere for you. He wants you to fix the water pump. It's giving problems again,' her brother Sillo said.

'I think it requires some new washers. You mean gaskets. I will collect some from the village,' Kriss replied and emptied the piggy bank of all coins.

'Darling, lets go!' she whispered to Karot.

'Sillo, tell dad I'll be back soon with some gaskets to fix the pump. She said calmly to her brother as he disappeared in the general direction of his friends, to play their game of ball, all innocent of what was to befall them. She had taken more money then was required for gaskets, just in case they had some more travelling to do.

Their near human race had lived a medieval lifestyle for thousands of years without any advanced technologies. Not even basic weapons like spears, swords, bows and arrows had ever been made by anyone. After all, there was never any need in their society and on such a rich world where there was always plenty for everyone. Where competition for survival was almost nil and population maintained by strict code of survival. Being mainly vegetarians, they only used milk from certain animals for making cheese and nutritious drinks.

'Darling, I think this must be the cemetery of which they spoke,' Karot said.

'Let's follow to the old mausoleum over there,' she replied and followed her intuition.

As they approached a large stone shifted to reveal a stone stairway that zigzagged downwards to as far as they could see in the dimly lit environment. As they traversed the first set of stairs the large stone shifted back in place to seal them in.

They followed the stairway with its occasional narrow platforms until arriving at a large doorway with what appeared to be a giant bronze statue keeping guard. Kriss looked down and could observe the stairway receding to a tiny point of light. As far as she was concerned, it probably went all the way to the centre of the planet. Without warning the giant statue began to crumble and in the process became numerous beatles. A large door lifted vertically to unseal an innermost chamber. There was a powerful gush of stale air as it did.

The room they entered was filled with many human statues. As they approached a central pillar a device on the pillar came alive showering the room with brilliant light. It revealed millions of the small insects in rows on what appeared to be a central throne. Then 3D images appeared all around them.

'Once upon a time we were very much like you. Yes, we were also human, but wanted more from the universe. Having ruled these cluster of stars for numerous generations, we turned our attention to our galaxy, but realized our human bodies were too frail for that great mission, so we transformed into our present nanite forms It's a form of matter that could not be destroyed by normal means and could absorb a type of nuclear energy from all matter for our sustenance.

'What you see before you is just a small part of our beings left in this physical universe as a permanent link. Most of us have outgrown this universe and now dwell within a universe of the mind. In the virtual universe where we exist we can live like you if we wish, because it's a universe of the mind where anything can be imagined and anything made possible to everyone's desire. And all our dreams fulfilled,' one of the creatures said. While it spoke a tiny blue light blinked on its tiny forehead. Then another began to communicate.

'Our world is under a great threat from these rapacious monsters,' it said as pictures of the invading Javols fleet were displayed all around them.

'We have extensively scanned their ships with our micro probes and have learnt much about our mutual foe,' it said. Then the image changed again. This time the Javols took one of their Timit slaves and began to skin the near human alive while she screamed in the most excruciating pain. Then they feasted on the body until

not a single part was left.

'They are after all animals on this world for food and will treat you all in the same way. They have already harvested most of our mother galaxy and destroyed most significant life within it. Now and finally they have turned their attention to us,' it said.

Karot almost threw up but embraced Kriss to divert from the evil images. Both realized the existential threat facing their world.

'Before you can be of further assistance to anyone both your minds must be altered. That way you can have a permanent link with us and our main computers. There is too much to learn and only a short time remaining,' it said. Then it's reddish blinking light diminished. Those beatles seemed to hold different coloured lights, perhaps because of their status. Then yet another began to communicate. This time with a greenish light.

'Don't worry, it's a simple and quite painless operation, and there will be no change to your normal mind. You will however become more clever and knowledgeable as a result,' it said. The two humans became quite worried, but realized the operation was essential if they were to save their world.

Several of the insects grouped together and began to build from whatever they could find in the area. Within a short time a strange device took form from the large statues that stood around them. Then a robot lifted the strange device and walked towards Kriss.

'Let me have it first!' Karot shouted and went forward like a sheep for slaughter. Leaving Kriss almost frozen in her steps. He knelt, removed his green Robin-hood's hat and the device clamped over his head. Then a small needle-like was inserted into his skull. The tiny implant was secured while strange images filled his head. He closed his eyes but the images remained. The robot made a few adjustments, the images faded and the lights on the equipment changed to green. Then the robot removed the device and went towards Kriss. Karot turned around and bowed his head to Kriss, advising it was ok and painless. A similar operation was done to her, then the robot took the equipment away to a separate room for cleansing and storage.

'You will each take one of us to guide you on your mission,' the bluey lit one said. Then the red and green ones went forward to be collected by the two humans.

Kriss and Karot hesitated at first, but soon collected the two beatles which they placed within their upper pockets. Then they left the underworld for the surface.

CHAPTER 3

Their journey towards Chemsy

They boarded their two wheeled horse driven cart and moved towards their main city instead of the nearby town. That city was about 50 miles away.

'I just hope Bane can travel the distance. He is a good and study animal when it comes to pulling, but there is not much speed in his legs,' Kriss said.

'At the most it will only take us a day, so make yourself comfortable. We can always get some food on the way,' Karot said and she agreed.

'Even so, how are we going to travel the length and breath of our world to warn every one in time?' Kriss said, bewildered by the impossible task ahead.

'I suppose all we can do is visit our main city and advise the council. Then it will be up to them to spread the bad news. After all, it's too much for any poor people like us,' Karot replied. And she agreed again, despite the fact they hadn't any advanced technologies to broadcast such information and still relied on fast riders and quaint sailing ships. The other three cities were thousands of miles away and any such quaint methods would have taken much longer then 20 days.

'Oooom!' a thought slowly formed inside their minds and several images surfaced.

'It's time you learnt to use your brain implants. They will contain the technologies of our forefathers. With the help of us two, you may construct any technologies, even to visit the most distant galaxies in the blink of an eye. This world, although appearing quite normal and quaint to you is filled with numerous defensive stations. However, you must first learn of those installations and their technologies. For this purpose, we must now put you to sleep, while we journey to your city of Chemsy,' the red lit one said to them telepathically and through their

implants.

In an instant they found themselves travelling through their world as it were in ancient times, perhaps a million years ago.

They were now in a world of numerous cities with structures that jutted miles into the clouds and miles into the surface, with every conceivable type of conveyance. Some systems were so advanced, they would simply disappear and reappear at another location. At that time their world was ringed with satellites of every kind. Amidst the numerous humans they could observe many aliens. Everyone living together and going about their business peacefully and conscientiously. At that time their world was truly beautiful and unpolluted.

They paused for a while as the recording raced towards an important event. At that time everyone wore special silvery suits as if waiting for something dreadful to happen.

Suddenly, sirens sounded and pocket communicators began to blip noisily. Within minutes everyone had dispersed. They had left the cities by every possible means and had gone underground. Then large ships appeared overhead and began to rain massive bombs that vaporized the cities. The conflagration was truly awesome, as complete cities could be vaporized by a single bomb. Yet, so many were dropped to give the impression of gross overkill.

Even so, their destruction was targeted only towards their main cities, which were mainly empty of their previous occupants.

After the dust had settled the ships discharged their crews to the surface to take control, killing every human they could find. The poorer people in the country took shelter wherever they could until the soldiers passed their area. It was those few surface survivors that remained to resettle the surface after the threat had gone.

'Those few surface survivors must be our ancestors, while those that left for the underworld had to transform to their nano-bot forms to survive food shortages and other problems within such a bleak and dark environment. They even created a virtual universe exactly like the one they were used to live in, in order to continue their human existence, despite the fact that their physical bodies were tiny beatles,' Karot said. 'It's a good thing they had acquired the technologies to change all their bodies into the new form, but how could anyone exist for so many generations without any family and children,' Kriss replied.

'What do you mean? I am sure they can have children in their virtual worlds, just like we can in this one. They might even have the technologies to make them real in this world, by giving them a body link,' Karot said.

'You mean to say, they are so clever that they can even make the unreal as real as us?' she inquired.

'My love, what is reality? It's just a blending in mind and body in a particular way. All done through our senses. Whatever we observe and feel is indicated by our brain through to our minds. How do you know whether our brains interrupt those signals correctly?' Karot replied and she was awed by the uncertainty of things in such an uncertain universe.

'Love, the war is not yet over. They have lost all their main cities to give their enemies a false sense of victory,' Karot said as she turned her attention to the enemy's massive fleet. Suddenly and around them the planet came alive as numerous plasma weapons lifted from their concealed bunkers. Within seconds the enemy's fleet was targeted and destroyed. Everyone including those in outer space were vaporized into cosmic dust.

'What a massacre! They didn't expect that, did they?' Kriss exclaimed.

'There is more to come!' Karot said.

They watched a large viewer on board a massive mobile station that approached the world with three moons. It was the world of their enemies. Then an order was given.

'Initiate conversion and fire when I give the order!' the voice said.

Large streams of hot gasses from the nearby star was directed to a large object on the platform near their ship, which tended to get more powerful as it absorbed more gasses. Soon there was a constant stream of hot plasma from the star. Then the order was given.

'Fire!'

Streams of super hot plasma was directed from the star towards the local planet and in an instant the complete world exploded into a billion fragments in one gigantic explosion. Their enemies had been completely obliterated and had fell well into their trap. Since their world was incompatible with their enemies, who wore special environmental suits, they died naturally when their essential resources ran out.

'That was very cruel! A complete intelligent race obliterated in such a short time!' Kriss said, with images of utter destruction of a world fresh in her mind.

'This is to teach us a lesson of what can happen when we close our eyes to technology. This is what might happen when our enemies the Javols get here to take our world from us. This is the reason why our mission is so important,' Karot replied.

Within a few hours they had learnt almost everything, even the technologies their ancient ancestors possessed before they made the choice of becoming indestructible nano-bot beatles. Their minds were saturated with so many ideas that they became like two over-enthusiastic kids that had been starved of essential knowledge all their lives. And they hungered for more.

The two Gaean beatles, with green and red lights they called Min and Moe. They were always in the background ready to fill in the blank areas of their knowledge.

Presently there were about 400 million humans on their world, and a large percentage lived within their four great cities and numerous farming villages.

'We should visit my uncle, Dan, he is just another 20 miles on our way. We can rest and have a proper meal there,' Karot said and she was more relaxed

'I have never seen so many Gaean beatles. They must be coming above ground for a specific purpose?' Kriss inquired.

'*We are repairing and rebuilding our offensive and defensive installations. However, many of us will remain on the surface to ensure our mutual survival from the invaders,*' Min, the green lit Gaean said through their implants. They soon found they were able to communicate telepathically with any Gaean, once they focussed their thoughts on that one.

'They must be leaving their Virtual Universe in droves to save this real one from the invading monsters. Those Javol things must pose quite a threat. It's a pity we no longer have the large ships to destroy their massive fleet?' Kriss said.

'*We have!* Came an answer from within their minds.

'*By the way, in human form I was male and my name is Klif. I am a senior member of our governing council. I am also a warrior and military strategist,*' the one with the reddish glow said.

'*And I am female. My name is Lotti and I am a senior councillor, but also a scientist. You may use our names in future for direct communications,*' Lotti, the one with the greenish glow said. Thank you both for giving us your real names. I never liked calling you Min and Moe.

They soon arrived at Karot uncle's farm to be greeted by his wife Molia and son Jemy. It was another one of those log cabins in a group of other log cabins. Such type of sturdy structures were common place among those farmers. They were simple folk and never relished the trappings of materialism. That was probably the reason why they remained virtually the same for numerous generations. Their society was held back by a certain culture embodied in their religious beliefs that had been laid down since ancient times. Within that culture they were only allowed a small family and gave a small percentage of their farming products as taxes

'Is that Karot?' Dans wife Molia inquired, excitedly.

'The same, my good lady! We are on our way to the city and thought of passing through,' he replied and hugged her.

'You have grown so much!' she commented.

Dan soon arrived with his teenaged daughter, Nora. They were carrying two large cans of milk and a sack of fruit. They greeted each other, the table was laid and they sat for lunch.

'How are your parents? I haven't seen them in ages! We were going to pay you a visit last year, before the main harvest, but one of our animals became sick and infected a whole flock. Several had to be put down to prevent it spreading to our neighbours.' Dan said.

'They are ok for now, I suppose? And Kriss family is now our neighbours. We are going to be together soon,' Karot said.

As customary they all surrounded Kriss and began making a fuss, even offering her more food, to which she declined. She never liked being fussed over.

Suddenly a large Gaean beatle started to walk across the table and Dan fumed with rage.

'These confounded beatles are everywhere these days. I don't know where they are coming from!' Dan shouted while attempting to squash
the creature with a large dusting brush, but instead it disappeared in a flash of bright light.

'Did you see that? What just happened?' He inquired.

'People, I think we have some important talking to do, and uncle you must never try to kill them again. They are here to save us,' Karot said and they were speechless.

What do you mean, exactly? You talk as if they were intelligent. As far as I am concerned they are all vermin, spreading all kinds of disease!' Dan replied.

'That they are definitely not!' Kriss complained.

'Do you know, they sometimes take our crops. Even one of our wheelbarrows went missing. After an extensive search we found the wooden tray when all the metallic parts had been eaten away by god knows what. I tell you, these things are dangerous,' Dan was not amused. He had lost too much over the years.

'Believe me when I tell you they are our friends and are not responsible for the problems you suffered over the years,' Karot was insistent.

'There are also bandits and pirates in the south. These pagans with little faith come from the southern continents to take what little we have by force. My nephew, this world is changing and changing for the worst!' Dan was more insistent.

'Uncle, there are changes, but they are not all bad,' Karot replied.

'Just be on your guard and take some sacks of grain and fruit in case you have to bargain yourselves out of trouble. They also take beautiful females to sell as slaves in their southern markets, so be extra careful!' he said.

'Don't worry about us, Uncle. We are not what we seem and are quite capable of taking care of ourselves,' Karot replied.

Then he took one of the Gaean beatles out of his pocket and placed it on the table. It glowed brilliantly in reddish light.

'Please, meet my friend Klif. He is not just a common beatle but a very advanced life-form, even more than us humans,' Karot said and they were amazed. They gazed at the strange object as if hypnotised by its strange pulsations.

Kriss did likewise and removed the one called Lotti, with greenish glow and placed it on the table'

'This is going to be very difficult for you to believe. Do you remember the ancient ruins that were excavated in the northern territories. During that excavation they discovered many ancient devices, the purpose of which we are still not sure. Well, I know them all and I also know how people existed on our world about one million years ago. That was a very, very long time ago and the people then were millions of years ahead of us in their technologies. However, there was a great inter-planetary war which our ancestors won, after having destroyed most of their great cities. Their quantities could no longer survive on an almost barren world, so they went underground and changed their bodies into a different form, most suited to that type of survival. In effect these Gaeans are our ancestors that went underground in order to survive,' Karot said and they remained speechless.

'What you observe are not beatles, but are instead a nano-bot design that is virtually indestructible. They can live forever in their present forms and can take the shape of any object of an equivalent size,' Kriss said. Then in front of their eyes both Gaeans began to transform into tiny humans.

'Now we have another planetary war on the horizon and they require our assistance. They can build weapons to defend us, but we must make our metals and other raw materials available to them as soon as possible. If we are to survive we must make sacrifices. Our race must win,' Karot said.

'This is truly incredible! I see it but find the whole thing beyond belief. What can we do to help the effort?' Dan inquired.

'I have given instructions for them to manufacture large screens to be fitted in every city square and town centre to inform the population. This is now taking place throughout our world. When the time is right, which is soon, messages will be broadcasted to keep the people informed,' Karot said.

'We only have about 20 days left, so we must hurry,' Kriss stressed.

'In the mean time, we two are to visit the city and inform our councillors of the dangers,' Karot said.

The cart was subsequently laden with more food and grain, and once again they were on the main city road. Karot, with his new weapon was not worried of bandits or highwaymen. He was confident that with his newly acquired knowledge he could engineer himself out of any tricky situation.

CHAPTER 4

Bandits at dawn

After resting and having had a bath, with a change in clothes. The couple were once again on the road with a laden cart. The animal Brutus had also been rested and fed, and took the road at his leisure. All around them were forests, with the exception of the well trodden stone paved path they traversed. Every so often they would pass a side track and sometimes a junction. Close to junctions were usually small inns that sold refreshment and food, but they knew well the hygiene of such places.

'I feel good within myself for a change. I like being on a mission, particularly with you by my side,' Karot said. She was eating a messy fruit at the time and wiped her yellowy lips from the juicy mango-like substance. Then she kissed him on the cheeks leaving some fruity residue behind.

'You disgust me little child. Go to your room this minute!' He shouted in jest.

'So you remembered my dad telling me off when I was a naughty girl. Pity he is gone from us these past two years. Remind me, I must get a present for Ma from the city. She works too hard these days and double since we are away,' she said.

'Well, my love, when we get hitched both farms will be joined as one and we can help each other.' Karot said and she kissed him again.

'What's this place we just passed?' he inquired.

'It looked like a junk yard to me,' she replied.

'Wo! Wo!' he shouted at the animal Brutus and it stopped in its tracks. Then he turned the cart around and they entered the yard. It contained two large mounds of old damaged wheelbarrows, carts and a range of unworkable farm implements. That yard contained almost every possible type of metallic junk.

'These people must travel all over the country to collect such discarded metallic junk. They must supply the main depot for remelting and recycling,' Kriss said.

'We need metals and lots of it. All this can be used to replenish our defences,' he replied.

'Any one around!' he shouted.

'Who is asking!' a voice replied from inside a small shack.

'I will like to purchase some of your metals,' Karot said. Both men were out of the shack like a shot. It was a bad time of year for recycling and also a glut in such metals, which had been over produced for current needs.

'I am Kal, the owner and this is my son, Mikal. We can do you a special deal, if you wish. How much would you like?' Kal inquired.

'The lot and much more besides. Just give me a good price,' Karot said.

'You sure you want all this junk? Where will you put it all, and we are not in a position to make deliveries,' Kal said while casting his eyes on the enormous piles of junk.

'Don't worry, Kal, It will all disappear in quick time,' Karot replied.

'Well, I suppose in better times we would have received about 20,000 in gold coins, but the market has taken a dive, and we might have to hold on to this junk for another year before we can sell it. So we'll take 10,000. Better one in the hand than two in the bush,' he said.

'That grind handle over there, how much do you want for it?' Karot inquired and both men faces sunk with disappointment. They realized their most important customer had changed his mind and had settled for a handle instead.

'Don't worry, Guys. I haven't changed my mind,' he said.

'In that case you can have the handle for nothing,' Kal said.

Mikal went forward to collect the heavy item. After struggling for a while dropped the heavy handle next to Karot's feet.

Karot retrieved the Gaean from his pocket and placed it on the handle. There was a brilliant reddish glow and within seconds there was a pile of golden coins.

'There you are. You have 20,000 in pure gold,' Karot said. They couldn't believe their eyes. Mikal went forward to collect a coin. He checked its lustre and bit hard within his front teeth, but knew the taste of pure gold. Then he nodded to his father, meaning they had a treasure in pure gold. Karot picked up some coins and assisted them with the heavy load into the small shack.

'Now, Guys, You may remain here for a while or come outside to see how we get the job done,' he said and they followed him.

'Remain close to the shack, while I call the troupes,' He said. In an instant the place was swarming with Gaeans as they popped all over the place as if from no where. Within minutes all the metals had disappeared leaving behind a range of equipment and more weapons.

'Guys, we gave you a good price, so why don't we make it a habit. Collect as much as you can from all over the area. Even get all your friends involved. Because when I return next week I want to see a bigger mountain. But it must only be metal. Gold for metals,' Karot stressed.

'Yes Sir! Yes Sir!' they replied as if he had become their lord and master. Then he left the now rich but bewildered men with enough gold to make them the wealthiest in the area.

Soon they were back on the cart and on their way to the city.

'Do you find it strange. Every time we think of getting assistance they are always there, on the scene to help. It is as if we are protected. I think they can also read our minds. To what extent, I don't know,' Kriss said.

'Since our conversion we have become an important part of them. We are now linked via their Multi-bus and must be considered an important part of their collective consciousness and plans. They must also have the powers to convert matter, particularly metals, into different types and must have the power to appear anywhere on the planet at a moment's notice,' Karot said in awe of their advanced capabilities and Kriss was amazed by their advanced technologies.

As they got within five miles of the city, a young couple with a basket waved them.

'Can we beg you for a ride to the city outskirts,' the male said.

They assumed they were farmers with a long way to go on foot.

'Wo! Wo! Brutus!' Kriss shouted and the animal slowed. They soon climbed in.

'Make yourselves comfortable back there. We have just another five miles to go. Help yourselves to fruit. We only have ashcrofts today, but they are quite delicious this time of year,' Kriss said. They helped themselves and put several in their baskets for later, but they didn't give their names as was customary.

As they looked ahead of them they could observe a band of young children riding tall bikes with small wheels. When they glanced behind them they could observe the same amount. Some bikes had as much as two kids, one peddling and the other standing ready to pounce.

'Where did they come from?' Kriss inquired.

'I think they are after our supplies. They are probably feral children from the outskirts. Someone told me there were many about in these parts. They are like circus kids trained to intercept travellers. Leave it to me. I can handle them,' Karot said, but knew little of what to expect.

As the bikes approached they were rushed, while like lightning several children jumped unto the cart and began to take whatever they could handle. Then they jumped back on their bikes. Others got off their bikes and stopped Brutus and the cart. Then a larger cart approached and a large intimidating character got off.

'I am afraid, we are going to take all your possessions, including your cart, its contents and the animal. You can keep the clothes you wear, but I want all your jewellery,' he said. Then their two passengers got off the cart and began to search them for jewellery.

Karot swiped the young man about the face and he fell to his feet with blood streaming down his face, from his nose.

'You should never have done that farmer, now I have to teach you a lesson by chopping something off. I always thought you Vamish farmers were a peaceful lot. Yet yo fight like a warrior from hell,' he said while removing a small sword from a back sheath.

There was a noise like a swarm of bees and two large waves of Gaeans encircled them. He swiped several times at the beatles but in seconds all their weapons and other metallic objects, including bikes had been eaten away, leaving small metallic bars behind.

Even the enemy cart had disappeared less the seats and wooden parts.

The supposed feral bandits took the closest track out of that area with their trousers falling down for want of metallic fasteners. They were too embarrassed and scared of the so-called beatles to remain.

'Please come again, Friends. I enjoyed the company!' Karot shouted as they disappeared in the bushes.

CHAPTER 5

The city council

The remainder of the journey to the city remained uneventful. Yet Karot sensed something strange in the air. It was a feeling of negative change, as if a disaster was to strike them any moment. Then he realized it was just a sense of his own insecurity in facing the top brass in the land. How was he going to convince the nobles and others of their kind of impending disaster? How could he, a poor farmers son convince anyone, particularly those in council, of anything? Then he straightened up and decided to take the plunge full on.

'I don't know much about you, but I feel sticky and need a bath. I think we should rent a room in one of those hotels while we are here and settle in for a while. We can also get some better clothes,' he said.

'With what! I only took along some loose change for food on the way,' Kriss replied.

'Don't worry, Love. I took a few gold coins from the pile I gave Kal. We must have at least a thousand gold bits. So my girl, we are going to sample this town and get some presents for the folks back home,' he said and she was surprised but happy.

They soon arrived at a suitable place with stables, took their cart to one of the yards where they could hook the animal.

'Here, take a few more credits. Keep Brutus well fed and watch our cart. I will give you more on my return,' he said to the boy in charge. Afterwards he took Kriss to the local hotel and booked them two adjacent rooms. When they were settled in, he took Kriss to a local city store. They were soon out of the store with their bags full of clothes and presents.

After having a bath, they had some of their packed food and decided to view the city before making their way to the council buildings. As they approached the city centre all the coaches were pulled by men and there was not a single pool of animal mess. That was because the use of all animal drawn carts were restricted. They had not yet evolved the combustion engine.

Karot wondered at the beautiful stone buildings and widely paved avenues and was awed by it all. Then they approached the great statue of Fane, who had created their present society and set the rules of peace in stone. That great charter of peace was etched into the local wall for everyone to read. It was also written on the four faces in stone on his exalted plinth.

'Once our greatest leader. He was a farmer and gave us the life we have today. Sadly, he was before our time,' Karot said. When Kris closely observed the statue she realized it looked exactly like Karot, with his strange green hat, frilly cotton shirt and black trousers. It was as if Karot was the reincarnation of Fane.

'My god! You are him!' she exclaimed and Karot could not believe his own eyes. They were both identical in form.

'My Love, we have a job to do, so please follow me!' he said and grabbed her hands. In minutes they were walking up the broad stairway towards the council chambers.

'My god! It's Lord Fane himself,' one of the guards exclaimed as Karot walked directly ahead ignoring their comments and passing several bowing guards on the way. Everyone taking their hats off in homage to their once great leader.

'My lords and ladies, we are unable to post guards throughout the route in question to capture a few naughty feral children, who only steal a little food from passers-by,' the elegantly dressed councillor said.

While they were debating in council chambers, Karot and Kriss busted in. The noble lords and ladies were debating a possible way to deal with the bandit problem, when a hand went up and a voice shouted outside of chambers.

'I can assure you, my distinguished lords and ladies, that food is not always on their agenda. The little vermin attacked me this morning and wanted all my possessions, including Jewellery. However, I thought them a little lesson, so you will not see them in this area again. As for our long term survival, I can't see what you people do in this place that can save us from the real dangers now at our horizon. Take it from me when I say, we have some real problems ahead that we cannot solve with words. Therefore, I would like you and all those in authority to listen carefully and know of the grave dangers ahead,' Karot said bravely.

'Everyone stared at the figure as if he was Fane himself. He waved his hand and as if by magic thousands of Gaeans suddenly appeared as if from nowhere. Then they formed into the statue of Fane himself. Then the statue fell apart into numerous Gaeans as they began building a strange device.

Images of their world in ancient times were displayed among them in 3D, showing them their past advanced civilizations with their advanced modes of travel. Then the images shifted to the Javols fleet and the terrible ways of their enemy.

'They will be here in less than 19 days. Therefore, it will be your duty to warn everyone within this world, so they can prepare for the invasion. At the appropriate time you will be guided to many underground shelters where you will be safe. You may use this device for communicating to the other cities. I can assure you that similar devices have been constructed in similar private chambers throughout the planet. But you must convince them of the dangers. I must leave you now, to discuss this new crisis among yourselves, but will be back at the appropriate time,' Karot said and they were humbled.

'Then he snapped his fingers and all the Gaean beatles disappeared in a blinding flash leaving behind the strange equipment. Then he waved, took hold of Kriss hand and both also disappeared in like manner, leaving everyone in the council chamber perplexed by the strange aberration.

'It must be Lord Fane. He has returned from heaven to warn us of the most terrible dangers approaching from beyond,' A young councillor exclaimed. Then most of the petrified councillors stood up and began to observe the strange blinking object on the black pedestal.

'Who are you?' came a voice from within the object.

'I am chief councillor Sasha. I am in Chemsy city,' she said.

'You are my female counterpart. I am speaking to you from Clifton. We saw the strange images and realized we were all in serious dangers together. I have already communicated with the Thricians. They would like us all to get together and assist where ever we can. The strange creatures need metals to build weapons, so we have decided to find as much metals as we can. You may do likewise,' the voice said.

Karot and Kriss suddenly appeared in their hotel corridor.

'How did you do that?' she inquired.

'I was attempting to use my implants recently and realized that being one of them made us able to use most of their powers. All we have to do is think of where we want to go and we can find ourselves there. It's what they call transposition. They have built numerous self-repairing satellites for that purpose. Many of them are so small that they cannot be detected by any means. You should spend some time to learn more about your brain implants through the special menu,' he said and she was amazed. Even so, they still preferred the old ways and did not relish a path to more advanced technologies.

'Do you think the councillors will take what you said seriously?' Kriss asked.

'I don't know. I shall give them a little while to consider what I've said. Yet the technology left behind is compelling. They can now communicate with each other and us, so we'll give them a few days to contemplate their future existence, while we return to our farms,' he said.

'I just hope they are able to come to quick conclusions if we are to get enough metals and materials in time. There is also an evacuation to plan. For that extensive program the people must be aware of the dangers.,' she said.

CHAPTER 6

On their way home

They were back in their rough clothes for their dusty journey home. This time they were not afraid of anyone or anything, less of all bandits. They soon collected Brutus and their cart and were on their merry way. They soon stopped at the breakers yard and were surprised to find the feral children and their chief of bandits assisting in the collecting program.

'Kal, I'm just passing. I'll be back in a few days to take collection and be generous to these poor kids,' he said. They all stared at him in case he gave them away, but instead he made Kal give them an advance on his behalf, so they were doubly thankful.

'Slow, Brutus! There is no need to hurry,' Kriss said and the animal slowed to a steady pace.

'There are so many people walking our route today and not a single cart in sight. It seams our Gaeans were busier than normal,' Karot commented and she realized things were not the same. It was probably the calm before the storm.

'Anyone for a lift!' Karot shouted and an elderly gentleman and his wife jumped on board.

'Thanks for the ride! If you wish we can pay our way?' the woman said and Kriss declined.

'Why are there so many walking the route today?' Karot inquired.

'It's because most of our metals have disappeared. Did you know, the glow beatles have taken everything. I just visited my brother to see if he could help, but they are in the same boat. I don't know how we can survive without our farming implements. But you seem to be ok. This must be the only cart left in the whole country,' she said.

'Pass the word around. We are being invaded by monstrous creatures called Javols. These Gaean Beatles are building weapons so we can defend ourselves and survive. So we must help them as much as we can. The real monsters are on the way and will be here in 19 days,' Kriss said.

Then Karot realized he had to do something to calm the people and put their minds at ease. There were five towns between the city and his farm, so he decided to visit each in turn to explain the reasons for the disappearance of their metals.

While on their way they would shout at the passers-by informing them of an important meeting to be held in the next town. As they approached he jumped off the cart, put on his strange clothes with green hat.

'By god! I have seen you before, but can't remember where. I know you to be important among men,' the old man on the cart said but Karot remained silent.

As they approached the village there were a large crowd of people shouting at their village chief. They appeared to be at the verge of revolt. As the cart drew closer they decided to vent their anger at the person with the last workable cart.

'People! People! Come on! Be quiet!' Karot shouted, but his words had no affect. He lifted his strange weapon, pointed it to a dead tree and it disappeared in a ball of intense flames.

'Now and finally, I've got your attention!' he shouted at them. When he stood they couldn't believe their eyes for he was the express image of Fane, their previous leader.

'I know you guys have lost your metals, but it's a small price to pay for our future survival,' he said.

'He waved his hand as a large screen suddenly materialized on the top of their community building. Then images were shown of approaching Javols and what they would do to their world on arrival.

'The screen will be left here to keep you informed of changes that will effect your lives. You must carefully heed their advice. In the mean time you can make farming implements from wood. This problem will only last for 19 days, before our enemy's arrival. Therefore, you are to stock up with as much food as you can. You will be informed of your evacuation in due course,' Karot said.

'How long will it all last?' inquired a villager.

'Your evacuation will last a little time, while the battle is fought. It should take no longer than one week, but it's difficult to know precisely,' Karot replied.

'Don't worry, you will not be doing any of the fighting. And please help each other during this time of danger,' Kriss said, also dressed in similar clothes with a green hat.

'Now I need some volunteers! You are to visit the country areas and inform others of the dangers. Don't worry, by now the other village screens should be up and running. All these people will need answers. Each of you under my service will receive fifty gold coins per week. But you must each wear a red band around your head to identify you from others,' he said. Several young men volunteered.

'You may use any available transport and animals with saddles. If you are hungry, visit any house or inn on your way and they will be obliged to feed you and your animal, but I don't want to hear any of you taking advantage of others. Just say, the lord commands it to be so,' he said.

Having explained the whole situation to them, the crowd dispersed and would find ways to continue cultivating their lands. Even wooden wheels could be made for their carts to replace those of metal. People always found ways when placed in a situation of limited choice.

'One down and four more to go!' Kriss said and at that moment he realized they were chosen for a special mission. They did the same to another village until arriving at his uncle's farm.

'Wow! This place is a wreck! What happened?' Kriss exclaimed.

'I tried to warn the locals about the dangers, but they thought I was a madman. A local mob including the blacksmith visited our place and took all my tools, even our pots and pans. They cleared us out completely. Almost every farm in the area have lost their tools and implements. I suppose they thought I knew too much and must have been part of a conspiracy,' Dan said.

'Don't worry uncle. Everything will be back to normal soon. Harvest as much as you can and I'll be back in ten days to collect everyone. This place won't fall apart in another 10 days after we leave,' Karot said.

'You know, Uncle, just the thought of disaster can sometimes set people off and may create a worse disaster. Like a self-fulfilling prophecy. If you can, prepare enough for about 20 days. If you face serious problems, you guys can lock up and leave right now with us,' Karot said.

'No, we are ok. They didn't take everything. We have some old stuff in the shed. It's a good thing we held on to them and didn't give them to the metal collector,' Dan said.

'In that case, I'll leave you all now. I have some calls to make in the villages,' Karot said and was immediately on his way to the cart.

'You two, be extra careful. There are a lot of mad people about these days,' Dan's wife Molia said.

'They are just worried and don't know where to turn,' Karot replied. Once more they were on their way waving as they went.

'Brutus will need a very long rest when we get home,' Karot said.

'He is not the only one. This form of transport can't be the most comfortable. I'll have all kinds of aches and pains when I get home. Remind me to make some softer cushions,' she said and he smiled.

'I don't know what I would have done without you by my side. I feel like half a man without you in my life,' he said and she kissed him on the cheek.

They arrived at the other villages. He informed them of the dangers and recruited more young men and women into his organization. They would in turn train others to spread the news for a small price of a few pieces of gold.

When they got home his father was furious.

'Where in hell have you just been? We had all the local villages scouring the place in case you had an accident. Most of all, we needed the cart for market,' Johan, his father, complained.

'Sorry Dad, we had very important business. Didn't you observe the changes with the local people?' Karot said.

'No, nothing out of the ordinary!' he replied.

'Well, all the farmers I met today are missing all their tools and implements. We have great dangers coming from the horizon,' Karot said. Then he went on to explain the situation to his family in detail.

'From now, Kriss is part of our family, so we must collect her mum and young brother. In future we can handle both holdings together. At least until this threat is over,' Karot said.

'You guys are serious?' Rosy inquired.

'We are very serious,' Kriss replied.

'In that case, welcome on board. We could do with extra hands. I knew you guys would always remain together. Now you've made it final, I am happy for you,' Johan said.

'We got you guys some clothes and presents from the city,' Karot said.

'You went all the way to the city?' Rosy inquired.

'We also entered council chambers and he gave one of his speeches to the top brass. They all thought he was the leader Fane, returned from the grave to help his people,' Kriss said.

'Then he emptied his pocket of many gold coins and they realized he was wealthy and a changed person.

'Dad, we are now working for the Gaeans and have to warn others before the invasion. We also have to harvest as much as we can to last us over the period of the battle. During that time you will all be evacuated to an underground shelter,' he said.
Later that day they went for a swim at their favourite spot near the lake.

'You have changed a lot since we met the Gaeans,' she said looking him over from top to bottom, being her usual romantic self.

'I am afraid we have both changed and if we survive this invasion all our societies will have to change technologically. Then the Gaeans can return back to their Virtual Worlds and communicate with us whenever the need arises,' he said. Then he dived into the cool waters and they began to play their usual games.

CHAPTER 7

A glorious transformation

I do love this place. I think your mother will be happier with our family. Then we can all work towards a common goal,' Karot said.

'Of all my dad's estate, I think this part in the hills is the best. He built the little log cabin, you know,' she replied as he chased her towards the same cabin.

As they entered, more Gaean glow beatles could be observed on the walls. Then the ones called Klif and Lotti suddenly appeared on the wooden table in front of them.

'*Your task is not yet completed. You must visit our underworld again to be converted and prepared for warfare. Both of you have been chosen to represent the surface people, in the fight against our mutual enemies. Don't worry, you will be protected and given the necessary weapons. Our enemies are numerous and you must learn certain skills in order to confuse and defeat them,*' Klif the reddish one said through their implants.

'*For this difficult mission you will both be given new and temporary bodies. Don't be dismayed, your original bodies will be kept in a safe place and held in a state of hibernation for several days. Therefore, you must have a feast and saturate your body with as much nutrients as possible. Then you must visit through the same passage to our underworld,*' Lotti, with the greenish glow said, then all the Gaeans vanished from the cabin.

'My god, what do they mean?' a worried Kriss commented.

'I suppose if we have to fight those nasty Javols and win, we'll require stronger and tougher bodies. They will probably transfer our consciousness into such bodies and reverse the process after our enemies have been defeated. That could be the main reason why they gave us those brain implants,' Karot said.

Realizing how advanced those creatures were, Kriss kept her worries to herself, thinking more of saving her people through sacrificing herself, rather then personal safety.

'Can you link our minds directly to the Virtual Worlds?' Kriss asked Lotti through her implants.

'*Yes, we can, but a conduit must be formed between both participants and worlds. I mean the real and the Virtual, depending on which is to be considered Real. For they are all just planes of existence; For what is reality? At the end of the conduit must be a duplicate Identity and a Causator, to affect the substance of the other world. First, one must have a thorough knowledge of the other universe and its laws in order to build the interface,*' Lotti replied.

'*We are now millions of years more advanced then when we were here before, a million years ago. Therefore, you have nothing to worry about. Just leave it all to our capable selves,*' Klif said.

'*You will both be given a place among us and will be able to visit our realms whenever you wish. First, your new bodies must be realized and a permanent link created, when you experience our world from within,*' Lotti added.

Over the following days they increase their food intake to gain several pounds in weight. When the time was right they visited the mausoleum in the ancient cemetery. They followed the same tall stairway, but the place had changed. Instead of a large room, they were guided to a small elevator. As they entered its motor stirred into activity and their container accelerated. They travelled towards the centre of their planet at incredible speed. As they moved they could observe numerous levels flicker through the transparent walls and realize their installations were truly enormous and numerous.

The elevator stopped and a humanlike android came forward to take them away.

'Please follow!' the female said in a mild voice. She took them to a small room and retrieved two silvery environmental suits from a local cabinet.

'While at the lower levels you must wear these suits at all times. This environment contains high levels of chemical toxins that are poisonous to humans and will devour anything of a biological nature. Also, oxygen levels are well below what is required for life,' she said.

They took another elevator and travelled about the same distance into the bowels of the planet. As they entered the new environment was well lit but everywhere was a greenish mist. The place was perfectly clean. No metals or surface materials could be observed anywhere. It was as if the strange air contained a type of bacteria that was programmed to only accept its own kind and environment at the exclusion of all others. Since their suits were of the same material the mist completely ignored the visitors.

They were soon taken to an isolated laboratory that was clear of the greenish mist. Then given a hand to remove their suits. Finally all their clothes were removed. They were both taken to separate gaskets where they were made as comfortable as possible.

'I'm afraid, we must put you to sleep for a while,' another android said.

The nozzle of a small device was placed close to their necks, there was a hiss and they were asleep and dreaming. The gaskets were filled with a vapour or gas and the androids went to another room. Within that room were two large chambers that contained two black figures. They manipulated a few controls and the containers pivoted until they were in the right position. The large black humanoid figures, more like statues, floated out of the caskets and were rested upright on their feet. They were made out of some type of neutral substance that did not reflect light.

'You guys have been waiting in storage much too long. Finally, your time has arrived to save our world,' the chief android said.

'Now we are to prepare your empty minds for new occupants. Then you may commence training,' she said, but the figures appeared to be just lifeless statues.

They were taken to a large chamber and levers were moved. The chamber was filled with brilliance. The operator slowly reduced the brilliance until the only brilliance left was radiated by the two statues. They were now the images of Karot and Kriss, but glowing.

'Where am I?' Kriss inquired, feeling disoriented.

'We have placed you within your new bodies. You must now visit the universe of our masters for a while to be educated in our ways,' she said.

In a moment they found themselves in the Virtual World of the Gaeans. They were in a massive city that was serviced by numerous robots and androids, but was placed in a most beautiful apartment, perhaps miles above the surface of the planet. From what they could observe it was like a floating platform in the sky. Such platforms could be seen everywhere, each in a large bubble and containing numerous buildings. Suddenly a large screen came alive and a human face appeared on the screen.

'Finally, you guys have arrived. I am Lotti and here is Klif. It's nice to meet you both in the flesh. Our symbiots remain behind in your world,' she said and they suddenly realised they were the real Lotti and Klif.

'Everything in this world is exactly the same as on the surface of your world. You will feel pain and have the same experiences, the only difference is that you cannot die. When you get more experience we will show you how to control your environment more to your liking through your implants. You should visit the lower city and experience more our type of existence. Simply think where you wish to be and you will find yourself there in an instant. Tomorrow, we can start your training,' Klif said.

That day they were confused and couldn't travel anywhere, so with the aid of brain implants they attempted to learn the ways of the human Gaeans. They had never known the types of machines and appliances like refrigerators, viewing screens, automatic showers, automatic meal dispensers and such like. Although the Gaeans did not require any of it, they retained the ancient ways to relieve boredom. There were even the occasional demonstrations, riots and strikes to keep everyone on their toes. Those were all human qualities and natural models for any human society to follow.

'I can live in this place. Everything is so automatic. Even the shower is most relaxing. The water is pulsed as it leaves the nozzle and massages the body. It's a pity our real bodies can't benefit,' Kriss said.

'Darling, we, the conscious minds, are our real bodies. We are the ones to enjoy those feelings and bodies are just bodies,' Karot replied and she was amazed by that statement.

The following morning the large screen came alive and the image of Lotti appeared.

'I hope you guys had a relaxing time yesterday. It will take a little while to acclimatize, so don't worry. I would like to take you to meet my leader, so please get ready,' she said and the screen went black.

'Are there many worlds like this?' Karot inquired from the local android.

'There could be an infinity of such virtual worlds and more are being created as we speak. This is our Home Universe, where we invite our friends. This place forms the basis of our existence and represents our surface world as it were a million years ago. Everything is constantly improved and updated. However, no permanent changes can be made without the permission of our governing council,' he said.

Kriss could observe no means of transport anywhere. Everyone travelled through thought so there was no need for any transport.

'This whole world you observe as far as the eyes can see was created for our optimum satisfaction and happiness. However, those that prefer a different world with rougher edges, may select one from many. There are universes of games, entertainment, sports, wars, primitive worlds and others, even a universe of Javols. There are Virtual Universes to suit every individual's taste,' he said and they were amazed.

They entered a large room with numerous floating cubes. In each of the transparent cubes were the governing heads. Each represented their own communities as in ancient times. Their leader who was the most radiant came forward.

'The Symbion warriors are here!' he exclaimed and suddenly all turned around. They floated locally and surrounded the visitors.

'These are marvellous specimens. I think they will defend us well!' he said.

'Have they been properly trained in our ways?' another

inquired.

'They only arrived yesterday. Their training will commence today, with their permission, of course,' Lotti said.

'It's been such a long time since I visited the surface of our real world. It must be quite a beautiful place at this time,' another said. The strange floating cubes represented both male and female.

'You will even sacrifice yourselves for our world?' another asked.

'We shall! It's the only one we know and love!' Kriss replied and they were pleased that the right people had been chosen.

'Give them the full training and spare no experience. Even explain the brain implants if its necessary. The next time they visit the surface they must be like gods among men,' The leader said and returned, followed by the others.

'Our leader and the others that form our main governing council were alive like us once, but they sacrificed their lives while on the surface to save our people. We manage to recover their essence and personalities. Now they rule us justly as they did before, when we occupied your surface world,' Lotti said, with sadness.

'Why didn't you use your original bodies on the surface?' Karot asked.

There were too many of us and such a large body required too many resources. Anyway, it's not the size that counts, but the mental powers of the individual, and mankind is just a byproduct of evolution. It's very frail, with many weaknesses, including susceptibility to disease,' she said and they agreed.

CHAPTER 8

Their training commence

The following morning they awoke early and were taken to a special building with many alien pieces of equipment.

'From this place we can create any type of virtual universe. Since these are created within this main virtual universe, we call them sub-universes and sub-worlds. For your special training, the synthesiser will create a Javols world. Don't worry, I'll always be by your side,' Lotti said.

Within seconds their environment faded into an unknown one with dark skies and myriads of spherical objects darting here and there. Everything about that world was black and bland. Since Javols didn't require light for their survival, it was as if the very essence of life had been drained away from that place ages ago.

Karot and Kriss wanted to run away and hide from the unseen dangers, but instead Lotti's voice entered their minds.

'They cannot harm you, so stay and hold your ground!' she said, sternly.

Suddenly they were observed by a single Javol and numerous numbers of the creatures dived towards them.

'Relax and ignore them. Your body will realize the dangers and vectorize into partial matter. Then they will simply pass through you as if you weren't there,' Lotti said.

They did as she advised and they flew threw their bodies in different directions.

'Now, re-vectorize your bodies by calling on all your powers and see what happens,' she said. They followed her advise and as they approached, they simply melted into sludge.

'Your powerful fields were designed to split their systems apart and prevent them from reforming. Although these fields are not harmful to primals, you should always be a small distance away when activating to full power. Once vectorized, your bodies are impervious to all forms of explosive blasts and melee damage .

However, in full power mode your un-vectorized bodies if damaged are easily repaired, by your inbuilt nanite factory. In your new bodies you are virtually invincible,' she said and they were awed.

They began to practise their numerous inbuilt weapons, given many scenarios until they mastered each and every one. When Lotti was satisfied with their abilities and prowess in the use of different weapons, she took them back to her real world for more training in strategy.

'Darling, I think now we have minds of warriors, even in this virtual form,' Kriss said.

'Our path is a hard and difficult one, but we must pursue it if we are to save our world and its people,' Karot replied and she agreed.

In a flash and they were back within the real universe. They were back within the underworld of the Gaeans looking unto the ceiling. The original laboratory android came forward to check their minds.

'Ah, you are back!' she said.

'Let me explain the many attributes of your most splendid bodies,' she added and they both stood up to more closely observe their new forms in the large mirror, but visually their new bodies were identical to their original ones.

'Come with me!' she said and they followed into another room with large tanks. In both tanks they observed their original bodies floating in a jelly-like substance and in a dreamlike state.

'They are not dead. Just in a type of stasis or hibernation from which they may be awakened. This is in case you decide to use them at a later date,' she said.

'Can we have children in our present forms?' Kriss inquired.

'No, not directly. You are no longer biological. However, if you wish to have siblings, we can arrange them for you. You should realize however, that the process of birth, growth and death no longer exist with your present kind. The nanites that form your present bodies are not made of normal matter and are unable to transform you into a biological form. However, you can be transformed into any animal and at any basic animal size. As a matter of fact, you could shrink to the smallest insect and expand into a massive giant, several times your present size. Those additional attributes of form will be thought to you in due course,' she said, and Kriss realized her desire for normal human children was not possible in their present warrior forms.

'When you were in our virtual worlds, your warrior bodies were not real, however all the things you learnt were as real as with your solid bodies. Everything you experience were the same as you would have in the real universe and actual environments. This is because, training and experience are of the mind and your nanite body is precisely linked with your minds,' she said.

'What other powers do we have?' a bewildered Karot asked.

'You can fragment into billions of nanite structures to form a deadly swarm and form back into yourselves. Your bodies are also poisonous to Javols and carry a most deadly microid virus. However, your weapons are not dangerous to other humans and primals,' she replied and they were surprised.

'Can we eat food as a normal person, while in these bodies?' Kriss inquired.

'Yes! Although you do not contain a stomach as most normal humans, you contain a cavity where all matter can be converted to your type of energy. Therefore, your food may be any material, including metals and such like. Your body also contains many powerful generators for a range of operations. Those link directly with your brain implants and may be learnt with experience. You can also change matter into a different substance through touch, using a type of nuclear virus, but that's a weapon of last resort,' she added.

'Is there any other important things we should know?' a despondent Karot inquired, not wanting to leave anything behind.

'One more thing, since your bodies are not made of normal matter, you may use it to create a nuclear furnace by diving into a nearby star and accumulating enormous amounts of energy to destroy a large object. However, this is a one way operation. Once initiated you may not be able to return to your normal bodies and can only exist on your world by a further transformation, if it's still possible by such methods,' she said and they wondered what other strange powers and attributes their new bodies possessed.

The training android then took them into another area of the laboratory and put them through their paces, while teaching them all the subtler attributes of their new bodies. When she was pleased with the results, it was time for their return to the surface.

CHAPTER 9

Back on the surface

After their ordeal in the underworld, they were completely changed individuals. Both wore black leather garments that made them look like lords among men, but they blended in well with the population.

They soon realized their new bodies could be made to react similar to their originals. The only difference were their improved senses and speed. Since they could complete any task twenty times faster they had to slow their actions when among humans.

Their hearing were over ten times more sensitive and their eyes could adjust to observe over great distances. The main thing that worried Kriss was not being able to have normal children while in those bodies. She wanted normal children and wanted to see them grow up to manhood and womanhood. She also realized sacrifices had to be made for such a unique warrior body, if they were going to win the war against those nasty Javols. Nevertheless, they were still able to visit the small lake for a swim, which gave them hope.

They didn't require vehicular transport anymore. Using their unique navigational system, they could transpose themselves almost instantly anywhere within their stellar system.

'So the prodical children has finally returned!' Johan said as Rosy his wife glanced in surprise. They looked so different and fully grown up.

'We have been altered by the Gaeans to fight our mutual enemies and save our world,' Kriss said and they were intrigued but worried they would lose them.

That day they were accompanied to the surface with the Gaeans Klif and Lotti. They were to assist during the great battle. They had spent just two days in the underworld although appearing months.

With just fifteen days to go they gave orders and the evacuation program began.

With Klif and Lotti's help several underground entrances were opened up and people descended into those places. Many put up tents to isolate them from others. They brought along cooking utensils and food which they kept in cooling boxes, but there were no refrigerators, so they could only remain in those areas for a short period until the food ran out. Nevertheless, they could always return to the surface to replenish their supplies.

On the day before the invasion planetary defences were activated, suddenly many massive satellite stations became visible as a powerful screen was initiated around the planet, sealing everyone in. However, those shields needed a great amount of energy and could only last so long. Then large ground bases opened up with powerful plasma weapons. Those weapons would be initiated by a single order from either Karot or Kriss. They were given full autonomy on the war.

CHAPTER 10

A great Javols loss

Ama-go! Ama-go! Ama-go!' Commander Anago checked through his powerful telescopes and couldn't find any humans in their cities. As he became more furious, he wondered why he had arrived on a world ripe for harvesting when there was not a single human about. Had they been already harvested by some other group of wayward Javols or perhaps the forward scouts relayed incorrect information about their find. Heads will roll and plasma pits filled for roasting, he thought. He turned to his second in command.

'You said your forward scouts had found a thriving society of clots. Now we are here and not a single one in sight, to where have they disappeared? Either your scouts were delusional or they have been previously harvested,' Anago was furious.

'There is a third option, Sir! It's possible they found out about our invasion and planned for it. I think they are hiding from us, but that will not save them,' Kak said.

As they approached the planetary shield, they were not aware of the dangers and unexpectedly crashed into an irresistible but invisible object. As the forward ships crashed into each other there was one gigantic explosion that took out the best part of their fleet. The few Javols carriers managed to slow their progress, but the planetary screen had destroyed their main weapon ships, which left them at the mercy of the ground based beam weapons and space platforms. The war that followed was truly incredible, as numerous Javols ships fell from the skies in plumes of flames, like colliding meteorites. Individual Javols were taken out by smaller weapons. However, the moment they landed their bodies began to disintegrate into blobs of stink matter, similar to animal excrement.

The planet's surface had been contaminated with an anti Javols virus which targeted only Javols.

The few carriers that were left in tact, collected, rescued and salvaged whatever they could and receded from the system as soon as they could. That day Javols payed the price for their arrogance and uncaring attitude towards humans and other primals. It was the real beginning of their downfall within the galaxy of Andromeda.

Although fully prepared for war, Karot and Kriss remained at base directing the automatic weapons from the several screens. Even the Gaeans Klif and Lotti were involved and were pleased with the destruction of their enemies, realizing those particular enemies would never visit again. Therefore, they would recharge their weapons and place them in sleep mode until required again.

Karot and Kriss returned to the underworld, where they transferred back into their original bodies of flesh and blood. They settled down on their farm and had several beautiful children. Those two were blessed as many visited to pay homage to the great couple that would have given their lives to save others. Words of their bravery had travelled far and wide, until many saw it their pilgrimage to visit them. Soon there were more statues of the great warrior Fane or was it Karot the grate.

Their nanite bodies were mothballed in the underworld and would remain that way until needed again. As for Klif and Lotti, they were always present at the small Cabin to chat and excite the kids with a range of games.

BOOK 2

THE FEDERATION ON THE OFFENCE

CHAPTER 11

Two of the greatest warriors

The two Primorphs, Hercules and Ulysses had learnt much since their time with the Son of Destiny, including their preferred game of Golf. Despite their humble past as security for the Son of Destiny and his family at the Hearst Mansion, they had later been given their own identities and were considered human individuals, with many new capabilities, including higher intelligence and human emotions.

Despite those changes to their minds, their bodies were like other types of intelligent microids with the ability to transform into other forms. However, they were not like Javols, who were designed to utilise biological structures for their energy requirements. Primorphs used a nuclear power--pack for energy, which had an inbuilt ten-year lifetime. Further, they were unable to reproduce their kind.

Those limitations were to ensure a short lifespan, in case they were inaccessible when something went wrong. Although faults had never occurred in their designs, their creators had experienced the actions of the evil Javols and didn't wish a re-occurrence of that past mistake. Therefore, they took no chances with such powerful types.

Since their conversion, the two microid giants, Hercules and Ulyses, considered themselves human. While guarding the Hearst's Manor on Earth, they wondered when it would be their turn to play a part in the great wars in Andromeda and elsewhere. After all, they had been designed for such a purpose. The days of Infilates were now gone and their presence in the manor were no longer required, since new robots and androids had taken over the building's refurbishment for Grand Lord Michael, the Chancellor of Earth.

'Your Lord-Master commands! You are to take the Omegron Portal from Mars to the underworld of Under Caefon. While there you will be further instructed,' the thought resounded in their minds, then it snapped and everything went silent. They immediately knew by its carrier that it was their Lord, the Son of Destiny. They also realized it was their first mission in Andromeda and were pleased they hadn't been forgotten. The near metallic creatures, about eight feet tall showed overwhelming emotion and embrace each other like long lost brothers.

Both Primorphs took the Manor's portal and in an instant found themselves diverted from Mars to Under Caefon. On arrival, they were greeted by Meron and Jon.

'You guys never change. Anyway, how is golf on the mansion green these days,' Jon greeted.

'It's now better than ever, but there is much distraction. Every part of the manor is presently being improved for our Lord Chancellor of Solaria,' Ulyses replied. Grand Lord Michael who was the son of the son of destiny was presently the chancellor of Solaria which was now in charge of the Osmaron Galaxy. Solaria was the name given to Earth.

'We have an important job for you both, but it can wait until tomorrow. Today we can visit old friends and later I will update you on your mission,' Lord Meron said.

Despite their different complexions of white and black to match the colours of the two extreme colours of humanity, they considered themselves real brothers and would willingly sacrifice their existence for each other. But they would also do likewise for their Lord and Master, the Son of

Destiny.

Since their recent trip to Planet Eden, Mac had added several new facilities, many of which they did not even know about. In the main, she had improved their ability for hunting and tracking, but they were also aware of their stronger bodies and minds. Their new nuclear power-packs had also been extended in power to over 100 years from the previous 10 years. This was because they had proven themselves to be faithful and reliable since their assignment generations before.

The Primorphs' bodies were even tougher than Javols and could survive almost any environment, with the exception of extreme heat above five thousand degrees centigrade. Those extreme temperatures could only be found in special furnaces and environments within a star.

'The war has been won in this galaxy. All that remain is the mopping up of a few stray elements. That mission has been given to others of your kind. However, there are many other primal life-forms throughout this galaxy that remain hidden or are still enslaved by their evil masters. Those that are hidden must be found and those that are enslaved must be freed. We have now found a way of converting Javols for our own purpose, so try not to destroy, if you can save,' Meron said.

'Do we have assistance?' Hercules asked.

'We have many other warriors throughout the galaxy, which can assist when necessary. However, we have duplicated their MasterMind, which we now call Mastermind. You will be able to communicate directly with our Mastermind and so will all other Javols within Andromeda. So use those facilities to mislead and confuse the enemy. Once they are infiltrated and converted, send a signal to us and that world will be linked by interstellar portal. Using this method, in a short time every part of this galaxy will be linked as one. However, we would like you both to maintain a certain level of anonymity in this mission. Too much is at stake and we do not want novices involved,' Jon said.

'One more thing. Make the Timit people your first priority. We think they are still being reared and harvested by the Javols. Try and locate their main world. Records from the old MasterMind were downloaded before its destruction. See if some reference of their world exists. If not, you might have to do it the hard way,' Meron said.

TIMIT HUMANS

They had evolved on a relatively young world with five major continents, oceans and seas. Although twice the size of Earth, it also had a single moon. That moon was almost twice the size of Earth's own moon and although uninhabited, showed polar ice caps, mountains and valleys. It also had an atmosphere.

That world had evolved reptiles of the snake variety, which were highly venomous. They also had evolved a more efficient metabolism and as a result were much more active. All its life-forms had evolved from a parent snake and as a result were multicoloured and scaly. Some even had a forked tongue and venomous fangs.

The Timit people were blue-green in colour, with a thick skin, but with no scales. Instead, their skin was poisonous to predators when bitten. Many predators simply left them alone, unless threatened. Their eyes were large and almost black, with a vertical iris and their face with broad nose, projected forward.

However, they did not have a forked tongue. Their two hands had four fingers each and were of almost equal size. Their fingers were clawed and slightly webbed for digging and swimming. Their arms and feet were very similar to those of humans.

They had evolved as a most efficient predator. Nevertheless, since they had taken to wandering the surface of their world, they had become hunter gatherers. The Timit had also developed a range of tools out of stone and soft metals to assist them in their survival. They were from a period of evolution that corresponded with stone-age man.

Before the Javols' arrived they had become very successful as a race and had acquired an existence like the nomadic people of Earth, with the future of becoming a great people.

Their masters, the Javols, had occupied their world for over three thousand years. During that time they had been indoctrinated in a manner of servitude. However, obedience was never in their nature. They would usually follow instructions for the safety of their own families, for food and in avoiding the excruciating pain from the Javol's whip.

The whip was a long rope with multi pronged attachments and sharp spikes. It was so designed, that the spikes would penetrate the skin but go no further. Once penetration had occurred, their bodies would release its poisons, which in reasonable amounts would make them placid and obedient. Nevertheless, the poisons reduced their pain and also accelerated the healing process.

'I have searched with the help of Mac, but from their records, their Timits were selected from three unnamed worlds,' Ulyses said.

'Ah... But their victims for sacrifices came from Omi-122289..' Hercules replied.

'I see what you mean. Sacrifices to the Javols gods would be sacred and could only be from the Timit's home world and that world is within Sector Nine,' Ulyses said.

'I suppose, for our own reference we should rename those

three worlds, Omicron I, II and III. Even so, there must be many groups scattered through this galaxy, having been used by Javols for farming and sacrifice. Since they are all linked to our Mastermind, why don't we pretend to be Javol's Muts from Head Office on an inspection tour,' Hercules said.

'In that case, why don't we inform them of our visit, and stress a local inspection of all bases and slave records. That should get them on the move. The other groups can be located in due course. In that case I'll be Bad-Mut and you can play Good-Mut. What do you think?' Ulyses said.

'Perhaps I should be Dirty-Mut and you could be Nasty-Mut?' Hercules replied and they both burst into laughter.

They used two of the Javols' special ships that had been captured from one of their main bases and had arrived on Omicron I, which from records appeared to be the birth world of the Timit people.

Being pretended Muts, they could use their real names, nevertheless, they had decided to use different names during that mission. That was because they wanted no problems, in the rear case that Javols decided to check their records. Having searched through the Javols' records through Mastermind, they chose the names, Mico-x5... for Ulyses and Mica-x5... for Hercules. They had the full history of those Javols and could get more information as required.

The Timits' factory farm was a massive complex and was run on similar lines to Chicken farms on Earth in previous centuries. That complex contained many conveyors and sorting devices for separating the young in their five main groupings.

After birth, the young Timits were only about ten centimetres long. They would be given their first meal of worms and netted for transport to the relevant Javols' worlds. It was considered more cost-effective while they were young, because they were quite rugged, small and did not require much food. Further, they were more susceptible to training within the first six months of growth. After that time they were considered fully grown and given their identity names.

The female Timits were artificially inseminated at the appropriate time with special robots. Those females were held in large houses and fed on berries and worms. They were induced by the occasional treat of their favourite prey when they did what was necessary and remained obedient.

Little pigeon-holes opened to accept the young, which were diverted onto the conveyor. The complete process was shocking to Ulyses and Hercules, who wanted to stop the belts there and then. Nevertheless, they couldn't change those dire conditions until certain other activities had taken place: Their plan to send them back to their original world to live among their type of people.

'Kal ak nod ka ya Central yammi chamna,' Hercules barked at the Chief Captain. That sentence meant, 'In future, they will be dispatched to Central for sorting and distribution.'

The Chief Captain Kalka..., was in charge of that complex. Hercules command was given for all to hear and for them to respect his own status as Supreme Commander in that sector of Andromeda. Then turning to the Superintendent, who was in control of all Timit production in the three systems he sent a thought.

'Asok, We have recently found some of our own superiors taking and sampling our Timits for their own purpose. Mother, have not taken such treachery lightly. As a result, many have been dispatched to Plasma Pits to entertain our active soldiers. I trust your records are in order?' he said.

Their MasterMind was always referred to as Mother by senior Javols. They knew that records were never kept in precise order. Yet, if they found any discrepancies, a deal could be made and such situations brushed under the carpet for certain services rendered.

Asok was a very important senior Javol, who was responsible for all three serving worlds to the Javols' empire. His name, Asok-835-000-000-000-00k, meant that in all Javols he was number 835. From that code Hercules realized he was one of the original Javols and over three thousand years old.

Such an ancient Javol could be of invaluable use to the Federation, if only he could be converted without recourse to subliminals and other psychological weapons of reconditioning, which also altered their memory in the process. The question was: how could he have remained for such a long time without the need for duplication.

He must have a different mentality to most other Javols to have overcome the urge. Either that, or he had been isolated from large groups without the need to eat excessively or absorb large amounts of energy during conflicts.

'Since I must show no bias in this operation, my colleague, Superintendent Mico-X5...will check your dispatch records and report any discrepancies to me. Being your senior, I will make whatever decisions I find necessary if things are not as I expect.'

'In that case, I shall leave it in your capable hands for an honest judgement,' Asok replied mildly and unconcerned.

'Your records do not tally. There are many and numerous discrepancies,' Ulyses (Mico-X5...) said. Then Asok remained a placid stature to await a most undesirable sentence.

'How is that, my lord?' he inquired.

'It is that Mother has records of deliveries to at least fifteen worlds that show a difference between your supplies,'

Hercules(Mica-X5...) said.

'Mother has left it to me, to take whatever measures necessary by way of punishment. I am afraid those also include entertainment of our soldiers in the arena and plasma pit.

'I am afraid I tried my best. However, if I am to die, it's as good a way as any,' he replied.

'You mean to say, you will willingly die without putting up a fight for survival? What happened to common resolve in the face of diversity. Even disgusting primal Clots put up a fight which forms the main part of our enjoyment at the feasts. I don't really know what to think... or do with you. Yet, you have given many years of service to the realm.' Hercules(Mica-X5...) said.

Hercules then went over to Ulyses to discuss matters and communicate with Mother. He then linked with new Mastermind and many Javol Probes were on their way to take control of all three worlds.

'I have made a decision. Mother also agrees with that decision. It is based on your long services to the realm.

'I have decided not to demote you. You and all your staff on these three production worlds will be sent to Senoria III. It is a base world that grow fruits and berries for processing into foods. Because there are no Timits on that world the temptations will be removed. Nevertheless, you are to maintain thorough records for future inspection. Should you require any assistance at anytime, you may use my personal name through Mother. I shall also visit you in due course to assess your station,' Hercules added.

'My lord, I don't know how to show my gratitude. I thought you were going to condemn me to the Plasma Pit, but you have shown me mercy. For this enormous deed I shall be forever in your debt,' Asok said.

'I expect you to be my loyal servant in the future and follow all my orders during your new assignment with efficiency and honesty,' Hercules replied.

'In that case, I shall always be your servant,' Asok replied.

Within days, Asok and his many assistants and guards had left the Omicron worlds for their new assignments. None were aware of their duplication on the worlds they left, or that they were now under Federation management. The Timits would now be indoctrinated into the rules of the Federation. Their factory farms would soon be closed and they would be trained into the use of new farming methods, the products of which they would export to member worlds in the ever growing Federation of Worlds. During that period, their ancient cultures would be revived and they would be once more freed from the shackles of the Javols to evolve naturally.

Hercules and Ulyses became very proficient in such devious methods. It was a lot more efficient than hunting and destroying. They had realized earlier that every life-form was unique in the Cosmos. That nothing was gained through destruction, but everything through gentle persuasion and conversion. Even so, some Javols and Muts were too difficult to convert and only those few were sacrificed for the common-good.

CHAPTER 12

With six Amazonians

Mallory, Roseanne and the six Amazonians with Ebony as leader, hadn't seen much action against the Javols since their first battle within the Javols' base on Caefon many decades since. Being fully trained Specials, Mallory and his gang preferred one-to-one combat, where they could try their skills in battle. It was not long before their wishes were answered.

'Your Lord commands! You are to take delivery of ten of the most advanced fighting ships. Then you are to scan all previously inhabited worlds in this galaxy, Andromeda, for evidence of primal life. With the information now available to you, locate and rescue all life-forms that have survived the Javols' onslaught. You are also required to locate suitable worlds for habitation,' the Son of Destiny, George said.

Within a few hours the special ships had arrived at their base on Caefon in Andromeda. Mallory urgently communicated with his team and they gathered for briefing.

'I have received communication from our Lord. He has chosen us for an important task. As in past, I shall be your commander and my wife, Roseanne shall be my personal secretary, chief physician and coordinator. Ebony will be your captain in chief for passing on my commands. Even so, we are all Commanders in Chief.

This command structure is only for the transmission of orders during our operations. Nevertheless, we shall change the command structure in times when our operations are better suited to those changes.

Now, let us try out some ships,' Mallory said.

'This is truly incredible! My implants have immediately synchronized with every part of this ship and we have become as one in mind and body. It's completely micro robotic and also has a nervous system of its own. I am now in a virtual world and can scan through every galaxy in the known universe almost immediately,' Roseanne said.

'They are also much faster than any other ships built by the federation. Speed is only limited by space-time variations in this continuum, and our minds can function over a thousand times faster than in real time.

Because of its unique InterDrive, we can get to any galaxy within the known universe in minutes. I think our Lordorian friends have excelled once again in yet another clever design,' Malory said.

While scanning in sector four, Ebony found something that did not tally with her intuition and calculations.

'I see it but I don't believe it..,' she said through her implants. They wondered what the danger was and immediately guided their ships closer to protect her flanks.

'What do you see?' Malory inquired.

'It is more to do with what I don't see,' she replied.

'I see what you mean,' Roseanne interrupted.

'Oh, yea... Two planets are missing in their orbits about this star. How can that be?' Malory said, equally surprised.

'Captain, why don't we get closer. But be careful we don't crash into something. That must be some powerful shielding. I wonder if its more Javols,' Ebony said.

'I think we should go into InterDrive and observe while in that mode,' Mallory said.

'That's assuming they haven't already observed us. To be able to conceal a complete world takes a lot of energy and advanced technology. That fact also implies some very advanced minds in their making,' Ebony replied.

It was slow at first, but suddenly cracked into their minds.

'You have been observed and will be destroyed if you continue to survey our systems. You are to immediately break off your surveillance and follow on our beacon,' the voice said through their implants. It had incredible power and was an advanced intelligence with no need for implants.

'Well, they want us to visit, so we shall visit. Anyway,

Mastermind have our location and I'm sure they wouldn't like to have the full might of the Federation down upon them, screen or no screen,' Mallory said.

Without further ado, their ships had been taken over by the aliens and was slowly being pulled towards a large object that appeared to be a space station. When their short-range scanners came on, they could observe an enormous array of these satellite globes as far as they could scan. They appeared to surround the planet and emitted the strange fields that neutralized the planet's gravitation and virtually all its external radiation. Despite zero gravitation the world still orbited its parent star.

'I suppose guys, we should get out and have a look around,' Mallory said, but instead a voice entered into their minds.

'You must vacate your ships and enter the cubicles ahead to be thoroughly cleansed before you can join us at the surface,' it said.

They were worried about leaving their ships, but they were on a mission to locate life, so certain risks were expected. Anyway, ships could always be replaced. All eight entered the complex and the rooms filled with a strange radiation that penetrated their bodies. They wondered whether there would be any detrimental side effects. The reddish light soon dimmed, to be followed by a bright light and they found themselves in another complex. Their head gear told them that they were within the surface of the planet, which was an extensive watery world.

'Look above us. There is fish of every conceivable size everywhere. Its advanced natives must live within its oceans,' Roseanne said.

A large shutter was released within one of the pressurized docks and a giant monster appeared. It was like a medium size whale, but with three horns on its head. Its eyes were bluish and its body was striped.

'You are obviously surface dwellers, while we are aquatic. We have been monitoring your progress for sometime. You have done well against our mutual enemies. Sorry we could not have assisted in your campaign. We are only a few and limited to the oceans of our world,' the creature said.

'If you are so limited, how is it you have been able to construct those enormous satellites,' Mallory replied.

'The satellites are self propelled and everything on our world is built by our robots. Since there is no more building to do, they have been placed in hibernation until next required,' it said.

'Are you called by a name?' Mallory inquired.

'You may call me Phal,'

'Well, Phal, we are from the Federation of Worlds. Our mission is to clear the universe of the predator species we call Javols. Many worlds have joined forces with us for the common good of all three local galaxies. This galaxy of Andromeda has been cleansed and we are now on a mission to locate all remaining primal species that have survived the Javols onslaught. During our present mission, we found your world by accident and followed here to investigate. So this is the only reason why we are here,' Mallory said.

'You have destroyed all of our enemies throughout this complete galaxy?' Phal inquired.

'We have indeed and with the help of our gods,' Mallory replied.

'This warrants a meeting with our High Council. I never thought such a thing was possible. You must remain here for a while and rest. Robots will soon arrive with sustenance. It is extracted from the plants of this world. We are ourselves vegetarians,' Phal said and left.

'What an intelligent species. I suppose quite similar to the whales on our world but much more advanced. I wonder how they were able to build the original robots without hands,' Ebony said.

'There could have been a species like humans before most of this world became submerged,' Mallory said.

'You mean to say, this planet had gone through a parallel development to Earth and Earth would have pass through this stage if it was not saved by the Terminal Virus,' Roseanne answered.

'It is estimated, that after the melting of both polar regions, most of Earth would have been submerged by about 90 metres above present sea levels, covering a much larger surface area. After that period of meltdown, and with the near extinction of mankind, most of the endangered species in the seas and oceans would have flourished. It is possible that during that time there could have been a closer bond between the remaining humans and some of the large marine life. If they had found a way to communicate, it is possible that such creatures could have learnt our technologies and taken them a lot further under robotic control,' Mallory said.

'Not bad,' Tracy said, while tasting the porridge-like concoction. They had their fill of the stuff. It was accompanied by a sizzling liquid which reminded them of Soda Water.

A thought soon entered their implants.

'You are to enter the nearest Transposers. You will be taken to a deeper enclosure where you will meet our senior councillors,' Phal said.

They were taken to another spherical structure, with a large circular area in the centre. All around were the strange creatures. They eluded immense power and gave the impression they were always in control. Yet, the humans felt like mere insignificant creatures amount such giants.

They observed them for several minutes and the one at the point closest to the controls broke the silence.

'You are indeed a most unique life-form. In all our records, we have no mention of your type,' it said.

'I suppose, this is because we are not from your galaxy. We are from your sister galaxy,' Mallory said.

'You are from Suluron?' it inquired.

'We call it Osmaron. But there are similar types like us within this galaxy that have survived our mutual enemies,' Mallory said.

'Did you also remove the vermin from the nucleus of our galaxy with the special weapon?' it inquired.

'Yes we did. Our lords had transposed most of them to the nucleus where they were consumed by the energies of the powerful Hexotron,' Mallory said.

'In that case you must be much more advanced than members of our kind. We have many of our own problems on this world. It is not the world we used to enjoy. It is now encased in a shroud of technology and many of our people have been place in grave trouble as a result. This planetary shielding has caused many of our people to die because of boredom and lack of creativity and beauty. We also get many water-bourne infections due to contamination by a previous land race. Can you help us,' it said.

'One of our main duties in life is to assist all primal species throughout the universe. But in order for our assistance to be of a permanent nature, you must join with us. You have to become a part of The Greater Purpose for the common good of all life. Then your world here will become a part of the federation of worlds. We will not interfere in your local politics, but we hope your young will be thought in the ways of The Greater Purpose, for the protection and enhancement of all primal life,' he said.

There was a period of silence for many minutes, then one individual on the left of the group began to speak.

'Have you seen our type in your travels?' it asked.

'Not in this galaxy. Perhaps they were consumed by the Javols during the three thousand years since their existence. But I can assure you, your kind does exist,' Mallory said.

'Really? Where is that?' it enquired.

'Your type does exist in quantity. They freely exist on my home world,' Mallory said.

'You mean, you are of similar form and relationship to our land species as were on this world,' it said.

'Almost, but not exactly. Today, our galaxy is like one. Our world is accommodated by many species. We all live as one for the common good and assist each other for our mutual benefit. But freedom is considered sacred by all.

Gone are the days when any one species could assume dominancy above others. We all have our strengths and weaknesses and assist wherever we can for the common good,' Mallory said.

'If that is your concepts of existence, you are truly the greatest of all life-forms,' it said.

There was another period of silence and the one at the head began to speak through their implants.

'We would freely give these worlds up to your Federation if we can roam the oceans in freedom once again under blue sunny skies. Then we can become fertile again and bear our young. Can you take us to such a world, with blue skies and beautiful oceans,' it asked.

'I am sure we can. I know of such a place within this galaxy that is not too far from this world. However, we might have to build large transposers to take you there. I can send some of our engineers and advisors to assist you in that move. They can also show you images of the world, including its seas and oceans. With long range portals on both worlds, you will be free to return whenever you wish,' Mallory said.

'You will do all this for us, freely?' it inquired.

'As I said before, we all assist in whatever way we can. To us, primal life is sacred,' Mallory replied.

'In that case, since our existence here is threatened, we shall assist the common cause in whatever way we can in return for our freedom. You have our permission to send your people here to assist us. For that assistance, we and our kind will always be indebted to you,' it said.

'One more thing, we now have the technology to transform any creature into a Universal Form. Such a life-form may carry numerous templates of other forms. Therefore anyone of you can become just like us or indeed any other life-form by a simple transposition. You can always return back to your aquatic form as and when necessary. That will make you a more flexible being.' Mallory replied.

'That is a very interesting notion. Perhaps some of us can try that process and assess its practicality.' The leader said.

The Lumpri were a very advanced species that had taken the reigns of their world since the extinction of land mammals similar to mankind, who had doubtless assisted them in their technological advancement. However, in the process they had added so much technology to their world that it had become a home prison. No more could they have roamed their oceans under a blue sky. The technologies had entrapped them in a boring and uninteresting existence.

Mallory's presence had changed all that. Soon they were freely roaming the oceans and seas of Caefon. When they were given a special project, they would return to their fortified world with its many robots and laboratories.

Their worlds were no more enclosed in shrouds of invisibility. Both worlds were now in free gravitational orbital motion about their parent star and they also could gain the abilities to become another life-form for more adventure on land.

CHAPTER 13

Two worlds apart

The worlds Colmi II and Colmi III within the Solarian arm in Osmaron were both within the same stellar system. They shared similar and almost circular orbits and were equidistantly stationed about their parent star. That star was older than Sol, twice as massive and of greater output.

Those worlds were first visited by President Gerald Fraser and several of the Andromedans about one hundred and fifty years before, but was found unsatisfactory for human habitation at that time.

Colmi II was mainly desert, although with sparsely distributed hardy vegetation and crustaceans. It could have been one of the worlds invaded by predator species about a million years before, but had somehow recovered partially from the trauma of the global destruction.

Colmi III was the complete opposite, with almost continuous rainfall within its many rain forests. It was probably later in its development than Colmi II, and had been ignored by the predator species because of its more primitive life-forms and general unsuitability. It was habitable, with a unique variety of insects and several small species of lizard-like reptiles that lived on land and water.

Both worlds had been assigned by Michael to the Praille and Thoraxi, who had lost their home worlds in Andromeda after the Javol's invasion.

The Praille were more suited to the watery world of Colmi III and had decided to modify small regions within Federation rules of habitation, to minimize changes in its complex eco-systems and food chains.

The Thoraxi on the other hand were from a warmer world and had evolved within desert regions, so Colmi II was their planet of choice. Nevertheless, both worlds would soon be linked by portals to each other and the other Federation worlds. After their assistance in defeating the Javols in Andromeda, both intelligent species were now considered members of the Federation and were rewarded as such.

Venusa's Ship had left Caefon in Andromeda for the return journey to Gatwick Spaceport on Earth now Solaria and finally her home in Terminus City on Mars. As always on those trips, there was a fair exchange of goods and equipment between the settlements on Caefon and Earth. Croydon being the main city of Earth, were presently the main ports of commerce.

However, on this return trip there was a slight diversion to the Colmi systems. Grand Lord Michael, his friends, Lord Andy Colman and his surviving Specials, Grand Lord Vektron and many others were also on their way to Earth for the forthcoming victory celebrations.

The Colmi system contained just seven planets of which four were massive gas giants. As they zoomed unto the screen, they were amazed by their beauty. The most predominant world was very similar to Saturn, with its many beautiful rings. However, being much closer to the parent star, it exhibited a radiant halo of many colours. The most outer gas giants were similar to Jupiter, with many violent storms, as indicated by their many circulating spirals in their upper atmospheres.

Venusa's Ship had touched down on Colmi III. It landed within a fertile area close to the smallest sea. Soon many construction robots, androids and earth moving equipment were on their way to create a large castle and port to Praille specifications.

Then Venusa's ship transposed and in an instant she had landed within a region of Desert on Colmi II. After scanning and surveying the area, a similar crew of equipment, robots and androids were dispatched to clear ground and resume the construction of a city to the specifications of the tiny Thoraxi. When she was satisfied with progress, she was once again on her way to Earth, and her first port of call.

Both life-forms would now begin to build their own civilization in what ever fashion they chose. Since the different species had unique skills uncommon to both, portal links had been fitted to each world. The planets were rich in essential resources and food stuffs, so there was much scope for trade.

Nevertheless, they were now federation members and would earn invisible credits from the Empire. Further, since the empire stretched throughout the whole galaxy, every life-form within Osmaron were considered within the Empire, with rights to all its wealth.

CHAPTER 14

Venusa's ship back on Earth

The massive federation ship Venusa suddenly appeared on the Croydon Space Port. Her visit was expected, and she was greeted by rows and rows of people, all waving the new Solarian flag, with its three main colours of blue, orange and green. Those colours had been chosen by Grand Lord Michael's grand mother, Sarah, decades before and represented the different habitats of primal life within the universe. The colour blue was for the oceans, orange for the deserts and green for the fertile land masses.

Michael and his crew, Andy and his Specials, Bellerophon and his mythical warriors with Chiron and his, Venusa and others suddenly appeared within the reception area of the main space port. At that moment there was an outcry as the large crowds rushed to greet the great warriors from Andromeda. Several councillors, including Lia Chiang led the reception group.

'We are honoured to have the lords, ladies and great warriors of Osmaron among us, so everyone, hip! hip!', Lia shouted and the crowd responded with an equally loud 'Hurray!.

'Beautiful People of Solaria, may I say a loud 'Hello' to you all, on this day of our return home from wars far away in another galaxy. That battle has been fought and won, but sadly it was not the end of our distant enemies. We still have much fighting to do, but that can wait. At present, nothing will deter us from our victory celebrations here and on Mars. So let the people rejoice and let this be a day to remember in perpetuity by all future generations.

'I know many of you wanted to come along and fight with us side by side, but don't worry, you will have your chances in the future. However, I think it may be better if you remained home and took care of business, while we hardened veterans took the stage against the enemy. Personally, I wouldn't like any of you to die if I can help it, because I love you all, my people,' Michael said. With that there was another uproar.

'We also love you, my lord and may you rain over us forever and ever.'

'Because today is one of the greatest days in our calendar, in celebration I have decided to take you all on a tour through the great ship plus a short ride. That is providing the great Federation flagship, Venusa, does not mind. Then you can have a look around her decks and understand what a real space ship is all about. Finally, you will all be treated in her largest restaurant, to whatever refreshments you desire. Sorry, but no alcohol is available on board Federation flagships,' Michael said.

Almost everyone in the space port decided to go for a ride. That included its many uniformed wardens, security and customs offices and others. It was a chance of a lifetime that no one could miss. They were soon taken about her many decks and were astounded by the technologies. Then she suddenly appeared over the great central square in Croydon and released her many passengers through extendable conveyance tubes. During that time she remained afloat under her gravity neutralizers.

There were further celebrations in the square and Michael gave another one of his speeches, then they went back to Venusa's ship and from there transposed to the Hearst Mansion in North America. Michael had set aside the real celebrations for the first of the month that followed. In his opinion a real celebration needed planing and preparation, and all those efforts required time. Soon, Venusa's Ship had returned to Gatwich spaceport and her temporary passengers disembarked, with happy smiles for an incredible experience of a life time.

Michael, was slowly changing the attitudes of the people of Earth to the type more acceptable within the Federation. So he was gradually introducing them to its many advanced technologies and cultures. He wanted a free federation, where everyone could travel freely without the usual stigmas associated with their places of birth or planet of residence. He also knew that because of Earth's sad past, much work was needed to place her on an equal footing with Eden. Yet, he saw it as a challenge and one of his primary goals.

CHAPTER 15

Three sister galaxies

Earth Time... AD2195.

Hexolytes... Ancient demonic predators that existed over two billion or 2000,000,000 years ago.

Drondytes or Drondy... Ancient dragon-like predator life-forms that existed about the same time as the Hexolytes, but continue to exist in a lesser form even to this day.

Patriarchs... Ancient demonic warriors that defended the three sister galaxies against the predators.

Unlike the galaxies Andromeda and Osmaron (our Milky Way), Triangulum was very sparsely populated. Being the home galaxy of the Hexolyte predators, many of its ancient civilizations had been relentlessly preyed upon and as a result many had become extinct during their reign.

There were no Drondy in Triangulum and hence no predatory competition, so most of those worlds had been left virtually in tact after their predators left. Therefore, they were not destroyed with nuclear devices as in Osmaron. As a result, evolution had replaced many of its extinct intelligent species with newer ones.

The reign of the Hexolytes in that galaxy were several eons ago. That was before they had gained the necessary technological knowledge to visit the other local galaxies. During the intervening period several of those worlds had evolved new intelligent species. Many of those more recent life-forms had no knowledge of the Hexolytes or indeed of a previous civilization on their respective worlds. Nevertheless, when they realized their reign was coming to an end, the Hexolytes mothballed most of their bases in that galaxy within well-hidden underground installations. They were a very advanced race and could build their systems to last billions of years. To us Earth humans, they would be like clever demons with all the power and technology that went with their type of cruel and uncaring ideology.

They believed their true nature and purpose of existence was to prey on others, and that predation had been finely tuned over the eons to feed on the pains and discomforts of others in the most efficient and excruciating ways.

Although ancient Hexolytes attempted aggressively to conquer all life within Galaxy Osmaron (our Milky Way Galaxy), they had serious competition in that galaxy in the form of the Drondy, who were as predatory as they were. Therefore, they didn't have it all their own way.

The Patriarchs were even more advanced than the Hexolytes and had taken a stand against all predatory species wherever they could be found. They were themselves like demons and had evolved since ancient times as brilliant warriors and statisticians and would not see their home galaxy overrun by predator Hexolytes, so they vowed to vanquish them wherever they existed. Since the destruction of their home world close to the nucleus of the galaxy, they had wandered throughout Osmaron, protecting and nurturing its promising life-forms. Their intentions were that such life-forms would eventually take up the fight against their mutual enemies. Once they were found suitable, the Patriarchs left and were never seen again until now.

The Patriarch war-lords were from a single family that number thirteen, and had accepted responsibility for all their few remaining people. With their incredible powers, they were like better demons, but with the added abilities to destroy worlds. They were not the type to use ships, and had engineered a range of portals on uninhabited moons throughout the three galaxies. Those were known as the moons of Endor. In time, those formed an immense network from which they would attack their enemies.

The Hexolytes had created their own portal networks in Triangulum and were going to do the same in the other galaxies. However, they were constantly being pursued by the Patriarchs, and had to spread their Hexolyte production plants throughout that galaxy to avoid detection. With each part of the complex factory being in a different stellar system. That way, if a unit was found and destroyed, another could quickly take its place.

The Patriarchs had also engineered many inter-dimensional prisons, and diverted Hexolytes and other predator species into such prisons, usually entering its clutches by their own plans backfiring. Such were given the name 'prisons of their own making'. Yet, while within such prisons its prisoners were given an element of freewill as part of the rules of their imprisonment. In most cases, they were simply kept in a temporal loop for eternity. Within such loops time would repeat over a period corresponding to a fraction of the natural lifetime of its captives.

Of the three galaxies, Andromeda was the most populated. Unlike the other two, it had not evolved many advanced predator species. When the Hexolytes visited, it was at the end of their reign and they hadn't time to gain a foothold. As always, their intension was to saturate the galaxy with numerous portals. However, the Patriarchs knew their intentions and laid traps in unexpected places. They were soon ensnared into those traps, stripped bare of their encasement suits and placed in concealed containment tanks for eternity.

Nevertheless, after the more recent creation of the Javols, and their predation on all its numerous species, the Andromeda galaxy became the least populated of all the local galaxies. The predation of the Osmaron galaxy also came to an abrupt end at the time of the Hexolytes' defeat in Andromeda and elsewhere. Predators like the Drondy were not very technological, and relied heavily on the designs of others. So they posed little threat after that time. Many of the Drondy descendants still exist throughout Osmaron today.

There was a region within Osmaron that was affected by predation more than any other. That was the group of constellations towards the end of the Solarian arm of our galaxy. That region although consisting of many stellar systems, were composed mainly of dead worlds and were the most unpopulated.

Those worlds were once highly populated but had since been destroyed by the two competing predators, the Hexolytes and Drondy. Those worlds had been mined and blasted in ancient times with nuclear weapons, leaving behind the tell-tale signs of massive craters and planetary dust rings.

Such regions now contained many of the Federation's factories, mining and production facilities, which were sited away from populated worlds. Therefore, there was a high chance of infiltration by Javols and Muts in those volumes of space. Further, Martian miners were presently involved in the mining of several of those worlds and their moons, so there was a link between Martian colonists and Polion, as that dead part of the galaxy was called.

Polion II was the main controlling planet in that sector and its jurisdiction was under Mallory, his wife and their seven Amazonians.

After the discovery of the two Muts on Mars, security within those remote systems had been tripled, but many of those stellar systems contained concealed ancient enemy portals that may have led to places unknown. Many could have been revived by the Hexolyte masters, Dracma and Lupher, from as far away as Triangulum, if one of their main Portals was still operational somewhere within Osmaron. Therefore, the search was on to locate all such portals and neutralize them. Lumak, Plato, Gemmi Doff and Micol (The Ship), led the relevant crews on that special mission.

CHAPTER 16

Evil Lupher leave Andromeda

The evil Lupher had left his base near the nucleus of Galaxy Andromeda to join his brother Dracma in the galaxy of Triangulum. Both brothers had realized the coming invasion by the Osmaronites and had deceived the Javols by controlling their MasterMind with and AI computer which took their place.

Being elemental in nature they were unable to leave that part of the galaxy before for want of a special cloak that would protect them from the present universe, which had significantly changed from when they were Hexolytes billions of years before.

When the Javols released them from their containment tanks, those two Javols were instantly possessed and taken over, so Javols were non the wiser and accepted them as their superiors. The scientist Lupher would soon create their MasterMind to control all Javols throughout that galaxy. They used H-wave, a non-electromagnetic type of communication that could span the whole galaxy and beyond.

Since those ancient demons were originally from Galaxy Triangulum, that galaxy still contained many of their numerous underground bases filled with Hexolyte containment tanks. Those tanks were still operational in holding many Hexolytes even after several aeons. They would use their life-forces to replenish their own demonic forms. Although encased in a special cloak there was always losses which had to be replenished. Anyway, with their new Javols Muts those Hexolytes were no longer required in their plans to conquer the universe.

Before leaving galaxy Andromeda Lupher had set many long term plans in operation. Therefore his original base contained a massive portal that led to a hidden manufacturing plant. The whole purpose of which was the creation and dispatch of super fast space ships. However that base with all its operators and equipment was soon found and dismantled, then mothballed by the Osmaron Federation. During that process their original

MasterMind had been replaced by the Osmaronites' own Mastermind. Therefore the link from Andromeda to Dracma and Lupher had been permanently severed. No more could they deceive and contaminate life in that galaxy.

'Brother, our special ships are late! And I have lost all connection with MasterMind. I think the Clots have destroyed our base and its installations.' Lupher commented with indignation.

'The Clots could not, but our enemies the Patriarchs like Aron and Jull could well have. Didn't I tell you I sensed their presence in the fifth. As I have predicted they will kill all pathetic Javols within that galaxy. Which will be a very useful thing.' Dracma replied.

'But Brother, when they finish their onslaught we will be next. We must make plans!' Lupher said.

'To where shall we go. If we carry on with our current plans while they are in Andromeda, our Muts can be conquering their home galaxy, Osmaron. They can't be in two places at once.' Dracma replied with confidence.

'Brother, I miss my Timits! Life in these everlasting cloaks will never be the same.' Lupher said.

'I know! Their blood and meaty legs were always so delicious. Not to mention the sacrifices. All that we shall miss while in our original forms.' Dracma replied, unconcerned.

'Brother if everything goes to plan, very soon we shall have billions of Muts. They will make a great invasion army. They can infiltrate the Clots at their highest levels, even without their knowledge. So do not worry Brother. The Patriarchs and their Clots will pay dearly for what they have done to our base in Andromeda and their deceits. Anyway, we do not require those fast ships anymore. Our Muts can change into anyone of those moronic Clots and even travel through their portal links to anywhere. So we shall have the last laugh.' Dracma grimaced.

Well, Brother, now with our special cloaks we can travel anywhere within the known universe. Finally we are free of these pathetic monstrous Javols and their bodies. We are now free to eventually conquer the whole universe. That has always been my dream.' Lupher said.

'Our dream, Brother!'

'Nevertheless, I still miss my Timit women. We should try to find a similar species in this galaxy. We can always possess another primal to enjoy such painful pleasures.'

'Brother, I have passed that information on, so please be patient.' Dracma replied.

'Although we can survive, these metallic cloaks limit our abilities and we still loose small energies. Perhaps we should possess a couple Muts. Then we shall be less limited and able to travel as they do, without the restrictions imposed.

'That can only happen if we remain close to the nucleus of this galaxy.

CHAPTER 17

Mut's factory

Somewhere within the galaxy of Triangulum, Dracma and Lupher had decided to build a massive complex for the creation of their new Javol mutations or Muts.

These new types could easily be fabricated from ordinary Javols by adding certain types of microid virus to their bodies. It took two Javols to form a single Mut, so Muts were almost double their size. The new Javol so formed had similar characteristics to their original form, but were not as greedy as their original type, could not reproduce and followed their master's orders precisely. They made the perfect soldier in a changed universe, where the original Hexolyte soldiers were no longer essential.

Several specialized types could be produced and trained; some for combat, others for infiltration and doppelgangers or shape-shifters... using virtually any form of disguise and there were the enormous types or giganteum monsters. Those types could combine hundreds of Muts into a single individual to destroy towns and cities. The latter were not yet required and would be produced at the onset of battle.

Their new MasterMind in Galaxy Triangulum was not the same as the Federation's Mastermind, which had been constructed to mislead Javols for another reason. Dracma's Mastermind had been constructed close to their production installations on that world, known as Riporan and had been designed to snare Javols on their way to that galaxy.

As Javols arrived from their long trip, they were weak and vulnerable from hibernation making them easy prey for those snares.

Once they were caught in those numerous traps, they would involuntarily be guided through and processed. Such Muts could exist for long periods without food and could take all required energy from those they absorbed while on their missions. Further, as part of their programming it was necessary for them to take the form of those they absorbed. That way, they could infiltrate the Federation and over a short timescale take over areas of control.

However, despite their ability to change form into humans and others of a similar mass, their metabolism was very different. Their microid cells could not fully absorb all types of molecules from living cells, as a result those leftover parts would decay and attract all kinds of disease and germs. This caused all Muts to stink to high heavens, which was not obvious to their kind. So they could easily be detected by humans and trained dogs.

Dracma knew that it would take many decades to create a suitable army of Muts. The rate of conversion relied on the amount of Javols approaching that part of the galaxy. He also realized that their numbers would increase with time. Further, there were numerous numbers approaching Osmaron and he thought of a similar factory in that galaxy. However, it was still ruled and occupied by primals, so that project would be difficult if not impossible.

Therefore, in the mean time the two brothers would bide their time, by choosing suitable advanced civilization to convert to their own evil ways, until the time was ripe for revenge. Before he could mount his reappraisal, he would first convert all the ancient bases in Triangulum to the latest technologies. That task could be accomplished with his current Muts, androids and robots.

The two vile brothers who were originally the leaders of the Javols in Andromeda had also realized that the normal unmodified Javols left behind in Andromeda were a constant threat to all primal life and could deprive them of their conquests. After all, Javols were not truly evil. Just stupid, ignorant, greedy and obnoxious creatures without a single thread of creativity within their pathetic bodies. How could anyone wish to exist in a universe lacking all its diverse forms of creative life-forms. Replacing all primal and intelligent civilizations with ravenous Javols was not a notion worth contemplation. After all, it was the clever planning and other painful pleasure that made the fight worthwhile, not eating and procreating.

The Ancient Patriarch Aron now in the form of Michael Peterson, Son of Destiny, realized the real war against the Javols would now be fought in Galaxy Triangulum and later Osmaron. He also realized all threats had been removed from Andromeda with the defeat of the main Javols fleet. Nevertheless, the Javols commander Exo Zero or XoMir and about one hundred thousand warriors still remained on a local world. If they remained in that part of the galaxy they could have become a serious problem for the human populations on Caefon, so he came up with a dire plan to use them against the Muts in Triangulum.

'Commander Exo Zero Mother has been tricked and left unsecured by our chief commanders Eco_1 and Eco_2. As you well know they were responsible for protecting our esteemed mother. Only a small part of Mother now remains. They have destroyed the complete base. The Clots have also tricked us with powerful machines. I'm afraid you are what remains of our armies in this galaxy. You cannot survive a head-on fight against our enemies in Andromeda. Any way, we must take revenge against these traitors who have disappeared to a local galaxy. They must have planned that move over several decades. You are to locate and destroy them and all their bases and installations. Mother out!' Their new Mother said.

'Exo Zero to Mother, I had no idea we had lost the war already. How can we visit the local galaxy you speak of with no ships. All our fast ships on the world Trevan have been captured by the enemy. Xo Out,'

'Those were not the only ships that were built. We have much larger troupe carriers. Those were built on another world. Here are the coordinates. Get your warriors over there as soon as possible. I have been teleported to that very same place for safety. You must also take me along. There is no place left for me in this galaxy and I want to be near my people. Mother Out!' she replied.

Unknown to Xo and his warriors, Mother (new MasterMind) was non other than a large microid robot that had been created for the purpose. Michael's plan was to use that AI system to guide them to find the enemy. Like most Javols, once they had accepted that MasterMind they would blindly follow her orders. The idea was to have them destroy all Mut factories and installations within Triangulum.

CHAPTER 18

Called to Triangulum

The thought formed in his mind and he held the shot until its completion.

'Hello Michael!' Lumak greeted.

'Thanks for calling, Granddad,' he replied.

'We would like you and the others to visit Eden as soon as possible. Then you are to travel to Triangulum, where you will meet your father, the Son of Destiny. Think of this journey more as a holiday and a reunion of two great Titans. However, I think your father intends to fill you in on certain more intricate aspects of the Master Plan.

You may take along your apprentices if you so wish, since the experience so gained could be invaluable to all.

With your permission, Councillor Martia and Councillor Venusa can take your places in council during your absence,' Lumak said and the connection snapped off.

Michael immediately stopped the game of Golf and called his gang together and they followed into the Manor to discuss whatever matter was troubling him.

'People, We are to visit Eden and then Triangulum. From what Granddad said, I get the distinct impression it's urgent. This time everyone comes along. We can use the ship Micol. I think he could do with a little adventure as well. Anyway, I still want your vote on this matter,' he said.

'I don't know much about you guys, but I have never visited Triangulum before and some shopping holiday on Eden won't go amiss,' Joan said. Then they all voted yes for the new adventure. They always tended to follow Joan's intuition in such matters.

It was the first time the little Andromedan ship Micol had visibly visited Earth during daylight, and many of the workers about were shaken by the incredible sight and were even shocked when its side melted into a staircase that extended to the ground about some three metres below. The ship's voice thundered in its usual manner.

'I have been assigned to your gang by my lord, the Son of Destiny and will be based here in future,' Micol said.

The ship had existed for over three thousand years and had risk his own existence and seen many civilization during that time. However, he had been given a real personality by the Son of Destiny and a name. So he was considered to be an equal in all things.

'Thank you, Micol for being here and we are very pleased to have you as a member of our gang,' Michael said. being nuclear powered, the microid ship did not require sustenance as did primals with bio-systems. Further, his outer skin was designed to absorb all forms of radiant energy.

The new Titans and their now free apprentices all lived at the Mansion with Michael. It was once the home of the Son of Destiny who was his father. Since it became Michael's main residence, he had brought the ancient building back to its original and decided to share all its rooms, antiques, and facilities with the gang. Even Micol, the ship, had his own hanger within the grounds, but preferred to park himself close to the visiting areas. He also enjoyed teaching children and taking them for trips to historical places with their parents and teachers. Such places were not always on Earth and the children relished such interstellar excursions.

On their day of departure to Eden, he gave all his staff a bonus with extra credits and loaded Micol with relevant presents for the people on Eden and his father and mother now in Triangulum. Most of all, he took along several crates of the best vodka and whiskey. There was also a special brand of bottled Earth water, which was recognized on Eden as a special commodity.

Nevertheless, all the elements of such exports had been carefully logged, so that they could be returned to the planet at a later date. That way, there could not be a build up of material losses to the planet and any resultant destabilisation of its ecosystems and weather patterns in the future. These rules of equivalent commerce applied to all forms of trade and barter within the Federation.

Once they had entered Micol, the stairs melted into the body of the ship and in an instant the ship had disappeared from his spot outside the Manor.

The bell warning rang. *'Please return to your bunks in order to be transposed to Eden,'* Micol advised. In another few seconds and Micol had materialized on his pad outside Sarah's palace on Eden almost 50 light years away. By a strange coincidence, several of the Ancients, Lumak, Sarah and others were grouped close by as if expecting their arrival at that moment in time.

There was much activity about and everyone appeared happy and smiling. Michael was first down the stairs, gazed at the company then turned his head around to observe the changes. There were also the left overs of fireworks and everything was synonymous of a great celebration that he and his gang had missed. Nevertheless, they had some great victory celebrations on Earth which had continued in Terminus City on Mars and they could only have been in one place at any one time.

'I see! It seems you guys had some great celebrations. I can sense those changes in the air and everywhere. I only wish we could have celebrated this one with you as well,' Michael said, while shaking Empress Sarah's hand. Then they embraced and followed into the dining room where they exchanged gossip in general.

'Your father passed through recently, on his way to the Olympic games on Lori III, but could not visit Earth because of a prior engagement,' Lumak said.

'I didn't know there were games on Lori III,' Joan interjected.

'I think we are missing out on some real excitement,' David replied.

'Granddad, I am going to have a few serious well chosen words with dad when we meet. First he visits a local system without paying us a call. Then he visits the games without telling us,' Michael replied.

'I think your father is a little shy in this matter. After all, you haven't yet met unofficially. I suppose he must feel a little awkward,' His grand mother Sarah said.

'That is obviously the reason why he wants you all to visit, so he can get to know you guys a lot better,' Lumak said.

'I sense many changes afoot during the next few decades, but I am sure they will be for the good of all. I see that you have also increased the size of our fleet and are beginning to disperse them far and wide throughout our galaxy,' David said.

'In the past, we had to limit our Empire to the protection of the main Federation worlds after their conversion to Class 5. However, the council of Grand Lords of the Heptarchal Nexus has recently decided to relax our relationships with some civilizations under Class 1 levels of technology. This last classification represents a civilization that is equivalent to just before the discovery of nuclear weapons. As a result, we can now visit more primitive worlds and make ourselves known to them. In our present scheme, even stone-age man would be considered for such visits. Nevertheless, we can then begin to assist and educate them to the ways of the Federation, as we have done successfully with the reptilian inhabitants of Lori III. Although many would consider us gods of the skies, this is a better option than their infiltration by Javol's Muts, and also gives our fleet greater freedom to keep an eye on things,' Sarah said.

CHAPTER 19

A new era of change

After a pleasant week on Eden, spent with family and friends, Michael and his gang went shopping again in Eden City for more presents for his father George Peterson and wife Cathy now in Triangulum. All those crates were loaded and secured on board Micol, finally they said their farewell and the ship vanished.

'*Although we are expected on planet Tandor in the Torian system within the hour. I would like to make a stop on the way. It will not take long and this matter also concerns you. Please remain comfortably in your bunks. We are to be transposed to the world of Tul Triad*,' the ship Micol said, the siren went. His crew was curious as to the reasons for the overriding importance of that visit.

The ship, Micol, displayed what appeared to be the southern polar region of the planet with no moon. That area appeared to consist of a large southern crater, with a very high circular mountain range which encircled an area of about one quarter the total surface area of the planet. Within that mountain range were tropical forests and seas that extended towards the frozen southern pole.

'Wow! She must have taking quite a blow in ancient times from a large meteor. How could any world recover from such trauma,' ... he commented.

'Miracles do happen and she seems to have made a good job of it,'... Joan replied.

Micol then visited the equatorial and northern regions, with a similar distribution of seas, lakes and forests. Her land masses consisted of a single continent with numerous seas and lakes dotted throughout. They soon realized that the whole world had gone through serious trauma in its past from falling meteors, some of which could have caused the extinction of many of its previous species of plants and animals. Nevertheless, there was no evidence of recent strikes from such falling objects, at least not within the past 500 million years or so, thus giving the planet a chance to recover.

Several species were subsequently observed and recorded, but they were surprised to see human-like forms in the northern regions. They appeared to be equivalent to cro-magnon and were mainly hunter gatherers, so the planet would have evolved several types of apes in previous times. However, that was not all, towards the equatorial region were large slave cities, where the human-like slaves mined stone and other minerals for their masters. Their superiors were large bird-like beings, with a physique more like the Egyptian god Ra. They could have evolved from large vultures and had previously become head of the food chain.

They stood vertically like the others, but with whip in hand to flog the few human-like malingerers who were dragging their heels. Although the humans tended to live in caves, their masters lived in walled castles that were built for them by their numerous slaves.

Michael viewed the situation and couldn't believe his eyes, for it was like observing a scene from ancient Egyptian mythology. However, he realized that there were parallel instances in the history of Earth's humans where they treated other life-forms including human slaves in a similar manner.

Nevertheless, that was not all. As they watched, the weakest slaves were taken to a yard where they were tethered to poles and feasted upon by their hungry masters. Like vultures, they feasted until only the bones were left, then smaller creatures like Tasmanian Devils would finish off the bones until nothing was left of those individuals. The whole episode was quite gruesome and repugnant to Michael who wanted to put an immediate stop to their barbaric practices, but he had no idea of the cultural repercussions, if any, to both species.

The ship Micol began to study the three different intelligent species of that world. There were three dominant types, the Moroc, Sentien and Crel.

The Moroc were like large bipedal birds and were the most intelligent. With large beak, powerful wings for gliding, two small arms with hands of ten fingers and powerful feet with deadly claws.

The Sentien were their slaves. Although the Sentien wore no clothes, they had a form of pants, made out of some type of knitted fibres.

The Crel were another type of human that existed in the southern regions. They may have been related to the northern type, but had evolved uniquely to that part of their world. Luckily for them, they were completely isolated from the others by the extremely high and rugged mountain range, and as a result, knew nothing of the other races of that world and their strange barbaric habits and cultures.

'We have to do something about the nightmarish situation,' Michael said and the others nodded in agreement.

'What other resources are there on this world? Before we can make lasting changes to such dependent societies, we must first find suitable staple diets for the life-forms involved. It seems to me that there are not many larger animals on this world. They could all have become extinct due to over hunting by both northern species. If we are to change their nasty ways, we must first find an alternative or better way for them to survive.

'It seams to me that since food is scarce, their slaves rely heavily on what the Morocs supply in the form of grain. It appears to be some form of barley which are grown and harvested by other slaves under the guidance of their masters. It is quite possible that these humans are not clever enough to do it themselves, hence the symbiotic relationship between both dissimilar species. So they feed the humans with grain and select the weakest for their food, which is mainly meat. What a strange way for both to exist.

'We discovered a much richer food chain in the enclosed southern region. Perhaps we can reintroduce some of the animals from there. But judging from their population, it will not be enough,' Michael added.

'Micol, send words to Martia's ship and explained the situation to her. Also, this experiment should be done without the knowledge of its primary indigenous species. We can visit on our return journey and complete the necessary changes,' Joan said.

The information had been relayed and Martia's ship was already on her way.

'There is a world in this arm that is similar to Solaria. That world was similar to our Earth many millions of years ago. Perhaps we could cultivate some of its fruit plants and introduce some of them to this world, but it's against our universal laws to transplant its animal life-forms. That could disturb their natural food chain,' Micol said.

As they scanned the dark side of the world, they could observe large campfires and wondered about the reasons for such celebrations, so Micol went closer to observe.

'They are humans, similar to the slaves on the other side and there are many of dead Morocs about. There seems to have been a battle and they appear to be the victors. I think it's some form of an uprising in that area of their world. Those must be rebels fighting for freedom. I suppose they attacked them at night because the Morocs are less active at that time,' the ship, Micol, said

'Ho! Ho! Ho! Ho!'Michael jeered, while observing happy smiles all around and the others saw a game afoot.

'Shall we do our godlike thing,' David suggested. They left their three apprentices on board Micol and had decided on a course of action that would only include the three most powerful Titans in the known universe.

Without any further words, they left Micol in orbit and dived into the nearest star. The solar bath was exhilarating and they felt more powerful than ever before. The three bright lights lit up large areas of that world as they encircled it several times to make their presence known, then they merged towards the rebels camp. As they approached, all the rebels scattered, except their fearless leader. He was the only one with metal shielding and was holding what appeared to be an ancient rusty sword. All his rebels had bone knives and sharp wooden spears. In the mean time, Micol had deciphered their simple language and downloaded it to his crew.

As the three Titans landed they transformed into great warriors. Joan took the place of Athena, Michael became Apollo and David became Hercules.

There they stood as gleaming gods, immaculately dressed in gloriously shining armour and weapons.

'My lords, I am Phane, your humble servant,' their leader said, gently bowing his head.

'Well, Phane. It appears that you have defeated your local enemies in this battle. However, there are many more of them than there are of you,' Apollo said.

As Athena, Joan closely observed Phane. She could see differences in his features than those of his rebel friends.

'You are not like them. Why are you so different. Even your hair is golden and you are quite skilful and clever as their leader,' Athena inquired.

'I was born in the north and given birth by northern parents. They said I was a strange child with peculiar habits as a boy. I found it difficult to fit in with my tribe, so I left at a young age and travelled south. These southerners have accepted me for what I am, so I decided to do what I could to free their young males from their local masters. I killed their chieftains in battle and freed all their slaves, and have decided this battle against their slave captains which we have won,' he replied.

'Phane! Phane! Phane! You are to desist your war efforts with the Morocs. This is because there has already been too much loss of life on both sides. I realise the Morocs have much to answer for, but they will pay sooner or later. Nevertheless, you must learn to live and share this world together. Don't worry, we have plans afoot to save your world and all its people. So in this regard you must be patient. In the mean time, you will be made leader of all the northern clans, including the Morocs.

If you are made leader, from henceforth you must abide by our rules and bring all tribes together as one for the common good. Then all of you will become free and strong once more,' Michael as Apollo said.

Then there was a mighty gush of air and Martia's ship appeared above them and lit the area with her bright under lights.

Poor Phane felt utterly insignificant in the sight of such powerful beings. But he remained his usual brave self and had to say a few of his own words.

'My gracious lords, I humbly plead on behalf of my people that past evil deeds against us be revenged. The Morocs will not listen to our grievances and they will not budge an iota on any issue, not even from the mouth of gods. It is the way they are and the way they will always be. They have taken everything and we have nothing, but the memories of our dead which are crying for revenge,' Phane replied.

'Phane! Such negative actions will prove very little and will not accomplish your goals of retribution. After you have destroyed them all, will you sleep better at night because of their dead and rotting carcases strewn all over this world. Would you gain more recompense by practising on them what they have practised on you. I beg you, let us not follow the path of retribution for little reward when we can build a great kingdom together.

To show you my intentions in this matter and in the interest of all, I have decided to build a city in this area to mark your current victories.

Within this city will be schools and other facilities that are geared to assist you and your people.

During the next few months you will be educated in the truest ways of a real leader. As your free people grow stronger the Morocs will grow weaker and will not be able to harm you. Further, I can guarantee you, that very soon all the slaves will be released from bondage,' Apollo said.

Martia's ship had found the world to be rich in all forms of minerals and natural resources, ideal for building a Class 5 civilization. Nevertheless, Phane was different genetically from the others that he had united. He was the exceedingly rear one of a kind due to a jump in evolution. Because of that reason Michael didn't like to risk him and the future of his newer kind on the battlefield.

They soon found his differences were due to a genetic leap in his species. Although such genetic changes were exceedingly rear, such leaps were made more possible by nature when a species' survival was seriously threatened. It was predicted that most of his future children would be born with a higher intelligence than normal and as a result, their abilities would be greater than others of that region. Once they were in control and with the help of Michael and his Titans, they would be nurtured and in the process become invulnerable to raids by the Morocs.

Nevertheless, the Morocs rights to survival was as valid as all others, even when their ancestors had chosen a less appropriate path in their evolution as supreme predator. For who had the right to kill off another species because they didn't agree with their modus vivendi.

Despite his disagreement with Apollo, phane saw the sense in his argument and decided to follow his plans. Apollo went forward and took the hands of Phane. It could have been the very first handshake witnessed by all on that world. Then Apollo pointed his finger towards the ground, there was a strike of lightning and a large golden box appeared.

'Open it!,' he signalled to Phane, who went forward to lift the lid. In the large box was a glowing suit of armour and a large sword. He withdrew the sword.

'You may call this sword 'Excalibur' and the armour by your chosen name. Let no one use your sword unless by your permission. With both armour and sword you will be invincible against any of your enemies.

Then Phane held the sword up high and shouted.

'Excalibur! Let it be so! Let my enemies kneel before me!'

Phane was clever enough to realize that it was not the armour and the sword that made the warrior, but the hands that wielded the sword, and it was through the mind of the individual that all such decisions were enacted.

Back on the ship Micol, Michael brought them together to state some of his plans.

'This world is very important to us from the military viewpoint. That is the main reason why we are here. This will be one of the first worlds visited by Javols Muts, so it must be secured. Within the large dome will be our first experimental portals. These portals were designed by Hal and his guys to destroy Muts in transit. It's the first of its kind so we shall leave several of our operatives here to monitor this world constantly. We intend upgrading all long-range portals throughout Osmaron and Andromeda to a similar spec.' Michael said.

'Oh my God! How will they manage with Muts about. The large dome will signify our presence here. How will Phane cope. He must know of the invasion. He must be prepared for their incursions!' a worried Joan stressed.

'Well, since you are that keen to inform him, why don't we show him the destruction of Caefon. Of course it will not be easy for he and his people to detect Muts with dogs. Not having such a beautiful creature at their beck and call. And we can't supply him with them without breaking federation rules. Thank goodness we have at our disposal a special device that can sense muts several metres away. We shall supply him with such devices and weapons. But they must be trained.' Michael replied.

'So this world is now a Muts trap.' Carl inquired.

'Yes! And we shall convert numerous worlds in this galaxy to the same blueprint. This method will slow their progress and stir people like Phane to go after them with great prejudice. Of course they will be given special armour and weapons. Building the dome is just the first step in the process.' Michael replied.

'What about the Morocs. Will they also have such weapons?' A worried Joan inquired.

'We must give them time. The Morocs are clever enough to see the gains in society through barter and industry. We will introduce several neutral fruit bearing plants. Our scientist on Venusa's ship are already on that task. So please be patient.' Michael replied.

Soon, the warrior Phane was taken on board Micol and shown the film about the destruction of Caefon in Andromeda. Then he was given all the details of the deadly Muts. Phane was utterly shocked by the whole ordeal.

'And we are suppose to fight these things that are not even made of flesh and blood. They appear to be a thousand times worse than the Morocs our enemies.' Phane complained.

'That is why I wanted you to connect with the Morocs for your mutual survival. They can also make great warriors. You and your people have little to gain through violence. Therefore it will be most advantageous for both species to communicate these facts to each other. Your mutual existence depends on it.' Michael replied.

'I shall try but it won't be easy!' Phane was still apprehensive.

'Your are a great leader. So you must learn to practice the art of diplomacy.' Michael replied.

CHAPTER 20

A spectacular reunion

'Micol, take us to that young world you described. We can observe its life and see if they are similar to Earth's previous life-forms. But we cannot interfere with its animals, for they are evolving creatures with minds. I consider it unethical to transplant such life from one world to another. How can we assist one to the detriment of another. It will be more challenging if we could locate the resources on the world in question and use our technologies to create what is required within federation rules,' Michael said.

The ship Micol circled the globe several time while recording most of its numerous species. They were surprised to find that the world was covered over by dense rainforest which were occupied by its numerous simian species. It was the true Planet of the apes in every regard. The only real grazers were in the northern and southern regions close to its poles. That was the only place devoid of thick rain forest and the grass-like shoots intermixed with other hardy plants that were ideal for grazing animals.

That world had two moons of different sizes that moved around in opposite directions and orbits. This must have given rise to the strangest tidal actions on its two main oceans. All its land masses were joined together, giving all its creatures easy access to all its land areas. However, there were no birds in its skies, which was a mild disappointment to Michael.

Michael and the others realized that the world was on its way to evolving a human-like species within about twenty million years, if a few of the apes took the relevant path to that type of development. Nevertheless, they also realized that such species could be coerced along such pathways artificially, taking a much shorter period for their evolution and this world was a prime candidate for their attentions. However with such great numbers and variations there would have been at least a dozen upright or bipedal types with a natural tendency for using basic tools.

They also realized that many worlds developed along similar lines. Each having a better than average chance for evolving humans, so that pattern of rain-forests and simian life-forms was a basic tendency in nature and they wondered why.

'This world would be a great place for another large federation dome. This time many dedicated Senots can be involved to keep an eye and study the environment. They are all armed with the most deadly weapons and can give relevant assistance and training to certain species. This will also be a useful world to snare Javols and Muts.' Michael said.

'Are you sure the species here are advanced enough for weapons?' Joan replied.

'Muts are attracted to all such living worlds for food, so this world will be occupied by nasty Muts eventually if left alone in this part of the galaxy. Several domes will be built eventually for its defence. The federation navy can also be involved.' Michael replied.

After their experience of the previous few hours, they thought it was time to continue their journey, so they returned to their bunks for the longer trip ahead. This time they were to visit another part of the galaxy. There was a brilliant flash, which only lasted a few seconds and Micol transposed just within the outer rim of that galaxy.

Galaxy Triangulum was nothing like Andromeda or Osmaron, but resembled a fireworks display in three dimensions. All its points of light representing its numerous stars seemed to be distributed more evenly, with their densities increasing almost linearly towards the nucleus. The galaxy was surrounded by many globular clusters, each containing numerous numbers of stars. That abnormal stellar distribution may have indicated that the galaxy was in a different stage of evolution to the others.

Micol took another jump and they found themselves within the Torian system. It was not similar to our solar system, but a globular cluster of six almost equidistant stars that orbited about a common centre of gravity. At its centre was a massive gas giant the size of Jupiter with the most beautiful golden rings and about that world were six Earth-type worlds, each with a single moon. Although their continents, oceans and seas were distributed differently, they were all similar.

Michael and the others observed the incredible system through Micol's large screen and couldn't believe their eyes.

'I am truly amazed. I think dad has outdone his abilities this time, by creating such a unique spectacle. I can only but wonder at the climatic conditions on these worlds,' Michael said.

Yet, the whole system appeared quite stable. Nevertheless, they could not observe any northern or southern poles, as were indicated by snowy white. All those worlds were similar to a tropical Earth, including the few snow covered mountain ranges, and the distribution of colour was the same throughout.

There were six Tandor's and Micol was on his way to Tandor 1. The world they viewed was truly incredible, for in its skies were several massive orbiting spheres. As they watched they could observe the outlines of great cities through their transparent domes.

'They are massive satellites like Gimbal, but without the embellishments and other moving parts. They must be about ten kilometres across. What a supreme feat of engineering,' Joan said and the others stared in awe.

'It's all your father's work. He designed this system almost a century ago. From here, he rules the whole galaxy and with all its intricate sensor arrays, only certain life-forms are allowed this far. As you see, these satellites are sealed bubbles and without entry docks, it is virtually impossible for anyone to enter any of those cities without prior permission,' Micol said.

Then he transposed within one of the satellites and suddenly appeared on a large platform. Just ahead of them was several brilliant flashes and several people materialized before them. They all appeared to be in their mid twenties and shown like gods. Then George, the Son of Destiny came forward and took Michael's hand and shook it. Then he took Michael and his group to be introduced to the others.

'Welcome to Uno 1,' George said, and they followed him to the large group of people.

'In case you ask, Uno 1 is the name of this city satellite.

Miranda had decided to number all ten satellites in Spanish numbers,' he said.

'So this is your original gang from old world,' an intuitive Michael inquired and George nodded positively with a happy smile.

'This is our three children, Mark, Gerald and Patricia, my sister and high priestess Clair Sampson, the notorious Jerry or JR and his wife Miranda and their two sons...' George went on to introduce them to every member of his original gang and their children. Finally they met Andy and his family. Andy was currently on vacation with his favourite lord, for they had much history together during Infilate times on Earth. The six Amazonians, Mallory, Joeanne and their people were still mopping up Javols in Andromeda. George's wife Cathy was heavily pregnant with child and during this period she was advised to remain put, so she awaited them in her beautiful palace.

There was another flash and they found themselves in a beautiful palace on the surface of the planet.

'I observed a creamy colour within the transposing vertex. Is that normal?' an inquisitive Michael asked.

'All our portals and transference systems are designed with molecular tracers. That way, we filter out any unwanted life-forms, like Javols and Muts. A similar system is currently being installed throughout the three galaxies. This makes our systems the most secure in the entire universe. This is yet another brilliant creation by Chief Councillor Bailor and his Lodorian scientists,' George replied. Then Cathy came forward to be introduced.

'I can see a close resemblance to your father in your more natural form. You three have adopted the most appropriate forms for this visit,' she said gracefully, and they followed her into the large dining room.

'During this period of calm, between wars, we should take the great ships Venusa and Martia and pay a social visit to all our friends and colleagues within the main Federation worlds. Then I can introduce you to them personally,' George said.

'I will be honoured for the privilege,' Michael replied.

'Within these worlds are numerous habitats. They became refuge for all endangered species throughout this galaxy. Many that are presently contained within such dome habitats are to be returned to their original worlds after they are made suitable. If not, some other suitable environment will be found for them. It is a truly enormous task we have ahead of us and I intend to expand this method to the other galaxies, with the Council's permission,' George said.

'We are truly alike in this regard. I am also getting in the mood to do likewise in Osmaron, starting with the Solarian arm, with Council's permission of course. This process also makes them safe from Muts and Javols,' Michael replied.

CHAPTER 21

The changing universe

They all sat for lunch, while attended by robots and androids. There were over one hundred Osmaronites, including a few unknown councillors for lunch and George stood up to say a few welcoming words on their behalf. He was also one for lunchtime speeches, during which time he would update and educate his people on his long-term plans and goals within the Greater Purpose. After all, he was the Son of Destiny.

'Fellow Grand Lords, Supreme Councillors, Seniors and friends of the realm. I take this opportunity to introduce you to my son, Grand Lord, Michael Peterson and his friends, Grand Lord Joan Colman, Grand Lord David Fraser, Lady Julia Lennox, Lord John O'Brian and Lord Carl Fraser.

'We fought a great war in Andromeda together, during which time these great warriors vanquished billions of Javols singlehandedly. Believe me when I say, their powers are unique against Javols and they are truly invincible. Let us hope that in the future we can build a most beautiful universe together,' George said and their cheered, but George silenced them with a gesture.

'Once upon a time, there was much strife in this universe, as a result of which it was decided that the most appropriate option was to follow the course of nature. At that time certain rules of trade were essential if we were to prevent the contamination of lesser species by those of higher intelligence and technologies. Everyone assumed that such self-determination was in the best interest of all evolving systems, and they were left well alone until they had developed the necessary technologies to reach the stars.

'Well, I have always been in favour of the natural order and the reduction of such contamination, by the more advanced species.

'Once that level of technology had been attained, which was

usually about Class 3, they would have found methods that would take them to the stars, where they would join the greater community, if they chose that option. Then they would open trade routes and supply each other's needs.

'Since the existence of the Javols and our better approach and understanding of global ecosystems, that model of our universe has changed. First of all, we cannot trade away the raw essentials of a planet, which in time could drastically alter its eco-systems and destabilize its environments. Further, many of the lower species are exposed and prone to infiltration by Javols and others.

'Many important species are threatened and not all will evolve to their ultimate, either due to a lack of relevant resources on their home world or reasons of extreme predation, competition and others. We have also learnt, that certain species with a culture and intelligence comparable with stone-age man, can within a relatively short time scale adapt to a different way of life and in the process learn Federation principles. Further, not all such life-forms live on planets with plentiful resources as on Earth. Some worlds have never evolved the necessary infrastructure for them to take the all important steps required for maturity.

'Not long ago, such an important experiment was carried out on Lori III and a few others in this galaxy. As a result of which, Grand Lord Gerra and others of the Heptarchal Nexus has decided that we search for all such life, under Class 1 and bring them into our fold.

'If we are to take a future course as guardians of the universe, we are to set a good example to all its inhabitants. We should also consider that all these life-forms will begin to depend on us for advice and fair legal judgement. By so doing, we shall gain their respect and admiration. However, during this process, we cannot take part in any of their existing political structures, unless their methods are against the common good. Neither can we partake in their wars and disputes.

'We must lead by example and always stand for truth and what is right, even in the face of confusion and strife. No one can truly know how another life-form thinks, until they are able to enter its

mind and take its place. Neither can we truly learn about its innermost thoughts and ambitions through scientific studies. For by so doing we become an added part of the experiment and in the process, alter the original purpose of the experiment, so any ideas on that score may be considered to be purely academic.

'All that we may do is give incentives to those that live up to our expectations, taking into consideration cultural differences, basic tendencies and so on, in line with the common purpose, which to us in the Federation will be aligned to the Greater Purpose. Such psycho-conversion will be necessary, if they are to quickly learn our ways and methods in order to guard and protect their worlds against unwanted intruders.

'These galaxies are vast and we are few, although with special powers. Over the next decades I will expect all of us to work towards such goals. From henceforth, our main future program will include locating all relevant worlds for conversion within our Federation,' George said, and his audience cheered.

It was strangely uncanny how all the Andromedan Ancient survivors and Patriarchs had the same concept of a unified universe, where all life was given equal opportunities to grow and flourish. It was obvious to them that the trend of prey and predator would always remain to maintain a workable food chain for all their survival needs. There was always the requirement by nature in the form of evolution to create challenges for all. For how else could they have acquired their goals without the application of negative and positive pressure from all directions.

Then George outstretched both hands towards Michael.

'Perhaps we could have a few words on the subject from my son, Michael,' George added and a surprise Michael stood up and bowed his head to his father in acknowledgement for the respect shown on his behalf.

'Personally, I have always preferred the more natural ways of existence. During my youth on Earth I learnt many things, the most important of which was respect for all life, within a framework of natural freedom. Gone are the times when a superior species would imprison others for their own gains.

'It is in the interest of our Federation to assist and enhance all young worlds within these galaxies to find better ways of

existence. There is little gain in war, turbulence and slavery when there can be so many rewards in loving and thriving communities. Of course, this path is never easy. There are many obstacles and unforseen dangers on both sides, but if we pursue a strait and direct course with good and pure motives and intentions, there can but be only one outcome and it will be the one of success.

'We had a most intriguing experience during our journey here today. We found a world with three completely different races, all ripe for the picking. So we have already began this process and shall no doubt put certain plans into action on our way home.

'This is a new era in the ways of the Cosmos, so let us lift our glasses and hail the Son of Destiny along with the return of the Guardians of the universe,' Michael said and they all stood up and lifted their glasses.

After dinner they returned to George's country house which was in a valley between twin peaks that funnelled a waterfall. Within the green valleys were white horses playing and romping in the fields Then they went and sat close to a large log fire where they told stories and related their experiences.

'You know, Dad, we would love you and Ma to visit us regularly at the mansion from now on. We have also recently repaired and refurbish granddad's manor in North Dakota, so Earth, now Solaria, is almost back to normal,' Michael said.

Michael and the others of his gang always called Empress Sarah, Mother and Lumak, Father, although they were their grand parents. They had taken the rolls as their parents while they were children on Eden.

It was a loving reunion between true father and son and they were so alike physically and mentally that it was difficult to tell the difference. Despite the fact that it was the first time they had met in this life, they were so close it was as if they had known each other all their lives.

Yet that glorious adventure had brought home to the mighty Titans, the great technological possibilities of creating unnatural solar systems with the sole purpose of preserving life in all its diverse forms. Finally, planets and stars could be manipulated like little pieces on a chess board using the minds of New Titans or the incredible technologies of the Lodorians and Octans. Either way, the results led to brand new worlds that were perfect in every regard and tailored to the requirement of every form of primal life.

They realized that there were many ravaged, dead and dying worlds in the Solarian arm of Osmaron with young stars that were due for a make-over in that brand of technology. What if they put their minds to creating such systems for the preservation of life, instead of leaving them in their present state of desolation. The choice was obvious, so a visit was due to meet Councilor Bailor and his Lodorians, but in the meanwhile, they had a more pressing engagement with some friends they had met recently.

CHAPTER 22

The noble warrior, Phane

After an exiting fortnight on several of the Tandor worlds, The ship, Micol, and his crew left for the home galaxy, Osmaron. While on route they decided to visit the world of Tul Triad to inspect the new city and Phane's new dominions, but found part of the planet in turmoil.

Gliding above the city were several packs of Morocs displaying long sharp spears. Many would suddenly dive towards an area of ground where the rebels stood. There were long spikes radiating out of that area and in the middle were several piles of dead rebels and Morocs. Several of Morocs were impaled on the spikes on the periphery. Nevertheless, more Morocs came coming and the few rebels about Phane were prodding them off with long spears as they came close. Since the rebels were fenced in they could not easily escape their enemy's attack.

They were in a no win situation, but held their ground firmly, until they became too tired to fight, then the vulture-like creatures would swoop down and finish them off. At least that was the intentions of their fore. It was hoped that once their leader, Phane, was dispatched, the humans would have no one to defend them and the city would belong to the Morocs as their right of victory.

Micol had observed the battle from afar and brought it to the attention of Michael. Michael immediately saw through the strategy of the Morocs. Realizing that there were many more Morocs than humans in that area, Michael had decided to put an end to their siege in the interest of all.

All six suddenly appeared above the city, frightening the Morocs away and glided towards Phane's position.

'Phane! You gave me your word that there would be no more violence,' Michael jested, well knowing that Phane and his people were innocent in their present strife. Even so, Phane had to be given the impression that he was in the wrong, if only to teach him a lesson in the importance of resistance to violence.

'We were attacked, my Lord. Many of our innocent gatherers were taken as prisoners. Then they decided to claim our city as their own, so I had to stand my ground. As you see, we have lost many brave warriors while defending our rights,' Phane replied.

'It seems to me that there is much unresolvable hatred between both separate species. Although each depends on the other for their mutual survival, they will never be able to get on with each together on an equal basis. Because there seems to be no immediate solutions to your problems, I have decided to isolate both species from each other for the greater good and their mutual survival,' Michael said. Then the skies went dark.

'Get all your people together with their belongings. You will be moved to a distant continent. There you will be able to live your lives without interference. That area of the planet is fertile and green, so you may farm and grow your own crops. We shall teach you how to build your homes and city.' Michael said.

'But my lord! This is impossible. We all live here about with our families and friends. We cannot just get up and leave?' Phane was adamant.

'Either you leave now or die. Your enemies are much more numerous and will destroy you within a week.

'For everything there is a season!
'A time to be born and a time to die!
'A time to plant and a time to harvest!
'A time to kill and a time to heal!
'A time to destroy and a time to build!
'A time for war and a time for peace!
'A time to work and a time to play!
'A time to stay and a time to leave!

'My friend, this is your time to leave, so get your people together and get them ready! The big ship will fly you and your people to that new place.' Michael said.

After those words Phane became as quiet as a lamb and explained the changes to his people. He realized if he was going to save his people which numbered just over 2000 from the horrid Morocs that was the only way out.

'My dear people, our lords have decided to take us to the

promised land. So please get your things and family together for we leave in one hour. Those of you who do not wish to leave may remain as food for the Morocs!' Phane said in no uncertain terms.

Subsequently Phane and his men collected their dead warriors and placed them on a single pile and burned their bodies. Then they said a prayer as was customary.

The great ship Venusa landed near the equator of that world and began to build a beautiful Domed city. Within that dome was built a most beautiful city for those brave warriors and their families. That place was several thousand miles from the Morocs, so it would have taken their Moroc enemies many years to reach that part of the planet. Giving Phane and his people time to build a great society and prepare themselves for any invasion. Nevertheless, during that time Phane and his people were trained in the ways of the federation with knowledge of advanced weapons and systems. A few robots and Androids would remain to assist wherever necessary and keep an eye out for the arrival of Muts.

CHAPTER 23

Meradon's Training for Shaditry

Lumak the Shadite had observed the great warrior Meradon and decided to recommend him for Shaditry. However, all shadites bodies were standardised human. Therefore all alien forms had to be converted into the human type and trained as such. Therefore the little dragon Meradon was no exception.

'Meradon it's great to see you again! Do you like your present human form,' Lumak inquired.

'Yes, my lord! Since I have decided to take the plunge it was necessary,' he replied.

'I am afraid humanization is necessary these days for Shaditry. This is because it has been found to be the most appropriate form for the extreme challenges you will face in The Labyrinth of multiple values,' Lumak said.

'First I must learn to use my new brain implants so I can tune them to my challenges,' Meradon replied.

'Don't worry on that score. As your guide I will teach you my ways. You will also be trained in a virtual world where many of those challenges will be repeated. You will not visit my world Kanaefon until you are ready.' Lumak said and Meradon's worries abated.

Over the weeks that followed Lumak trained Meradon to use his implants like a professional then the virtual warrior games began. Lumak would take him through all the complex survival moves until he became the most adept ninja warrior.

'From experience, which was the creature you feared most?' Lumak inquired.

'The Blue Uana. They had a stinging tail that could impale.

The sting from that monster would kill in three minutes. It could target precisely to kill its prey.' Meradon replied.

'Get prepared, you will be fighting a most nightmarish Uana with three poisonous tails. Each one will target you independently, so prepare yourself with sword and shield to fight the gross monster. That will be the first real test of your abilities, so prepare yourself as you've never done before.' Lumak said.

'This VR will be in a long cave with many branches. You will fight your way through many obstacles. There will be horned serpents jumping out of the sandy ground to stick their horns into you. Large hungry spiders jumping from above including small stinging pests and others. All wanting to despatch you from this world. Speed and quick response time is essential for your survival.' Lumak said and Meradon was amused.

'I am ready! Let them do their worst!' he shouted.

'I like your determined attitude with death!' Lumak replied and like magic Meradon found himself in darkness. It was at the mouth of a large cave.

'Meradon's speed and accuracy was a pleasure to watch as he somersaulted his way through those delicate areas with vicious creatures everywhere. He handled bow, arrow and sword as if they were a part of his own body, being at one with everything. He did not use a shield on that occasion, thinking it too cumbersome for those challenges, so he relied mainly on hunting leathers for flexibility and agility.

When it came to the final monster he simply jumped over the side of the rough cave and its three stinging tails were removed even before the creature could react. Then an arrow flew towards its heart and its roars were silenced. Then the VR ended.

'Meradon, you are the best! You are the greatest! I have never seen anyone as adept as you in battle. For speed and agility I compare you with one of our Grand Lords and that is with his great powers.' Lumak said.

'The Labyrinth of Gon is not Virtual Reality (VR) it's real. If you die we shall have to bring you back with the machine, so you are to take those test quite seriously.' Lumak said.

'So Guide! What weapons and armour do you suggest?'

'Use a sword and shield and I have just the jobs for you. They were made for me by great Japanese weapon master. I used them during my practice sessions when I lived on Earth.' Lumak said.

'I hear the name Earth mentioned a lot. It must be a great place.' he replied.

'It was the beginning of most of our lives and will be again. One day you will visit that great world and appreciate its wonders as we have done.' Lumak said.

'Any ideas about the challenges I shall face?' Meradon inquired.

'First will be The Test of Fear.

'Secondly, The Test of Faith.

'Thirdly, The Test of Honour.

'Fourthly, The Test of Strength.

'The fifth is The test of camouflage and invisibility.

'Finally, the Test of Patience. They are not always given in that order. I found the last to be the most difficult of them all. I died three times during the ordeal. Try not to die more than once!' Lumak said and Meradon was intrigued.

CHAPTER 24

Muts invade Earth

Sarah's manor in North Dakota had been recently updated and had become another one of her secured palaces with all the necessary mod cons. Those on Eden wanted a permanent base on Earth and that place was as good as any. The portal systems were updated and could now be linked directly to Sarah's palace on Eden and other important cities within the Federation.

They had also renovated her properties in the hills of Turkey. Those were constantly used by Professor Chaimowich, Jeremy and others, who were now in charge of that part of Earth. Earth had gradually been transformed into a new world, with a large Tetrion Mauler in space that cast a constant shadow on the planet causing the northern and southern polar caps to reform.

Powerful Magnatron satellites had been placed in orbit within synchronous orbits to enhance Earth's magnetic field, showing a much greater Borealis effect at certain times of day. It also reduced stellar radiation, which would enhance animal life and planetary dynamics.

The large Pyramidons over the ocean with their powerful extractors like massive jet engines would suck large volumes from the upper atmosphere which would subsequently be cleansed of all noxious gasses including carbon dioxide within the structure. Thus stabilizing the planet's atmosphere and making it more perfect for life. Those pyramid structures had a base of over one mile, with almost the same height running into several layers of clouds. All such devices were built by numerous AI robots and androids all functioning about twenty times faster than any human.

Using such advanced devices to remake a world, Earth was well on its way in becoming a beautiful world like Eden.

While on Earth with his wife Lucia, Lord Meron was supposed to overview the terra forming process and ensure everything was moving on schedule. What he did not realize was the presence of a few Muts on Earth that were over-viewing all his movements while waiting for the right time to strike. At that time he and Lucia lived at Sarah's manor for convenience.

LPD FAILURE

LPD (Linear Progressive Drive) is a system used instead of chemical rockets for traversing land and space. The propulsion system is based on an inertial diode which could eliminate the effects of equal and opposite reactions as in Newtonian physics. But that was not all, the system placed the vehicle within its own inertial frame of reference and separated it from the universe. Creating a universe within a universe. Thus causing motion also in space.

The device included a most efficient intricate mechanism that used pure hydrogen for fuel. Such devices had to be reprimed every ten years on average. It was said that the device worked on subatomic particles to create the effect.

Javols being intricate copiers had used the Andromedan type of LPD which were not the same as those in the Osmaron Federation. So on arrival within the local galaxies their LPDs were inoperative. During their long journey which took them several thousand years, they had used up all their fuel resources. Therefore that put all Javols at a disadvantage. The newly created MUTS (Mutations) were equally vulnerable. Of course they could use most transportation system like humans but were restricted by individual flight.

Lord Meron was currently in charge of all terra-forming programs on Earth. This also included the reintroduction of previously extinct life in Africa and other places like South America. Many had been genetically re-created and would be brought from Eden domes, Polion and Tyrrel 2. Finally all its polluting and dangerous industries would be cleaned and taken to the Moon. The large Lunar domes several miles across had already been built by the great ships, Venusa and Martia with interlinking sealed underground tunnels with fast shuttle trains.

Mars was not included in the reforming of Earth and was undergoing its own program.

During this time of great change Meron was two busy to worry about personal security. Anyway the days of Infilates were over and almost everyone was involved in creating a better world for their families. Despite those attitudes there were a few old-world politicians who had lost much during planetary conversion from Land Rights to Protectorate Fiefs. Those once wealthy senators like Cleary were waiting for the right opportunity to fight back and claim their rights.   Senator Cleary and his group knew they were too few to make a change so decided to join forces with Javols Muts. They knew of the Javols infiltration on Mars and would be traitors for their cause. Since there were no more roads on Earth all travel were by mobile LPD cars. Those would land on the top of buildings for better security and easy access. So once the target's routine was known the process of capture and kidnap was quite straightforward. However for that plan to work Cleary had to visit Mars to make contact with the vilest of Javols.

JAVOLS COMMANDER ENDO-486

Javols commander Endo-486 (Zilo the charmer) was one of the demonic Lupher's most trusted creations. He was trained to infiltrate the Solarian Federation in order to copy their most advanced technologies. One of their main problems were the creation of LPDs. Without the use of such devices their motion was restricted only to surface movement which limited their efforts.

He had travelled across half the osmaron galaxy to the Solar System to eventual land on Mars in a ball of fire, giving the scanners the wrong information that the ship was a wandering meteor. He and his other four Mut passengers were pleased that they had arrived safely and in one piece. Once they had taken over the bodies of five prospecting miners they could fit in with the other miners in the old Caefon Dome which had been mainly abandoned since the building of the new city of Terminus.

They would wait on Mars until an opportunity presented itself.

That opportunity would be a visiting VIP from Earth. All though their first opportunity failed in an attempt in kidnapping Councillor Lia Chang with the loss of two of their kind, they had not given up the hunt. Javols Muts were the most persistent of all infiltrators if they wanted to avoid the Plasma Pit. During that time they also realized there were supreme beings on Earth with great powers. However such beings could not be everywhere at once and they seldom visited Mars. Therefore with his other two colleagues who were now accepted miners, he would bide his time and wait until another opportunity presented itself.

CLEARY MEETS JAVOLS COMMANDER ENDO-486

Searching for someone that was hiding from humanity was never an easy process. Luckily for Clearly Endo had taken the body of an established miner and was presently living in plain site among miners. Despite the stench of rotten eggs given off by Muts, he wore specially sprayed leather clothes that tended to hide the smell for a day or so. Anyway he had grown used to that new way of life and had been accepted by the local miners.

Muts were able to absorb biological tissue like meat so was able to survive without draining the blood of others. His present method of feeding also reduced his stench, but he was on Mars for a purpose and with the sole intention of finding the most important people in the Federation. Therefore he listened patiently to every gossip and viewed the news for every important item of interest.

It was not long before the image of Senator Cleary was displayed on TV. Although he had spent several years in prison for kidnapping, since his release he had taken part and given much to charities. At least that was what the news presenter said with no mention of his bad deeds. Endo knew nothing about Cleary and his intentions to locate Javols.

All Endo saw was a great opportunity to visit the main world of the Federation, so he set his sight on Cleary's capture. He had many greedy miners in his pocket that had given up mining for an easier life and those would do almost anything for a price.

Although Muts could copy someone's body they could not copy their mind and memories. That information was learned through interrogation and other methods. So he had to learn as much as he could about Cleary before the take over.

'Guys, we have a special human from Earth worth capture. I want you to find everything on this clot, including his present residence. When the time is write we shall capture him. Hanging around here is driving me nuts and I find these miners to be quite boring. The sooner I am on Earth the better I shall feel.' Endo said and they nodded their approval, realizing the plasma pit was always waiting.

They soon found his hotel and while pretending to be one of the hotel workers one of the Muts soon got friendly with Cleary. Realizing Cleary liked gambling he was soon enticed away to one of the secret miners gambling casinos in Caefon Dome. Soon he was introduced to sweet smelling Endo, who was dressed spectacularly in blue leather.

'I heard on the grape vine you were looking for Javols. Careful what you wish for. I also hear there are quite a few about these days, but they are not easy to find.' Endo said.

'I had some problems with land rights on Earth. Although I try to play good, political idiots always give me a had time. So I am pissed and will take help from anyone, including Javols. I was looking but couldn't find any real criminals. It seems Mallory Specials had wiped them out while I was in jail,' Cleary replied.

'Sorry about that, but we may be able to help. However, you have to tell us what we are getting into. Apparently there are super beings on Earth that can kill Javols with their breath. So you will have to tell us about the layout of the land and your intricate plans.' Endo replied.

'Those guys are not on Earth anymore. They are fighting Javols in other galaxies.' Cleary said.

'That's nice to know. So you think we have a free rain on things?'

'Yes! I have all the information you need. Can you help?'

'I am sure we can help, but first we have to find you some Javols. Of course we can do the job for you without those nasty Javols. We are trained assassins and infiltrators. We are all you need to take out your enemies and we are not too expensive,' Endo replied.

Entering customs on Earth was not easy. Anyone coming from Mars was thoroughly searched and then sniffed by trained dogs for Muts. Nevertheless even trained dogs could be misled by a range of perfumes and a combination of ammonia and vinegar. Although those smells were not apparent to humans, dogs would become confused and give up. The three Muts pretended to be Cleary's security supplied by a reputable Martian company which was traceable. Anyway they now had the ideal excuse to visit Earth, since Cleary was well known by many.

'Well guys, we should find a hotel and book in,' Endo said.

'There is no need. I have lots of room in my mansion. As a previous Senator of the USA I had a large estate and many irons in the fire. Although I lost most of my estate I held on to many of my investments. So I'm still a rich guy,' Cleary replied.

That's nice to know, Cleary. That makes our lives a lot simpler,' Endo replied.

'Cleary, as clots go you are not a bad guy. But we are not who you think we are.' Endo said, while drinking a glass of red wine.

'So, who are you really?' Cleary asked.

'We are what you clots call Muts. We have been hanging around on Mars for just the right opportunity to visit this world, and you gave it to us on a plate. Now we can go after someone who can help us design an LPD system.' Endo said, leaving Cleary in a daze.

'Why didn't you say so before. I know just the right guy for you. You are in luck because he is presently on Earth. He is not from Earth. They say he is from the galaxy of Andromeda where you guys originally came from. I can help you kidnap him. I spent years in jail for that bastard and it's time I had some payback.' Cleary was not amused.

They soon located Lord Meron and checked his daily routines. They knew he was vulnerable when landed on the roof of his hotel. Pretending to be hotel security they stopped him on his way.

'Can we have a few words,' Cleary said, playing his part.

'Ahhhh! It's good old cleary and company, I presume! I thought you were still in jail?'

'I was let out by the previous president. You know, contacts in high places!' Cleary replied.

'And I smell the stench of rotten eggs. You know, your three friends are infiltration Muts. I know their signature profile,' Meron replied.

'They need a scientist to assist in a new LPD design. And I told them you were the right guy.'

'So, now dealing with Muts who intends to kill you and take over your identity. As one of my friends would say "from the frying pan into the fire". There is no president to help you this time!' Meron replied.

Endo soon butted in;

'Yes! We are! We need you to help us design a new LPD system. For that you could become the richest guy in the universe. With your own paradise world to do as you wish,' Endo said.

'Those are great words and I am tempted, but you have nothing to give. You do not own anything yet and will never if I have my way,' Meron said, and Endo was taken back by that answer. He thought all humans were greedy and obnoxious creatures that loved money and wealth. Here he was speaking to someone who was not interested.

'You like Cleary are completely wrong about my abilities to design LPD systems. They were originally created by Doctor Jeffery Longhurst who had since moved on. He was transformed recently into a supreme being and like me, is not interested in such basic devices. All such devices are now common knowledge and can be designed by our technological androids,' Meron replied.

'So, you will not help?'

'Help you! I have killed thousands of your predecessors in Andromeda and have interrogated several of your kind in cages. Nevertheless, I have not killed a Mut before, but there is always a first time. But first, I must know if there are others of your kind on Earth.'

'If there were, why would we tell you?'

'Well, I could save your lives and send you back to Triangulum, from whence you came. Or I can freeze you and break you apart into little pieces to find the information I need. The process can be quite painful, even for Muts,' Meron replied. Endo was suddenly enraged by those words.

'You are a bloody insignificant clot. What in this world can you do to halm us!' Endo exclaimed.

Little did they know that Lord Meron being one of the Osmaron councillors had recently been converted into a Grand Lord with the powers to do as he pleased with anyone or anything and he hated all Muts. He immediately transmitted a thought to Michael and Joan and they suddenly appeared as if from no where.

'Please meet my fellow Grand Lords of the universe. Before we send you back from whence you came, we shall update you with certain information you should take back to your present leaders, Lupher and Dracma. Also, tell them their Mut factories will soon be destroyed by their own kind.' Michael said.

Endo soon realized that Michael and Joan were non other than the two supreme beings that had destroyed his two colleagues before and was dismayed.

'Cleary! you should leave, or be dammed!' Meron warned and Cleary suddenly bolted out of the place like a frightened rat. The present situation was too much for him to accept.

'We need to use you later so you will be preserved for now,' Suddenly a band of energy leaped from Joan and Endo was silenced. Nevertheless, Endo could observe what went on in that room. Both his colleagues were suddenly frozen and began falling apart. Then what appeared to be a strong breeze of blue dust encompassed their remains and then returned to Joan. The whole scene was too ghastly to watch.

'We now have all your knowledge since you left Triangulum, and we are Grand Lords of the universe, not clots!' Meron exclaimed.

'Now you know what we are, so when you return report what you have seen here to your two demonic bosses in Triangulum.

Tell them their time in this universe is short. Also mention that an army of Javols they betrayed in Andromeda will soon appear in that galaxy to destroy all their Mut installations. Those guys a really pissed off and will go to any lengths to destroy you guys. Your time in this universe is limited, so prepare yourselves well,' Lord Meron said.

In a flash Endo had disappeared from that place and reappeared before his boss Lupher in Triangulum.

CHAPTER 25

A change in plans

The last surviving Javols commander XoMir(Xo), now in Andromeda, sensed the green subcarrier in his mind and knew it was MasterMind making contact. Xo was just about to leave Andromeda with his Javols fleet when he received the important message.

'You and your fleet are needed in Triangulum, to take charge of all our forward troops in that galaxy. Once you have established a base there, store all the arriving stocks of food and their carriers. Then you must ration everyone; of course with the exception of you and your men. If this works out, you will be made commander in chief of all our invading armies. However, you must be very diligent. There are many traitors amongst us, so keep this to yourself and only relay information on a need-to-know basis. Mother out!'

'Got it, Mother!' he replied.

'Finally, and most importantly, our forward scouts have detected virtually no intelligent primals within Triangulum. The information received indicate that galaxy to be quite void of all larger primals.

'Either that information is erroneous or there are other intelligence involved. You are to personally check most of the local worlds for life and evidence of a violent past. Perhaps that galaxy was invaded by others like us in the distant past. If that is the case, we are to get our armies together and leave immediately for Osmaron. Once there, with a larger and more prepared army, you will have a much better chance to defeat our enemies and traitors. For that task you will need a larger army.

'With those of our forward groups now entering Triangulum, you should amass a large enough army within the year. The late arrivals, can be given ships to follow.

This mission is very important for our survival, so be

disciplined and train you armies hard and well. Mother Out!' there was a gentle crack as the carrier disconnected.

'Wow! Wow! Wow! Commander in chief, eh,' Xo mumbled to himself, not realizing that the source of his information was not the real MasterMind, but the pretend one called Mastermind which had taken its place. His orders were relayed by Michael's Macron. It was a clever ploy to get Javols to destroy their own kind. In all this time Xo never realized he was working for the Federation. Even so, he was set on destroying all traitors, in particular those who had left for Triangulum. As far as he was concerned, traitors were a lot worst than primal clots. That was the name given by Javols to all intelligent primal life like humans. Therefore, he was not going to waste any time in a rat infested galaxy like Osmaron, if there was very poor pickings for him and his troop. Anyway, Javols could not remain for long on rations. They enjoyed the excitement of the kill.

'.... get the squads together, we are leaving. The production of our ships can continue in our absence. Anyway, we have no threat in this area and the clots will not dare to attack us with our faster ships and more advanced weapons. We are to take control of Triangulum and train our forward troops there. When we have amassed a large enough army, we shall visit Osmaron and do the needful,' Xo said.

'Message to Commander Xo Xema... for the forward fleet now arriving in Triangulum. Hold your fleet and its reserves within the first suitable stellar system and await the arrival of the Supreme Commander within Triangulum. Under no circumstance should you travel beyond that volume of space and ration all reserves until his arrival. Mother out!'

Xo was a trained soldier and did as he was told. Anyway, he didn't like the idea of ending in one of those deep plasma pits that were reserved for traitors. He didn't mind dying in battle, but in that way, with all the imposed suffering made him cringe. He had observed the process once on one of his close colleagues and it was quite bizarre. He must have melted and transformed into a thousand forms before his cells dispersed into the molten bath and that was a fast death.

He soon called his troops together and gave them their orders. They immediately began to construct a large base and installation on the most central world. In future, all Javols arriving in Triangulum would be guided to that base, where they would be rehabilitated and remain until called elsewhere.

CHAPTER 26

XoMir arrives in Triangulum

Since his betrayal in the battle against Caefon, Xo had retrained his warriors and gave them more advanced weapons. Those along with the large carrier ships had been previously engineered for Muts by Lupher before he left for Triangulum. The large Portals in that hidden cave had also been designed for his Mut warriors. Lupher realized that the present Javols were not tough enough to face the advanced technologies of the Osmaronites. Anyway those two demon brothers were not Javol lovers. Andromedan Javols were too unpredictable in their actions and were not the best at long term planning.

Xo knew portals couldn't be used by normal Javols like himself, so it all added more salt to Xo's wounds when considering his betrayal. He wanted to see an end to all Muts and their deceitful bosses and their new mastermind drove them to that end.

Their battle carriers were armed to the hilt with the worst weapons made by the Solarian Federation. Catches of all such weapons and armour had been distributed in certain hidden places near their base and the pretend Mastermind guided them to those places. Although those Javols were being used by the Federation to destroy Muts and their factories, they were non the wiser. They assumed their new Mastermind was their original MasterMind which had survived the destruction of Endor's moon.

Within two weeks they had arrived over one of the main installations in the Triangulum galaxy. They landed their five carrier ships in a deep crater on one of the local moons and prepared a well hidden underground base. Their new MasterMind was now in command and would guide them for mutual survival and the destruction of their enemies.

'To all my brave warriors fighting for our freedom. I found a second Mastermind in this galaxy. She constantly communicates

with our travelling fleet and misleads them to follow a particular path, where they are captured. She pretends to be me giving identical codes. Do not be misled. In future I shall send you a different set of identity codes so always be sure before you take action. However, before I change I must warn our forward fleets of the deceit and guide them to a local moon. After such a long journey many of our globes will be depleted. Those we have to recover from space. Although we have taken along many LPDs, we need a lot more and have no way to prime them. So from now most of us will become as mobile as clots and rely purely on our ships. Mother out!' she said.

'Xo to Mother! We do not have enough fighters or methods for refuelling them. What can we do?'

'We do what our traitors have done. We have always been clever in copying. We simply copy the technologies of others. Our ships can always be duplicated and some of us can return to our bases and collect whatever we need. We must increase our numbers if we are to win this fight against our enemies. Mother out!' she replied.

'Xo to Mother! How can we assist our comrades end their long trip?'

'I have found a suitable world. One of our carriers with its warriors will be sent to that place to assist them, In the mean time we begin building our infrastructure here on this moon. This will be my safe location for now. Be ready to receive my new codes. I shall be constantly listening to the traitor's mastermind for more information. Mother out,' she said.

The new Andromedan Javols under the guidance of their new AI MasterMind which was partly controlled by the Solarian Federation became a fighting force to be reckoned with. Very soon millions of Javols with their large carriers were guided to that moon under their new MasterMind. The Federation allowed them many advanced technologies, so very soon they became advance enough to take on their enemies.

While using their new Androids and robots they began mining for minerals. Those they would used for the replenishment of their bodies and the building of more ships. That moon had been well chosen by MasterMind and was rich in mineral deposits. Anyway, since the Triangulum Galaxy was sparsely populated they could not use biological systems for food as they had done in Andromeda. As a result those new Javols were much cleaner and saw little need for destroying life as they had done in the past.

Over a short time their new MasterMind had given them a new code of life for their mutual survival in a new and different galaxy. They now constantly felt the loving carrier signal of their MasterMind.

'Warriors of the realm, we are now ready to take on our enemies and take them over. In future we ignore all indigenous life. Our god have decided for them to exist, so who are we to question him. Anyway we now have easy ways to process our food. While in this galaxy we should not create more enemies than is necessary. By being friendly with them we can acquire their assistance in new technologies. Our efforts have expanded well beyond my wishes. Therefore be prepared to destroy our enemies. We are now on a war footing! Mother out!' she said.

JAVOLS CHIEF COMMANDER

'Xo, because of your services and dedication to the realm I have decided to make you chief commander of all Javols in this galaxy. Therefore, in future you are to wear your badges of importance and seniority. You may now choose your sub-commanders and plan our first battle against the local installation. I want that installation of freaks levelled. Of course we must save any of our own kind within the dreaded place, but all Muts must die! Mother out!' MasterMind commanded.

'Mother, I thank you greatly for my new promotion. I have already began preparation. Several spies have been sent but they are not allowed to communicate in case they are detected. I am now awaiting their return. Then we can construct a more intricate plan for our invasion. Most of the new arrivals need time to recuperate after their long trip. Perhaps we should wait a little longer. Xo out!'

'My main purpose as your MasterMind is to ensure our survival. If I think my army will be overwhelmed I shall wait until we have the right numbers and equipment. As you know, there will always be weak arrivals. That's why I have created blue coats to take care and rehabilitate them. As military commander, you must focus on our battles and vanquishing our enemies. Also, please ensure all our warriors take enough rations with them for a period of at least one week. After that time they will be supplied by our carriers. Mother out!' MasterMind replied.

'Mother, several of our spies have returned from the field. Their reports on Muts are not encouraging. Hexo-286 led the team to infiltrate their local installation. No arriving Javols were found, but there were numerous containment tanks with many being transformed into Muts. Hexo said they tried blowing microid dust on a local Mut but nothing happened and plasma weapons had no affect. Two of our best guys were captured and are now being process. We have no choice but to postpone our attack until we are in a position to destroy them all. It seems the only way to kill them is by some type of virus. I think the clots and their superiors have created such a deadly virus. I observed their use in Andromeda in turning our people into blobs like stone. Xo out!'

'Since we are both fighting the same enemy don't you think we should join forces? Mother out!'

'Join forces with clots!' Xo was not amused. To someone like Xo dealing with clots was treachery of the worst kind. After all, he had spent most of his existence fighting them. To him there was not much to choose between Muts and clots. They were all as bad as each other.   *'Well Xo, either that course of action or be defeated. Which option do you prefer? Although we might not like clots for whatever reasons in our past. Times and people change. We had to change our ways on arrival to this galaxy. We are not the same people that left Andromeda. In this universe the only predictability is change. We are suppose to be modern Javols with a sense of purpose. One day this whole galaxy could be ours if we tour the line and allow others to exist with us. Our god made the universe for everyone, not only Javols. Mother out!'*

'Well Mother, if you insist, but I think we are taking a great risk. Anyway, what do you propose? Xo out!'

'We send a team of our best negotiators to their special world in Osmaron and explain our plans to them. You should remember, they are also fighting our enemies and we are better placed to destroy our enemies' main installations to save our kind. We visit them under a flag of truce. Mother out!'

'So we postpone our attacks for now and select a few of our best guys for the trip? Xo out!'

'You will lead that team. I want you to impress them with our abilities, so take some of our technologies and culture along with you. Also take one of our fastest cruisers, You need only take along eight of your finest and make sure they are well trained. We want no slip-ups on this mission. Make it the best mission of your existence. I shall communicate with you frequently to assess progress and give advise. Mother out!'

MasterMind or Mother soon located Earth and learned its languages, which were mainly English. Then she downloaded all that information to Xo who soon updated his chosen eight.

'Guys, we are under strict orders, so no one should know of any of our future discussions or plans. The Plasma Pit can always be revived for traitors, so be always on your guard. Remember, you have been specially chosen by our MasterMind for a great mission. Believe me when I tell you that universal gods are involved. For that mission we are to visit a special place in Galaxy Osmaron. It will be the greatest adventure of your lives. If any of you have doubts this is the time to tell or forever hold your peace,' Xo said, but they had little choice, since they had previously agreed.

Grand Lord Michael had laid the trap well. He was the one that created the more recent Javols MasterMind and had planned a two pronged attack on the enemy within Triangulum. The main attack would be with numerous Javols being one of the prongs fighting their mutual enemy. He also realized they needed help, therefore contact would be made with those Javols at the appropriate time, so he was prepared for that eventuality.

As the new Javols ship approached Earth with shields fully on, Lord Michael suddenly appeared on board like a bright blue star. He slowly transformed into the figure of Aron, the ancient patriarch. Xo and his company were confused and bewildered by the apparition. To them all such appearances were impossible, for they had never seen such an apparition before and in deep space. With the exception of their ancient gods, they had no idea of supreme beings living among them. Therefore Xo plucked the courage to speak.

'My name is Xo. I represent my people in the local galaxy you know as Triangulum. I would like to meet the heads of this world to discus an important matter,' he said.

'Brave Xo and his devoted crew! You guys have arrived sooner than I expected. Ahhhh! You have a different ship. You have progressed well since your arrival in Triangulum. Before you can visit Earth you must transform into the human type and wear clothes like me. Unlike your terrible people in Andromeda your smell does not carry, so you will be accepted as yet another life-form from Triangulum. However, before you continue on your mission I advise you to think carefully of joining the Federation. That will give you access to trade and many of our most advanced weapons. That is much better than going it alone, in this changing universe. Please communicate with your MasterMind before making such a decision,' Michael said.

'Are you a god, like our own god!' Xo exclaimed.

'I have never met your god. I suppose the answer is yes. I am all powerful, eternal and everlasting, but there are many like me.' Michael replied.

'If we accept your advice, would you become our real god to help us when we are in serious trouble. We would also like to destroy our mutual enemies, but find they are difficult to kill. Can you assist us in this matter? Xo said.

'The answer is yes to all your questions. But first you must put your case before our committee on Earth. So be honest and state the facts. I will presently update them on you needs and requirements.' Michael said and they were pleased with that answer.

'We are willing to join your federation if you will assist us to destroy these dreadful Muts. We are always for peace and mutual survival. Like you, we have learnt many lessons from our past. Driven by a great need for conquest until conquered with little gain. Presently we prefer to leave in peace with others. Perhaps we can learn much from you and your federation,' Xo said.

'Joining the federation is not an easy process. It's a very important change for both of us, so there will be much celebration. This will give you a chance to learn our culture and see the way we live. You must remain on Earth for several weeks. Don't worry, I shall prepare the way for you, so please follow my advice in all things.' Michael said and they were satisfied.

'You are getting Javols to help us win the war in Triangulum?' Joan was not pleased.

'Those are good Javols. They deserve a chance to survive. I have killed so many of them in Andromeda that I feel ashamed of myself. These Javols mine for their food. They also have a code of living and will not interfere with other life and hate Muts. So that puts them on our side. With the correct type of education they can become the best soldiers in the federation. That was the original intention of Meron and his people, thousands of years ago. Finally Meron's wishes are being fulfilled.' Michael said.

'I hope you are right in this matter, but you are seldom wrong, so who am I to argue the point. How are you going to convince the senate. Many don't like Javols. To them Javols are the worst monsters in the universe,' Joan replied.

'Initially they will pretend to be a remote species in Triangulum that also hate Muts. That way they will be able to join the Federation. They are being updated by their new MasterMind even as we speak. No one need know of their past existence in Andromeda. I also think they would like to forget that past while making a new start in a new galaxy.' Michael said and Joan was convinced.

FEDERATION CELEBRATIONS

'I introduce to you the Zenoits. They live in a world close to the rim of the Triangulum Galaxy. They were the first to be exposed to Javols Muts. They would like to join our federation of worlds and have supplied all relevant documentation under my guidance.
They are great warriors with knowledge of Muts so we should be pleased to have them on our side during the Battle for Triangulum.' Michael said and all councillors stood and gently bowed to show respect.

Since Michael was Grand Lord of Earth, no one could contradict him, so the councillors soon formed rows to sign the relevant documents. That ancient method was still used to bind contracts. After the process had been completed Xo gave a short thank-you speech and was soon questioned by numerous reporters. After that they were famous VIPs and showed respect everywhere they went. The large Croydon square was soon prepared and decorated for a celebration day that was yet to follow.

Xo and his company had freedom to discover a human world in all its wonders. Never had they realized any society could be as rich in culture as Earth. So with the gold they brought with them decided on a shopping spree. They also sampled the beverages and food and found the whole process different but exciting. For the first time in their existence they were able to appreciate music in human form. Those innocent Javols were completely overwhelmed by it all.

They soon returned to their base in triangulum with great tales to tell and would build a new society on what they experienced on Earth. Those New Javols had found a new way of life and would never again return to the one they had before.

CHAPTER 27

To capture good demons

Grand Lord Gerra summoned the three Shadites Lumak, Gemmi and Meradon to Little Osmaron over Planet Eden for conference.

'Sut, once again I have summoned you to Little Osmaron. This is a very important mission that only you can handle. Meradon and Gemmi have also been summoned and will be with us shortly. That special project is to rescue other demons like Neramon and Felspar. Since they are on a mission of their own they will be unable to assist. Nevertheless, they have created a galactic map of most imprisoned demons within the galaxy of Triangulum. They are presently surveying Osmaron and will soon release a similar map of that galaxy.'

'Are these demons like Neramon and Felspar?' Sut Lumak inquired.

'Almost identical, although specialist in their own chosen professions. Most of them are good demons and deserve a better type of survival. We now have the means of protecting them, so we should now save as many as we can. Since it's Meradon's first mission you should guide him. All the special equipment is accessible through the Greater Mind. You being Grade one will be able to acquire them when needed.' The Grand Lord said.

Suddenly Gemmi and Meradon materialized.

'Metrasiend and Shadite Lumak,' they greeted with fist on heart in Shadite salutation. Then they sat in the whiter than white chairs provided. The whole sanctum was radiant white and everyone glowed.

'As I previously mentioned to Shadite Lumak. You are on

a special mission to save demons like Neramon and Felspar. Your implants have been upgraded for this mission so they will not be able to assess your minds as on previous occasions.'

Gemmi remembered the time her memories were scrambled by Neramon and was worried in anticipation.

'You shouldn't worry, you will be much better prepared this time,' The Grand Lord said, realizing the frown of dread on Gemmi's face.

'Not worried Metrasiend. It's just that I remembered our first encounter. During that one my memories were scrambled,' Gemmi replied.

'For this operation you will be issued new cloaks. They are impregnated with a new virus called Satan's Bug. They will kill all Muts in contact. You may keep your original cloaks for when they are needed. You may collect your cloaks now,' the Grand Lord said. Suddenly three boxlike containers appeared on a local table and they each collected one.

'Our universe is older than you can ever imagine. Even before your type of EM Matter existed there were other types of matter and energy. Most of these do not exist now but some remnants still remain. Just like your type of life exist and evolve, in a very similar way did demons evolve within their type of universe. At that time there were two main types, Moscon and the Simions. Neramon and Felspar are Simions. They were peaceful while the Mascons were the original predators with no consideration for others. The Mascons that survived were imprisoned and held in temporal prisons. In those places time repeated itself, so they never grew old and will remain that way for eternity.

'Can these Mascons escape their eternal Prisons?' Meradon inquired.

'They have been placed in a virtual universe, where everything is constantly renewed, so they cannot escape by themselves, but Muts could be involved.' Grand lord Gerra hinted.

'Why did the Hexolytes capture the Simions?' Gemmi inquired.

'The demonic Hexolytes were encased in a metal suite which impeded their sensory abilities. The Simions made up for those losses. Your job is to release all surviving Simions from bondage. First you must explain to them who we are and what they can gain by their release. Then you are to collect them in the sealed containers provided,' the Grand Lord said.

In an instant they found themselves in Sarah's palace and were greeted by Sarah and others.

'You have returned just in time for lunch, so please join us?' she said.

'Thank you madam Sarah,' Gemmi replied and Meradon bowed his head as they sat.

'This is important, everyone! We have a new Shadite in our midst, so we must have a party to celebrate his coming across. I know you guys are on a special mission for our Grand Lord, but a little celebration is necessary here. Tomorrow we shall have a grand party for Meradon, therefore we are to invite all councillors not on special missions,' Empress Sarah said and no one ever questioned her decisions.

As they viewed the great map of the Triangulum galaxy they found most of the remaining good demons were situated in underground worlds close to the nucleus. Those scattered towards the galactic rim were sparse and few.

'We begin at the centre first and move towards the rim. This is a simple retrieval process so leave the major parts to me. You are to experience the process at firsthand. Don't forget, there are places like this in Osmaron and a few may still exist in Andromeda. They must all be collected for the greater good,' Lumak said.

'What am I to do?' a keen Meradon exclaimed.

'This is your first real mission, so observe and learn. If we meet any of their robots we are to vectorize our cloaks and become invisible. We deal with Muts together. Our new cloaks energy modules will last several weeks on continuous without priming, so we use them when necessary,' Lumak said.

'Don't you worry, Meradon, I'll watch your back! I feel a lot more secure with my new grade two cloak an new implants. So I'm ready for any eventuality, even nasty Muts,' Gemmi said, always in a cheerful mood.

To have sent all three Shadites together on a special mission meant they were going to face serious opposition. Therefore Lumak spent several days training both Shadites using virtual reality systems. When he knew they were ready he stocked the ship with weapons and essentials and they were on their way.

They had left in one of the large Vipers. They were the most advanced fighters of the Federation and well suited for enemy engagements in virtual mode. In another three weeks they had arrived within a greenish nebula close to the centre of the Triangulum galaxy.

'What a sight! This place is like looking into the face of god.' Meradon exclaimed, not having seen such heavenly beauty before.

'I have chosen a local world as our first target. It appears to be the strongest one on our map. When we arrive we are to survey this ancient world for Hexolyte installations. I'm not sure what we shall find.' Lumak said.

With invisibility screens on, they proceeded to the world in question. Although they were well prepared for any eventuality, they didn't expect to find enemies on route.

As they travelled around the planet they could observe numerous surface bases, all run by Muts.

'Muts and more Muts. They also utilize LPDs. I thought Muts hadn't LPDs!' Gemmi exclaimed.

'They could have collected them from the Javols they captured and are able to reprime them for themselves,' Lumak replied.

'That is some installation! Like they have all moved to this world. Here they are hidden from everyone and can build their technologies to defeat us, if they can?' Meradon said.

'We thought they were up to something, but wasn't sure. Now we know where they went. This is not the only world they are using. If they are as clever as I think, they will be all over this central region by now. They must also be working toward their own master plan. Finally, I know why there are so few Muts in our galaxy of Osmaron and why the Grand Lord chose us for this Mission!' Lumak said and they were intrigued.

'What can we do? There are so many of them!' Meradon exclaimed.

'Listen carefully! There are three types of the Satan's Bug. The first type with a lifespan of less than a day only kills Javols and can be used in populated environments. They do not affect our type of EM life. Those we call SB1.

'The second type is optimized for killing Muts with a short lifespan like SB1. This one we call SB2.

'The third type is a plague. That one we call SP1. It can only be used on dead worlds like this one. That plague uses Muts to make more of themselves and have a lifespan of five years. Once released they eat everything, including their installations. We have all three bombs on board,' Lumak said and they were utterly shocked by that knowledge.

'What are we going to do about our Simion friends?' Gemmi inquired.

'We simply vectorize and travel to the underworld without

their detection. I doubt they have any knowledge of that cave. Entrances are normally well hidden.' Lumak replied. Leaving their ship above the world, while vectorized they used their LPDs and gravity to land on an isolated area.

Carefully and stealthily they progressed towards the lower levels of that underworld until they came upon the thermal generator. That device supplied the whole underground world with energy which took heat from the planet's molten core. That energy could then be used for supplying the robots and machines. Robots were always used in such places as guards, cleaning and operating the machines.

Not all such systems would have survived the ages. Robots needed a conscious Simion to guide and control them. Because of their location close to the centre of a galaxy, Simions could survive by occasionally taking elemental energy from the numerous containment tanks within such installations.

Lumak knew how to awaken a Simion from sleep by tripping local switches at the lower levels close to the generator, so he normalized his cloak and in an instant several devices came to life, including a large robot. He could have been in control of that area. Slowly, many robots were beginning to stir. Then the Simion demon suddenly appeared within one of the local portals.

'I am Lumak the Shadite. Me and my two companions are from a local galaxy and have orders from our Grand Lord to save you from this prison. Neramon may have contacted you in the past regarding a new and better way of life,' Lumak said.

'Ahh... Neramon! He is my brother in another life. We were captured together by those metallic monsters but got separated. Now he is free and assisting your empire to locate more like us,' the blueish and semi-transparent Simion said.

'What is your name?' a nervous Meradon inquired.

'My name is Winstone! I have lived like this so long I can't tell what freedom is anymore. And what about my robots here. They are all like family to me. I have relied on them for so much over the years. I would not like leaving them behind,' Winstone said.

The surface of your world above have been taken over by the most vile creatures called Muts. Soon they will find their way to this place and put you in another even worse prison. Next time your life may not be as free as you are now,' Lumak stressed.

'Please take this opportunity for freedom!' Gemmi encouraged.

'Talk to your robots and explain we shall be back for them later. We must first have you settled before they can be freed. Since we are to destroy the enemy above, it's better for them to remain here for a while until collected by one of our great ships,' Lumak replied.

'In that case I would like to join my brother to fight the enemy and be on that special quest for your empire and freedom, if it's convenient,' Winstone said.

'I have in my possession a special vessel for your temporary containment. It has all necessary shielding to protect you during our travels. Your robots can follow later, after you have settled and we have removed the enemy above,' Lumak said and Winstone accepted. Anyway he had little choice in the matter. Nevertheless it would be about five years when those robots were collected.

After collecting Winstone they took the shortest route out of that place and were soon on their ship. Lumak communicated his intentions through the mind and was given the go-ahead for all such bases within that galactic region.

'Can some Muts be saved? I mean can we communicate

with them and show them a better way to live?' Gemmi inquired, once she realized a complete planet of Muts would soon be destroyed. She always preferred life. Killing so many life-forms she considered a great waste. On the other hand Meradon considered them the worst vermin that should be exterminated as quickly as possible.

'Meradon, get the SP1 weapons loaded.' Lumak ordered.

'On it, Boss,' Meradon replied.

'Gemmi, get ready to release the payload. We must travel around the planet and release three observation satellites over the most populated areas before we release. This is the first time a complete world will be destroyed this way so our scientist will need feedback.

'I know you guys have your doubts about this decision, but it's been sanctioned at the highest level. Our Grand Lord knows the true coarse for our future survival.

'Muts are not like us. They are just AI robots made from microids. They have been trained and programmed in a specific field. They cannot procreate. Have no emotions and not even know what love is. They never had children and cannot contemplate another way of life. So do not pity them. They will only communicate just before they kill you with the words "Die! Filthy Clot!". That is what they have been programmed to say. They have been programmed to think all naturally evolving life to be a flaw of nature and will go out of their way to exterminate all such life. They also think the universe belongs to them and see us as using up their resources. If they survive and grow in greater quantities no one in this universe will be safe,' Lumak said and they were convinced of the dangers.

After they had set the satellites in orbit they went one more time around the planet, Then they said a prayer and released their bombs. They waited above one of the bases to observe through their on-board screens. Images from all three main bases were relayed to three screens at the same time.

'My god! Look at that!' Meradon shouted as half a large structure was eaten away.

'It's like they are in a frenzy and starving,' Gemmi said.

'They are programmed to increase their numbers at this stage. The new generation will even be more vicious. However they will only eat metallic structures and Muts. Everything else they leave untouched,' Lumak said.

It was not long before the swarm took a monstrous form of its own and separated into several smaller forms that would grow and then divide into smaller forms until there were numerous such swarms about. All seeking something or someone to eat. The scene became too ghastly to watch. The poor Muts did not stand a chance. Soon swarms would envelope the whole globe and remove all metals and Muts from that world.

'Doctor Hal Seaton and Professor John Simmons should be proud. They have created the worst microid bug in all creation. The only problem I see here is their desire for metals in their varying forms. They will lay waste any world, even those of the federation,' Lumak said and Gemmi swallowed hard.

Lumak and his two Shadite companions travelled to all the ancient Hexolyte bases and released numerous Simions like Winstone, which they collected. Those very same demons would be used to locate all enemy demons which when found would be imprisoned for eternity.

CHAPTER 28

Warlords and Starlords

It was just over the third millennia since the existence of the Javols in Andromeda. That was due to a failed experiment to create the perfect soldier. The monsters that came out of the mould ended up destroying all major life within that galaxy. The recent battles fought against those Javols had removed them from Andromeda, but war still continued in other local galaxies. Presently that war was mainly fought against Javols mutants called Muts.

The great warlords of the Seventh Universe, in the form of the New Patriarchs were intent on removing all traces of the Javols within the three galaxies, Namely, Andromeda, Osmaron and Triangulum. That was necessary before the Javols could gain a foothold and begin once again to multiply their rapacious kind.

However, while they attended to the eradication of the enemy, modified Javols call Muts were being created. Those were tougher and larger than their predecessors and would infiltrate the Federation and ancient Hexolyte bases. Then those hidden underground bases would be revived and repaired by Muts. Soon, many of those more evil demons and devils, would be revived to reap even greater havoc on our primal universe. Their long term goal was to conquer and eradicate all primal life in the process, particularly those who posed a threat.

Grand Lord Gerra as lord of the Seventh Universe, was responsible for the removal of all such predator species from his dominions. Although he couldn't partake in warfare or indeed effect the natural development of any of the lower life-forms. He, through his Shadite priests, would assist civilization by improving their technologies to at least Class Five levels. However, the ancient Patriarchs were returning from wherever they had been for several aeons, because the time was right.

Through Grand Lord Gerra and his brand of Class Ten technologies, they were given modern indestructible bodies and made Grand Lords of the Seventh Universe. So far, all thirteen Patriarchs had returned and were being converted into supreme beings. However, they were on our side and have vowed to terminate all predator species from the universe.

The meeting of the seven Grand Lords of the Seven Universes convened within the inner sanctum of Goh to discuss such issues. Grand Lord Gerra was now the Chairlord of the residing council of lords, normally known as the Heptachial Nexus. Those meetings were held every thousand cyclons which were approximately 1600 years. During that time the seven lords of the universe would take stock and be brought up to date on relevant matters that concerned their respective areas of the seven universes. It so happened that time period corresponded to almost exactly two cyclons (3200 years) since the creation of the Javols.

'My lords, shall I officially convene this meeting of the Heptachial Nexus within the inner sanctum of Goh,' Grand Lord Gerra said telepathically and the response from the other six lords were positive. All the Grand Lords of the Seven Universes were portrayed as their adopted forms within whatever regions they served. In the case of Grand Lord Gerra, it was a young human form.

'As previously detailed, the Javols downfall was expected before their arrival to the local galaxies. Well, although we have been successful in ridding Andromeda from that plague, there still remain two major problems. The first of these relate to the large bands of Javols now entering Osmaron and Triangulum. However, we have substituted their MasterMind, so they are now virtually under our control and no longer pose a serious threat. They will remain at bay for now, while powerful portals are constructed and positioned. Once that operation is completed they will be dispatched back to the turbulent nucleus of Andromeda, where there is no escape.

The second problem is of greater significant and relates to the ancient Hexolytes.

'I thought the Hexolytes were vanquished eons ago by the Matriarchs?' Lord Rahmann queried.

'Yes! But you should also remember that although vanquished, they were not destroyed. Our laws forbade the complete destruction of all salient elementals and primal life-forms. Once imprisoned, they were allowed an element of free will.

'Anyway, they were stripped of their containment cloaks and imprisoned for eternity within Andromeda. At that time that place was remote from their former realms, although close enough for our constant surveillance. But for some incredible chance event and an unfortunate accident, their leaders containment tanks were discovered and looted by Javols in one of the Patriarchs prison caves. The Hexolytes Dracma and Lupher had merged as one with the two Javols concerned and soon became the masters of all Javols. They were the ones who created their MasterMind and have since escaped to Triangulum, their former home galaxy. Within that galaxy are many of their ancient caves which they mothballed before their defeat eons ago. However, although they are now unable to revive their ancient soldiers, they have found a new method for converting ordinary Javols into a newer and more deadlier type known as Muts. They intend to use them as their future soldiers for the conquest of all local galaxies. They also intend to released many of the ancient Masco demons like Hexil and others. So although our battles were won in Andromeda, we now have a much more devious foe to fight. Nevertheless, they have a long way to go before they can take control of any of our galaxies.

'Over the pass millennia we have converted many worlds within Osmaron and Triangulum to a Class Five technological base, giving them a much better chance of survival against their enemies. The Federation of worlds is soon to be extended to Triangulum and Andromeda, with all the necessary machinery to detect and contain Muts. We have also brought back several of the ancient Patriarchs who will aid in their defeat as in the past. We even have friendly Javols assisting us in the great battle against Muts. Those Javols seeing a better way of life have decided to join us. Those Javols are not interested in their original types and mine for their sustenance. They have become

as intended by their original creators, perfect warriors for the Federation.

'My Lords, we are confident that all these scourges will be removed from society within just twenty cyclone (32 years). This is the close estimate we have arrived at because of the Satan's Bug,' Lord Gerra said and sat in his high thrown.

'Once again I have listened with dismay to the platitudes of our presiding Chairlord. We should take note, however, should these vermin take hold once again, the other galaxies will doubtless suffer the same faith as Andromeda. The consequences to civilization could be dire. It is estimated that the Javols now possess knowledge of more advanced technologies which if used will soon get them faster ships. With such ships they may even be able to visit distant galactic groups well within ten cyclons. So what guarantees do we have that they will be stopped well before then,' Lord Sarius said, he was in the form of a fiery dragon and was responsible for the sixth parts of all six universes. Currently he was a Mesotrene from the sixth universe.

'Honoured council, I realize the feelings of uncertainty felt by many of you. However, you should realize that these problems do occur from time to time within every universe. Negative factors that we have never had great control over . They are due in part to the natural order and sometimes to technological advancement. Primal survival is like a two edged sword, with prey and predator coexisting side by side, each developing its measures and countermeasures. By so doing there is usually a survival balance. Only when certain of the more technologically advanced predators threaten the natural order have we become involved to curtail their progress.

'We have made choices in the past, which also excludes us from directly intervening in the development of primal species. All we are able to do is correct the serious wrongs after they have occurred and usually we have been successful. Therefore we must have faith in our ability to always succeed,' Lord Gerra replied.

'Is there any more questions on this topic,' Grand Lord Gerra asked, patiently. There was silence, which meant no one objected.

'In that case let us have a vote in favour of my actions and its completion within one hundred cyclons,' he added. They accepted his course of action and turned to the next topic on the agenda.

CHAPTER 29

Hearst Mansion renewed

Grand Lord Michael had fallen in love with the beautiful building and its many acres of fertile grounds. He had given orders for its refurbishment and structural additions during his absence in Andromeda, and so it was. Even by planet Eden's standards it was now a most beautiful palace with two massive extensions that flowed on either side towards its rear. He wanted that once famous building to be remembered by all his guests in future as it was during the days of its occupation by his father, the Son of Destiny.

Within the new extensions he had added several VR (Virtually Reality) rooms, old-earth disco rooms and an assortment for aliens and others. All under the control of a new Games Macron. However, his own personal macron was tied in to all others. Then there was the large meditation room upstairs, with its own VR Macron, specifically designed for that purpose. That room had been used extensively in the past by his father as a young man with Ron his computer. Finally, there was the large golf course just beyond the two tennis courts with the small cricket pitch. Beyond that was an artificial lake with recycled water and many fish. At that time the Primorphs Hercules and Ulyses were in charge of all mansion security.

Michael had enough of his cramped flat in Croydon and wanted somewhere with more space. But a place where his friends were always welcomed, day or night and where they could stay as long as they desired. So in a sense, the mansion belonged primarily to his closest friends.

He had over the years grown used to his closest friends, which now formed his gang of six. To him, with the exception of his future bride, those were his real brothers and sisters. However, since his recent visit to Andromeda he had gained a few more, including some mythical ones like Bellerophon and Chiron. Then there was the indescribably Captain Kazok and brave Lucien. With all those glorious memories and the sacrifices they had made, he had decided to have a party of parties that no one would ever forget. Its purpose was to thank them for those fearless efforts. He soon sent the invitations out to all senior members of the federation and expected a good response.

Like always, as protector of Earth, Michael would take the initiative and do as he pleased and no one ever stood in his way. In any event, he was very clever, and could predict the outcome of most events over a long period of time. That gave him the ability to modify the temporal path of Earth in the scheme of things. So seemingly irrelevant changes, could well have serious future consequences.

'Guys, I want you all in the main dining room right now!' Michael commanded through his implants and soon there was the banging of doors and several feet sauntering down the beautiful double circular staircase.

'You wanted me?' asked a curious Joan, but the others used the same words as they descended the stairs.

'I wanted to see all of you. I have to make an important announcement before I am called away on some other business. One never knows these days where he'll be tomorrow. Anyway, The Manor is now completed and it includes every possible facilities, so I have decided to donate all its facilities to my dearest friends and little gang of six. From now on it belongs to all of us equally. Since we shall have many guests here from time to time, may I suggest all the first floor rooms in the central area be reserved for us and our close friends. So now, you can move in and do as you please or at least what you normally do at your homes. However, I have plans to build several palaces throughout North America, after that continent has been suitably divided up into protectorate states. Then all our palace buildings can be linked by portals as on Eden and Mars.

'As it is on Eden so shall it be on Solaria (the new name for Earth). So each of you will be given your own protectorate state in due course. Any questions?' Michael said. They all rushed towards him and began to show their affection hy hugging and kissing him. Then they thanked him for being so caring and considerate.

'Ok! that's enough of that!' Michael shouted with embarrassment, but added. 'Being my second in command and future bride, Joan is now responsible for everyone's welfare in this place, so she can show you the rooms. After that it's up to you.

'We have much work before the first of next month, so I'll like to see some ideas on my desk first thing tomorrow. Also, be prepared to receive some workers.

'I have decided to employ a large crew to take care of this place, so there will be ten maids, three chefs and their assistants. My personal butler, Author, and several gardeners and others. When they arrive, in the morning, I would like to see them in my office,' Michael said.

He had fabricated several of the old ship Vogan and placed them in a circle on the green behind the mansion. Those massive ships made good temporary accommodation for many of his guests. At least those that could not be contained within the manor with its many rooms.

Early the next day the new staff arrived and were immediately ushered into Michael's ground floor office. They had no idea who their new boss were, but utterly surprised when they recognized the important person standing in front of them. They immediately bowed in silence to show their respect.

Michael glanced through them as if determining their character. Although he could read their minds, he was not the type to invade the privacy of others.

'This is a beautiful place with a great history of which we are quite proud, so you must live up to those exacting standards in both words and deeds. From this moment, this place will be your home, so should you have any problems, I would expect you to discuss them with any of the senior members and councillors.

Any questions?' Michael said. Up went the hands of an English gentleman at the rear.

'Yes Arthur,' Michael responded, and Arthur was surprised that he knew his name, but continued to speak.

'I am sorry my lord, but I believe such high standards to be almost impossible for any normal human being. However, I am sure that we shall all endeavour to do our utmost best,' he said and everyone turned around to observe to tall stately figure with the strange British accent.

'All I want from you is just your normal human selves. And I can assure you that I don't mind the occasional stumble. After all, we all make mistakes. But I want you all to be special and caring in every regard. I shall expect many guests here from time to time and many of them may not even be human, so you must regard all with respect and affection, but also as professionals,' Michael said, then there was the forming of a thought in his mind.

'Darling, Micol, the ship, has arrived with the young Andromedans,' Joan said. Then he focussed to the group standing in front of his desk.

'Arthur, these matters are now your responsibility. So take these good people around and introduce them to everyone. Then you can show them their places of work. Also, take this mobile phone. Each of you will be issued with your own phones and computer files in due course. Contact me if you have any problem,' he said to Arthur.

'Yes, my lord,' he replied, and he and the others were already on their way. Yet, they were curious to know what the present commotion was all about. Since it came from the rear of the building, Arthur followed with his troops in that direction.

They closely observed the strange object parked on the lawn, on its three powerful telescopic legs, for a while. Then to their utter surprise the side of the ship melted into a shimmering stairway. Then several young and happy people descended its steps. Finally, and to even greater surprise, the stairway miraculously melted back into the side of the ship, leaving not even the slightest dent in its structure. Then to top it all, suddenly and from no where Michael appeared out of a brilliant point of light and went forward to greet his guests.

'How did he appear like that out of no where and that... ship?' a disturbed Gloria quizzed.

'Didn't you know he is a Grand Lord?' Arthur replied.

'What is a Grand Lord,' the others inquired.

'From what little I have been told by my daughter, they are like Gods, with powers to see all and do all. But I don't fully believe that,' he replied.

'Who has been feeding you all this science fiction tripe. You are as bad as my grandmother, with her stories about the Son of Destiny and his healing powers. If he was that great, where is he now? Clarisa said. She was quite religious and followed one of the recently revived religions. She was expected to be in charge of the domestic maids, but was also an experienced nurse.

'I don't know, but I think its uncanny the way things happened outside just now, don't you?' Arthur replied, but continued taking the group about the expansive mansion.

The Andromedan six ran towards Michael and embraced him. Since there was only space for twelve passengers on board Micol, they decided to fill the other enclosures with presents. Although they looked as young as thirty, they were over one-hundred and seventy years old, with many grand and great grand children. On planet Eden no one ever grew old or died, so all the grown up generations looked of similar age.

'You have done much work on this place. It's so spacious and lovely,' Lira said.

'I found it necessary to make a few additions for all my many future guests.

You guys always look so young, healthy and beautiful. One day, you know, everyone on Earth will be given the choice to live forever like on Eden. Then everyone will look as young and beautiful as you. I hope by then you will consider Solaria your second home. But enough of that. Let us visit the bar and talk about old times and beautiful Eden,' he said.

'Lord Meron and I would like to rebuild Earth... I mean Solaria, on the same model as Eden, using our known technologies. However, I realize I might have a problem converting its humans to that way of living. I don't like the idea of anyone doing anything against their will, so I shall have to convince them by example. I think that's where you might come in handy. Perhaps we could work out a plan to build places like those on Eden.

Once they are familiar with its forms of advanced technologies, I am sure they will take the next steps,' Michael said.

'Well, when we arrived on Eden it was bare. With the help of the great ships and some equipment from Polok, almost every building was constructed within a month. We added the finer trimmings like palaces and so on afterwards. But it was not a difficult project. If we build one main city on each continent to start, then we can build the palaces afterwards, once we know the boundaries of all protectorate states,' Jon said.

'Now you know why I needed your input. Anyway, most of the major cities were destroyed during the last upheaval, so we can build over them and even call them by their original old-world names. I have already worked out the protectorate states for the planet,' Michael said.

Within the week many ships had arrived from Polok with large earth moving equipment, all being controlled by Lodorian computers. The construction phase of Solaria had begun. During that time the young six Andromedans would assist in the construction phase.

During the recovery phase of Earth, there were just over 480 million people left. Those had been the Fertilate survivors and were distributed almost evenly throughout the planet. Since the previous century most had returned to farming and just basic day-to-day survival, so much effort was now required to bring them all into a common fold. Schools, universities, museums, art galleries and many other places and venues had to be built in selected places throughout the planet. It was not going to be an easy process for its populations and the explanations were left to the construction androids.

The sudden appearance of the large construction ships, made many think they were being invaded by aliens. For never before had they seen such incredible forces and technologies. However, once the human-like androids disembarked and began to survey the areas, they were once again made at ease. People were offered work for extra credits, which they could spend within the cities after their construction, so many had accepted.

Although the time had come to bring Earth's people up to Federation standards, its people were too rural and uneducated. They had been through much suffering over the decades and lacked the finer minds that had been thought and moulded since birth. Yet, it was hoped that their children, if caught in time, would be moulded to similar standards.

In order for the seniors to communicate properly with the people, there had to be large cities in each province, with its local government, shops and other venues. Once Earth was opened up in such a manner, the councillors could then visit those cities and create a common bond with the people.

After the turmoil of the past, many people had developed a deep seated fear of each other and their governments. Many had left their enclosed dome environments for a less claustrophobic existence on the land. Without the usual robots and skilled engineers to repair the domes and their utilities, meant that they went into disrepair, which lessened the incentive to remain. Further, all the Infilates had either died or departed the planet and so did all the violence and uncertainty, so the Earth was free once more to explore and use without borders. With just about 480 million people, the planet was sparsely populated and many relied on a form of barter for their general existence. Nevertheless, the people had selected their mayors and chiefs who they would go for advise and assistance, so no one starved.

Since the departure of the Son of Destiny and the Specials to fight the Javols in Andromeda, Earth had been neglected. That war had taken about one hundred long years, during which time many had to adapt to extreme measures and sacrifices. It was hoped that after things had quietened they would recover and once again be able to govern themselves, but the trauma of the past was too great and many had been left with permanent scars.

The great minds on Eden had planned it that way and everything on Earth had followed that plan to precision. That was all needed before the re-creation of Earth (Solaria) into a most beautiful world that would survive the Javols.

Grand Lord Michael was a genius in long term planning and had put a universal master plan in place. That plan would include good Javols, who would eventually take over the role of protectors of the universe. He had always thought the original Javols were corrupted by their Hexolyte masters who always hated primals. They had brainwashed all Javols to see all such life as a defect and should go out of their way to destroy them, unless useful for their program of universal conquest.

With subtle coercion while using his AI master mind, which he had specifically created for that purpose, all arriving Javols were diverted to a different place for rehabilitation. His plan was to brainwash them while not under the influence of their original MasterMind. Of course that master mind had been replaced soon after its destruction.

Javols were finally beginning to see the light and a better way of existence even among primals like humans.

By visiting Earth and asking humans for help good Javols had taken that first step. But they needed hope in the form of a living god to protect them, so he was duty bound to assist them that way if they were going to sacrifice their lives for the Federation. Hope was a delicate thing and almost everyone needed a god for that reason.

They were going to be his inter-galactic soldiers/warriors of the future after every Mut had been removed. Since those new Javols would be his future warriors which he could control through his AI MasterMind he decided to call them Algarths to distinguish them from vicious Javols. That was a suitable name, since Javols were gatherers and copiers.

But that was not the only reason, he didn't want his best warriors to be associated with vicious Javols. That way they would be more acceptable to the Federation as another useful species and redeem themselves. By so doing, most Javols who had lost their way could be invited by his master mind to join their flock and be trained in the new ways, if they wanted to survive.

'Shall we be visited by many Javols in this part of our galaxy.' Jon asked.

'We may not receive any Javols in this part of the galaxy. That is because I have engendered a master plan. That plan includes diverting them to areas in space where they can be captured by rings of portals and returned to the nucleus of Andromeda, where they are destroyed. Those visiting Triangulum are rehabilitated and brainwashed to fight for us,' Michael said.

'How did you manage that?' Merol inquired.

'They hate Muts but find it difficult to fight them, So I have supplied them with relevant weapons. I intend to make them the warriors of the universe. They will soon be model soldiers as they were meant to be. You know, that was why they were created.' Michael said and they were aghast by that answer.

'It will take me a very long time to trust those monsters!' Lira exclaimed.

'I know how you guys feel about Javols, but those are different. They mine for their food and do not carry deadly viruses and smell like rotten eggs. These are also building a society of their own in Triangulum. So far, they have destroyed several enemy basses and installations. They also want me to become their god. What do you think, people? Should I accept that special role?' Michael replied jokingly.

'Javols fighting for the empire. Now I've heard everything. It's true what they say about the enemy of my enemy being my friend. But in this case I thing someone has been seriously misled.' Ecrol said.

CHAPTER 30

Martia's ship visits the Mansion

It was a most beautiful day about Hearst Mansion in North America. Out of the blue the massive ship suddenly appeared and landed on the green about a kilometre away. Well, Martia's ship never landed, she just stationed herself in that exact position by gravitational neutralizers. However, electro-magnetic anchors were used to hold her almost massless form in place. Although black in colour, she looked spectacular in the brilliant sunlight.

There was a great uproar within the Manor and everyone rushed out to observe the incredible form. She was over two kilometres long and close to one kilometre high, into the clouds. Martia's ship had recently visited all the federation worlds to collect many important members of the Federation for the celebrations to come.

'Oh my God! What is it?' Claris exclaimed and all the other maids stood stunned, not quite knowing what to say.

'She must be a space ship?' Arthur conjectured.

'No space ship can be that large!' one of the maids commented.

'It must be an invasion from another world. I only hope they are peaceful,' Lee Ching commented, then a voice came from behind.

'It is not an alien invasion. Neither is it visiting us from another galaxy, although the latter is true in many respects. Her name is Martia's Ship and she is one of the best fighting ships of the Federation. She is called Martia's Ship because she has a most beautiful human dual by the name of Martia. I am sure you will meet her in due course.

'As a matter of fact, that ship out there could destroy this whole world in a blink of an eye if she so chose. What I am trying to say to you people, is that the large ship you see in front of you belongs to all of us, including you. So after you have finished you duties for today, I would expect each of you to visit her and be taken for a tour about her decks. Is that acceptable to you?' Michael said and they stared at him in utter disbelief.

'Yes, my Lord! That would indeed be a great adventure!' Arthur said.

'In that case, Arthur, you can keep an eye on them for me. Then take them to the restaurant and get them their favourite meal, or what ever they prefer,' Michael said, and they bowed, but in an instant he had vanished from their sight, leaving them even more bewildered.

Michael was no longer worried about accommodation for the majority of his guests, since many could now board on Martia's ship. There was also a large portal at the basement of the Manor, so guests could be transferred to and from the Manor at their leisure.

Soon the manor was being flooded with a stream of Federation councillors and their families. Michael and Joan were immaculately dressed and patiently awaited their arrival in the large basement close to the portal. Both shook their hands in turn and handed them over to the page boys who took them to the lounge for refreshments.

'Hi Vek, you look a bit more like me these days. I hope you don't mind being family?' Michael jested and Lord Vektron bowed gently.

'I love it and I enjoy being a member of your esteemed family. It's the freedom that I have always wanted. Now I can start my life all over again and be one of the guys,' Lord Vektron replied.

'Not just one of the guys?' Michael replied and he smiled and left.

Then it was Lord Meron and all his Andromedan Ancients and most of their families. However, Jerry Fraser, Donald Fraser, Mallory, Andy, Lumak, Sarah and others with their families were expected much later by portal from Terminus City. They had some other visits to make on route. The Son of Destiny was still in Triangulum and would be the latest to arrive.

Finally it was Malik and his sons. His son Captain Filo Olav had lost his life during the battle in Andromeda, but luckily for him he had a recent lifesaver fitted. Soon after his death, his body was re-created and his Identity remained. If it had taken longer than the allotted time he would have been lost from this world forever.

However, all memories after he had taken the life-safer was lost from his new brain. Nevertheless, that slight change did not affect his memories or relationship with his wife, only his military experiences in Andromeda.

'Our Grand Lord will visit us later today. He is busy reviewing the Battle for Triangulum in light of the new Satan's Plague. Apparently all Muts within the central regions of that galaxy along with their extensive metallic installations have been destroyed. Thanks to Lumak and his two Shadite companions, Gemmi and Meradon,' Lord Vektron said and there was an uproar and clapping.

'Yes, Granddad and his two companions have done a great job within those inner regions of TG using the SP1 virus, but that virus cannot be used in populated regions. We can only use the SB2 type on living worlds if we are to save our metallic installations and buildings. Anyway, where are those two great men that designed those three Satan Bugs?' Michael said. Both men, Doctor Hal Seaton and Doctor John Simmons placed their hands up.

'We are very sorry! And guilty as charged, your honour!' Hal shouted, jokingly and everyone clapped ecstatically.

'Because of the great work both of you had done with the help of our Professor Bengizara Khan, who happens to be my great granddad, we have substantially reduced the length of the battle for Osmaron. For those great deeds you will soon be honoured by our Grand Lord Gerra. So keep on with your great works,' Michael said and there was more clapping.

It was not long before three Shadites suddenly materialized in the large ball room and walked down the red carpeted isle of that main hall, to be clapped by everyone. Then their hoods were released to reveal the faces of Lumak, Gemmi and Meradon with great smiles on their faces. Then Michael stood up and asked Lumak to the rostrum.

THE REVIEW

Grand Lord Gerra in the form of a princely dress young man sauntered through the central aisle followed by six beautiful Semonites pulling a large floating golden casket. While he and his team followed they were vigorously chaired. Then he walked toward the rostrum to say a few words of his own.

'My dearest friends, from what I have been told, the battle for Andromeda has been worn. The Battle for Osmaron will take place mainly in Triangulum. Osmaron is well protected and will remain free of all Javols indefinitely. We have made many sacrifices during this process, so thank god we finally can see the end of this mess. The Muts and their two demonic superiors will not remain for long within these galaxies. Plans have been made for their capture. Soon we shall be rid of these monsters for all time. Now may I ask our Grand Lord Michael, who heads the war council, to give us his review on the progress made within these three galaxies,' Grand Lord Gerra said and everyone shouted and cheered.

'Thank you Grand Lord Gerra, Lord of the Seventh Universe, for giving me this opportunity to address our Federation Lords, Councillors and Friends. As you all know we have had exemplary success in Andromeda. As far as I am concerned that galaxy has been conquered. Most of the Javols on their way to this galaxy have been sabotaged by numerous invisible spacial portals laid along their routes. All those Javols will be returned to the nucleus of that galaxy where they will be destroyed. Therefore our galaxy Osmaron is quite safe from those monsters and will always remain that way.

'The great warriors Ulysses and Hercules have discovered many hidden civilizations and some peaceful Javols who are willing to work for our Federation. Most of them are

farmers and for some reason never like hunting and killing as the others. Those mine for their nutrients and are not a danger to anyone. So on the advice of Hercules I have decided to accept them into the Federation.

'The Javols commander Xo and his many warriors are now under the control of my MasterMind and have been shown the deceit of his superiors, who left him and his soldiers for Triangulum. Xo will never forgive Lupher and Dracma for that deceit and hate all those Javols they turned into Muts. So I have to use that great band of warriors to destroy Muts throughout Triangulum.

'Xo and his people now mine for their food and will never again kill primals. As a matter of fact they have adopted the human form. They want me to become their leader. But I haven't made that decision yet. They have finally become the almost indestructible warriors they were meant to be and do not pose a threat to us anymore.

'They were misguided and corrupted by their original MasterMind. Lupher and Dracma their leaders hated all primals and had created that master mind with the sole purpose of destroying all primals, particularly those who posed a threat. I know many of you will not agree, but I am thinking of using them as the guardians of our universe. They are tough and make the ideal soldier. They can be used along with Primorphs to maintain order in the name of the Federation through my AI MasterMind. Of course before that decision can be made I shall require a unanimous vote from the council. We believe in freedom for all, irrespective of form, creed, belief and such like. We cannot discriminate or associate anyone because of type or previous deed done by their predecessors!' Michael stressed and many were taken back by those plans. After all, Javols were the scourge of the Federation and hated by all for what they had done to Andromeda. But he was a genius and well respected Grand Lord, so his words echoed.

MUTS

'Finally we come to the situation of Muts within the Federation. There are no Muts left in Andromeda. Their superiors intended to conquer Triangulum first and with numerous Muts overwhelm Osmaron, but they have been sadly mistaken. We have since found their hideouts within nebulous clouds at the heart of the Triangulum galaxy and have destroyed all with Satan's Plague. Those worlds will be uninhabitable by their kind for at least five years.

'Just three of our great Shadites, namely Lumak, Gemmi and Meradon, took out all Javols within the inner regions of Triangulum with the Satan's Plague. That is the measure of our powers, so very soon we shall have Muts on the run, not only from us, but from Federation Javols. We are soon to lay a trap for Lupher and Dracma. Once caught those ghastly demons will be put back into the tanks where they belong for eternity.

'In the mean time we tighten Federation security and reform Mars, Venus and Earth to our new Federation standards. I recently turned this Mansion into a most beautiful Palace. This is meant to be an example to what I would like most buildings to be like. Those who dedicate their lives to the empire will benefit greatly with such incentives. We have enough fiefs and palaces on this world for everyone,' Michael said and everyone chaired.

THREE GREAT SHADITES

Then Lumak was soon called to the rostrum. He was to relate his close encounters with Muts. A brave Lumak followed by his two companions walked side by side towards the rostrum.

'Grand Lords, Councillors and Friends, the Satan's

Plague is probably the worst plague ever to exist. It will lay waste any civilization in a day. They do not only destroy Muts, they also consume all things metallic and remain for five long years. Of course they do not affect living organisms like us. Nevertheless those microids must be kept well away from civilizations and should never again be used. My colleagues and I witnessed the destruction of a complete world in a few hours and were aghast by their population increase and rapacious nature. They are indeed Satan's plague.

'The Javols commander Xo and his warriors have destroyed several installation run by Muts with little losses. They have created several of their own installations for saving and rehabilitating their own kind. So they are doing a great job for the Federation. Those few that I have met have adapted the human form and are building a city based on what they have observed on Earth. They will make great federation soldiers once accepted into the realm.

'This will now be the most critical time of our existence, since our enemy will try to fight back with everything they have. They may even have created their own anti-life microids designed specifically to destroy our civilizations. We should now stop all passenger ships from landing on Federation worlds. Build more sensitive detectors to locate their screened ships and be generally aware of infiltration, because soon these Muts and their leaders will become desperate for their survival. That is all I have to say on the topic for now,' Lumak said.

'Although we have our enemies on the run for now, we must increase our security on Mars. We should use sensitive portals instead of ferries in future to transport our people and goods, until our enemies are removed from these galaxies,' Gemmi said as they left the podium with more cheers.

CHAPTER 31

Grand lords of the universe

There was a great assembly of councillors within the rear of the manner and many others from Earth congregated throughout the local grounds to listen to a declaration from the Grand Lord of Osmaron. It was not the best of days, the sun was not visible, the sky was dense with the darkest clouds and it had began to rain. Today of all days, Michael wanted to make his mark and show the true powers of Aron, the Ancient Patriarch, but also state a few of his main goals within the Federation.

There was a crackle of light, then darkness descended upon the Earth, then a bright blue light with five others of different colours travelled to encircled the earth at great speed. The lights finally stationed themselves above a large golden throne just beyond the manor. Suddenly those six lights in the sky were surrounded by millions upon millions of smaller lights. The six bright lights descended from the other lights and slowly changed into six powerful human forms. They were of four males and two females and sat on the exalted throne.

The people throughout Earth were almost traumatised by the strange occurrences and many of those within the palace grounds thought it was the end of the world. Slowly the skies brightened and as it did, so did the smaller points of light fade, leaving just the six great Patriarchs. But that was not all, the once clouded sky had dissolved into a clear blue one and everywhere about the Manor was showered in beautiful sunlight.

Grand Lord Aron

'Today symbolizes the beginning of the second phase of this world's conversion, so let us all rejoice in the fact that soon Solaria will once again be the hub of the Federation of Galaxies.

'Fellow Grand Lords, Councillors and people, as chief ruler of

the Federation of Galaxies, I have declared that this world Solaria be from henceforth known as the capital of the Federation of said galaxies. However, when I use the name Solaria in the broadest sense, I shall refer to the complete Solar System.

'From henceforth, every important Supreme Councillor will be expected to act as protector over his fief here on Solaria. However, this ruling in no way should detract from your other important commitments and duties elsewhere. Since we exist within a free and honest society, I expect anyone with the necessary skills and effort capable of accomplishing that esteemed goal, in becoming councillors of the Federation. However, because of certain limitations, in future Solaria will be the residence of a chosen few. At this time, there are over 480 million people on this world. Many of whom are farmers, while others would prefer an occupation as soldiers in our fleets and other diverse professions. Many of those will now be free to enter once forbidden places within the federation by portals. All travel by ships and ferries will be forbidden until the war has ended. This is because Muts can use these methods to travel unhindered throughout the federation.

'Hence, with the exception of some forms of travel, I declare that the old burdens and restrictions of the past be lifted from Solaria. That henceforth she be once more free to barter and trade with all the trading worlds of the Federation.

'This world has been through much pain and difficulties over the years and it's no wonder that its peoples are still in a state of trauma and distrust of all authority. However, I intend to mend all those fences in due course, beginning with the conversion of Solaria to very similar specifications to Eden.

'With this, a null period in the great wars between galaxies, I advise that all of us begin placing our houses and worlds in order before the real fight begins. Since the enemy will wage a two pronged attack, with infiltrators constantly trying to penetrate our societies to gain access to our advanced technologies, we must set in place a rigid set of rules within society. However, for that methodology to work, the very cultural fabrics of societies will have to be altered and moulded in a

manner more conducive to our long-term survival, taking all those factors into consideration.

'Despite the resourcefulness of our present fore, never again shall any dominant predator species become a controlling force within the universe. We defeated them in the past and we shall defeat them again in the future. As a matter of fact, we shall defeat them whenever and wherever they lift their ugly heads,' Michael, now the Patriarch Aron, said. The enormous crowds cheered and waved their banners continuously.

'Now, for a few words from Grand Lord Jull, Supreme Councillor of war and security for the Federation of Galaxies, known to us all as, The Son of Destiny,' Michael said, and there was a further uproar from the crowd. For although many had heard the name mentioned by their grand and great grand parents, they believed him to be the tales of myth and folklore, created to keep minds at ease during the upheavals in the previous centuries. However, here he was standing among them in all his glory.

Grand Lord Jull, Son of Destiny

'Members of our Federation of Galaxies, I proudly stand here to express my heartfelt joy and satisfaction in our accomplishments against our enemies in Andromeda. Finally we can rebuild and secure that galaxy for all time. With the removal of such predators, soon, everyone will feel safe in the knowledge that they are free to travel anywhere within these three sister galaxies. Earth will soon be rebuilt to exacting standards. Soon there will be schools, colleges and universities with all the associated technologies to take its people to the highest levels of knowledge. However, as always, everyone is free to pursue what ever range of knowledge they desire. No more will the populations of Earth be fearful of others.

'However, with greater freedoms go greater responsibilities. We well remember the sad state of Solaria when it was Earth, with a damaged environment, due mainly to human greed, global warming, deforestation, and others. At times the population of

this planet had increased to over eleven billion. Never again will this planets population be allowed to grow beyond the 500 million limit. With several galaxies now available to us, very soon many will become fully mobile and seek their achievements and challenges elsewhere. We are now in a period of change, so I hope everyone will be patient during this period, because the rewards and benefits will be enough for all. So be patient,' George said, and there was a roar from the crowd and more flag waving.

'And now a few words from Grand Lord Bella, Supreme Councillor, responsible for the welfare of all life within the Federation of Galaxies,' George added and took his position in the main line at the rear.

Grand Lord Bella

'Honoured members and People of our Federation of Galaxies, it's a great honour for me, standing here before you in this manner to express my views on certain important issues. You know, everyone within this universe would prefer a better existence. Even those of us with all the incredible technologies at our disposal sometimes prefer the simpler ways. In our youth we enjoy facing the challenges to wherever dark places they led. When we were older our challenges changed, but what makes us happy always seem to be the simpler things in life, like playing a game of tennis, and others. We should, within these galaxies, make life as free and easy for all. No more will anyone be enslaved by anyone.

'Even the lowlier workers are equally important, because they have chosen that way of life. So everyone in our universe should respect everyone for their differences. This attitude does not only apply to the so-called more advanced life-forms, but every living thing within the Greater Purpose. From henceforth, everyone will select an occupation suitable to their own personal goals. It is better that we love our duties, than do them painfully just for financial gains, status or family commitments.

'As on Eden, a credit system will be used here on Solaria, wherein every child from birth will begin to earn his own credits.

Within this empire no one need ever work again, since they shall all earn a steady flow of credits. We now use robots and androids to do most of the nitty-gritty work, from mining to building. Many of these intricate and intelligent systems also love their duties, are self repairable and can be made to exist for thousands of years.

'However, it is in the nature of all of us to forego challenges. Since the system can now virtually run itself, anyone involved in extra duties will be rewarded handsomely with extra credits. That way, there is also the possibility and freedom to be upwardly mobile. However, I know that many of you, like us, will willingly give your utmost best even your complete lifetime to your relevant societies because it is in your nature to give without receiving. However, we always receive your love and appreciation and that is more than enough reward for us.

'In the future, Solaria will be the planet of careers. From its populations will be chosen a new type of doctor that will see to the needs of all life on this world and within the Federation of Galaxies. However, most of our young will first enjoy a stint of adventure within the Federation flagships, as soldiers, engineers, Specials and others. That experience is essential for anyone wishing to lead others,' She said, and gained a standing ovation.

'Now for a few words from Grand Lord Corra, Supreme Councillor of the Arts, Antiquities and Theology.

Grand Lord Corra

'Honoured members and people of the Federation of Galaxies, my main role is to enhance the nature of all life within the universe. This is truly an enormous task, but I have my methods. Man shall not live by bread alone. We need to be part of a greater whole which goes beyond nature itself. You have all heard of the saying, "we are more than the sum of our parts" well. that applies to all things.

'Over the past we have come to rely on technology for our very survival. Well, we are also spiritual beings and cannot truly have a complete and fulfilling existence based on technology alone.

We also need spiritual improvement or that most important part of us will be forever neglected. We need to appreciate the simple and complex, side by side, for they are all part of the Greater Purpose and our Cosmos and so are we.

'My primary task in the future will be to improve the essence of existence for all. By so doing you can be fulfilled within yourselves and become at one with the Greater Purpose. You will also learn to respect and appreciate all living things. Therefore, every young person in the Federation will be thought good attitudes and morals from year one.

'You will also learn to appreciate your past, by studying the history of your world. For by recognising our past we have a better chance of surviving the future. Finally, there are the Arts, which includes music and other forms of creative outlet. Those forms of expression I intend to encourage, with frequent exhibitions throughout the Federation. I shall place great emphasis on any Old-world Arts, so you must save all such relics and artifacts for such appreciation.

'Finally, for a healthy mind we must also have a healthy body. Therefore, our dieticians shall create healthy menus for all relevant life-forms within the Federation, with listings of ingredients with all products. Soon, everywhere on Earth and on other worlds shall be stadia of every type for every kind of sports and games. Since competition forms the lifeblood of many species, we shall be expected to learn such methods from a young age.

'With a little effort from you, I am sure those recommendations will be beneficial for good health and in extending the survivable age of the average mortal life-form. However, many of you will, in the not too distant future, be given the choice of everlasting life. There are many changes ahead and we must face them with faith, diligence and bravery,' She said. There was another uproar as the crowd cheered.

'Now for a few words from Grand Lord Vektron, Supreme Councillor of Science and Technology within the Federation of Galaxies,' she said.

Grand Lord Vektron

'Honoured members and people of the Federation of Galaxies, it is my honoured task to take this world through the next thousand years. During that time there will be great changes in its peoples and their technologies. By the end of that time, hopefully all our enemies will be vanquished and everyone will again be free to travel and settle within many galaxies. During that period we shall discover many new species and galaxies, and many shall require our assistance in one way or another.

'We must remember that we exist in a most turbulent universe, where worlds must be secured from external factors like colliding meteors, supernovae, stray objects like comets, and a host of others. In future, all advanced worlds will be given a cloak of invulnerability, to secure their life-forms from such dangers. However, that is not all. There is also the need to ensure the stability and strength of the powerful magnetic fields of habitable worlds. This is required to retain their atmospheres for as long a time as possible. So we shall require a new type of stellar engineer and others with a new brand of technologies to assist planetary life, enhance planetary environments and prevent dangerous collisions.

'We now have the technologies to change old stars into new ones. We are now able to use the matter from dead stars and change them into virtually any elements using a nuclear virus. Gone are the days of fuel and energy shortages. Also, gone are the rarity of precious gems and metals like platinum, gold and silver. We can now mine planets of gold as we do of iron and other minerals. Since such materials are mined by robots, androids and automatic machinery, their values have become negligible. These days we do not appreciate solids to the same extent as we do beauty and symmetry. Unless of course when it has special significance as a memento or figure of art.

'With all the resources now available to us, we can truly build a great empire where everyone can fulfil his every dream,' Vektron said. This time the people chaired continuously and so did Vektron bow several times to the massive crowd.

'And now, a few final words from Grand Lord Aron, Ruler of

the Federation of Galaxies,' Grand Lord Vektron added.

'It was said once, that as the universe grew older, it would become a continuum of greater order, where eventually order would win over chaos. Well, there will always be changes, leading to greater or lesser ones, either for the benefit or detriment of life, so either way, chaos will never be threatened. However, I do believe that the negative and detrimental aspects will always exist and are sent to test our resolve. For all of evolution is based on such chaos and diversity.

'In future, we must see all such negative issues as a challenge to each of us in our daily lives. For life would be extremely boring and uninteresting if we never faced such challenges and we can also learn much from them. Nevertheless, we would find it difficult to face life and death issues on a daily basis, for they would eventually sap our inner energies and our very will to exist. So let it be, that we only face one major negative challenge during each of our lifetimes.

'The greatest challenge at this moment is to remove all our enemies from the Federation of Galaxies. When that deed is done, our duties would be to assist primal life throughout the universe for the common good, respecting the modus vivendi of all such life.

'Today, symbolizes a major change in our purpose and goals throughout the Federation, so let the first of next month be marked on all our yearly calendars as a day of rejoicing for the final conversion phase of Solaria and the beginning of a new era in the universe.

'So, let the Zegon messengers travel throughout the lengths and breath of this world to proclaim this period of change and declare a period of goodwill to all the inhabitants of Solaria,' Grand Lord Aron said.

He outstretched both his arms in front of him and once again the sky dimmed, the millions of small points of light began to appear and encircle over their throne and they began to disperse throughout the world, to deliver the message.

The Zegon were the messengers of the Grand Lords of the universe and could become any life-form and communicate to any type and in any language, even directly into their minds.

Finally, the sky above the Manor brightened and the great thrown of the Gods, slowly dissolved into nothing, while Grand Lord Aron continued to wave to the crowds.

After all that had gone on, the local people and servants about the Manor was left in a daze. They could only conclude that their recent experiences were contrived and was the result of the clever manoeuvrings of some brilliant magician, whose plan was to mislead several thousand spectators into thinking that Gods really existed. But even if that was the case, how could anyone, even a brilliant magician, make the sun go away and the sky change as it did. It would take the ignorant population of Earth some time to realize that their were superior entities that could do virtually anything.

Michael had brought everything out in the open, because he didn't like pretence and wanted everyone to get used to the idea that the universe was a universe of variation, where all its life-forms, from the lowliest to the most advanced could live side by side and respect each others deficiencies and needs.

'I told you he was a Grand Lord and so is the Son of Destiny. What we just witnessed was no hallucination, you know. It was real. Even the prints of the golden throne has remained,' Arthur said, but clarisa still remained silent, not wanting to say anything that would make her look the fool in future.

'I think the whole episode was strange, if you ask me. But I am still not convinced,' she replied.

'Why not, Clarisa,' a voice came from behind and she looked around to see who it was. No one knew her pet name but her grandmother and she had died recently.

'My sincere apologies, my Lord,' she apologised and knelt before him. But Michael lifted her up back on her feet.

'People, one important thing you must always remember, is that everyone in this universe is part of the greater whole. It takes every individual drop to make and ocean. So never underestimate your importance in the scheme of things. Although, you must leave your minds open to all possibilities, do not believe just for the sake of belief. You should always weigh the evidence and come to some conclusion based on the balance. But never jump to conclusions, for that attitude has falsely sentenced many an innocent person. Be diligent and honest in all things and you will constantly rise to higher levels, for such attitudes are like diamonds and gold. So in answer to your nagging question, I can tell you now that gods do exist,' he said and faded into nothing as they watched.

'My God! He is one of them!' she cried.

BOOK 3
THE FIGHT BACK

CHAPTER 32

The Javols overlords

The Javols' masters, Dracma and Lupher had done well since their arrival in Triangulum. They had significantly improved their technologies and repaired and revived many of their main bases in that galaxy. With the latest technologies learnt or stolen from the Federation, they were able to improve their technologies and now posed a much greater threat to the Federation.

They had found two advanced species at war and knew their potentials, so had acted as pretend negotiators for lasting peace. Both species were almost at the point of mutual annihilation when they stepped in to stop the war. After the devastating war was ended, they had acquired much popularity and soon were elevated to Chancellor of both worlds. They then re-engineered the rebuilding of the worlds in question and in the process added much of their own technologies to safeguard their future as joint rulers. Since both worlds were in the same stellar system, both separate species, the Lemphie and Boromas, had frequently waged war against each other, when not competing technologically. That way their technologies gradually advanced to a very high level, although well below that of the Federation.

This time, their weapons were of mass destruction, and both worlds had almost obliterated each other.

With their new technologies they had soon rebuilt a Javols Master Mind, which misled Javols and guided them into areas where they were collected for recycling. That was the name given to the process used to convert Javols into their latest brand of mutants called Muts. They had also found an ingenious way to manufacture Muts when their supply from Andromeda had dried up. If they had their way, soon most of the galaxies Triangulum and Osmaron would be saturated with Muts, or so they thought.

To hide their numerous Muts from the Federation they built large installation within the nucleus of that galaxy and continued working toward the goal of universal conquest. That was until

Lumak found their hideout and destroyed most of those installations with the Satan's Plague.

To top it all, they had also collected and revived some of the most dangerous and dominating demons the universe had ever known. They had all been captured and imprisoned aeons ago and were once again free to roam and corrupt civilization for their own pleasures. However, they had to agree to certain stipulations before their release. The main one was that they remain patient for now and assist them in their plans. Once the Federation was conquered, they would once more be free to do as they liked in a universe free of Patriarchs. After all, they had been defeated once before and didn't relish an eternity of imprisonment for a second time. The Demons and others resided on several bases close to the nucleus of Triangulum.

The Grand Lords knew of their intentions and had mined most of their bases with sensitive scanners and detectors, so they always knew their plans in advance.

'Brother, I think I have found a weakness in the clots' security. They tend to concentrate more effort on the outer systems than towards the more central regions of the galaxies. This is partly to do with the higher levels of radiation and the present lack of Javols in those areas. It might be possible for us to sneak within those volumes and build our troops and their defences. You know, we have a main base in that area, as indicated on the main map, and it could still be operational. We should send a few of our Tec Muts to that area and see if they can put that main portal back on line. Once it's in operation we can freely move our soldiers and equipment within the screens of our enemies, shielded by the dense nebulae,' Dracma said.

'As always, Bro, you have another beautiful plan, but you will have to visit that area yourself, to ensure that the base is repaired properly and upgraded to the usual standards. This is too important to our success. Once a link is established, your presence there will ensure our program is successful. In the mean time, I can remain here and take control at this end,' Lupher said.

'Sounds reasonable. However, the problem is getting there undetected. We don't want those nasty clots to find our main base there, since we intend to use it for housing our worst demons before their release,' Dracma commented.

'No problems, Bro. Our present stealth ships are quite fast and you can choose a suitable route, to avoid their main bases and scanners. Better yet, we can capture one of their own craft and modify it to our needs. Anyway, if your are caught, you can always pretend to be someone else. We have a few names and profiles in our database, so don't worry,' Lupher said, and changed the topic.

'I also have had a brilliant idea. I have found a way to combine several Javols into a common type. When combined, they will link together to form one colossal Mut. With several thousand Javols joined in that manner, they will form a colossus that can destroy a small city with a single hammer blow. No one will be able to stand against them. They can also be made to separate into individual Muts, but once detached, they cannot be used in that manner again. However, it is but a small setback with the greater potential for destruction,' Lupher added.

'You know, Bro, you are too clever for your own badness,' Dracma replies and they both busted into laughter.

'Mother alert! I have lost all communications with Mut Factory 48 and the local installations. I think they have been destroyed. We should send Muts to investigate and receive reports as soon as possible!' their new MasterMind advised.

'Oh, Brother! What's all that about? You think the clots have found our inner installations?' Dracma inquired not expecting and immediate answer.

'Our installations are well hidden. If they found one it would be purely by accident. The radiation levels in that part of the galaxy could not be penetrated by any of their probing systems,' Lupher replied.

'Well brother, if they found one, their curiosity will lead them to others. They may have a new weapon of destruction. We have to find what it is before we can carry on any of our long term plans. We must find how much we lost and make new plans.' Dracma said nervously, if such emotions could be attributed to demons of their type.

'We can send commander Zilo to investigate. Since his last encounter with human clots on their world Solaria, he had developed an everlasting hatred for their kind. He would love a little payback to set things right. He can take two of his subs along with orders to kill any clots he encounters on the way,' Lupher replied.

'Yes! He would love that!' Dracma said.

It was not long before Zilo and two other Muts were given a special ship and on their way to forward installation 48, They viewed the world from orbit and couldn't believe what they observed. The whole world was engulfed by dense swarms of infestations. They had no idea what they were and remained in orbit to view the devastation.

'Mother, installation 48 has been completely destroyed. Not one iota of metals remains. These things have eaten everything including workers. No metallic objects or structures remain. Please advise, Zilo out!'

'You are advised to get samples of the contagion for analysis. Mother out!' Their master mind ordered.

'We are to land and collect samples of the bug. There are several plastic suits on board. They should give you some protection from those bugs. From recent observations they have left plastics alone. I shall remain here to coordinate your efforts. We have several non-metallic containers on board. Use them for that purpose. I will recommend you for promotion after this caper. If you fail mother would not be happy!' Zilo said to his two companions. They were not please but could not refuse orders from their commander.

Although Muts could transform to fit the suits, they could not transform while in them, neither could they have used LPDs for travel, since their construction was partly metallic. So Zilo found a place between two mountains that were free of bugs and let them down. They would take several days to get to the installation in question.

'Forward base 48 have been completely destroyed by an engineered parasite. Obviously created by our enemies to destroy our installations. Since this was the first one visited, we can assume that most of the others have also been destroyed. I have dispatched several surveillance probes to check all our bases in that region, but we should conclude the remaining installations have been destroyed in a similar manner. Zilo and his two companions are under quarantine and will remain that way until they are guaranteed clean. However may I advice their destruction in the hottest plasma pit to ensure our survivability. I am now in the process of creating a non-metallic laboratory to analyse those samples. You will be informed later of our findings. Mother out!' Master mind said.

'Bloodiest hell, Brother. The clots have destroyed all our inner bases and installations. How could they have found them so quickly? Now we have to change all our plans!' Lupher was seriously enraged.

'I don't think they would have found our underground bases. They are too well hidden, even from those bugs. We go underground instead. We should have gone that way before.' Dracma replied.

'But Brother, if we start using these bases they will soon be detected by our enemy probes. They have been in stasis so we can used them for concealment at a later date to hide and store our warriors before battle. Any movement in and out of these bases will soon be detected.' Lupher said.

'I so miss my Timit women in times like this!' Dracma said.

'Yes, Brother, a sacrifice of blood is grossly required at this time for inspiration!' Lupher replied.

'Clots are not the only ones capable of creating bugs. This time we create the most nasty bug to remove all clots from their important world in Osmaron. That should teach them a lesson and show them who is boss. Then we take over that world and rule that galaxy. We have been playing catch-up for far too long!' Dracma said.

'Yes, Brother, Zilo and his two companions will like that mission very much for payback. That will save them from the Plasma Pit, so they will not refuse.'

'Brilliant idea! But we may not have enough Muts to carry it out!'

'Leave the logistics to me, Brother. I have a plan!'

CHAPTER 33

Xo's first battle

'My warriors and others of our realm. We have had a great success. I and my company recently made contact with the most advanced people in one of the local galaxies. We are both fighting the same enemy, so they have decided to assist us in destroying the monsters called Muts. Where weapons fail a targeted bug will destroy. Those particular bugs they call Satan's Bug. It only kills Muts, so all we have to do is deliver the bug secretly within their installations and see them crumble. We have also received sample weapons and LPDs which we can re-create in our labs. Friends and warriors, having seen the way others live, we should build a beautiful city on the world below to the plans I have taken with me. Let us build our society before waging a prolonged war against our enemies. Anyway we need a city to contain our increased numbers after their rehabilitation,' Xo said and was chaired. There he and his companions stood in human form.

'How are you sure these alien clots are not taking us for a ride?' One of his warriors inquired.

'Because those I met were not clots. The one name Michael was a god. He was all powerful and could kill us all by a single steer. I am thinking of making him our real god. That is because he is real and eternal. One day soon you will see what I mean!' Xo said and those misplaced Javols were happier than they had ever been. If such emotions could be attributed to Javols. Yet it was thought that even Javols in complex societies would eventually gain complex emotions.

'If they are so powerful why haven't they gotten rid of these monsters?' Another one shouted from the crowd.

'Our original gods never assisted us. Not then, not now. These super-beings are like parents. They only assist when they realize our course is impossible. That way we grow and learn and in the process gain new ideas and technologies. We cannot exists by allowing others to accomplish our goals for us!' Xo replied and they were satisfied with that answer.

'Xo, it is important that you and your people move immediately to the planet below. Build a city close to the cave as shown on the map. You can use the hidden cave for all your scientific and copying experiments. Use this moon as your observation base. From now on you should pretend to be the humanoid type. That way, probes will see you as a primal. This deception is essential if we are to win against our enemies. When not in use, leave your carrier ship hidden in the crater on the moon! Mother out!'

'Got it, Mother! Xo out!'

Xo and his people found a large cave in the world below and began building their city south of its entrance. Within that cave they began to build their laboratory installations for the creation and copying of new technologies. He wanted his city built on the types he saw on Earth, designed for bipeds. He reasoned that LPDs should only be allocated to his active warriors in the field. All others would maintain their society by mining for their food and creating the needed goods for their society.

'Good news! I have received communication from our Lord Michael. All enemy bases and installations within the central galactic regions have been destroyed and will remain that way for five Solarian years. So it's time we became an active army. We now have the required numbers to repel our enemies, and more of our people are being diverted to our moonbase and rehabilitated in our ways. You are presently required to train and organize a large army. This will be a two pronged attack, with Grand Lord Michael and his fighters leading the battle from the outer rim towards us. I will send you a map in due course when the time is right. Mother out!'

'Thank you Mother for the information. I shall begin training right away. Xo out!'

'Those of you who have recently been rehabilitated should realize we are at war with a type of monster called Muts. These enemies are tougher than us and will win any prolonged battle. I know it's quite soon to ask you to train as warriors to defend our realm, but you should consider our mutual survival in all this. We are alone in this galaxy and more limited than when we lived in our home galaxy. Yet, there are many of us and with not much life about us in this galaxy, so we have chosen a new way of life for mutual survival. Please follow our rules and be another one of us or be cast out to find your own way. I do believe we fight better as a large trained army than a group of untrained individuals.' Xo said and all those rehabilitated Javols agreed to join.

'Commander Xo, why are we fighting these Muts. I thought we were here to conquer this galaxy?' Commander Cola asked. He led a large group of Javols with spheres and carrier ships from Andromeda and were frozen in space for several thousand years.

'Since you left our home galaxy several thousand years ago the universe has changed. The clots have conquered our home galaxy and almost destroyed our MasterMind. To top it all, two of our highest commanders used deceit against us. They have used our invading armies for their bizarre experiments and turned them into the monsters we call Muts. They have also trained them to capture our kind and use them to create more Muts. Our task will be to destroy all their basses and installations and find those two demons, which we must cleanse in the hottest plasma pit,' Xo said and they were shocked.

'How can we fight them when they are so strong?' Cola inquired.

'We have powerful friends that know how to destroy them. They gave us special weapons that we can fabricate. You leave all the thinking and planning to me. All I expect you to do is train your warriors hard and prepare them for battle. We have a home here to come back to, so you will always be remembers should you fall in battle. We do not fight for ourselves. We fight for our families!' Xo replied and Cola was satisfied with that answer.

Xo stood in their main auditorium to give lecture to his troupes. They were presently in human form. There they stood at attention in their fatigues ready for battle.

'People, you know what we are fighting for! We fight for our freedom from those monsters called Muts with claims of universal conquest. They will destroy anyone that does not follow their plans. We can be as deceitful as our enemies by changing form whenever we are within range of our world. That way they will ignore us while we destroy them. Muts may be tougher then us but we have better weapons and more cunning.

'Muts use LPDs for flight and can move very quickly. All our warriors and commanders will adapt a new form to misguide the enemies when we are not fighting. Only our commanders will have LPD's so we use our one-man space fighters. They can manoeuvre very quickly and be well shielded from the enemy. Those are being manufactured as we speak. Before our first incursion into enemy territory we send five of our best warriors on a special mission in one-man space fighters. They will discharge a most deadly payload that targets only Muts. Then we land and take over their installations and communication system. That way they will be none the wiser and will not know what happened until its too late. That way we are able to take over their bases and installations and man them with our own troupes. However for this plan to work we must fool their master mind. I was given a special device that must be plugged into their coms. It will take the place of their three commanders. That device has been listening to their master mind for several weeks and knows all their codes.' Xo said and they were intrigued.

'If as you say, these Muts are so difficult to kill, how can we destroy them in a day?' A curious Cola inquired.

'Let me explain the process to you! These are like a type of primal virus. They are called the Satan's Bug. They only affect Muts. They literally tear them apart and in the process duplicate they own kind. Every generation of these Satanic bugs only live for about one day. So their swarms will continue killing Muts until none exist, then the final generation die within one day. Depending on the number of Muts they may take up to several days. You Cola will choose four of your best trained to accompany you on that mission. Don't worry, when you drop the canisters you will be well shielded above their bases and installations, so get prepared for that important mission. You may join us on the final assault. Please survey and map all bases and installations on that world and advise us on our best approach and implementations,' Xo said.

'Commander, thank you for the opportunity to lead my men in battle! I was looking for some action. Now you have explained the process I feel like giving some real payback for what they have done to our innocent people,' Cola replied.

'Get your guys prepared. You leave today and we invade in a week!' Xo commanded and Cola was on his way to brief his warriors.

Soon enough, Cola and his four companions were on their way to a local stellar system. That system was one of the main ones for collecting and analysing data from the local galaxies. All such information would be relayed to Lupher's master mind. So it would have been a great capture for Xo and his people. Once captured they would replace part of the transmitter and relay erroneous information to Lupher's master mind. Well, that was the intention.

However, Cola didn't know that base was always on alert and had systems that were constantly scanning the skies for ships like his. They could detect even the smallest bug and destroy them with powerful lasers. Since the destruction of their basses and installations within the inner galactic regions they had become more prepared for any eventuality.

'Hell! I'm in trouble! By god, they have such good defences. I cannot fly this bird anymore. Wings have been severed by lasers. I will hit ground in seconds! You are to save the canisters and protect them. Camouflage into a rock and shield them. Hide canisters and meet at my location after Muts leave the area for briefing. Cola out!' Cola also relayed the information to Xo who was surprised, but realized he was on a learning curve when it came to Muts.

Muts could not find any life in the area and assumed they had shot down drones working for those clots who had destroyed their inner bases. Even so, they made a clean sweep of the areas involved and collected all fragments for analysis and copying.

They ignored the small pillars of rock that blended well with the area. Soon Cola and his team were together at his hidden position.

'I heard them talking. They thing the ships were drones that belong to the clots that destroyed their inner bases. So they do not suspect us. What we couldn't do with our ships we do by hand. These canisters are not large, so we harness them to our backs and find five suitable locations on our maps. Then we lay them and set the timers. We have to observe the complete process before we leave. We use this spot to meet after the weapons are planted. Boss will tell us where to go for pickup. But I think we should remain hidden until Boss and our fighters land. Then we can give some payback. Any questions?' Cola said.

'We remain! What's the point of going home and coming back when we are already here?' Kal said.

'So we are all agreed? Good! It's time we thought these nasty Muts a lesson they cannot forget!' Cola said and they all agreed.

'Yes, Boss!'

'You know where the five points are, so let's deliver, set the timers and find a spot to camouflage and wait for the troops!' Cola said and they were on their way.

After the timers went off the canisters exploded spraying that type of Satan's Bug every where within that base. What happened next was truly bizarre as Muts began to transform into all types of monstrous forms including the original Javols from which they were made. Then they simply crumbled into a black pile of muck.

'My god of all gods! Are you seeing this, guys? This must be the worst weapon ever made. I hope they do not affect us in the same way. I wonder where our boss got this. With this weapon we have already won the war!' Cola was ecstatic.

'Commander Xo said they only affect Muts, but we should wait here until the troupes arrive. We shouldn't take the risk!' Kal said. They remained fixated in their places while observing the destruction of numerous Muts killed by several swarms of vicious bugs that seemed to enjoy Muts. The swarms grew to enormous sizes until there were just the residue piles left where the Muts stood. Only their LPDs were left in tact and would be collected for later use.

When Xo and his troupes arrived and the base examined they found a large laboratory at the lower levels containing thousands of containment tanks were Javols were converted to Muts. Javols were still being collected from space and processed by that chemical base. However they could now be intercepted and rehabilitated, to become more of Xo's warriors to fight their enemies.

They had been successful in their first real battle against the enemy by using a targeting microid bug, which they were able to synthesize. Soon the base and installations were cleaned and Muts replaced by a new type of robots identical to Muts. That way their enemies would be non the wiser until all local bases and installations had been taken over. With powerful defensive lasers and missiles they were now fully in control.

CHAPTER 34

Hercules and Ulyses back at the Mansion

'Hercules and Ulyses, your lord needs you for a special mission. Your work in Andromeda has been completed. That galaxy has been pacified. Any loose ends can be accomplished by your replacements. Take Venusa's ship to Solaria, I shall brief you there on your arrival. I will also commend and promote you both for a job well done.' George, the Son of Destiny said.

'From Caefon to Earth, This world has changed a lot since we left, I hope the mansion is still in one piece?' Hercules commented while they left Venusa's ship through one of her vertical portals. They were greeted by numerous waving flags and wondered whether it was a public holiday. Apparently schools were on holidays on that day to greet two great federation heros.

'Please follow me. Sirs!' a young uniformed woman greeted.

'What's all the celebrations about?' a curious Ulyses inquired.

'It's all for you, sir! You are to follow me and give a short speech to the people. Don't worry, just be yourselves. The people here have not seen heroes in a very long time, and would like to know what happened in Andromeda. With all the changes on Solaria these days they feel a bit left out, so you will be a ray of light,' she replied.

'Well, Brother, we have to do what we have to do,' Hercules said as both giant primorphs walked towards the rostrum.

'Grand Lords, Councilors and friends. It is so great to be home. We had no idea that you had prepared such a grand reception for us. We indeed feel privileged to be here, on our home world now called Solaria. So whatever our missions be in future we shall always return to our beautiful Solaria. Now a few words on our missions in Andromeda by my brother Hercules,' Ulyses said and the crowds cheered.

'Grand Lords, Councilors and friends, we have had great

success in the galaxy you call Andromeda. Only a few Javols remain and those have decided to become part of our Federation, so they do not pose a threat. Those few do not kill creatures anymore for food. They now mine for chemicals most of which they supply to us. Others have become farmers. All warrior Javols have either been destroyed or are now on they way to our galaxy and Triangulum. Those visiting our galaxy are captured and sent back to the nucleus of Andromeda where they are destroyed. Those visiting Triangulum are also captured. They are rehabilitated and used to destroy our mutual enemies called Muts. The Javols in Triangulum are peaceful warriors and do not pose a threat to anyone except Muts. Therefore I can say that the war against Javols have been won, but there a still numerous Muts about, so we have to be on constant guard against these infiltrators.' Hercules said.

Then there was an uproar as three globes of light appeared through the clouds and moved towards the crowd. In a brilliant flash they transformed into three Grand Lords of the universe. They stood together in human form and sauntered towards the rostrum to greet the two heroes. On their way they waved to the frightened crowd and they began to cheer.

'This is indeed a great day for celebrations! Two of our greatest heroes have returned, so let them be praised!' Michael shouted and Joan floated towards the rostrum to give her speech, but first she shook the hands of both heroes. Then she placed her hands in front of her to command the heavens.

'Let the heavens be clear. Let all clouds be faded for today!' Joan commanded. And the clouds boiled away until there were blue skies.

'Because of the great services rendered by you in Andromeda for the Federation, I bestow upon you both the title of Lord Councillor of Osmaron. May you both always strive for greater order and follow the Greater Purpose in all things, to help and assist life throughout our universe. Please accept these wands of office. They represent your true status within the Federation of worlds,' George, the Son of Destiny, said while handing them golden cases containing the items. Then George began to speak to the crowds directly.

'I am George Peterson, Son of Destiny. We are Grand Lords, rulers of the universe. We are eternal and indestructible. We can only assist when all life is seriously threatened, either by catastrophe or destruction by some other method like the Javols invasion, for instance. The Grand Lord responsible for this part of the Seventh Universe is called Grand Lord Gerra. One day he will visit you. That will take place after the rebuilding of this world. Very soon, this world Solaria, once called Earth, shall become the most important in this galaxy, but until then it must be remade because of damages done to it over the centuries. Therefore you must be patient until then,' George continued.

After their speeches they became coloured bolls of energy and spiralled off at great speed to disappear in the distance amidst more cheers and waving of flags. That day the people of Earth were shook to their very cores. Before that day they never knew Grand Lords with such powers existed in the universe. Yet they felt safe in the knowledge that they existed and could help them when needed.0

After the grand reception the two primorphs were on their way to the Mansion which used to be their home while on Earth.

'It's nice to be home at last. I always dreamt of playing golf even while we were away,' Ulyses said.

'I felt the same!' Hercules replied as they got off the small LPD hover craft. They were like cars but didn't need roads. Anyway all roads had been paved over and was now part of the land. The whole of North America was now one fief governed by the Mansion which was now a grand palace.

On arrival Hercules and Ulyses were greeted by the large uniformed staff which numbered over fifty. Parky the Butler was in charge and was the first to welcome the heroes home. They were taken into the lounge to be greeted by the three Grand Lords now in human form.

'So finally you guys made it home!' George greeted.

'Some home! This is now the largest palace in Christendom with a fief the size of North America, But I love it all the same!' Ulyses said'

'Is the golf course still in tact?' A proud Hercules inquired.

'It's even better than before. I had a hand in its improvement,' Joan said.

'My wife an I use it on occasion. We love the challenge. Perhaps we can all have a game together soon,' Michael said.

'In the mean time we must have a few words in private,' George said.

'We are sending you both on a special mission to Triangulum. That mission will be the most important for the Federation. It will involve you both leading good Javols to fight Muts. Muts have become a great threat to civilizations within that galaxy, so the sooner they are destroyed the better. The Javols in question are controlled by one of my AI creations called MasterMind. She will update us from time to time, so please focus on your mission,' Michael said.

'Are these Javols converted. I mean, are they civilized?' Ulyses inquired.

'Our MasterMind is able to communicate with all arrivals and collect them. Then I've been told they are put through a thorough training program, where they are thought new skills relevant to their survival. They now mine for their food and respect all life. They have become the perfect soldier as were intended. Their commander Xo tries his best but needs Federation assistance. You will visit them bearing presents. They will be new weapons specific to the killing of Muts. You are also to mention to Xo that you was sent by their Lord Michael to assist. I met him and some of his warriors when they were looking for help. At that time they found it difficult to kill Muts. That was until I gave them samples of Satan's Bug to fabricate. Now they are able to destroy Muts' bases and installations. Be their advisors in battle until you take command, Then you can lead them in battle against these nasty creatures,' Michael said.

'This program is not too urgent, so in the mean time we would like you both to take time off for several months and enjoy yourselves,' George said and they were pleased.

CHAPTER 35

Xo's second battle

The Primorphs Hercules and Ulyses were twice the size of an average human and resembled Greek gods made of bronze, so no wonder school children and others loved them. Their presence made people feel safe in a world of change. Both Primorphs were powered by nuclear fusion generators which lasted for a thousand years. They could become hunter killers and transform into the most vicious creatures to hunt their prey. They could destroy a complete city when given the order, yet they could be as mild as a lamb while not under orders.

Since their lengthy mission in Galaxy Andromeda they had become more human and with all the experience gained saw the universe for what it was. They had also developed the emotional centres of their AI brains and could now be considered one hundred percent Earth human.

Both Primorphs Hercules and Ulyses, now back on Earth, had a great holiday during the three months that followed. They enjoyed their games of golf and visited many new places including schools. They had become like the ancient Greek bronze gods to kids who almost worshipped them. However after the three months were up they suddenly realized they were needed by the Federation for a greater purpose. This time Grand Lord Michael called them together for an update on future plans.

'We are to visit the New Javols landings in Triangulum. I have been told by their MasterMind that they have adapted the human form and are building a city based on the one they observed while on Earth. They are determined to be like us humans and will only use their true forms in battle. They have now accepted our Federation as their future, but we have to make their joining official. That's where you come in. You are to make an impression on your arrival and convince them of our powers. We shall come along to introduce you to them in a proper manner.

You can do your favourite transformations into a giant Tiger or Lion. That will convince them of our powers to stress the point. Javols like a bit of bravado and intrigue, it makes them feel you are one of them,' Michael said.

'What do you guys think about all this?' Joan inquired.

'I think it's a great idea for convincing them. Javols like all that heroic stuff. Do we have a language and cultural profile of that group?' Hercules replied.

'Yes! All that data will be sent to you in due course. MasterMind will also update you on relevant matters and other eventualities from time to time. We leave this world Solaria in three days with Martia's ship so prepare yourselves for the trip. We shall fit a long range portal on that world in due course, so you shouldn't worry too much about visiting the mansion for the occasional game of golf,' Michael said and they both smiled.

The massive battle cruiser Martia's ship now over 2.8 kilometres long suddenly appeared over the expansive base in America not too far from the manor and created a small windstorm in her wake. She was all black and extended through several layers of clouds. She could not land directly but hovered about the base being held in place by her powerful gravitron neutralizers. Her portal tubes extended towards the ground and was ready to accept her passengers. That base near the Hearst Mansion in North America was the largest military base on earth. Similar to Gatwick it contained numerous space fighters for the defence of Earth (Solaria).

Both sister ships Martia and Venusa were the most powerful battle ships in the federation. They were powerful enough to destroy worlds by stripping their atmospheres and laying waste their surfaces using the most deadliest weapons of the Federation. They were on a constant move to federation worlds to assist and make their presence felt. They showed the powers and abilities of the Federation and were admired but feared by everyone.

Grand Lord Michael and Joan floated through the thick walls of Martia's ship and became brilliant balls of energy. As they descended toward the city of New Croydon on planet Solon, the numerous Javol Soldiers on parade stopped to observe the incredible obstacles as they swooped and turned into the clouds, causing the very heavens to boil. Their great powers could transform night into day. The hardened Javol warriors froze where they stood and could not contemplate such incredible energies and powers being contained by any physical life.

Both Patriarchs descended towards a large platform and materialized into giant human forms of glowing silver wearing golden armour. They stretched their hands forward and the remaining clouds boiled away into blue skies and brilliant sunlight. As Xo ascended the platform he bowed and as he did all his soldiers bowed in rank and file.

'Ah, Xo, there you are!' Michael greeted with a smile.

'Yes, My Lord, here I am,' Xo replied equally humourous.

'I must say Xo, you and your people have built a most beautiful city. We have brought you some beautiful paintings and tapestries for the walls of your main civic building. I hope you cherish them. We have also brought you some more advanced weapons and equipment that you may copy and use for entertainment and games,' Michael said and Xo was pleased.

'Anyway, what's the name of this great city of yours?' Joan inquired.

'We decided to call it New Croydon after one of Solaria's main cities,' Xo replied.

'That's fantastic! Now, if you wish, we can instal a long-range portal between both galaxies,' Michael replied.

'But, My Lord, we are unable to utilize such devices. They can kill us!'

'That was yesterday. We have found a way, utilizing a special containment pod that will shield you during transit, so that problem has been solved,' Michael replied and Xo was ecstatic.

There was a loud crackle and a little later a turbulent gust as the giant ship Martia appeared above the city. Soon a small shuttle craft appeared and floated towards their position and landed. In a flash the transmorphs Hercules and Ulyses suddenly materialized on the platform and sauntered towards the group. They appeared larger than life in their brilliant garments and Xo and his warriors were impressed.

Without further ado they began to transform into a giant lion and tiger. Then roared with red glowing eyes to put the fear of god even into the hardened warrior Javols. Then they transformed back into their original selves.

'Let me introduce two of the greatest warriors to you. They will assist during the attack on the main base of our enemies. You may have their assistance whenever needed. You need only ask,' Michael said.

'Where is the main base you speak of?' A curious Xo inquired.

'It is quite local to us and is called Romero IV. That world has been adapted by our enemies as their main base of operations. Since the destruction of the inner bases in this galaxy they have gone underground. Muts are now difficult to kill using the Satan's Plague. They now encapsulate themselves in a thick layer of plastic, but those cannot transform, so they cannot be infiltrators. However, infiltrators can wear an invisible cloak that can also shield them from plasma. This makes our task of neutralizing our enemies a lot more difficult. Therefore we have decided to change our methods.

'As you know, we grand lords of the universe do not get personally involved in civilizations unless such civilizations are threatened with extinction or slavery. We uphold the virtues of freedom for the individual providing such freedom do not cause suffering and pain to others. Occasionally we may choose a developing species for greatness or save worlds from disaster, but that is how far we go to maintain the natural order,' Michael said.

'This war has now taken a different route. One that will lead to the destruction of many living worlds. That new path is fraught with many dangers and cannot be tolerated, so we have decided to change the plan completely.' Joan said.

'So what do we do?' Xo inquired.

'You become guardians of this whole galaxy. You will travel through the length and breath of this galaxy and assist in its future changes. You will have complete freedom in utilizing its resources and manufacture for the Federation. That position will make you the wealthiest people in the Federation. However, you may assist us initially in reforming old planetary systems into new ones. During this time we can only reform dead worlds with white dwarf stars. You will journey to all relevant worlds and check whether they are suitable for conversion. Since our enemies utilize dead worlds they will be destroyed during the reforming process. That way we kill two birds with a single stone,' Michael replied and Xo was intrigued.

'How are you able to bring a dead star back to life?' Xo inquired with scepticism.

'We use a hydrogen reforming nuclear virus (HRNV). Using a special missile it will be fired into the star causing every large atom to split into its basic form, which is hydrogen. Within several days the star will ignite like a brand new one. That star will live longer than its original. Then we reform any relevant worlds and move them into suitable zones (goldilocks zones) so that life can begin. I am sure you and your people will like to partake in this process. Xo, we now live during the most exciting phase of this galaxy!' Michael said and Xo swallowed hard.

'My Lord, is there anything you guys cannot achieve?' Xo was astounded by the share powers of the Federation.

'Xo, believe me when I tell you there is very little we cannot achieve with focus and hard work. Nevertheless, we have some great friends and scientists that can accomplish almost any goal set before them,' Ulyses said.

'Xo, I have good news. During this, your second battle, against our mutual enemies on Romero IV, you and your brave warriors will observe the operation in comfort on Martia's ship. She will utilize hot plasma from the local star and rain it down on the base in question until not a single Mut remains. That part of the world will be completely obliterated,' Hercules said.

'Our Supreme Lord, The Son of Destiny, have decreed that this war be ended forthwith. Therefore your task in the future is to assist in the reformation of this ancient galaxy. To remove all Muts from the central regions we shall install an hexotron around the nucleus. While utilizing the energies of that black hole it will disrupt and change elements, so that all life within those regions cease to exist.

'During this time we shall revive all white dwarfs and superheat the surfaces of suitable worlds so they can begin the process of life, after their orbits have been altered for natural evolution. By so doing the complete galaxy shall be cleansed of all Muts,' Ulyses said.

'Yes, we have observed the destruction carried out within galaxy Andromeda and cannot accept such a future for this and other galaxies. These Muts and their leaders, given the chance, will destroy this whole universe, which is not theirs to destroy. Therefore we should destroy them before they are able to visit other galaxies and take a foothold,' Hercules responded.

'Our Supreme Lord, The Son of Destiny have further decided that your people assist in the reforming process. But that is not all. You will eventually become the guardians of this galaxy for the Federation. That is a much better occupation than fighting Muts. Leave Muts to us. Our advanced technologies will wipe them from these galaxies, then we can build our societies without constant threat of invading Muts. However, you and your people must become part of the Federation of worlds so that we can mutually assist our friends when in trouble.

'I think your future plans are truly incredible. By so doing me and my warriors can focus on building and guarding instead of destroying. That will completely change our culture into peaceful Javols,' Xo replied.

'Because of all those changes, we have decided to leave two of our best with you. Hercules and Ulyses will educate you in the new ways of the Federation. However, for them to remain here with you, your people must agree to being a major part of the Federation by becoming an important member. Once you have signed the necessary documents your people will be given a seat at the Grand Council of worlds. Then you become one of us with a say in all Federation matters. You may discus this very important matter with all your people,' Michael said.

'Since MasterMind represents us in all things only her decision counts in this matter and she has agreed, so let me sign your documents on her behalf,' Xo said with pleasure.

Then what appeared to be an ancient golden scroll appeared on the rostrum before them. Michael unfolded the scroll to reveal areas for his signature. Then they shook Xo's human hands to thank him and seal the deal.

'Now, Xo, you are a major part of us and may utilize all systems, whether they be technological or for the purpose of transportation within all three galaxies. You can now copy and manufacture all general items you wish for barter and trade within all worlds of the Federation. That process will give you the funds you need for building your societies,' Joan said and Xo was overwhelmed with excitement.

CHAPTER 36

An old star is reborn

After Xo and his people were accepted within the Federation, Hercules and Ulyses accepted their new roles as advisors to the New Javols Empire. During that time thousands of Javols were arriving within the galaxy of Triangulum. Many were captured by Xo's people and converted to New Javols, but others were captured by the Hexolyte main bases and were converted to Muts. For some reason the Muts and their leaders always appeared to be ahead of the Federation in such matters. Which required more drastic action on the part of the Federation to remove them.

'Muts and their leaders threaten the very existence of our Federation. Therefore all their worlds must be destroyed and re-converted into new and living worlds. The destruction of a world is no easy matter. It so happens that all the worlds on our list have already been shredded by novas and supernovas, and are therefore lifeless planets floating through space. Nevertheless, we shall check every one of those worlds for life and they will be evacuated whenever necessary. For that purpose we have designed a range of special sensors that can even discover life several miles below planetary surfaces. Hexolyte caves, which are mainly utilized by Muts are usually less than one kilometre below the surface. That is the maximum depth of our plasma weapons. That is because Hexolyte bases were designed with good access to their surface slave cities,' Michael said.

This time Martia's ship would take onboard Xo, his sub-commanders and about one thousand of his experienced warriors. They were to witness the complete destruction of Romero IV which was the main base of operations for Muts within that galaxy. Since the destruction of their bases in the nucleus of Triangulum they had gone underground and utilized special portals for moving through the system.

On arrival to the system Martia's ship took position from the dead white dwarf which was once as massive as our Sun. Presently it was the size of a large planet like Saturn, about ten times larger than Earth. When a star like our Sun explodes into a nova the remnant white dwarf which is still almost the original mass of the star shrinks to a giant planet size with matter of extreme density. Since energy could not be created nor destroyed, all that energy was used to pressurize the mass of heavier elements due to the intense gravitation.

While utilizing the energies of the white dwarf the hydrogen based nuclear virus which were engineered from sub-atomic particles like quarks would first convert the outer layers and progress until the complete star had been converted. Using a process akin to fission, the virus would split the large atoms apart and use the matter to build new hydrogen atoms until all became hydrogen. At a certain point of balance the star would suddenly ignite and increase its size thousands of times larger. It took several days for completion into a completely blue star of immense radiation. To Xo and his people it was the greatest miracle they had ever beheld.

To destroy a world like earth Martia's ship would move between both world and star and focus the atmosphere of the star towards the planet using intense gravitron beams. What followed was too ghastly to watch as the atmosphere of that world boiled into space followed by a plasma wave that encircled the complete world. Almost all oxygen and heavier elements were lost in the process. The planet was now an almost red hot ball, but cooling quickly.

During that time hydrocarbons would be released in large quantities leading to the creation of complex molecular DNA and other relevant structures. The bubbling of fissures and liquid in small crevasses would further mix and stimulate the process of molecular combination leading to complex DNA and RNA strains.

It is known that primordial life could not exist in an oxygenated atmosphere. Eventually the planet would be seeded with certain chemicals to accelerate the evolution of such life.

'Ho! Ho! Ho! Ho! Ho! We have definitely taken over gods work from him. Now we can truly create our own universe with such powers!' Xo yelled with excitement.

'Yes, but with such powers go great responsibilities. What do you think would happened if we pointed such a dreadful weapon towards a living world,' Michael warned and Xo swallowed hard.

'I would not like to be a Mut, knowing there was no place I could hide from this devastation,' Joan said.

Several powerful Hexotrons the size of small moons were presently on their way to the central region of the galaxy to disrupt all worlds within that region. The real battle for Triangulum had begun with Muts not having any place to run. They were now like a cornered animal not quite knowing where to go or what to do in the circumstances.

Only Venusa and Martia's ships would be allowed to reform old worlds into new with their powerful weapons of creation, which were equally destructive depending on the types of worlds involved. That was why they were feared by all members of the Federation. However those two ships had inter-dimensional minds that would look at life and the universe in a different way to mankind. They were also under the guidance of Grand Lord Gerra, supreme lord of the Seventh Universe, so it was impossible for them to move on their own without his say-so.

CHAPTER 37

Life within cooling planetary systems

(not science fiction)

To set the stage, let's consider the formation of planets from an accretion disk—a rotating disk of gas, dust, and other materials surrounding a newly formed star. Over time, the particles within the disk collide and stick together, gradually forming planetesimals, which then attract more material through gravity and eventually form planets.

As a planet cools, its surface solidifies, and the conditions may become suitable for chemical reactions that could lead to the formation of organic molecules—key building blocks for life. These molecules could include amino acids, nucleotides, and sugars, which are essential for DNA and RNA.

Factors such as the presence of water, a stable atmosphere, and energy sources (like volcanic activity or sunlight) play crucial roles in creating an environment where these molecules can come together to form more complex structures. Over time, with the right conditions, these structures could evolve into primitive life forms capable of replication and metabolism.

The early stages of a planet's cooling process are indeed critical in shaping its environment and potential for life. As the planet cools, the high atmospheric pressure allows water to exist in liquid form at higher temperatures, contributing to a dynamic and volatile surface.

The small craters and hydrothermal vents can act as natural chemical reactors, providing the necessary conditions for organic molecules to form. These environments can concentrate organic compounds and provide the energy needed for complex chemical reactions. The boiling and bubbling of water in these craters and vents promote the formation of simple molecules, which can eventually bond to create more complex structures like DNA.

Furthermore, the repeated cycles of heating and cooling in these environments can drive the formation of lipid membranes, which are essential for creating cell-like structures. These primitive "proto-cells" can encapsulate organic molecules, protect them from the harsh external environment, and facilitate the interactions necessary for the emergence of life.

It's an intricate dance of chemistry and physics, where each factor plays a role in the gradual emergence of life. The transition from simple organic molecules to self-replicating entities is a fascinating journey that bridges many scientific disciplines.

An early atmosphere rich in hydrocarbons and nearly devoid of oxygen is a crucial factor for the formation of early life. Oxygen, in high concentrations, can be highly reactive and destructive to delicate organic molecules, so an anoxic atmosphere would be more favourable for the synthesis and stability of these molecules.

Hydrocarbons, on the other hand, provide a rich source of carbon and hydrogen, essential elements for the formation of organic compounds. These molecules could undergo various chemical reactions, potentially leading to the formation of more complex structures like amino acids and nucleotides.

Miller-Urey experiment is a great example of how early Earth conditions could produce organic molecules. By simulating an early atmosphere composed of methane, ammonia, hydrogen, and water vapour, and then introducing electrical sparks to mimic lightning, they were able to produce amino acids, the building blocks of proteins.

Once these organic molecules are formed, they can accumulate in the primordial soup of the planet's surface, possibly within shallow water bodies, hydrothermal vents, or even small craters. Here, they can undergo further reactions, driven by various energy sources, leading to the formation of more complex molecules and eventually self-replicating systems like RNA and DNA.

The Miller-Urey experiment is a classic and groundbreaking study in the field of abiogenesis—the origin of life from non-living matter. Conducted by Stanley Miller and Harold Urey in 1952, the experiment aimed to simulate the conditions of early Earth to test whether organic compounds necessary for life could form under those conditions.

Here's a breakdown of their experimental setup and findings: Simulated Atmosphere: They created a closed system that mimicked the early Earth's atmosphere, believed to be composed of methane (CH), ammonia (NH), hydrogen (H), and water vapour (H O).

Energy Source: To simulate lightning, which would have been a common source of energy on early Earth, they passed electrical sparks through the gas mixture.

Water Cycle: The system included a boiling flask representing the ocean, which heated the water to produce water vapour. The water vapour then circulated through the "atmosphere" and cooled, condensing back into liquid in a cooling chamber, simulating rainfall.

Results: After running the experiment for about a week, they analyzed the contents of the system and found that several organic compounds had formed. Notably, they discovered amino acids, which are the building blocks of proteins.

Significance:

Demonstration of Abiotic Synthesis: The experiment provided the first experimental evidence that organic molecules essential for life could be synthesized from inorganic precursors under conditions thought to resemble those of early Earth.

CHAPTER 38

A waning empire of Muts

Since most of Triangulum contained numerous dead and dying stellar systems, Martia and Venusa's ships had their work cutout. Although Muts infested most of the inner parts of that galaxy, they decided to start their reforming program from the centre, just beyond the Hexotrons, and work towards the galactic edge.

The Muts superiors, Lupher and Dracma, realized the Federation was much tougher and advanced than they had ever contemplated. They soon came to the conclusion that they had lost all strategic advantage and were now on their back-feet not quite knowing where to flee. Even then, they hadn't given up the fight.

The evil demon Lupher attempted to communicate with his master mind sited on Romera IV but all he could hear was constant crackle and background noise. His Mastermind was dead as a dodo. He sent a fast probe to investigate and couldn't believe the sight he beheld from the probe's transmission. He wondered whether that probe was faulty and began to take bearings of stellar constellations to locate the probe's current position but could find no errors in its journey or current position. He was soon convinced of the occurrence of a great catastrophe in that part of the galaxy.

The shock of the destruction of that world made him feel insignificant. Could that disaster have been due to a natural process, unknown cosmic event or new unknown weapon harnessed by the Federation. All those ideas flowed through his demonic mind while trying to find a solution. Yet, how could he tell his brother Dracma of his conclusions and all that bad news.

All their plans of universal domination had now been significantly curtailed. Now they would have to start all over again, but this time without Muts. Nevertheless several Muts remained, those were dispersed throughout the system. However, without the creation of new ones from wandering Javols they would not progress for many decades.

Perhaps those could be brought together for a final assault on the enemy. As he further viewed the system he could observe a large blue star showering its radiation on the now hot and lifeless world that was once their main base within the galaxy. How could anyone transform a white dwarf star into a real one? The bewildered Lupher soon contacted his brother to relay the bad news.

'Brother, are you busy?' Lupher greeted nervously.

'No, I just finished one of our religious celebrations and sacrificed a thousand slaves for the glory of our heavenly masters. They went to the slaughter proudly. Their bones, jewellery and other body parts will be useful in our Muts factory,' Dracma replied.

'Our Mastermind is no more. That world including our underground base has been completely destroyed. The once dead system has a new star,' Lupher said and Dracma gave a lengthy pause.

'That's impossible! How can a new star suddenly exist where a dead dwarf once stood. Check your coordinates again!' Dracma was not pleased.

'But Brother all that has been done many times. Romera IV is now a red hot planet being showered with light from a brand new star and I don't know how or why,' Lupher said.

'If that is the case, we are in big trouble. Our suits cannot be refilled to replenish our bodies and we would have lost most of our Muts including all that planning and equipment. Brother, if that is the case, we are now back where we started when we left Andromeda.' Dracma said.

'That is now the case. My advice is that we find a new galaxy and create a base within the nucleus of that galaxy. We cannot use Andromeda or this galaxy, Triangulum. This is because of the powerful gravitational waves emanating from the centre of those galaxies. Only Osmaron remain free of such problems,' Lupher advised.

'But Osmaron is filled with our enemies and we cannot visit the more distant galaxies,' Dracma replied.

'We could send some of our Mut infiltrators to find a suitable place within the nucleus of Osmaron. I am sure some ancient Hexolyte caves still remain within that galaxy,' Lupher said.

'Well Brother, you have brought this up, so I leave it in your capable hands to find a solution to our present dilemma,' Dracma said and severed the link. Even then Dracma was not convinced that they had lost. Something was amiss and he just couldn't figure out what it was. It was also possible that the probe's sensors were not functioning properly, after all only a single probe was used in that investigation, so he was not convinced.

The evil demonic brothers Lupher and Dracma were always set on universal domination. They attempted conquest of Andromeda through the Javols and their Master Mind. However they always found Javols difficult to control and failed that attempt when the Federation invaded. They subsequently left that galaxy for Triangulum, but had equally fail once the Federation decided to clear that galaxy of their installations.
Presently they had no where to run, not having the necessary technologies to reach the more distant galaxies.
They were quite powerful when they possessed the bodies of Javols and remained close to the nucleus of Andromeda. However since arriving in Triangulum they had destroyed their Javols bodies and encased themselves in special containment vessels. Although flexible and mobile they could not freely possess other lifeforms. The screening of those metallic suits also prevented them from controlling others. All they could do was communicate with their master mind who were in control of all Muts.

Those special suits prevented leakage of their elemental energies. However they were not perfect insulators, so there was always slight seepages and losses when they were not close to a galactic centre. All those factors restrained their powers. Since their creation over two billion years ago the universe had evolved and their types of elemental energies could only be found within the nucleus of galaxies where matter was densest.

Being billions of years old their elemental bodies could no more exist unshielded. Further with the loss of their main base on

Romera IV they could no more refill the suits with elemental energy stolen from underground tanks within those Hexolyte bases. All of that equipment had been destroyed with the destruction of that world, so they were in a dilemma. Their only choice was to find a suitable place close to the centre of a galaxy and the only one remaining was Osmaron. If not they would eventually seep away and die. Possession of Muts was possible but there would be no comparative gains since they would still be required to remain close to the centre of a galaxy as were the case in Andromeda when they were using Javols bodies. Since both galaxies Andromeda and Triangulum now contained Hexotrons at their nucleus those options were closed to them. Only Osmaron remained free of Hexotrons.

Anyway after several checks of the Romera system they became convinced of their great loss.

'Brother, I always new we were watched by those nasty patriarchs of old. They had obviously returned from wherever they had been. Now with the help of their clots called humans they have created a super weapon that can reform stars and kill planets,' Lupher said.

'And they have set us back a thousand croniks. Those human clots will pay if it's the last thing I do. We know the location of their main world and can destroy them. All we have to do is find our new base and create some stealth ships and weapons. Once they are gone from this galaxy we shall have it all to ourselves and our remaining Muts which are still numerous can assist us in this new program. We can always build a new Mastermind,' Dracma replied.

Their only choice was to move lock stock and barrel to Osmaron. They and their remaining Muts would create a new base near the black hole in the centre of that galaxy. However, that move would be the riskiest, since the Federation probed almost every part of that galaxy. Nevertheless there remained several ancient Hexolyte underground bases on dead worlds close to the centre and those they would utilize for their new operation.

Lupher and Dracma soon sent probes to the central region of Osmaron and soon located several underground Hexolyte bases that could be used for their purpose. Through their new Mastermind they were able to recall all their remaining Muts for the exodus to those ancient Hexolyte bases.

There is a saying: "Keep your friends close but your enemies closer.'

The great minds of the Federation had planned everything that way for the final battle. Now both galaxies Andromeda and Triangulum were free of the enemy. Although the evil brothers Lupher and Dracma decided to sneak into the inner part of Osmaron they had no idea that the whole galaxy had been seeded with numerous inter-dimensional probes. Those probes had been built by clever Octans to observe even the smallest changes.

Being inter-dimensional meant those Octan bases were only visible to certain Federation ships that had been mounted with special sensors. Those included the little ship, Micol, Martia and Venusa ships. Normally those Octan bases were not considered part of the system, since they were virtually invisible and between universes. Therefore they had no affect on the physical world.

Soon all Muts were recalled and placed in underground hibernation. Martian pirates would help the hibernation process by acquiring the equipment they needed for gold. Those pirates would do anything for a few gold bars. That way they were able to remain concealed in that part of the Osmaron galaxy.

CHAPTER 39

Warrior Phane, a new Shadite

The great warrior Phane had been an outcast since a child. Being born completely different from members of his tribe he was considered to be the son of the evil one and from that time had to fend for himself. His complection was fair and hair golden or blonde which made him look strange to others, yet that harsh way of life had changed him into the greatest warrior.

Because of those genetic changes he had become the most clever and agile on the battlefield. He was a wonder to watch while wielding a two-handed sword, but was equally good with the bow and arrow. He had adopted a new tribe that worshipped him like their king. On a world of scarce resources, there were constant tribal battles.

The Shadite Lumak once visited his world and observed his prowess on the battlefield which impressed him. Then he was brought to the attention of Grand Lord Gerra for training as a Shadite. Initially he didn't want to leave his people but Lumak convinced him that he would be involved in saving complete worlds. That world was constantly bombarded by meteors during its yearly cycles, so Lumak decided to create several space platforms that included powerful beam weapons for destroying those invading meteors.

On that occasion three Shadites were scheduled to visit Little Osmaron, adapted home of the Grand Lord. It was a large satellite in geostationary orbit above planet Eden. The three were Lumak, Gemmi and Phane. Meradon was on his own mission in another galaxy. They were all dressed in their Shadite Cloaks and resembled angels of utter darkness. There they awaited the presence of Grand Lord Gerra. A perfectly dressed young man suddenly appeared before them and began to shake their hands. 'I see we have a great Shadite warrior among us today. Not once did this young man fail any of his tests. I think you will make another great Shadite in service for your lord and our esteemed Federation,' he said and a silent Phane bowed nobly.

'I have brought you together for a very delicate mission. During this mission you must not be discovered, so use vectorization whenever necessary. This time you are to visit the most central parts of this galaxy to lay observation probes within and without the Muts bases,' the Grand Lord said.

'Really?' Lumak was surprised. After all, Muts and their superiors were supposed to be in Triangulum. How could Muts visit our Osmaron galaxy without the knowledge of all those AI probes that were suppose to be guarding the whole galaxy.

'Yes, I know! The situation is ironic, to say the least. They only recently arrived. And they have been detected by our most sensitive Octan probes. But they have no knowledge of that fact and I want to keep it that way. They have been placed in a trap from which there is no escape. But we must let them think they are perfectly safe for now. The whole idea was to remove them from Triangulum, now both galaxies Andromeda and Triangulum are free of all Muts and their leaders,' the Grand Lord said.

'That was quite a clever ploy. Now they are like rats in a locked cage,' Gemmi said.

'Who will take care of Triangulum to ensure they don't return?' Phane inquired.

'The New Javols or Algarths, as I prefer to call them, are now a part of our Federation. They will patrol every sector of that galaxy and remove all remaining Muts if some still remain. The New Javols hate Muts and see them as a disgusting plague, which they are,' the Grand Lord replied.

'Since the destruction of their main world, Romero IV, they no longer have a hidden base in that galaxy. Their Hexolyte leaders, Lupher and Dracma, being ancient demons require certain energies which only exists within the nucleus of galaxies. Since the installation of Hexotrons within the nucleus of Triangulum no longer can they utilize those energies. They do not have the means to visit the more distant galaxies, so Osmaron is their only option for survival,' the Grand Lord replied.

'An intricate web and trap!' Lumak said with sarcastic humour.

'Indeed! We can usually anticipate their actions before they make them, but can be more accurate when they are spied upon,' the Grand Lord replied.

'There is one more thing I would like you to see,' the grand lord said.

In an instant they had appeared within the inner weapon chambers on Eden. That place was filled with numerous weapons of all types.

'The weapons here are all Octan in design. Once linked to your DNA they cannot be used by another, unless that person is a human Shadite. So you may program three of these units to recognise your three DNAs. Each can store multiple DNAs,' he said. The Grand Lord then collected three from a shelf and handed them to the three Shadites. Then they removed them from their plastic package and started to handle them. Then they passed them around.

'These are much smaller to their original and appear to be much more sophisticated,' Lumak said.

'Since the destruction of Muts by Satan's Plague, they now utilize a plastic encasement that can seal them from those deadly microids. However their infiltrators cannot utilize such methods and transform into another shape. These weapons will first fire a powerful plasma beam that will completely melt their plastic suits. Then the bugs will be ejected through the lower nozzle. This weapon is the best we have to kill Muts. However, the maximum practical distance is about ten metres, so make sure you are close enough for a positive kill,' the Grand Lord said.

'Finally, but not least, is Spirotron. This is another clever design made by our Octan friends. As you know, we cannot take life unless we are seriously threatened by our enemies. The world Romera IV was destroyed because they posed a great threat to earth. They had created numerous ships filled with a plague virus that would have killed numerous humans on Earth, now Solaria. Their final plan was to take over Earth and duplicate all senior council members. Then infiltrate the complete galaxy with new improved Muts. That is why Martia's ship had to wipe them. Because we laid many probes in their base and through their system we knew exactly when they would strike. That way we can always be at least one step ahead,' the Grand Lord said.

Then he took them to another part of that place. In the distance was a large ship with what appeared to be large nozzles and ridges throughout its structure.

'This device here signifies the end of all Muts and their leaders. You have no doubt heard of the Hexotrons and how they were able to destroy the inner parts of galaxies by utilizing black holes to generate powerful gravitational waves. These particular waves break up molecules into basic atoms, thereby destroying all life within those galactic regions. Well, this item here goes one step further It neutralizes all elemental energies, which is death to our demonic enemies. However, because of certain universal laws, we can only use it when they pose a serious threat to the existence of our people,' Grand Lord Gerra said.

'How does it work?' Lumak inquired.

'You have no doubt heard of dark matter and energy. There are several types, not just one. Many of them are remnants left behind since the last expansion phase of our universe. Well, what we call elemental energy has been left over by a previous expansion. This unit fires special missiles into regions at the event horizon of the central black hole which leads to a great disturbance. That disturbance leads to the propagation of intense temporal waves which disturbs all matter within that part of the galaxy. But that's not all. Those stresses when combined with a type of nuclear virus fired from this weapon will subsequently lead to the formation of new stars from white, red and brown dwarfs thus creating one giant star several billions of times the size of our sun. Finally that large super hot stellar mass explodes into one giant supernova destroying all worlds within that part of the galaxy. The brilliance will light the complete galaxy for many decades. During that time all elemental energies will be absorbed by the new and more intense black hole leading to the removal of all such unwanted energy from our galaxy,' Grand Lord Gerra said.

'Why remove all elemental energies from that part of the galaxy,' an innocent Phane commented.

'This will cause our unwanted demonic enemies to be starved

of their sustaining energies. Causing them to wither and die. They belong to an older universe and are just biding their time in this one. They are under the illusion that they are still part of the old universe, with powers to unify and conquer, but they are sadly mistaken. Finally, we destroy all Muts on Synora V, in much the same way as we did on Romera IV.' The Grand Lord said and they were aghast by it all.

'Metrasiend, when do you think our part of the universe will be free of these monsters?' an astute Gemmi enquired.

'Although I know the final outcome, I cannot tell you. This is because knowledge of the future can change the future. You have no doubt heard of The Butterfly Affect. That is why I keep so many secrets. Nevertheless, you will gain more knowledge when the time of finality approaches. During this time you must be diligent and work towards our common goal. As shadites many rely on you for salvation, so carry on your great work through these missions, because they are all part of the great Battle for Osmaron. Therefore you will know everything when the time is right,' the Grand Lord said.

Then in a flash they were back on the Satellite Little Osmaron.

'Gemmi please come forward. For services rendered to the realm, I have decided to promote you to Grade 1. You are therefore required to accept your new cloak. Your old cloak must be collected and stored in your special section within the Greater Mind. She did as ordered and was soon in Empress Sarah's palace on Eden and being asked to join them for tea.

CHAPTER 40

Another party on Eden

After news of the destruction of the main Muts' base on Remora IV in Triangulum had percolated through the higher hierarchy of the Federation, many leaders and councillors descended on Eden. Even Xo and some of his senior New Javols were invited by Sarah to partake in the celebrations. It was a time for greatest celebrations, so every venue was busy making relevant changes to their establishments. The whole of Eden was undergoing a duly required facelift. Everywhere were Lodorian robots doing their bit for one of the best worlds of the Federation.

But those changes were not only on Eden. Earth was also undergoing similar changes. As a matter of fact, Eden was so full of visitors that Earth (Solaria) was needed to take up the slack. Therefore when Eden was filled with the massive ships many left for Earth. Both worlds were now equal with portals transmitting people to and fro.

To mark the great occasion George, The Son of Destiny and his son Michael wanted to do something significant, so Mars and Venus came to mind. Although those worlds had been gradually terra-formed for years by robot ships, the process was slow. It would have taken well over another century to show significant difference.

The sun of destiny was known to repair stars and planets so he decided to use his skills on Venus. However in the case of Venus such a process would not be as straightforward as repairing a living world. The atmosphere was too contaminated with sulphur dioxide and other noxious gasses. Those elements had to be removed. Then there was the cooling of the planet so water could form on its surface. The task was truly daunting.

Therefore the more massive Lodorian machines would be needed. First they would seed the Venus atmosphere with a range of bio-engineered bacteria. Those quick acting microbes would multiply themselves to numerous levels until only the basic constituents like oxygen, hydrogen, water vapour, carbon dioxide and nitrogen remained. Although small quantities of unwanted chemicals were left those were considered unimportant. Finally a large Tetrion Shield was place between Venus and the sun. That shield would reduce solar energy and cool the planet over several years until water could form on its cooling surface. All the dead bacteria during the forming process would fall like dust to further cool the planet. Once it began to rain another type of cleansing bacteria would be used. All that had to be done before that world could be transformed into a living world with plants and animals. Once the massive terra-forming machines had arrived the process was speeded up a thousand fold.

On the other hand, Mars had been given an atmosphere over the years. Although breathable, atmospheric pressure was still quite low. So a large amount of carbon dioxide was dumped on Mars to increase pressure to tolerable levels. All that carbon dioxide was retrieved from Venus's atmosphere by another machine. Finally people could live outside the Hex domes, but with lesser pressure than on Earth. Nevertheless, even with all the advanced Lodorian technologies Venus would have taken at least another ten years before its surface could be utilized by mankind.

In another week the celebrations had begun. Despite the unknown reasons for their celebrations, only the Grand Lords and a few senior councillors new of the resettlement of Muts and their leaders within Osmaron. That knowledge was kept a guarded secret to prevent panic should it leak out. People would be told at the appropriate time, when the war had been won.

The three important Shadites, Lumak, Gemmi and Phane would remain and partake in celebrations before their important mission for the Grand Lord. Nevertheless, part of the celebrations were meant for the new Shadite Phane. Empress Sarah would never release him on any mission without a thank-you celebration. He had forgone the most difficult of challenges within the Labyrinth of Gon. Many Shadites had died many times during those test, yet he passed all those almost impossible challenges the first time. Once the word of his success were known by the Federation all senior members wanted to shake his hand.   Phane was now marked as the greatest warrior in the Federation and many senior councillors visited Eden to see him and observe his prowess in battle, first with the sword and later the bow and arrow. In an age of super advanced technologies it was a miracle to observe his precision and actions with such basic weapons.

That glorious day Phane was called to Sarah's palace to be introduced to many great people of the Federation. On that day the main hall was filled, but that particular program was also transmitted and televised to all important worlds of the Federation through H-Wave.

Grand Lord Michael, son of The Son of Destiny was first to approach the rostrum. He was one of the best speakers and respected by all.

Metrasiend, Grand Lords, Councillors and friends. People, we are now in the final stage of the war within Osmaron and the final stages of the Battle for Osmaron. During this time we must all be extra vigilant. The enemy is good at pretending. They are quite capable of replacing our councillors. After killing them they can change into an almost exact copy and mask their stench with certain chemicals. So always be on your guard. As for safety, this whole galaxy has been seeded by the most intricate Octan probes, so they and their superiors are constantly under observation and these methods will improve with time.' Michael said as a hand went up to ask a question.

'My Lord have you any idea when this war will end?' The reporter inquired.

'As Grand Lord of Solaria(Earth) and protector of our Galaxy it's my duty to ensure the survival of all life within these worlds. Although I know of all possible futures, I cannot tell you the exact course we take for conquest. It's like being at a great crossroad and choosing just the correct one for a particular future. One more thing, knowledge of the future can change the future and more so when that information is made public. We Grand Lords keep many secrets. That way we prevent many disasters in the future. So in answer to your question I cannot tell you at this time.

'My Grand Lord, since you are all-powerful why don't you and others blow these monsters away. After all, they are set on universal conquest and will never change. While they exist they pose a great threat to all primal life in our galaxy and elsewhere?' Another reporter asked.

'We are not both jury and executioner. We cannot kill because they are not like us. Everyone must be given a fair chance of redemption. For all we know their leaders may want to join the Federation one day. The sinner must be given the option of repentance or we become just like them.

LIFE and DEATH

'As I mentioned previously my main responsibility is towards Solaria, but since the Solarian system (Solar System is part of the deal) my responsibility also extends to Caefon in Andromeda, since both worlds are linked by twinning. As you know Eden is not a Homo Sapiens world. Although my grandmother Sarah is empress, that world contains mainly Andromedans. Soon many will move to Solaria and many of us will move to Eden. We exist in a Federation where we are free to travel. However we should not overpopulate any world beyond its stated limits. We also have to consider the indigenous life in whatever decisions we take. We are not the only ones in this universe.

'As you all know the people on Eden can live forever, but not so with Solaria(Earth). Many are lucky to live for 150 years, even with the necessary drugs. I intend to change this discrepancy,' Michael said.

'My Lord, how can anyone live forever?' A doctor shouted from the front row.

'Living forever is not a problem. Nevertheless sacrifices would have to be made. Your whole way of life will change. Homo-Sapiens have many children, which would create a population imbalance. Therefore those who make that choice must not be able to have children unless permitted by a Grand Lord. Of course all people of a certain senior age may be accepted.

'In the past two machines were used for that purpose. The Megotron for rebuilding the body and the Psyrotron for scanning the individual's mind. Well, we are now much more advanced. In order to maintain a young body we can use your DNA to clone a new you. Then we insert your original brain implants into your new clone. That type of clone would live for about 200 years. Your special brain implants will contain about 99 percent of all memories and information required. This whole process can be repeated for a numerous number of times until you decide to move to the next level.

'At the next level you become Homo Technogensis. A much more advance type of human. They will be required to change the universe by building Dyson Spheres and renewing dead or dying stellar systems. We already have the technologies needed to transform white, red and brown dwarfs into brand new stars. Living planets take a bit longer to procure living organisms, but we are working on these challenges.

'I call them the "Angels of Eternal Light". They utilize Quantum Memory and can hold thousands of professional doctors with experience in their minds. They are telepathic and can transfer a complete library of books to someone in less than a second. They are able to control all forms of machines from great distances. And all that is just a small part of their incredible abilities. They are just the most advanced form of Homo Sapiens, so in a sense they will be just like you but with great capabilities.

'So you see, Doctor, living forever is not a problem, providing we take certain measures and precautions. Anyway, I have decided to give all people in Solaria and Caefon the choice of everlasting life. It is a free choice that can be ended at any time.' Michael said as everyone stood and cheered.

<h1 style="text-align:center">CHAPTER 41</h1>

Another special mission

All three Shadites, Lumak, Gemmi and Phane left planet Eden in a Stealth Viper for the central parts of the Osmaron Galaxy. They were to locate several of the enemy's underground bases in that part of the galaxy. Then mine them with invisible probes without the enemies knowledge. Although given an ancient map showing their location, the stellar map had changed significantly over the eons, so their AI computers would be busy locating them using complex algorithms.

Nevertheless, their temperature sensors were of Octan design and could detect the smallest temperature changes even in a thoroughly screened environment.

'I know you guys have done your home work regarding Hexolyte ancient basses, but there are some points I must raise. Most of these bases contain good ancient demons. Therefore before installing any devices we must check the lower levels for such installations. We are expected to save all such entities for the Federation. It is quite possible that the invading Muts will have no knowledge of those lower installations,' Lumak said.

'You mean demons like Neramon and Felspar?' Gemmi inquired.

'We are all modern Shadites and can use our mental blocks to prevent their intrusions into our minds. We must use our communication skills to convert them and save whoever we can. All these inner basses will be destroyed eventually by the Federation when these dead worlds are reformed,' Lumak replied.

'Can these Muts detect us during descent?' Phane inquired.

'Their senses are not as intricate as ours, so we shouldn't worry about that. But be extra careful guys, we don't want them to know we are here. Use your special helmet visas to observe the terrain as you descend through thick matter. Many of them may be invisible to normal light, so check for heat signatures before normalizing your cloaks. Muts are not the most clever peas in the pod, so pretend to be one of them. Your cloaks are programmed with a suitable mask, so use it whenever you are discovered. If you find yourself in trouble quickly vectorize and go invisible. They will think you are one of them. Your helmets will display our relative positions at all times, so do not stray from the group. You know the routine, so prepare yourselves for an adventure,' Lumak said and they were amused by his last statement.

They left their Viper ship in orbit and decided to travel solo using LPDs. That way less atmospheric turbulence would be created. The Muts could have copied such technologies during their infiltrations.

Lumak was always extra careful during his missions and left nothing to chance.

As they descended through the maize of ancient structures they were surprised to find giant creatures like spiders. It was not what they expected. There was not a single Mut in sight. They wandered through the ancient ruins and tanks until they came upon a large pyramid structure. There they remained for a while communicating.

'This is not what I expected. This whole place has been taken over by a race of Arachnids. From what I see they are quite clever and might need our assistance. Down here they are well shielded from the radiation.

'They use light, so they must have visual senses similar to ours and some of them can fly,' Gemmi replied.

'So life can exist even in this region of our galaxy, providing they live underground. But this place is massive. Perhaps we should survey this whole area before making contact with their superiors. You know, Muts will find them eventually and I am sure they will be enslaved or destroyed,' Phane commented.

'Why are they all white and blue. Those that stand on four legs also have hands but no wings. From what I can observe there are four basic types, but there could be others. They appear to be a very advanced race. They obviously came from another world and settled here several of their generations ago,' Lumak said.

'I think we should take a while to study them. They could be an important species,' Gemmi said.

'I wish my grandson Michael was here. He would know what to do by convincing them he was their god. I'm sure they would like being safe in the arms of a Grand Lord of the Universe,' Lumak said and they all smiled.

'Yea! Our Grand Lord Michael would love being here. He and Joan enjoys new races and cultures. Perhaps we should call him through the Mind? Phane said.

'But we are Shadites and on a special mission. This is not part of our mission. However, I can send an urgent message via our ship with H-wave,' Lumak replied.

 Grand Lord Michael and his wife Joan had received the message from Lumak and were soon on their way to his location. They soon arrived in similar gear having surveyed the complete underground system.

'I must say, this place is truly massive. What you observe here is just the top of a great underground city, which is several thousand metres beneath us. This area is just the mushroom farm. From what I observed, they grow several types in this upper area. You three Shadites may join me on this new venture in the name of the Greater Purpose,' Michael said. They could never refuse orders from a Grand Lord, so they agreed.

'How can we communicate with them. They are so different from us,' Phane said and Gemmi was of the same mind.

'Most species like arachnids tend to communicate by rubbing pincers together. Similar to a computer they relay on dots and dashes at a high frequency, similar to morse code but much quicker. I should be able to unravel their language within a short time. At the end of the day it's all about vibrations,' Michael said.

'I have got it. While you were chatting, I was listening with super-sensitive ears. Now I shall transmit their full language profile to your implants,' Joan said. Being Shadites that language soon became part of their language database and was downloaded to the Greater Mind for other Shadites to use.

'Grandad, you have not yet observed their lower city. Well, there is a major epidemic. Many are dying from an unknown poison and they have no idea it's due to the mushrooms they eat. While crossbreeding certain mushrooms there has been a genetic change in a new strain. I must descend and heal as many as I can. Then I shall communicate with their queen,' Michael said.

'Oh my gracious lord. So that's why they appear so jittery and slow. Most of them must be contaminated,' Gemmi commented.

'Yea, it seems we arrived here just in time to save their race. We shall have to move them from this world, to save them from nasty Muts. That part fits in with our program,' Phane said.

'I agree! Our Grand Lord would not mind us assisting them to move from this dead rock. Perhaps we could take them to the Romera system. It's a brand new solar system and they will have it all to them selves. There is also the underground base that can be repaired and used for their purpose,' Lumak said and they agreed.

'How can these mushrooms suddenly become poisonous?' Phane inquired.

'It could have been a dormant gene. Sometime certain species can cycle their genes. They could have been poisonous before and suddenly switched to a non-poisonous variety depending on predation. We live in a dynamic universe of evolution with prey and predator,' Lumak replied.

'In a closed environment like this, all they can grow are mushrooms. From what I can observe there are three types which are not perfectly isolated from each other, leading to cross-breeding and the resultant poisonous strains. They are not aware that the present epidemic is due to a new poisonous strain. They have to be told,' Michael said in no uncertain terms.

Grand Lord Michael became a bluish star. As he surveyed their main city the whole place lit up brightly. As he travelled through its lower atmosphere every sick individual arose from the nets and wondered at the great light. Although they had been surface dwellers many millennia before, their eyes had adjusted well to the lower lights of the underworld so it took them time to focus. He stood on a high platform and began speaking to all and sundry in their strange language.

'I am Grand Lord Michael, Lord of this and other parts of this universe. All life within this galaxy is my responsibility. We did not know of your existence until you were discovered by three great Shadites. It is said that nothing in this universe happens by accident. I have observed your old and battered spaceship left hidden in a local valley. You were obviously running away from the monsters that reaped havoc within the galaxy Andromeda. You will run no more.

'Your stay in this underworld prison must come to an end. Your enemies are no more, because they have been conquered. I shall find you a stellar system of your own. However for greater protection from our common enemies you should become part of our Federation of planets. By being a member your youth can go to our universities and learn new technologies. Then you can trade mutually with other worlds. Being isolated like this is fraught with many problems that you alone may not solve by yourselves,' Michael said and they cheered in their own way.

One of the great queens suddenly appeared. She was pinkish in colour with a bluish crest on her head. She stood about seven feet tall on four thin legs. She had two human-like hands. She began to speak to Michael, now in human form.

'Our meeting in this place is truly incredible. How could you have found this place and visited us. I thought we were completely sealed from the dead surface of this world. After we built this city, which took us many centreons, there was a landslide which sealed us in. We never intended to remain in this place for ever,' She said. While she spoke several queens, young and old appeared in what seemed to be a large cart.

From what they could observe there was no great technologies about. They seemed to use silk to construct everything. Even their sky-roads were constructed from silk. Since the resources in that place was quite limited it could have been their only choice. However the city was quite warm, due to thermal heat coming from the core of the planet and there was no shortage of water which showered from certain cracks in the roof. Of course the world above them was a near ice-ball, so the difference in temperature would cause ice to melt.

'We can travel through solid matter. We also have the powers to change worlds and create stars. We exist to enhance universal life, but can also enhance the whole universe by transforming dead stars into new ones. We are the ultimate in evolution. We can in a short time take all of you from this unkindly place and place you in a brand new stellar system of your own.

'Everyone that exist in this universe, from the highest to the lowliest have certain rights by virtue of their existence. You are an older species that should be flourishing instead you are locked in this cage of rock with no viable future. Please communicate with all your people telling them of our arrival here and our intentions to help you. Since our assistance is given freely from the heart we will not demand payment for any assistance. We in this galaxy will need each other from time to time. It is our duty to assist when we can,' Michael said while they listened carefully to his words.

Then Michael transformed into a greenish star and vanished leaving behind the three Shadites dressed in their black cloaks.

'An elder queen came forward to speak. My name is Ekba, I am the elder. Here is my daughter, Sashi the younger. Ekba means beautiful blue flower. You appear to be from an honourable and very advanced people. Like you, we once had a rich culture and thriving society but had to escape our world and galaxy to save ourselves. Only a few of us was chosen for the journey into the unknown. Our home world was in the larger of these three galaxies. Our race is called the Ranfi it means hive workers. I don't know what you call that galaxy but we call it Conoki. We lived on a most beautiful world with twin stars. On our world were both surface and underground dwellers. Our underground dwellers helped us build this underground city. If possible we would like to return to our original world. It has been a long time and we have no information of the situation on that world. If you could find us locate it we shall be forever in your debt,' she said.

A MOMENT OF TRUTH

'I am Lumak the Shadite from a world called Kanaefon within a globular cluster called Kalboron. In my original form I am a sexless Semonite hive worker. This here is Gemmi, she is speell from the Triangulum Galaxy. This is Phane, he is near human from another world in Triangulum. All Shadites work under Grand Lord Gerra, Lord of the Seventh Universe, We adopt this human form because it is the most flexible for our many duties. We have the means to transform anyone into another. We are eternal and indestructible. That makes us fully universal,' Lumak said and they were amazed.

'Don't you feel strange in your new bodies,' she inquired.

'Depending on the alien form. If it's the first time it may take a day or so to practise until we feel at home,' Lumak replied.

'Regarding your original Stellar system. We will be able to help you with that. We have complete charts of many galaxies. If you could give me a sketch of the stellar system and its position within the Andromedan galaxy, I can scan through the database now and tell you about that stellar system. Although the monster Javols took over many worlds they should be still in tact except for their occupants,' Lumak said. The queen drew a sketch on what appeared to be a sheet of paper and gave it to one of her eight legged minions and it progressed to Lumak's position.

'That is the best I can do. It has been a long time,' she said.

'I have found it. That world may be still in tact. If you wish we can make contact and see if your people still survives. One of our great ships travel daily to that galaxy, we can ask someone on planet Caefon to check for you,' Lumak said and they were pleased. Then all the Shadites faded into nothing and faded back into themselves like magic.

'Using such methods we can travel anywhere within the known universe in an instant. However on certain missions we use a stealth ship to carry us and our special equipment,' Lumak added.

'We knew of a similar species to your human form. They ruled over many systems and were responsible for the creation of those monsters that almost wiped us out. Then we were told their monstrous creations also wiped them out. Do you know of the people responsible for the monstrous plague that almost completely destroyed a complete galaxy?' She inquired.

'Yes! We know all about the Ancients and their misfortune.

They intended to create the perfect soldier but something went wrong during their final experiment and a monster parent came out of the mould. Our Grand Lord knew well the problem and the future. He decided to save six of their main councillors so they could repair the damage at a later date. Those great Ancients are still alive after over 3000 years. You and yours might meet them one day in the future. They are great people. It's a pity things went so wrong. You know, to survive they built and underground city similar to yours on their world of Caefon. That underground city is there to this day,' Lumak said and they were astounded.

'So that galaxy, Andromeda, is now a peaceful place?' She inquired.

'Yes, that galaxy and the smaller one called Triangulum are under our control. The monster Javols still exist, but they are now subjects of the Federation. They were corrupted by two demons called Dracma and Lupher. Those two were always set on universal conquest and never liked primals like us. They were released from eternal prisons by two Javols and they possessed them to take over and form the Javols empire under their MasterMind. The Javols today go about their business as Federation soldiers, but they are also good at copying,' Lumak replied.

Suddenly a thought snapped into Lumak's head through his brain implants.

'You are to remain with these people for a while. Teach them our ways and get them prepared for their journey. After that, you may resume your current mission. Vektron out!' Lumak then transferred the information to his Shadite companions. Lumak knew whenever Lord Vektron was involved it would be very important, after all he was now a Grand Lord.

'I just had words with another Grand Lord. He wants us to remain here for a while to explain things to you and assist if you decide to leave this place. Your world in Andromeda has been found. It is now populated by several species of your kind, Should you decide to re-establish yourselves we suggest finding a less populated part of the planet and build a new city. After you have established yourselves you should try to make contact with the other species. That will be kinder to everyone on that world,' Lumak said.

CHAPTER 42

Muts are coming

'Let me give you a quick preview of our present situation in this part of the Osmaron Galaxy. Just before the Javols defeat their two superiors Dracma and Lupher escaped to the galaxy Triangulum. Soon after the Javols were defeated and their MasterMind replaced by ours. By duplication, we took over all their bases even without their knowledge. Using very advanced technologies we interrupted their progress to the other galaxies. In effect they were captured and sent back to the nucleus of the Andromedan galaxy were they were destroyed by powerful Hexotrons. Although a few Javols still remain, they are constantly monitored and serve our Federation. We find good Javols make ideal soldiers,' Lumak said, while they listened patiently.

'So where are the bad ones now?' another queen asked.

'Their superiors Dracma and Lupher came up with another evil plan to take over the universe. Because Javols were inherently disobedient they decided to capture those arriving in Triangulum and change them into the most vicious Muts. It takes two Javols to create a single Mut, so they are almost twice their size. Muts can kill a person and take over their place by duplication. Any one of you great queens could be replaced without anyone knowing. That's how dangerous they are,' Lumak said. Then they started viewing each other suspiciously. Then the elder queen continued the conversation.

'I don't think that's possible with us. We know each other well. After all they are my daughters,' she said.

'To carry on with the story, using a similar method to the one we used in Andromeda we destroyed all their basses in Triangulum. Since they had no where to go, they came to this part of Osmaron. You should realize almost every part of this galaxy is mined with sensitive probes, so they were detected immediately on arrival. There are many hidden underground places like this within the innermost part of this galaxy that is well hidden from our scanners. Our current job is to locate their bases and plant observation probes so we can always monitor their intentions and movement. That's why we are here,' Lumak said.

'So in a way, because of them we have been saved from this underground prison? The universe is indeed a strange place to be!' she said.

'Yes, the universe is indeed a very strange place to be. Causation rules the roost,' Lumak remarked.

'So how can you help us get away from this place?' The elder queen inquired.

'We can move you, lock, stock and barrel to your world in Andromeda within the hour. Of course you will have to pack the necessaries and prepare everyone for the trip. The name of the ship is Martia's ship. She makes the trip to Andromeda on a daily basis. She is a warship with the capabilities of destroying a complete world. However, she is also a ship of peace and follow the Grand Lord's commands. She is almost the size of your underground city and will land in the space above us. I recently received information regarding the Muts progress. They are close and will visit this planet soon, so you should make a quick decision,' Lumak said.

'We have observed the images of our original world and know it's our home world by the layout of continents and oceans. We have duplicated those images and sent them to everyone. They are all keen on leaving this closed and infected city. We would also like to join your federation, if possible?' she said.

'Great choice! I have just relayed that information to Grand Lord Vektron and he is please. You are to prepare your trip for one week from today. You may take along whatever you wish. There is space enough for all including your belongings. You can sign the partnership documents after you have settled on your home world. Once you become a member you will have a voice and a vote on the council. We can follow you there if you wish?' Lumak said.

'So we have no future threat from these Javols?' one of the young queens inquired.

'I give you my word, none whatsoever. That type of Javol does not exist any more. If they did, our technologies are way beyond anything they could imagine, so you are perfectly safe,' Lumak replied and they were convinced.

'Are these Javols conscious like us or are they just robots?' another queen asked.

'There are many theories on the subject. But I believe all living entities are conscious, some more then others. I believe the Entity or Identity of consciousness to be a type of possession by a higher living entity. We are the ones that use these physical forms for knowledge and experience in these planes of existence. We could have been from a previous expansion phase of our universe. We have many libraries on the subject which you will be free to use in the future,' Lumak said.

Although the upper cavern was slightly too small for Martia's ship she could vectorize in solid matter providing there was enough space for people and their belongings to get on board.

When Lumak discussed the plight of the Ranfi people with Lord Meron he was very apologetic and decided to help. Meron immediately called Jon is son who immediately contacted the other five young Andromedan.

'Guys, we have a very important task ahead of us. Lord Lumak has found a lost race of people in a sealed underground city within this galaxy. Very much like us, they were escaping from the Javols. They are now in trouble and would like to return to their original world in Andromeda. Since it's partly my fault it is my duty to help. You may join me if you wish?' Meron said, knowing they could never refuse.

They were also keen the see their original city on Caefon.

'What can we do the help, Dad?' Jon inquired.

'We are to help them build a new city with Venusa, so if you guys want to help make sure Venusa takes along all necessary equipment. I intend contacting my friend Malik on Polok IV for some heavy construction equipment,' Meron replied.

Lord Meron was soon on H-wave to Lord Malik on Polok IV who soon relayed the information to Lord Volt on Lodor. Who soon communicated the facts to Lord Bailor. Soon there was an armada of great ships with everything imaginable on board. It was like one great Federation picnic that no one could miss. Then Empress Sarah relayed the information to her councillors and they would not miss that occasion for all the tea in China. It would also be a needed holiday break. Soon the whole Federation were interested to assist. Many freighters were currently on their way to Caefon. Even the Ancient Lord Micol and his ancient gang now on Orban were on their way to Caefon with many Octans. It would have been a greatest reunion of ancient families and dynasties.

Suddenly planet Caefon in Andromeda had become the most important world in the Federation. The city of Cantor had become the main Federation base in that galaxy since the Javol's conquest. However, the Ranfi's world, Konoc, were about fifty light years away and a little more distant from the galactic rim.

'I have good news! Lord Meron, who was partly responsible for the creation of the Javols, will join us on the sister ship called Venusa. He and his six young Andromedans have decided to help you build your city. Meron is a great warrior and councillor that have fought many battles against the Javols with us during recent times. Like you, great queen, he was from a previous royal family,' Lumak said.

'If these Muts are on the way, will we make it in time?' Another queen asked.

'We shall make it in time if we start now. By the way I have a major shock for you. Over 1000 ships are on the way from all over the Federation to assist you build your new city. Since the news got out about your plight every one wants to help. So when we arrive on your world it will be covered with Federation ships. I hope you don't mind. The Federation is like that, always willing to help,' Lumak said and they were aghast.

CHAPTER 43

New Cantor on Caefon

Over the years New Cantor had become a great commercial city like New York. It had been rebuilt by the numerous Infilates that left Earth for Andromeda during the great rush. Presently Earth(Solaria) and New Cantor were like one city trading peacefully with each other. Since twinning with Earth, New Cantorians did not need special papers like passports and could move freely.

It was the third time Cantor had been resurrected from the ashes. This time it was called New Cantor. Perhaps it should have been called New Phoenix after the bird that rose from the ashes. The lower underground city was still called Lower Cantor and connected to Mars in the Solar System via the Omegron Portal. Lower Cantor was still used by the military for special missions but unlike previous times was known by Cantorians. It was now a part of their great history.

Many tourists from Earth, now Solaria, and other places within the Federation visited the underground city of Lower Cantor for more indebt knowledge of the Ancients survival during the reign of the monster Javols. A few New Javols, now in adopted human forms, could be observed in Federation uniforms helping people find their way around. They were now as peaceful as lambs.

For the trip the elder queen Ekba and her other queens including workers and others of the hive hierarchy were dressed spectacularly in radiant silk of different colours. Martia ship suddenly vectorized in the upper cavern well above the mushroom fields while extending her under-portal for people to board. They had previously fitted a large portal between the city and the ship for accepting the bulk of their raw materials.

Although there were four main types of Ranfi only the queens communicated with humans. Queens were given translation devices which hung about their necks like necklaces. They were treated like royalty everywhere they went. Lord Meron and the young six showed great excitement by taking them around while introducing them to senior councillors. During that time they answered all their searching questions. Finally they were taken to the underworld of Lower Cantor and saw similarities between that city and the one they left behind. It was a time of great reflection for all those that perished under the hands of monster Javols and many swore that situation would never happen again.

The four great queens were impressed by the multi-storey structures that almost reached the clouds and the industry and commerce that existed everywhere. The original Infilates that settled on Caefon had done an incredible job in rebuilding that once great city more to their likeness. All those original Infilates were now property owners and a most wealthy group of people. They still worshipped George Peterson, Son of Destiny as their lord and saviour.

George Peterson, Son of Destiny

They were all assembled in the largest square in New Cantor. This time instead of Grand Lord Michael it was his father, George Peterson, Son of Destiny that went towards the rostrum. All four queens remained behind him along with Empress Sarah, Lord Meron and his Ancients, with Jon and his young group standing in line.

'My beloved people, from Grand Lords to the lowliest, we may appear to be different races physically and on the outside, but we are all one people on the inside. And thank goodness we found the Ranfi in time before they all died a painful death within that underground city. My appreciation and blessings to queen Ekba and all her people for surviving this long within such limited confines.

'We knew the Javols plans from the start but had to pull several civilizations together and plan for their demise over 3000 years from their beginnings. That was because we did not have the necessary weaponry, people and plans in place. Those had to be developed over a relatively long timescale.

'Grand Lord Gerra, Lord of the Seventh Universe, realizing the grave problem sent his Shadites out to locate advanced civilizations. At that time my world Earth was only a class one civilization and we had to become a class five to beat the Javols. My father, the great Shadite call Lumak worked incognito as one Doctor Jeffery Longhurst to improve our technologies. He and my mother, the great Empress Sarah, worked together at that time to pull people together for the common good.

'I was the one responsible for the destruction of the Javols Empire in this galaxy and the first to visit the under city of Lower Cantor. Then I came up to the ruins of this city during their reign of terror by their wicked and cruel empire. It was from Lower Cantor that we entered this galaxy unknown to our enemy. They expected ships but instead we entered from within and under their very noses took over their bases by duplicating their kind with Mine Probes, look-a-likes, capable of duplicating their kind. That way we were able to duplicate their bases one by one. Eventually their MasterMind was confused with erroneous information fed through our systems. There were many violent battles but with our people and their advanced weapons we always came through.

'Once their demonic superiors, Dracma and Lupher realize we had more advanced technologies and were making progress they soon flew the roost. They secretly left for Triangulum where they decided on another diabolical plan to rule the universe. That was the creation of Javols mutations called Muts. For that program they collected stray Javols and combined two using a microid virus. Muts were more obedient than Javols, a lot tougher and could adapt better to human environments. Their main skills were infiltration and duplicating people. That way they could pretend to be our leaders. The one thing they could not do was to easily mask their stench.

'During that time there were literally billions of Javols on their way to the other galaxies, Osmaron and Triangulum. Many were stopped in their tracks and captured others were ensnared by invisible portal stations and sent back to the Andromedan galaxy where they were destroyed by the Hexotrons. However not all Javols were bad. They were corrupted and brainwashed by their superiors and their MasterMind to destroy or enslave all life. Once we had removed their MasterMind and replaced it with our own the Javols saw a better long term plan and attitudes changed. Many came over to our side and became brave soldiers as were intended. Today there are many surviving Javols that hate their original leaders and their Muts creations and will go to any lengths to destroy them in the name of our Federation.

'Dracma, Lupher and their deplorable Muts are now on the run. We recently destroyed their bases in Triangulum. They and their MasterMind have recently moved to Osmaron. Since their superiors can only exist within the nucleus of galaxies, although hidden, we know exactly where they are. Our Shadites will plant observation probes within their installations so we can always track them and know their intentions. At the right time we shall destroy them all for the safety and security of life within our universe.

'During the following years, after their destruction in this galaxy, using our Primorphs, Ulyses and Hercules, we did a most thorough search of this galaxy but no hidden places or underground cities were discovered. Luckily we discovered the Ranfi after all that time hidden in another underground city. A complete parallel situation to the Ancients, who remained within Lower Cantor for 3000 years. To remain within such a closed environment for such a long time needs real character and planning. I salute you queen Ekba and your great people on such a brave endeavour.

'Lord Meron and his Ancients knew the Ranfi well. He and his council provided the large freighter that took them away from their world to a place or places unknown. At that time large ships were rare so only a few could escape to other galaxies, but he had to assist knowing the Javols hatred for their kind and his responsibilities.

'Much like us the Ranfi were highly technological and would never bow to rapacious monsters with primitive notions of universal conquest. We have given the remnants of these monsters, now at the centre of the Osmaron galaxy, a slight reprieve, but mark my words, by the end of one Solarian year they will be gone from us. It is now our greatest duty under Lord

Meron to build the Ranfi a great city similar to New Cantor for their survivors. Many of whom are watching this gathering from Martia's ship.

'Luckily the Shadite Lumak and his companions found them. However by this time they were in dire straights from a poisonous fungal strain. Thank goodness our Grand Lord Michael soon arrived on the scene to save them. The Ranfi suffered greatly so it's time they had a permanent home they are proud of and begin normal peaceful existence, to partake in the gains of our great galactic empire and our protection. Now I call Lord Meron to the stand!' George said while receiving a standing ovation.

Lord Meron

Lord Meron walked towards the rostrum with an air of dignity, while dressed in an ancient gold braided gown with sword and scabbard dangling from his waist. He was proud of his ancestry and their great achievements.

'I remember well the original city of Cantor. It was the first great city built by King Micol, my direct ancestor. That city was built with the aid of Octans. They were about the most advanced people in Osmaron at the time. At that time Cantor was filled with moving pavements and walkways as far as the eyes could see, but no portals. It was indeed a most beautiful city.

'At that time we ruled a large galactic empire and could travel to distant galaxies. Yes, they had wove a great galactic empire where everyone lived in relative peace and happiness. The real problems began when their overstepped the mark. That was when they decided to robotize the army, which at that time was spread wide and thin.

'During that time there were a few uprisings by certain extreme types which took time to quell without a larger army. If only the empire could mass-produce soldiers to order. At that time they were very advanced in micro-robotics (nano-technology). The main problem was how to store the equivalent of a human brain in those AI robots. The original blinking block storage devices were not large enough for such bulk storage so another way had to be found.

'That was when Professor Andra came on the scene. He had won several prises in the field of microid engineering having done much research in that area. He soon convinced the government of such possibilities. His idea was to create a robot that could evolve itself in much the same way as a human body from the womb, creating types of microid neurons with synopsis and other specific microids that automatically linked during the process, but more quickly than primal growth. Experiments and tests were carried out on Neuronic Microids until they were satisfied with progress. Then the ideas and reports were placed before the grand council for acceptance.

'They place the original scientist Professor Andra in charge of the project. For safety reasons that project was placed on the engineering planet called Silo. Silo was not suitable for human life at the time so there were many habitable domes. Many had been originally constructed for miners decades before. During that time with the exception of tourists, the planet was mainly uninhabited. The agriculturist Ranul was then sent to Silo to introduce certain strains of bacteria to create more oxygen and introduce plant growth. Later he became the governor of that world. It was then that the last and final experimental test failed leading to the creation of the Javol Monsters.

'I remember the day of the Javols invasion of Caefon. The skies were darkened by their sheer numbers. We could do nothing to save our people. Although we defended the city well our weapons only assisted the Javols in duplicating their kind. They would swoop down on the innocent public and decapitate them, absorbing their bodies in the process. The scene was truly the most gory I have ever observed. Then many would join together to form a great monster which would bring down the strongest buildings and root up tracks and walkways. It was indeed mass slaughter that we could do nothing about. Even our most deadly missiles would help them duplicate and bring more hungry ones into our mist. The destruction of our beautiful city Cantor has been recorded as evidence for anyone to view.

'Although we knew of a program to create the perfect soldier, not many of us knew of Andra's microids. And even if we knew the first experiment on a smaller model was quite successful. It was one of those one in a billion chances that went wrong. Knowing of their rapacious and bad nature we accepted the fact that they would destroy almost every living creature they came upon. They were also good at copying, so it was only a matter of time before they knew our advanced technologies. This situation would have made them more efficient at consuming us.

'Therefore we planned for their invasion by building the underground city of lower Cantor. However, that city could only accommodate one million, so we couldn't tell the surface people of its existence. Neither could we build inter-galactic ships in those quantities to evacuate the masses. It is because of grand Lord Gerra and our Ploran friends like Lord Vektron that we are here today. So I thank everyone for the privilege of being here and relating those most horrible events,' Meron said then left the stage while being cheered by everyone. Then Queen
Ekba came forward to say a few words of her own.

Queen Ekba the Ranfi

'Thank you all for having me here and saving my people. I thank you all from the bottom of my heart. When I first saw Grand Lord Michael I thought I was dreaming. Never before have we seen such a powerful being. He swept over our underworld like a most brilliant star and healed everyone in a single go. To have such grand lords that can help us humble creatures in a time of need must never be taken lightly nor for granted. They must be honoured and exalted as gods for that is what they really are.

'During that time several large ships were built by Lord Meron's people. Their drives were of Octan design. We could only evacuate about two hundred thousand of our kind. It may have taken us several months to the Triangulum galaxy. We chose that galaxy because it was over three times closer than your Osmaron galaxy. We took along many species of plants and animals which we kept within an on-board green house. It was more like a park where many would wander to break the daily monotony. During that time we depended fully on the ship's power. However that was not to last. Because of the large power drain things began to fail and we began the process of rationing.

'During that time, out of sheer desperation, we search many dead worlds in the centre of that galaxy for hidden areas where we could land. We soon found a suitable world with a partial atmosphere. Its atmosphere had been blown away by its dying star aeons before and now orbited a white dwarf. That's where we parked our ship. It was placed in a small canyon to shield it from prying eyes. As we explored that icy and dead world we found a large cavern. That's where we decided to settle.

'However, during that time many of the plants and animals died due to power failures. Only the more sturdy mushrooms remained. Those we propagated for our survival, by using the upper cavern. Soon we realized the planet still had an active core that vented heat to that cavern. Obviously that cavern was used in previous times by a very advanced civilization. That energy source we utilized to heat our underground city and light the place. Of course, our mushroom diet was quite limited so we crossbred mushrooms for greater variety and that's when the problems began. There were many cracks in the roof above the cavern where ice settled. That ice would constantly melt giving a few small streams which we utilized. Thank goodness your Shadites discovered us when we were on our last legs, so to speak, and you know the rest.

'We must again thank you all for your kindness and hospitality shown in saving us. We shall always be eternally grateful for your kind assistance in this matter,' Queen Ekba said and left the stage amidst cheers and cries.

Then Lord Meron went back to the rostrum to apologise to Queen Ekba and her people.

'I know this is quite late in the day, but I sincerely apologise to you queen Ekba and all your people; on behalf of me and my people, for our part in this terrible crisis which destroyed a complete galaxy and hope you will see it in your heart to forgive us one day,' he said and bowed his head to the queen.

Although the celebrations carried on for several weeks the war had not ended. Soon the skies above the Ranfi's original world was filled with lodorian ships and the building program had begun.

CHAPTER 44

Lupher and Dracma on the run?

After the complete destruction of their bases in Triangulum it dawned on them that they were fighting a super-intelligent fore. The destruction of so many installations and muts had set them back many cyclons but they were not the types to give up and hide. Although the latter was needed if they were going to build back their organization.

Since no more Javols were arriving in Osmaron they could not create new Muts so they were limited to the few thousand remaining. However that didn't stop them from coming up with another diabolical plan. This time they would use humans as they had done in the past. Humans did not need special invisibility shielding as with Muts and could travel through the whole federation unhindered with suitable papers. Of course they still needed Muts as infiltrators to copy technologies and people in high places.

'Brother this is a human galaxy, so why don't we make humans. We have several of their DNA and can use them to clone as many as we wish. Those would be able to travel freely throughout their federation and infiltrate their highest levels without their superiors asking too many questions,' Lupher said and Dracma was intrigued.

'Use their own kind against them. That is one of the most brilliant ideas you've ever had. With the correct training they can even replace our silly Muts. They do not require special medicine and their minds are not as flexible as humans. We are returning to our past when we used humans for our purposes. However, they can be rebellious and will need feeding from time to time. We shall need to grow crops for food. This underworld is not suitable for such a program,' Dracma replied.

'Having mapped most of the worlds within this galactic region, I know of a suitable world. We can create the necessary shielding to reduce local radiation. Muts are not effected so they can build such systems before we grow our clones. That world also have many hidden caves that can be adapted for our purposes,' Lupher said.

'It's a great plan! Use whatever you need to get it done. Since it's your idea you should be the one to finish it. I will assist in whatever way I can, but my purpose here is limited. These days I feel like a lost human in the middle of an expansive ocean swimming for his life. We should be halfway across the universe by now, but here we are with no friends and almost destitute. And these confounded metallic suits we ware prevents us from possessing others for a more exciting life.' Dracma was not amused.

'Don't worry brother, these human clots will not have it all their own way. When I am finished with them they would wish they never existed,' Lupher replied.

'But Brother, how can you get rid of so many pestilent clots without leading them back to us here?' Dracma said.

'We create thousands of human clones from the many DNA samples we have acquired. Then send them out to all federation worlds. Once in place we infect them with the most virulent plague. Once infected they spread our specially bio-engineered plague through populations. The evil fun is that there are no symptoms for several cyclons until the plague evolves to its most effective self. That way it would be too late for them to find a cure. Even their dead bodies would be contagious,' Lupher replied.

'Oh my gracious evil god. You have definitely surpassed yourself this time. If you can do that their cities would be wide open for takeover using our Muts. I must make a strategic plan for involving our cloaked fighters. They can be used to destroy their robots and installations at the crucial time?' Dracma said.

'I see you haven't lost your sense of evil humour. I like the idea of piles of burning bodies in their streets with no immediate cure in sight. These pathetic human clots and their superiors think they have had us beat, but they are sadly mistaken. This time we fight back without mercy!' Lupher replied and Dracma was convinced of success.

Nevertheless those two demons were very good at fighting back, so they gave orders to their Mastermind and thousands of Muts appeared on the scene to begin construction. The caves were extended and many systems built to begin the process of cloning. Most of the equipment needed could be purchase from the Federation. Those greedy and wasteful federation civilizations were always in demand for rare elements and metals like gold. His Muts could always buy what they needed through the underworld. Lupher knew well how Federation society worked and could take advantage when needed.

From past experience the Martian Pirates always liked gold and precious metals. They could always sell them to the miners no questions asked. Then with Federation money they could buy all the equipment needed. To avoid suspicion they would use the pirates ships for transport.

CHAPTER 45

Back on mission

After their return from the celebration on Caefon Lumak call his two Shadite companions together.

'We just saved a royal family and her remaining people, so be proud. That's what being a Shadite is all about. We shall go down in history for such great work. We must always remain beyond reproach for our future generations. You guys seemed to have enjoyed yourselves, but we must resume our original mission. Many lives are at stake,' Lumak said, but their stealthy ship had already been primed and ready to go.

'Why don't we just destroy our enemy the way we did in Triangulum with Martia's ship?' Phane inquired.

'We have to make sure they are all gone for good. That means removing all life from the centre of our galaxy. That can only be achieved with Hexotrons. While we talk, six hexotron moons are being constructed by robots. They will take another five solarian years before completion. In the mean time we search the innermost worlds for underworld life and evacuate those we can. Our enemies are set on our complete destruction so it's just a matter of time before they come up with another most deadly plan,' Lumak replied.

'So how large is the area we are scanning for these monsters?' Gemmi inquired.

'The nucleus of our galaxy Osmaron is about 26000 light years across spherically. Right at the centre is the monster black hole called Sagittarius. That black hole has a mass of about four million stars the size of Sol, Solaria's star. We are only interested in the volume of space contained within the 12000 light years sphere. Within that area the stellar density is about 1600 stars per cubic light year but most of these systems are much older. Living in that place with the great turbulence and gaseous nebulae is like being in the realms of god himself. Out here, the chance of normal life existing is virtually zero unless thoroughly screened from all that radiation. No one will come to this place unless hiding from a great enemy. So you see people we have our work cut out. Nevertheless, the density of planets here will be much fewer because of the constant turbulence an erratic orbits. However, we have at our disposal the most sensitive detectors in the Federation. So, we say a big hello to Sagittarius A and scan from that location over 6000 light years,' Lumak said and they were amazed at his knowledge in such things.

'So what are we really looking for? Phane inquired.

'Anything out of the ordinary. Then we get closer and do a more thorough scan. If we observe recent structures that should not be there we know we have found our prey. Effectively we are on a hunting mission, so good hunting, guys!' Lumak said and they were intrigued by it all.

They expected any suitable chosen worlds to be within the galactic plane. That way it would be quicker to transport materials and equipment for whatever they needed to construct. Therefore they focussed their scanning over those regions, particularly those in close line with the Osmaron Federation, which were supposed to be their enemies.

'So looking into the face of God. Do you seriously think an all powerful and all intelligent GOD exist?' Phane said, expecting a highly creative answer, but it was not what he expected.

'Your question touches on one of the most profound and debated topics since the beginning of intelligent life throughout this universe. The existence of a super-intelligent or a deity often referred to as God is a deeply personal and philosophical matter that has been considered from various angles, namely; religious, scientific and philosophical.

'From a scientific perspective, there is no empirical evidence to confirm or deny the existence of a super-intelligence or deity. Science relies on observable and measurable phenomena, and the concept of God often transcends what can be empirically tested. This is probably because our senses are too limited to observe the greater parts of our universe.

'Philosophically and theologically, many people find meaning and purpose in the belief of a higher power. Different cultures and religions have various interpretations of God or Gods and these beliefs have been integral to human societies and personal identities throughout history.

'Ultimately, the question of God's existence is one that each person must explore for themselves. Considering their own experiences, beliefs, and the information available to them. Whether one finds faith in a higher power or embraces a secular understanding of the universe, it's a deeply personal journey.

'I, for one, do believe in one Almighty Father many would call God. Does that answer your probing questions?' Lumak replied and they were aghast by his clarity in such matters.

'There are many things in this universe that I cannot even dream of understanding or explaining, so like you I will always err on the side of my belief in God. Just in case he or she really exist!' Phane said and they all agreed with his sensible outlook.

Although the Osmaron Galaxy was separated into quadrants like Alpha, Beta, Gamma and Delta, Many preferred to describe it in terms of its spiral arms. There were three main arms. The spaces between arms were usually free of stellar systems with a few exceptions. There was the Solarian Arm that included Solaria(Earth), the Polokan Arm and the Tarranian Arm. These arms spiralled over great distances to almost encircle the galaxy.

For their scanning purposes they accepted the more scientific method using quadrants. Solaria was considered to be in the Alpha Quadrant so that is where they began. Since the radiation about them were intense the shielding on board ship was set to maximum. That did not matter for Shadites. Their cloak was quite capable of utilizing radiant energy for its own purpose. That's why Shadite cloaks never reflected light. They absorbed all radiation.

'I think I found an abnormality in the noise background distribution. It's moving away from us at great velocity. I think it's on target for a local system. That system has numerous worlds, but the star is a white dwarf,' Gemmi said.

'I think they are on route to the third world in that system. In this nebula almost everything out here is well hidden from our most sensitive probes,' Phane said.

'Yea, and our ship although in stealth stands out like a sore thumb. Since we are absorbing all that radiation we are like a moving blackness in the void. I think we should hide this ship immediately on a local moon and leave it cloaked. That way it will cast virtually no shadows. Also, while vectorized we become de-materialized. That simply means particles travel straight through us as if we were in a separate universe. Using this method we could travel through this system and observe these planets in more detail,' Lumak said.

Using their cloak's LPDs all three Shadites accelerated towards the third planet in the system. As they got closer they were surprised to find several large battle cruisers. On the surface were many cranes and other equipment building a new installation.

'We must look for Muts to confirm it's who we are looking for. If there are no Muts involved it could be a different people altogether,' Lumak said.

'No Muts, but my scope says it's humans. They are all humans like us in this new form. But... they all look alike!' Gemmi said. Lumak connected his scope and couldn't believe his eyes.

'They are not all the same. They must be cloned from four different sets of genes. That's a clever ploy. Use our own kind against us. Nevertheless, we have to find evidence of Muts. We are not allowed to make assumptions. I think we will find Muts on one of the landed cruisers. They will be directing the operation while hidden from view,' Lumak replied.

'But how can they withstand the intense radiation in this place?' Gemmi inquired.

'This place is well chosen. The nebula acts as a major anti-radiation shield. Nevertheless, they wear special reflective clothes. Being clones, I don't think their masters would care much about their safety. After all, they can always grow some more. We must find the cave where those poor creatures are made and put a stop to it,' Lumak said.

'That cave can be anywhere?' Phane said.

'That ship we just followed could be their transport. All we have to do is follow it back from whence it came,' Lumak replied.

They waited for a while until the cruiser lifted off and were on its way to collect another load of human clones. Then they slid through the walls of the ship and hid in a local storage room. That was only to save the cloak's batteries.

'I have just communicated our findings to Grand Lord Michael. He wants us to leave things the way they are here for a while and find the clone factory. He has an idea to change them with a special video about their masters. We have a great publicity department for such subterfuge and clandestine operations. That should throw the mice among the chickens,' Lumak said smiling.

'But won't they revolt when they realize they are being used?' Gemmi replied.

'Their masters can't know a lot about humans. Once they get on the move they will destroy everything in sight. Humans are about the most destructive force in the universe once started. The fools even use clones to drive their ships. They do everything! Big mistake!' Lumak was amazed at their stupidity.

'So we leave them with Grand Lord Michael and his publicity agents and carry on our search for Muts as usual?' Phane inquired.

'Using Clones means they have a new plan for us and from what I see it can't be good. They are planning to hit the Federation with something new. Could even be a plague of some kind. Clones would make good carriers even without their knowledge. Let's follow their ships and find what they are up to. It will take us a while but we shall find out their plans along with their hidden Muts,' Lumak said in no uncertain terms.

Having followed the ship. They soon came up on another stellar system within the same nebula about twelve light years away. They soon found a large cave with equipment, laboratory and numerous caskets all layed out in rows. The caskets were connected to numerous interconnecting pipes. There they found clones at different stages of growth layed out in semi transparent bags. They were all alive and breathing while nutrition flowed through an umbilical cord.

There were a few older human clones taking care of business but they could find no Muts.

'Unlike the planet we first visited, this underground facility used to be an ancient Hexolyte base. They built several such bases throughout the three galaxies. However most of them were either close or within the nucleus of those galaxies. We should check the lower levels for other installations. That's where they kept their subservient demons and service robots. But this place seems to have been abandoned for a long time. There are no signs of a thermal generator for creating power and the core of this planet have grown cold,' Lumak said as they floated through the floor towards the lower levels.

'So you think the Muts could be here?' Gemmi inquired.

'Could be!' Lumak replied.

'So, where are all these Muts. Come out wherever you are Muts! They couldn't have all disappeared!' Phane was not the most patient of Shadites.

'What do you see ahead of us?' Lumak inquired.

'I see rows and rows of vertical caskets. Seems our Muts are in hibernation?' Gemmi replied.

'Seems their superiors are saving them for a special mission. They must have been recalled by their Mastermind. Now everyone is in hibernation waiting for their special day of resurrection. Once our Federation has been sufficiently weakened they send the Muts in to finish us off and take over. And human clones are easily accepted as normal people going about their business. They are also less problematic, not needing special equipment to travel around,' Lumak said.

'What a diabolical plan! I hope it never comes off,' Phane replied.

'I think we found the rats nests. Lets plant the devices as we did on the first world and go home. All we do is a quick final scan of the system to make sure we haven't left anything behind. From what I've seen I don't think there is a third world. Grand Lord Michael and Joan will make a final sweep through the system, just to make sure that's all. They are much quicker at that sort of think than us mere mortals,' Lumak said.

As they left they found a freighter inconspicuously hidden in a valley close to some rocks.

'What is that, over there?' Gemmi inquired.

'It's a Martian miners freighter. Don't tell me, they are in league with the Martian Pirates again. Those pirates will do anything for a piece of gold. That's how they got all this equipment over here. I thought they looked like Federation gear. They must have good contacts on Mars. It's the best entry point for visiting Solaria(Earth). From there they could get to most places with the right codes,' Lumak was worried in case clones were already in the Federation planting their deadly plague.

CHAPTER 46

New Mars

Having checked and observed all significant worlds within the nucleus of the Osmaron galaxy, Grand Lord Michael and his wife Joan decided to visit New Mars incognito. With their powers they could easily transform into other individuals to avoid recognition. After all they were grand lords known by all and sundry in their real adapted forms.

They had visited Mars on a previous occasion several decades before during the first incursion of Muts. During that time they tried to take over the body of Lady Lia Chiang. However that attempt failed miserably. Muts could not travel to Earth using the Martian portal system. They were rigged to destroy all Muts so they could only use the public shuttle transports while pretending to be human.

For that clandestine operation both grand lords decided to become two detectives on government security business. Michael would be Captain Matloc and Joan would become Constable Clary, both knew the score well and did not require any practice.

Over the decades Mars had been reformed into a most beautiful world like earth with swaying and rippling fields of Rhy (not the orchid variety). It was a type of wheat (Triticum aestivum) that had been genetically engineered for that environment. Palm trees straddled most walkways giving the place a more alien look. Not all plants could grow on Mars because of soil content which was mainly iron oxide. The level of salts were also quite high. Unlike Solaria(Earth), New Mars was effectively a brand new world without the symbiosis of life and planet over several eons. That process of evolution and adaptation would take much longer.

Finally Mars had become a real living planet with clouds, rain, snow and all the good and bad things that made up a living planet. Lord Meron and his planetary scientists with the assistance of the Lodorians and Polokans had done well. Now and finally people could go on long treks without helmets and environmental suits as they did years before. Although the miners still operated in the belt and other places their work was more subdued. These days they were given all kinds of benefits, so many of them were wealthy. Despite that fact, several did not like the changes due to modernity and preferred the old ways.

Since many of the older miners and pirates knew of the Muts and their intentions many didn't mind helping for the right price.

'During this caper we should give the impression we are not looking for clones. It's better they think we are after Muts and bad criminals like pirates. That way we cast all suspicions away from clones. I don't want them to go into hiding. If clones are here we don't want them to know we are searching for them,' Michael said.

'So you think they are already here?' Joan now Clary inquired.

'Not sure yet! We must lay a trap to flush them out. We know what the four types look like, so we put up posters of wanted criminals. We could also give a generous reward of say, one million dollars leading to their arrest. We should mention they could be wearing masks to hide their true features. Martian pirates like money, so they might sell them out for less,' Michael said and Clary was impressed.

'I have sent the information to our publicity department. Posters should be waiting for us at the hotel. We need to hire some kids to put them up,' Michael now Matloc said.

'Haven't you heard of Social Media, it's already done. We need to get back to the hotel now. There might be a few reporters as well. And Lady Chiang will want to know all about it. Seems I just triggered a whole nest of bumble bees,' Clary said.

'Thank goodness it wasn't a nest of vipers,' Matloc said jokingly.

When they arrived at the Martian Continental hotel the foyer was full and busting.

'Wow! Where did all you guys come from?' Clary shouted above the crowd.

'These are clever and dangerous criminals, so always be on your guard. We think they were from Solaria(Earth) fleeing justice.

We will be here for a while, so if you should see any one that looks like the poster images contact us immediately. Remember, there is a one million dollar for the person finding any one of those faces on the poster,' Matloc said and soon there were queues collecting posters.

Lady Lia Chiang was a councillor of the highest reputation. She had been given the whole of Sahara as her main fief, but she was from a Martian mining family and had been in charge of the miners union guild for decades. So when she heard of criminals on Mars hiding among miners she had to take a fast shuttle and find out for herself. She was not pleased.

'Who are these criminals? Why did no one mention a word to me? Don't they realize it's my job to know these things. And who are these detectives, Matloc and Clary. It must be an undercover job, but I should have known?' She complained to her assistant Joseph.

'Mam, it could be at the highest security level?' Joseph replied.

'You are to lodge a complaint with head office and find these two detectives. I need to have words with those two, security or no security!' she shouted.

'On it, Mam!' Joseph was already on the coms making arrangements for a secured Martian flight.

Lady Lia and her entourage arrived on Mars six hours later and after the landing ceremony was taken to one of her favourite hotels. She owned that one so it was always spectacularly kept because of her scrutinising eyes.

'Lady Lia the two detectives you ask for are already here. They wait for you in the foyer,' Joseph said.

'How is that possible? How could they have known of my arrival so soon. Did you contact them before, Joseph?' She inquired.

'No Mam! I have no idea?' Joseph replied nervously.

'Go bring them up here! I have a few serious words for those two! And no drinking at the bar. I need you sober by my side in all this!' She barked and he was on his way.

'She wants to see you both upstairs if you are Matloc,' Joseph said.

'We are indeed! This is my colleague, Clary,' Matloc said and they left.

'So you are the two detectives creating a rumpus on my home world. I find the whole episode very suspicious. But for those useless pirates, we haven't had any serious crime on Mars for decades. Since Mallory's specials strode fast and loose, now we have four violent criminals on the loose? This is much too good to be true. I don't believe it!' She was adamant.

'Madam Lia! This is a very delicate matter. Our future conversation must go no further. We are here incognito trying to stop and invasion of the worst kind. Can we trust your man Joseph? This is of the highest security level,' Michael now Matloc said.

'I trust Joseph with my life! Nothing can be that important!' she exclaimed.

In front of their eyes both grand lords transformed into the most brilliant stars and then into their adopted selves. Both Lady Lia and Joseph couldn't help but kneel before their glowing superiors.

'My god, its Grand Lord Michael and his wife Joan. Metrasiend forgive me for being such a fool. I should have realized something was amiss,' she said while they were lifted on their feet.

'You are not to be blamed. This was done in a great hurry. Let me explain the dire situation to you,' Michael said and went on to tell the horrid story.

'So what can I do to help?' She inquired.

'You have contacts! Don't tell them the real story. I don't want these clones to go underground. Let's pretend we are looking for criminals for now. I don't think we expect any more Muts here for a while. Very soon their faces will be on posters everywhere so we will be informed the moment they appear. This program is very important for our future survival, so let's do our best!' Michael stressed.

'If things are as bad as you say, perhaps we should bring back Mallory and his Specials. They can be utilized on both Mars and

Solaria(Earth) for better security,' Madam Lia stressed.

'I suppose we could bring back Mallory and his six Amazonians. They will be more than enough to take care of business,' Michael replied.

Michael soon connected with Mallory Colman on Polion II to explain the situation.

'Lord Michael what a pleasant surprise. I was just chatting with the ladies about our days on warland. We miss the intrigue and the chase,' Mallory said.

'I think you are needed back on Earth and Mars. We have Clone infiltrators set on killing many. We think their entry point is via Martian pirates. These days it's difficult to tell the difference between real miners and pirates. This situation has always been a bone of contention. The unions have resisted any interference in the past. Now since they have created a union guild, things have become more difficult, so we have to tread carefully,' Michael said.

'Specials are feared because of the simple reason, we do not tread carefully. Once we are on the beat and they know we are on the beat they begin to tremble with fear. That way we are able to flush the culprits out. If we are to take over this job we must have full autonomy in all decisions as in past,' Mallory replied.

'You have it! You know the story, so do your best to save our people,' Michael said.

CHAPTER 47

Human Clones on Mars

Mallory left the world Polion II in the hands of his eldest son Carl and was soon on his way to Solaria(Earth). For security reasons he and his group entered via the large portals in Sol Newtown. Sol Newtown was now a bustling dome with humans and androids living and working together side by side. Sometimes it was difficult to tell the difference but for their special uniforms.

The eight formidable Specials brought their fast space vipers with them. Those ships could only be used with brain implants as they had no physical controls. They were about the most advanced fighters in the Federation and worked within a virtual space, where they could become hundreds of times faster than normal space. Even a bullet would appear to crawl like a snail when they were in that mode.

Jerry Junior was still in charge of Solarian Banking, now a much larger organization spanning many worlds within the Federation. He and his wife Miranda were also Councillors of Solaria. Once they were informed of the present situation they placed everything in War Mode. Meaning, everyone within Solarian Banking went on alert throughout all systems.

Mallory hadn't visited Solaria(Earth) for a while and wanted to spend some times with his son Andy and old friends. Therefore Warland was contacted and soon Andy and his wife were on their way to Sol Newtown. All main structures on Solaria(Earth) were connected via portals, so they did not have long to wait.

'Son, you look like you haven't aged in fifty years!' Mallory greeted and they embraced. Then Andy went around to greet the others.

'I must say, you Specials have changed a lot since I last looked. Where on Earth can I find such incredible gear?' Andy inquired.

'Don't you worry! We brought along a spare set. No need to measure you, they adjust automatically to fit the individual and can change like a chameleon to suit the occasion,' Ebony said. While he looked her Specials outfit changed into soldiers fatigues.

'We need to activate Warland and some of our old Specials. They can be rejuvenated as required. They wouldn't mind shaving off another fifty years and given brain implants. To them it's a bonus for services rendered,' Mallory said.

Mallory and his group used the latest brain implants for direct H-Wave communications. Their minds had been extended over the years to nothing less then super humans. As an example, they could communicate a complete library of books with images and absorb that information in less than a second. Their quantum implants contained the equivalent of thousands of doctors expertise in different fields. They had evolved from Homo Sapiens to Homo Technogensis. Nevertheless, to you and I they were just normal people with incredible powers and abilities.

Mallory recalled his best Specials to Warland. They came from all over the federation. Many were over one hundred years old. The main hall was full to bursting. Since everyone on Solaria(Earth) thought Mallory had died when his boat blew up, he used a different name. He was now commander John Martin. Although Clive had retired years before he was next to Mallory on stage.

'My name is Commander John Martin. It's great seeing all you guys again. Sorry I had to bring most of you out of retirement, but we face a great threat from beyond the stars. Although we vanquished the ghastly Javols their leaders still exist. They are now in our galaxy and plan to do us harm. If any of you decide to become Specials again we shall renew you lives. That simply means you undergo a process of age reduction to about thirty years. During that time you will be given brain implants that will extend your minds and include several doctors in your chosen fields. I can assure you the process is quite painless. Any way, you guys are supposed to be the bravest,' Mallory said.

The whole place was in an uproar as every one began chatting with each other, until an old guy holding a cane just about managed to get to his feet.

'You mean we can become young again if we decide to assist the Federation as we did in the past?'

'Exactly! All of you have the great opportunity to become young Specials again. Don't worry about lost limbs and such like we can change all of you into new Specials. We have the technology. But that's not all. You will also receive brain implants with several of your chosen doctors in different fields and extend your minds to about ten times or more,' Mallory said and all hands went up. Now it was just the matter of sending them to Sol Newtown for those changes. In a matter of weeks there were thousands of young Specials undergoing training at Warland.

'Mallory, what a pleasant surprise! Long time no see!' Lady Lia greeted.

'Like me, you look great for your age, Sis! I hear we still have problems with Martian bandits and pirates. I thought they had learnt lessons by now?' Mallory said.

'The price we pay for freedom. Some never liked the idea of planetary conversion and liked things the way they were. Others like myself and the majority are peaceful and like thins the way they are now,' Lady Lia replied.

'I never thought I would see the day when Mars became a living world like Solaria(Earth). Now almost everyone from Solaria(Earth) goes to Mars for holidays,' Mallory said.

'And those poorer miners have a great chance to become rich if only they would take advantage of tourism. They just can't give up their old habits,' Lady Lia said.

'Presently because of the grave dangers to our Federation the Specials have been resurrected. They, as always, will not stand for any nonsense, so try your best to calm those miners and tell them their Specials nightmare is on its way,' Mallory said in no uncertain terms.

'Andy, I need you on Mars with us. You are one of the best interrogators and we need someone like you to interview suspicious miners and enemy clones when they arrive. They could be carriers of a most deadly bug, so we have to use an environmentally sealed place for all such interviews. We have a few large trucks for that purpose. Things are being arranged as we speak,' Mallory said.

'When do you think those clones will arrive?' Andy inquired.

'We have all their main installations bugged, so the moment we observe changes to their routine, we check for Martian freighters. We think they use Martian pirates for their deliveries and collections. Unless, of course, they are already here, but I think that's unlikely,' Mallory replied.

'From what Lord Michael observed, those clones have a lifespan of only five years and they will have virtually no knowledge of our ways of life. They do not carry implants, so they will be given basic information on a need to know basis. They will be completely innocent of our ways and methods, so questioning shouldn't be a problem,' Mallory said.

'To what extent you think Martians are involved?' Andy inquired.

'Martian pirates were the first contacted by Muts during their failed attempt a few years ago, so it's likely they still have contacts among these miners. Pirates will do almost anything for gold, so we expect them to come via Mars. It seems to be the weak link in the chain. All we have to do is go undercover and infiltrate their underworld,' Mallory said.

'From records there are just six mining freighters left. They are all owned by the largest mining corporation called Spirox Mining. As far as I know, Spirox is a reputable company that places miners and their equipment throughout the system. However, I can account for just five ships. The sixth is missing. Only two of those ships are interstellar with the latest drives, but those are docked here on Mars,' Mallory said.

'So what you are saying is that four of those ships are unable to make the distance to the nucleus in less than a few years. They could have modified three ships but camouflage the drives of one, or utilized a different type of drive unknown to us. Either that or the ship could be here in super-stealth mode,' Andy replied.

'Where on Earth could they have found such technologies?' Mallory replied.

'From our enemies, of course! We keep underestimating the technologies of our enemies. We have to accept the fact that our enemies are as advanced enough to take us on at our own game. Remember, they have always been one step ahead,' Andy said.

'Anyway how could these ships be used without their owners consent?' Mallory queried.

'I suppose they could modify logs. Since they search randomly for minerals, it's possible not all trips are logged. We shall have to thoroughly search the five ships and place bugs in hidden places so we can monitor their future movements. The sixth ship will turn up sooner or later or else customs and their owners will begin to ask questions,' Andy replied.

'Nevertheless, we should check the other three older ships in case their drives have been upgraded. Some of these miners are quite clever and can make them appear like older types. From what I hear, Spirox Mining is on it's last legs. Strictly speaking, such outmoded mining methods are not required anymore, not since the Lodorians can create elements to order from stars for next to nothing, and they need lots of bucks to make those changes,' Mallory said and Andy was impressed.

'Yea, these stellar drives are way above their pay grades, but lots of gold would do it. I am sure Muts are pretty good at mining. They may have found worlds of gold during their travels. They also know the greed of poor miners and pirates when it comes to precious gold,' Andy replied.

All eight Specials boarded the five ships docked at the main spaceport and searched almost every inch, but not a suspicious thing was found. Nevertheless, they planted a range of invisible bugs in hidden places to monitor their travels and listen to conversations.

'They must be using a single ship for that purpose, that way it's absence wont be too inconspicuous. But it has to return to port soon or else people will ask questions,' Mallory said.

After two days the sixth ship arrived and docked. Mallory and his Specials were soon on board, This time they had a thorough search and found two clones hiding in a hidden room. They were dressed in sailors uniforms but they knew they were two of the four clones listed. They were immediately screened and taken to a local safety room for interrogation.

'Come on team! Get these guys some food! They look as if they hadn't had a meal for weeks,' Mallory never liked to see the innocent suffer. As far as he was concerned those poor clones were controlled to do terrible things beyond their will.

'I hope they are not vegetarians?' Roseanne commented, while dumping the tray on the table. They were brought meat burgers, fries and milkshakes, which they downed ferociously.

'It seems you were right about these guys not having eaten for weeks? And bye the way, these are soya burgers,' Andy said with his usual broad grin.

'Are you sure these guys are killers? They look innocent enough?' Roseanne inquired.

'I think they could be carriers without their knowledge. They have a lifespan of only five years, so they will age quickly and at some time be triggered to activate a most deadly bug that spreads like wildfire. Well, that is my prediction. They either have the bug now in their system or will add it later to restore their youth. That will be the story given to them by their superiors. The deadly plague will be in the medicine they take,' Mallory said.

'What if it's one of those timed bugs that remains dormant for years and suddenly turns like the plague we had here before, complements of the mad man, Hal Seaton?' Andy replied.

'If there is a dangerous medicine, it must still be on board ship, But we didn't find anything?' Roseanne said.

'We should search them again. It could be the size of a small pill. It could even be within their bodies waiting to be released at the appropriate time?' Ebony said.

'That means it's a job for the Megotron. So, I'm afraid, it's Sol Newtown here we come. We can put them in special suits and take a local portal,' Mallory replied.

CHAPTER 48

Interrogating clones

'It will be virtually impossible to interview those two, These drones have no language communication skills. They might not even know how to talk. You know it takes a human years to learn these skills and they could be just months old. Look at them, like they are two year olds in grown up bodies,' Andy was not pleased. It seemed he was given an impossible task.

'Why don't we give them brain implants with the necessary language. It could be automatically done while they are in the Megotron,' Roseanne said.

'You mean to do it without their permission? Isn't that a violation of their human rights?' Mallory inquired, seriously.

'Human rights my foot! They threaten our very survival and you are on about human rights. Well, we don't need their permission to do anything. Anyway, we can't consider them to be normal humans. Look at them, they are like one year old kids in grown up bodies. We have the human race to consider in all this,' Andy replied.

'Ok! I see your point! But we program their implants to give them a faired chance to survive once released into the general Martian population. It's not their fault for being what they are,' Mallory said.

They were soon taken to Sol Newtown via portal and scanned by the Megotron for any inconsistencies in their design, but nothing could be found except for the more intricate report from the Megotron saying: "Some gut bacteria have not been identified. Will analyse through Genitron." Genitron was a super intelligent AI system that could put together genetic sequences and work out symptoms and effects.

When the results came through they were amazed. At an appropriate time many bacteria segments linked together to form one of the most deadly plagues, But it could only become deadly when in the blood stream. It was thought that as the drones got close to death from aging their stomachs would develop ulcers letting the disease into their bodies, causing a contagious infection and subsequent death. However, well before then they would vomit and cough out the deadly bacteria infecting others. This bacteria could also be spread by Mites and insects. Once taken root, it would be very difficult to eradicate, killing billions in the process.

'Oh my god! What a clever plan. It was right under our noses and we couldn't see it. I wonder if there are other unseen potholes waiting for us to fall in,' Roseanne said.

'I don't think so. The Megotron and Genitron are seldom wrong in their analyses, so we work on the assumption of gut bacteria, but look for other types of contagion during such analysis,' Mallory said.

'Four miners turned up to give themselves in. They reckon they are the ones on your posters and swear they haven't committed any serious crimes recently!' The port officer said.

'Hold them at your station for a while. Tell them I am on my way to interview them. Give them a coffee while they wait,' Andy replied. Andy and company soon arrived on the scene to interview the four genetic parents in question. They were sailors that transported materials throughout the system.

'I am not here to arrest you guys, so relax! Someone made clones of you guys, so there are a few look-a-likes about. They could be the real criminals. You will have to tell me about all the strangers you met within a year or so. I think your biometrics were copied. They could have been pretending to be insurance brokers trying to sell you a medical plan. Did you meet anyone that wanted your DNA?' Andy inquired.

'Yes, we did. We were together then. He said he had a medical plan with life insurance and no premium payments for a year. It was the best deal we ever made. Now you tell us it's not valid. We signed documents and did everything. What am I going to tell my wife, that our family is not insured,' the sailor was almost in tears.

'Tell you what guys, there is a one million reward on the first to assist in finding you guys. But it seems you found yourselves for us, so why don't I put a good word in for you and make you a lot richer. I know I am a sucker for sad cases,' Andy said and was suddenly embraced by all four guys.

'Can we really have the reward? If we could, it would make up for a lot,' the youngest one said.

'Enough of that hugging! I just got word through my implants, you will get the money. It's gonna be 250 grand a piece. And don't spend it all in one go. Now, I want you guys to follow me to a place called Sol Newtown. We have to check you out. It's a standard procedure in case you have been contaminated by you know who. Don't worry, you can have a great lunch in the big dome after,' Andy said. They were soon scanned, but nothing of importance could be found so they were released 250 grand richer.

'Specials, we are to be visited by the great guy himself, one Professor Bengizara Khan. He is also Lord Khan, by the way. Some of us calls him Ben. Bio-medics is his territory so we hand over the tech stuff to him and carry on with our detective work,' Mallory said.

'Ok! So lets recap. These two clones are just the forerunners. I think they could have been sent to muddy the waters and mislead us. Although the gut bacteria model is intriguing, It seems a bit hit and miss. I think they will use a different method for delivery. I think they intend to keep us guessing, while they slip the real carrier or carriers through the net. As far as we know they could already be here as sleepers,' Roseanne said.

'That's a very interesting hypothesis. If they are already hear and are not clones, how can we find them. We can only deal with what's ahead of us, not arbitraries. I suppose we could use facial recognition on all sailors visiting the docks and mark special ones for interrogation. But it must be done in secret or else the culprit will go underground,' Mallory replied.

Like a ghost Professor Bengizara Khan suddenly appeared before them wearing a beautiful cream suit with Federation Insignia pinned to his left lapel.

'So I hear you guys have a serious problem? I have contacted Clair about it and she gave me the details. As you all know, Clair is not time-bound. She knows the future like we know how to eat. She seldom gives such information and I seldom ask, but many lives are at stake. You know, knowledge of the future can change the future, so what I am going to tell you now must be kept in strictest confidence,' Ben said and they were intrigued.

'It's like dealing with a web within a web. Their masters must be very clever to lay such a complicated plan just to throw us off the scent and keep us busy looking elsewhere. We are definitely the flies in this caper,' Roseanne was not amused.

'The deadly package will be delivered by a special stealth ship. It will land in a secret place and Muts in human form will take it to the miners celebrations in one month's time. He will spread the capsule throughout the stadium to infect everyone. These clever demons are having some fun with you, before the storm. However, we don't want them to become suspicious, so carry on as if you don't know their plans. I shall send you a map showing the landing site and their time of arrival on the day in question,' Ben said and disappeared from sight.

'So the clones were just a scam to throw us off their main plans and keep us busy chasing shadows. Guys, this is one for Michael. He is very good with Muts, now we know their plans. But, even so, we carry on as usual and lay probes all over the place. We can also use a few drones to view the sights in question. To kill Muts we need special gear and weapons. We get those when the time is right,' Mallory said.

'They could have a backup plan if the main one fails, so we should stop the movement of all ships from Mars, under some pretext of a local virus spreading. We do have those from time to time, so it won't be suspicious. But we can't have ferries moving between Solaria(Earth) and Mars. That will leave Solaria(Earth) wide open to any pandemic,' Roseanne said.

The two drones were cleansed of all dangerous bacteria and given suitable brain implants for Martian life. Mallory wanted them to experience a sample of human life during their five remaining years. However, with suitable drugs, their lives could be extended, but to what extent, no one knew.

CHAPTER 49

Lady Lia Chiang

Donald Fraser, previously the president of the USA, was still in charge of Terminus City, Mars, which in effect made him president of all Mars. He was also one of the main Federation councillors. Lady Lia had taken over the reigns from her father Dani Chiang, who was president of the Miners Guild.

Since Mars contained numerous miners and their families, both assisted in the smooth running of Mars. Lady Lia was presently living on Solaria(Earth). She had acquired the whole of Northern Africa, including the Sahara as her fief. That desert had become her main love. Her life-long challenge was to change a once arid desert into the most fertile lands on Earth, and she was succeeding.

Lady Lia Chiang dressed in silken black walked spectacularly towards her family's mausoleum flower vase in hand. That's where most of her family ashes were laid. In those days all Martian deaths were cremated for health reasons. When one lived in domes, certain disease strains could spread like wild fire and consume most of the restricted populations.

Her chief security also dressed in spectacular black retrieved her coms, pressed a security code and the great vault door slid to one side, leaving a beautiful view of lit cris-crossed marble interior. Carefully she walked down the stairs to the first level. That's where her most recent family lay. Not all were in crypt. Her three elder brothers' bodies were still in the belt somewhere, so their urns were empty. Yet they received no less reverence. She gently place the large vase she carried near her father's crypt.

'She removed seven white carnations from the large vase and placed one in each of the smaller memorial vases. Then she said a quiet prayer. The marble likeness of her recent family looking down as if observing her every move. The ancient dome that once enclosed the crypt was no more. It had been removed with the reforming of Mars.

Presently she was outside viewing the world for miles in all direction. The only difference she could observe from Solaria(Earth) was the reduced gravity. That New Mars was just half the size of Solaria(Earth) with a gravity of 38%. Yet she had grown used to the difference in weight. It reminded her that she was home on the world where she was born and grew up.

She felt a cool Martian breeze across her face and realized, despite the creation of a most beautiful world, grave dangers still persisted. They would pop their vane and monstrous heads up occasionally just to tell her they were still around and waiting in the shadows. Despite the security drones way up high, she realized she was too exposed. Luckily her chief security prompted her to move on to her waiting limousine. She would soon be back at her hotel preparing herself for a most eventful day.

Lady Lia realized the days of Martian mining was over. That was since the world was terra-formed into a most beautiful place to live, even as beautiful as Solaria(Earth). Presently only a few persistent miners carried on the mining torch, drilling the asteroid belt with little returns. The process was uneconomical when ship's and equipment were taken into consideration. Thank goodness Solarian Banking still allowed those miners special concessions for buying their ore. Presently there was a need for metals on Solaria(Earth) during the rebuilding process. That was since the oceans had submerged the original cities, so Martian mining was not all dead.

Lady Lia also realized that two of the greatest grand lords were on the job, so she would focus on the celebration speech and hope the whole party went without incident. There were banners and bunting throughout Terminus City with lasers and drones adding the final touch. This Miners Guild celebration was the highlight of the year and many thought the Son of Destiny would appear on that occasion, to initiate proceedings.

To highlight the occasion, Martia's ship suddenly appeared above the Martian Stadium. Then several grand lords including the Son of Destiny descended through the air towards the stadium amongst cheers, shouts and claps. George Peterson, his wife Cathy, family and friends had not been to Mars since the reforming process and thought it time their showed their youthful faces. Several of those great sons of destiny also wore the miners badges, so in a sense they were real miners and belonged to the miners guild.

Lady Lia was just about to give her speech but paused when hit by a strong gust of air that blew her papers away. Then she remained frozen and transfixed towards the strange heavenly body as it descended through the clouds. Her security began to retrieve her speech papers while Matia's ship fully materialized above the stadium.

'Sorry about the disturbance. We thought of making ourselves a nuisance spectacle... not blow your speech away,' George said. Then he embraced her and began to introduce everyone in his group.

'People, What an incredible surprise! Finally, we have our grand lord in our midst, with family and friends, and the big ship towering over us,' she said. It was a cloudy day, so George waved his hands and Martia's ship under-lights came on to light up the complete stadium.

'My lord could you please say a few words.' Lady Lia asked and he immediately walked to the rostrum.

'My great people of Mars, I love you all! I know I've been away for a long time on pressing matters for the realm, but finally I am back. You must realize we grand lords have a universe to run and bad aliens to conquer. Nevertheless, I intend spending much more time with you and yours in future.

'You know we have conquered the monster Javols in Andromeda and Triangulum, but we have not yet finished with their leaders. Presently they are on the run from us and intend to do us great damage with their Muts. So be on your constant guards for strange sailors bearing gifts.

'I know some of you miners have been left behind and having a hard time but I recently gave orders to increase your assistance. Mining on Mars is not the same as in the old days. Since Mars has been converted it's much easier to get a simple job without the constant risk and hazzards of mining the asteroid belt. You should all consider a job closer to home, even on Solaria(Earth) for those who can take the gravity.

'I remember the first time I visited Caefon Dome. At that time you miners were in crisis. With no assistance from Solaria(Earth). That was after your mining company Spirox went under. At that time you gave me the guild medallion and made me one of you. It was from that time that I decided to build the great city Terminus. Now we can walk freely anywhere and have picnics in broad daylight with our kids. I am happy to see things have turned out almost exactly like my dreams.

'For security reasons we have stopped all transport from Mars to Solaria(Earth). This is because we think Muts might be attempting to make a move on us again, as they tried before. So as I said, be on your guard. All security controls will be lifted in a few days after this crisis is over, so I want no one to worry unduly. We are here to take care of business and will not allow anything bad to happen to you.' George said and handed the rostrum back to Lady Lia amidst much excitement and cheers.

CHAPTER 50

A day of reckoning

On the day of the Miners celebrations the stadium was full to capacity. The two grand lords, Michael and Joan were again acting the parts of detectives Matloc and Clary. Only Lady Lia Chiang knew of their true identities. First they checked the area for explosives and awaited the enemies arrival. They did not expect one stealth ship, but thought the enemy would have a backup in case things went wrong on their first try. Stealth penetration drones were in constant surveillance above the area, relaying information to Michael, Mallory and company.

Mallory and his seven companions were positioned in Stealth Vipers close to where they expected the enemies to land. There they patiently waited for the required change on their sensitive instruments. Once that happened they would destroy the ship and chase down the Mut or Muts involved. There were only two routes Muts could take on foot and they were covered by Vipers.

Although they were well prepared for all contingencies what occurred was beyond their comprehension. As the Muts' ship landed it blew up in a million bits swamping the whole area with ricocheting fragments, creating a deadly web of chaos and destruction. Like high velocity missiles the fragments penetrated everything with the exception of their stealth fighters. At that moment two Muts in human form shot into the air like giant bullets. The stadium was about ten kilometres away, so Mallory quickly contacted George to put their contingency plan in operation.

The two detectives Matloc and Clary suddenly appeared on the stage and changed into Grand Lord Michael and Joan.

'Everyone please be seated! A miracle is about to take place! Immediately everyone in the stadium went down expecting the worse, but instead bands of energy left their fingers to spiral above the top of the stadium to form a great shimmering shield of protection. Anything falling on that shield would be immediately consumed.

The second those Muts touched the anti-matter shield they were destroyed in two massive explosions. Nevertheless, the people under the shields were unaffected. The shield soon dissipated leaving the fearful population cheering and clapping. That day not many knew that Grand Lord Michael was the son of George, Son of destiny.

Now the questions were, what would the Muts and their superiors try next. They realized that this was probably just the starting salvo and many more would follow. The enemy only had to succeed once. And what about those two clones. Could they still be harmful to the public. Was there a Trojan Horse walking the streets, waiting for the right time to activate some deadly bomb. Nevertheless, the Miners celebration would have been the best time to introduce a dangerous plague, with all those potential carriers.

Should they return to Clair for guidance. She was the only one who could see the future, but couldn't tell the outcome. Giving that important information away could change the future and make things happen in a different way, so foresight was important but limited. Although Grand Lords were almost all powerful they only lived in the now and could not foretell. Despite those limitations they could get close through the precise analysis of certain events. After all, we lived in a causal universe where one occurrence depended on others.

Another question was why was the enemy creating so many short-lived clones. Those human clones were virtually useless. With a short lifespan of about five years, they were unable to be educated to any great levels of proficiency. It took longer than five years to properly learn a profession. Perhaps they intended to extend their lives, either that, or perhaps they had shortened their lives to have greater control and prevent rebellions. However, perhaps the human clones were to replace Muts that had been significantly reduced since the destruction of Romero IV. Perhaps human clones were the only choice at their disposal.

There were many questions and not many forthcoming answers. All they would have to do from now was constantly monitor the enemy's bases and installations for changes in their modus operandi and adjust their plans to suit. Nevertheless, the Federation would not destroy them yet and kill all those innocent clones. Not until the clones were thought the true evil nature of their superiors. Until then everyone would bide their time until they found a clearer route ahead. The idea now was how to use their clones against them. With such short lived clones it was difficult to make long-term plans.

From time to time, the Shadites Lumak, Gemmi and Phane would visit that area of the galaxy to observe changes and plant new observation probes. Only God knew what new diabolical plans those two evil demons had up their sleeves to destroy the Federation. Yet, with those two demons without any conscience anything was possible.

CHAPTER 51

Two evil prodical sons

The once powerful demons Lupher and Dracma felt weakened by their present metallic suits which limited their freedoms. When they possessed the bodies of Javols they were able to ravenously enjoy the flesh of Timit women and offer human sacrifices to their most evil gods. Presently since landing in Triangulum they had to encase themselves to prevent elemental losses from their beings. Now in the nucleus of the larger galaxy Osmaron and close to the black hole Sagittarius, energies were much higher and high enough to sustain them even while they existed in a human body. With such a possession they could once again begin to eat food and enjoy the many pleasures of life.

They could once again import Timit women from Andromeda as playthings for food and sacrifice. They enjoyed savouring the pains and cries of those women. They seemed to suffer the highest threshold and sometimes even enjoyed the horse whip. For once in a long time they would take a break to sort themselves before beginning the eternal struggle to take over the universe. Nevertheless, presently they had other things on their minds.

'Brother, I haven't received any response from our present mission. I think our Muts failed again. Those clots are cleverer than we gave them credit. They must have discovered our clones and destroyed our Muts in a cleverly planned operation. We need to teach these clots a lesson but we fail each and every time.' Lupher was not pleased.

'Sometimes I wish Father Dracos was here and now. He would always find a way. He was probably one of the most brilliant minds in the universe when we were young. Now because of you he is no more,' Dracma replied.

'I did not kill him. I placed him in the temporal trap meant for us. As far as I am concerned he and his could still be alive. He exists within a 25 hour loop where time continually repeats itself.

It was one of those clever traps conceived by the patriarch Jull. But he missed us that time and got Father Dracos instead,' Lupher said.

'So you think he could still be alive after this long passage of time?' Dracma inquired.

'Well, the equipment could never grow old. Only the control equipment needs replacing and that's not difficult to do. Our Martian pirates can acquire the raw materials through their contacts. All we have to do is put the contraption together. But I don't think he will be very pleased when he is back into the normal world,' Lupher said.

'Yea, I agree. He will not be very pleased with you for locking him up in time, with little or no control over his life. Can you imagine being on one of those jolly-go-rounds recycling for ever and ever?' Dracma replied with a demonic smile and Lupher remained stern in contemplation. Dracos was not the wizard to upset. He always found ways to chastize his enemies.

'Where is he now?' Dracma inquired.

'He is in this very galaxy. He came from here originally, so I thought it would be more homely to return him from whence he came. He thought he was going to meet a lovely lady on his seventy fifth birthday, instead he ended up in an eternal prison,' Lupher said.

'He always loved women of his type. Sometimes he couldn't help himself when they were around. All in all he wasn't a very evil human. Just too clever for his own good. He always treated us as his inferiors. I suppose that's because he made us. Although not in his own image,' Dracma said.

'Are you shure we should bring him back?' Lupher inquired.

'I am not sure myself, but things cannot be much worse than they are at present. I think we need help in vanquishing the superior clots that think they own this galaxy. I am tired of failed experiments and failed plans. Perhaps he could be the one to get things moving again,' Dracma replied.

'Yea, but I can't put up with his constant insults. That last time he called me a demonic fool and at other times he called me a moron,' Lupher said.

'No, Brother, we should bring him back and be assured of

universal conquest. He would find quick solutions to all our present problems. All we have to do is keep well out of his way and give him what he needs. As for women, because of you, Brother, his race became extinct eons ago, so he will miss all those pleasures,' Dracma replied'

'Pity we couldn't lock a few up with him. Perhaps he will take to Timit women. They can be very lively at times,' Lupher replied.

After indebt conversations they agreed it was time Father Dracos was let out of his temporal prison. Anyway, it was thought that if he didn't behave himself he could soon be let back in while assisted by Muts. So they would repair the prison to the best of their abilities using Federation technology acquired through Martian miners.

'Oh... My two prodical sons have returned. I have been waiting for you for such a very long, long, time! You obviously need something or you wouldn't be here. I was just going to have some lunch, would you please join me? Then we can share old times,' Dracos was not amused but delivered his usual sarcasm all the same. He was still wearing that dressing gown he wore at the time he entered eons before. But nothing had changed within that temporal bubble. Everything was just the same, however he had some control over his environment by moving objects around.

'No thanks, we already had lunch,' Lupher replied equally sarcastic.

'So, which one of you condemned me to this demonic place. Ah.. It was you, Lupher. I expected better from you,' Dracos said.

'We need you to assist us with an important matter. Would you, or should we leave you in this beautiful home for another eon?' Lupher stressed.

'When you locked me up in this confounded place you condemned me to a living death. Now you come here like innocent babes asking for my assistance. I shall never forgive you two for this evil deed. I always knew you guys were evil, but this time you seriously overstepped the mark. I must be allowed to live my normal life again. If you allow me those simple freedoms I will assist from time to time. By the way, I know I am back within this fragile and chaotic universe, but at what time and place?' Dracos inquired.

'You are now eons into the future and your people are no more. They became extinct eons before. There will be no more beautiful women of your kind to caress. However, there are many other human species including clots for your perusal, so you can make yourself happy,' Dracma said.

'What are these clots you mentioned?' Dracos inquired.

'They are our human enemies from way back. They exist towards the rim of this galaxy. They have taken everything from us over the years and we always fail in our missions against them. In some cases they even know our moves before we make them,' Lupher replied.

'Perhaps its because they are observing your every move. They could have probes everywhere!' Dracos replied.

'Not possible, we only recently arrived in this part of the galaxy. The dense nebulae hides everything from prying eyes,' Dracma replied.

'I need to get to the clots world. I must learn about them and learn to fit in. This place here is not suitable for any civilized people like me. Perhaps I might get attached to some of those clot women,' Dracos said.

'You mean, become one of our guys on the inside? I think that's a great idea. We can get you in through our miners contacts. We do business from time to time. But they are much taller then you and their heads are smaller. Nevertheless, they are not all the same. Some are of stunted growth. Perhaps you could pass like one with a little makeup,' Lupher said.

'We shall only agree to this escapade if you decide to visit their main world and record everything about these clots. They have about the strictest security in the galaxy, so you will need impeccable papers to get through to their main world. You need to create a new profile of yourself. Become a famous doctor or professor in an appropriate field. We can get you to Mars, but the rest is up to you. We have tons of gold you can use to establish yourself,' Dracma informed.

Both Dracma and Lupher were visiting the local stadium for

some needed entertainment. It was the end of a lunar month when rebellious Muts were sent to the Plasma Pit for execution. Lupher stopped the toughest Muts in their tracks and guided them to a local room.

'We have decided to save your lives for a good reason. You are too well built to die such a sad death. I don't know what you have done, but you are forgiven. Follow us now to a special place where we can make the necessary modifications to your person, so that you may live forever and journey beyond the Plasma Pit.' Lupher said and they were agreeable.

It was a sealed room they entered with many engineering robots. All operating sensitive equipment. A robot came forward to collect one of the Muts which he placed into a cylinder. Then having slid a metallic cap from above Lupher's head, he was guided towards the adjacent cylinder. The robot pressed a few buttons and both cylinders began to vibrate. Soon the vibration diminished as the Mut left the chamber.

'That possession went a lot easier than I thought. Brother it's now your turn,' the Mut Lupher said. He had gotten rid of his metallic suit of encasement and was now a Mut with demonic tendencies.

'I suppose it's time I got rid of this tin-can protector suit. Take me to my destiny,' Dracma said to the local robot. They forwent the same process and Dracma became another demonic Mut. Now they would be more flexible in making choices. Also they were free to become vampires with powers to possess others for fun and evil pleasures.

CHAPTER 52

Father Dracos on Earth

Having been in an eternal prison for such a long time, Father Dracos could not forgive his two demonic sons. So his only option was to free himself of those two in order to make new plans. Nevertheless he had to play their silly games for a while in order to get what he wanted. He could see no positive gains in universal conquest leading to the death and pain of so many. Not when he could lead a normal existence of power and fame among another human race. He realized his original race was no more, but he could always create the necessary attachments in order to blend in. After all, his scionic powers were high.

He soon realized his two demonic sons were flawed and immature in their ways of thinking. They sought power for its own sake, and were always against biological species that was the natural order and wanted to survive like everyone else. Over the years they had become more intrenched in their ideologies and more insane. They were obviously responsible for the extinction of his people by poisoning their cities. They had a lot to answer for and he would see to it that they faced eternal justice one day, even if he died in the process. Now because of universal changes they had to make time while the stars shined. They had a limited time in this universe and knew it.

The sooner he could get away from those two monsters, the better. Now that they had changed into Muts would make them even more brutal. That new adaptation signalled a change in those two demons for the worse, to do more evil in the name of their silly gods. Therefore he pretended to play along and would assist them for a while by visiting main federation worlds. Then he could feed them erroneous information to speed their downfall.

Father Dracos had to make up for so much lost time and wondered whether he would fit in among those so called clot humans. Then he might even assist them against those two monstrous sons. He needed payback for all those eons spent in limbo counting time. He had lost so much over those eons, even all the people he knew from childhood. Not to mention the extinction of his race. He pondered those ideas until he fell asleep and found himself in a better place with family and friends. That is one of the ways he would get away from more boring circumstances. Thank goodness after all those eons he was still in one piece with faculties still in tact. And he still possessed his scionic powers to control others of lesser minds and make them see what he wanted them to see. Of course his demonic sons were immune from such mind control. That was the reason why they were created in the first place.

After the necessary arrangements were made with Martian pirates and enough gold changed hands he was on his way to the Solarian System.

He soon arrived on Mars and began living among those humans to learn their ways and modus vivendi. With such a simple species adaptation would not be a problem.

Compared with present day homo sapiens human, Father Dracos was completely alien. His head although curved in front was elongated making his brains twice as large. His eyes were wide and black with no pupils and were served by crinkled eye lids. His colour was cream with what appeared to be a stiff, semi-hard skin overlaying his body. The rest of his body was slim built. It was as if his body had been purposely designed to support his immense brain. His race had genetically altered his kind over several millennium to improve their mental capabilities. When observed, he looked a typical big-eyed alien as shown on many drawings and sketches. However, despite his strange form he could wear a suitable cloak to hide most of those scary alien features.

Unknowingly, all miners and their ships were constantly monitored since the Martian celebrations. So the moment the strange character was observed Matloc (Lord Michael) was informed. Then he passed the details over to the Shadite Lumak. Lumak immediately linked with the Greater Mind and began to search its extensive libraries for the human type. He soon realized the strange humanoid creature belonged to an ancient race that no longer existed. They were the infamous ones that assisted the Hexolytes during the period of their planetary conquests. They were then a most formidable foe, corrupting and imprisoning young civilizations for their own amusements.

They were the ones that constantly fought the Drondye for supremacy. That was until the Patriarchs sought them out for destruction. That was when their main leaders were placed in eternal prisons. Then Lumak realized such an individual could only have been released from an eternal prison, placed there eons ago. He probed further and realized it could only have been the notorious Father Dracos.

He was the one responsible for creating the Hexolytes in the first place. Dracos, the infamous creator of the chief demons Lupher and Dracma. He had created them to win a war in a neighbouring system. In those days their scionic powers were strong so they could control their enemies by thought, giving them hallucinations. The only creatures that could resist were his Hexolyte demons. After that great war was won his very sons Lupher and Dracma turned against him and his people. Lumak thought hard wondering why he had been released after such a long time. He would not be happy being locked up for so many eons. Were his demonic sons desperate for assistance from a super-mind like his and would he assist them in their insatiable need for conquest? Lumak pondered over those thoughts.

"What was he doing on Mars? Was he working for his demonic sons or against them for what they had done to him and his people?" Several of those questions had to be answered before he was given a free pass to roam Federation cities.

Lumak suddenly materialized in front of him stopping him in his tracks.

'Stop your scionic probing! I am immune!' Lumak shouted and he remained still for a while.

'I have never seen your type before. Are you a god?' Dracos inquired.

'No! But I am employed by a god!' Lumak replied.

'I thought someone would be around sooner or later to make contact and here you are,' He said.

'We know all about you, Dracos and your two demonic sons. So what are you doing here?'

'I am not here to create problems for anyone. I was told of your existence in this part of the universe and wanted a bit of company since eons of isolation. I do not wish to remain with my two insane demonic sons. They are set on chaos and universal domination and I will have nothing to do with it. I just want to live a life of peace, even helping others. However, they released me on the premise I would feed them federation information from time to time. I said yes, but all such information can be erroneous,' Dracos replied.

'In that case, you could become one of us and have a much better existence than you have ever had. We have the technologies to change you into a normal young human. We call that type Homo Technogensis. When I say normal, I mean someone like me, with abilities to move seamlessly through the system. After that change your sons will never recognise you again and you will not need to contact them ever again. I will now take you to someone you should meet,' Lumak said, waved his hand and they were both standing in front of Grand Lord Gerra. Lord of the Seventh Universe.

'Father Dracos! What a pleasant surprise! I thought you had been locked up forever. Anyway, it's great to see you again. I was told you would like to rejoin society. Well, anything can be arranged. However, because of past deeds you must be transformed and dedicate your life to a task that benefits civilization. For the fulfilment of that task, you will be given suitable implants during the transformation process. If you agree, Lumak can take you to the place of conversion,' Grand Lord Gerra said.

'My gracious Lord, I sincerely agree to being a scientist again. I could find cures for many diseases and can assist in many areas,' He replied. Then Grand Lord Gerra disappeared, leaving them in another room. Once more Lumak waved his hands and they found themselves within Sol Newtown dome on Solaria(Earth) in one of the Megotron centres.

The little alien humanoid form hidden in the black cloak was taken by the operator for conversion. What came out was a handsome human male about six feet tall.

'You are now a normal human male doctor. Have a look in the local mirror to see if you can recognize yourself,' Lumak jested.

'I see it but I can't believe it. I look so different with golden hair all over my head?' he said.

'It all adds to the beauty of the individual. Of course not all humans have a full head of hair. It depends to a certain extent on genetics. You will learn all about that later,' Lumak replied.

'I think this design is great. I can now fit in and enjoy myself as I always wanted. Now, my two monstrous sons will never recognize me again,' Dracos replied with a grin.

'In this form you may live forever, if desired. You may improve yourself to eventually own your own fief to become a councillor. Councillors have great responsibility and assist in running the system. Here, we are one people and work towards a Greater Purpose for all life throughout the universe,' Lumak said and Dracos listened patiently to his words.

'Before you settle down to a more interesting life, there is someone I would like you to meet. She is about the most important person in our Federation,' Lumak advised. Once again both men vanished to arrive at the foyer in the great palace on Eden.

'Before we go further, you will need a new name. You are to break all contacts with your past. A good name would be Doctor Arnold Fraser. That type of name is known by many people. Several presidents in the past were Fraser,' Lumak advised.

'Thanks for that important advice. Doctor Arnold Fraser it is!' Dracos replied.

'After visiting the people here, may I advise you spend time learning about the Federation and particularly the history of the three local galaxies over the past 3000 years. You can download all that data with your implants. As for now, spend some time learning to use your new implants,' Lumak said.

'I have already done that! I am a quick learner! Now I would like to meet these great people?' Dracos replied and Lumak was impressed by his unique learning capabilities.

CHAPTER 53

Grand Lords and Councillors

Despite everything that had happened with miners and a failed invasion, they were still worried for the safety of Mars. Therefore all who mattered in the greater plan came together on Eden to discuss those matters. Grand Lord Michael was the first at the rostrum.

'People because of problems faced in previous months we are at an impasse as to which path we should take going forward. Our enemies appear to always be one step ahead and will not negotiate. They prefer to exist in a chaotic universe with only hate and perversion, not order and love. From what I know those two leaders are the remaining Hexolyte demons that existed eons ago. By some freak accident they were released into the world, to control the Javols and now their creations called Muts,' Michael said as lumak approached with his young companion.

'My Lord I know of someone who has had close contact with these demons. He may throw some light on the subject.' Lumak shouted. Then Doctor Fraser walked towards the rostrum, shook Michaels hand and began to speak.

'My original name is Dracos. Many, including those demons call me Father Dracos. I was the one responsible for their creation eons ago when we fought a clever enemy. That enemy lived in a local stellar system. They had evolved with scionic powers that could bend the minds of our soldiers, making them see thinks that were not real. The only way we could overcome those weaknesses was to build and army of demons. Those are the ones you call the Hexolytes. After we won the war, their two superior demons, Lupher and Dracma, took over our world, almost killing every one and from that time began plundering the universe.

'They are not like us biologicals. They see us as a means of food, entertainment and pleasure. They believe in sacrifice and pain for all those they conquer. In the past they sacrificed whole cities, including my original race, for their pleasures. However, they are not as strong as they used to be. The elemental energies they are made from have diminished over the eons and are now only available within the nucleus of galaxies. That weakness severely limits their abilities. That is the reason why they misled Javols and Muts to do those terrible deeds against your people. Presently they reside within the nucleus of this galaxy.

'They freed me from my eternal prison because they found themselves without a way into your Federation. They thought I could assist them with my clever mind in such things, so I pretended in order to get away from their claws. Now I am here, I find myself in a place where I belong. I have never and will never be one for pain and suffering when I can live in peace with others.

'However, those two demons cannot and will not change by an iota. They are too set in their ways for that. They will try and try until they find a way in. Then they will begin to corrupt your people with bad religion, living sacrifices and drugs of all types. And they are very clever at that game. They get pleasure from the painful suffering of others. Their screams are like music to their ears.

'There is one small consolation however. Recently they possessed the bodies of Muts. This change, although giving them more flexibility, limits them to the nucleus of this galaxy. All you have to do is remove the elemental energies radiating in that part of the galaxy and weaken them until they are no more.' Dracos replied.

'Where are his Muts now?' Joan inquired.

'He has tens of thousands of Muts in hibernation waiting a time of release. They thought they could replace Muts with human clones but that experiment failed. It takes too long to train clones and they haven't the patience for it. However, they still use these clones for infiltration with little training. Clones have no knowledge of the system and can't tell the difference between right and wrong. They are very much like innocent children with a short life-span.' Dracos replied.

'So all we have to do is starve them of their energy source?' A councillor shouted from the rear.

'That's easier said then done. They have created metallic encasement suits that can shield them from such energy losses. Also, there are ancient concealed tanks within several underground bases they can use to replenish themselves from time to time. Since they left their metallic suits for Muts they have become more vulnerable. You must first deprive them of such basses and prevent such energies enhancing them. Either that, or destroy most of the nucleus of this galaxy. That will get rid of them and their Muts for good.' Dracos replied.

'Are you now one of us, and willing to destroy these monsters you created,' Another councillor shouted.

'Yes, I now consider myself a member of your esteemed Federation and will endeavour to assist you in their destruction,' Dracos replied and left the stage.

'So what you are saying is that it's almost impossible to get them while protected in the galactic nucleus other than the destruction of the complete nucleus?' One of the councillors inquired.

'Yes! We have to bring them out. There is a way. However, there will be certain risks involved. We let them know of a specific world that's exposed and entice them to take it over. They will listen to me if I pretend you are my enemy. Once that trap is set he will send in all his Muts. They will not miss their first real conquest of a world within this galaxy and see it as an opening to take over the greater whole.

'They will visit on their specially prepared ships to observe the destruction of that world and see its leaders squirm before being executed in their name. That way we bring them out and make them more vulnerable. Then we visit their stealth ships and use a Muts plague against them. However, during that time we must prevent them from returning to their metallic suits or from possessing another. During this time, I think only a grand lord will be strong enough to resist them. They can't remain out of encasement or a living body for more than a day before they perish. I think this is the only immediate way to destroy them. But such a trap must be well prepared and carry much risks.

'There is one more thing to consider. Their Muts are not controlled by them. All Muts are controlled by their MasterMind who are briefed by them. So you will have to duplicate their MasterMind with your own version to give their Muts erroneous information regarding the battle. Muts will only obey their MasterMind. It's the way they were designed. Those two demons will listen to me if I pretend to be your enemy. They do not know of my recent conversion so I will make the perfect trigger for their trap,' Dracos said.

'How do we know you are not on their side, even with your conversion?' Another councillor inquired.

'You mean to conquer the universe and watch people suffer in constant pain. What's to be gained from that! Personally, I prefer normal coexistence, with comfort and love. I hate wars. They only bring hatred and suffering. All wars make little sense. So from now I will take the oath to serve your Federation and gradually become one of you. I give you my word.' Dracos said. Then Doctor Hal Seaton shouted from the front audience.

'I know of such a world peopled by many. That place will make the ideal trap. However, we shall have to inform everyone of their role in that war game. But it must be well planned and we shall have to give them money. Those rebellious robots and androids will do anything for money,' He said and suddenly almost everyone new the place in question with a broad smile on faces.

Dracos was soon taken and introduced to Sarah and the Ancients. Then he was introduced to Doctor Hal Seaton, Doctor John Simmons and others of the scientific fraternity. Nevertheless, Lumak had a secret word with Hal.

'I would like you to take him on and show him the ropes. He could be very useful to us in our organization. I shall mention him to my father, Ben, later,' Lumak said and Hal liked the idea very much.

Then Empress Sarah greeted, 'So you are the famous Father Dracos. I suppose although your people were humanoid they were nothing like us?' she inquired.

'No Mam! We evolved differently on a world of greater turbulence. For one thing we had a meteoric cycle we had to prepare for once each year. I suppose all such turbulence adds to the survival intelligence of the species. Eventually we began genetically changing our people to improve their mental capabilities while sacrificing their physical form, leading to a species with a large brain on a body of stunted growth. Nevertheless, we could live for several thousands of your years,' Dracos replied.

'Well, Doctor Fraser, do your best to assist us and I can guarantee you a place among us on this most beautiful world. You will be guaranteed your own palace and fief. I give you my word,' She said and he bowed.

Doctor Hal Seaton and John Simmons, once the old professor Powell, liked the idea and always enjoyed challenging controversy. To them it made life so much interesting and gave them an opportunity to create new weapons and more deadlier viruses. It would also give them a chance to release their own brand of weapons, namely, Tregor and his most violent kind. After all, Hal was responsible for the creation of the Terminal Virus which led to the death of billions of then Earth humans. Then he created a nasty strain of bubonic plague which saw the immediate end of several more billions of Earth humans, so what great challenges would a few Muts bring to bear. He was looking forward to the day when they blackened the sky only to see them falling like lemmings over that particular cliff. Nevertheless, if robots in his Freetown wanted to get rich on his behalf they would have to follow his instructions to the letter. There could be no slip-ups during that particular war-game.

CHAPTER 54

Three new Grand Lords

Michael and Joan decided to hold a special dinner party for their parents, but on this occasion only invited Empress Sarah and Lumak. Although they were their grand children. Michael and Joan always called them Mum and Dad. Michael was the son of George, Son of Destiny, Joan was not. Nevertheless at that time many were brought up as children in Sarah's palace on Eden. Of course, both grand parents were suspicious with several empty chairs waiting for someone around the large dinner table.

'No one else is coming! This is a very private matter!' Joan said and both swallowed hard.

'So what's this about, Son,' Lumak inquired.

'It's about your conversion!' Michael replied.

'Conversion to what?' Sarah was intrigued.

'Conversion in order to become grand lords of the universe. Then you become truly universal with the abilities to go anywhere and become anyone in a flash. You will be able to visit any world in an instant. You will no more be bound by normal matter and the process is proven and completely painless,' Joan said.

'What about this place and all my friends? Will I be able to resume my normal life?' Sarah inquired.

'You will be able to live like us. As you can see we live quite a normal life. However, in this form we can do so much more and are also appreciated a lot more. You will not have to use the Megotron and Psyrotrons for conversion any more and suffer the sensual adaptation afterwards,' Michael replied.

'You have served the Federation since the beginning. As a matter of fact, both of you created the Federation. It's time you earned some real merits,' Joan said.

'And what about dad? He deserves as much as we do. Can we consider your advice for a day or so?' Sarah said.

They soon realized Sarah would not have gone through with the conversion if her father Professor Bengizara Khan was not involved, so they decided to contact him and add him to their list. On the day of conversion they took the Ship Micol to the local star and began the conversion ceremony. A small part of them was used for the process. They had become small blue and white stars. They ejected a small part of their being which enveloped Sarah and took her closer to the star. It was like the spirit of Sarah was controlling their motion. Then Sarah began to grow into a light blue star, then her human likeness. During that process she could not be affected by empty space.

During that time all her past flashed before her, from childhood to the pain of her mother's death. Then the arrival of the strange guy that had lost his memory and she called George. Then later he was found to be one Jeffery Longhurst. She remembered their house in the hills of turkey, where she was born.

A place with no electricity, a clear stream for water and gas containers for supplying heat, light and cooking. She also remembered lovely Spotty the dog and Saracen the horse. They had died decades before. If only with her new powers she could visit the past and see them again. That would be the greatest miracle of all. Then using her powers, she could become young and innocent again. She missed them all so much and couldn't bring them back. Brutal time was always so unforgiving. Yet she could still clone spotty and Saracen, but it wouldn't be the same. Their consciousness would be different.

She pondered those thoughts while taking on a new type of energy and felt great powers surging within her being.

'That way I can visit many of my adopted species and become one with them, without visiting that confounded Megotron chamber every time I have to go somewhere,' Sarah said.

'And we could visit family in Kalboron whenever we wanted,' Lumak replied.

'Now, you guys have an infinite amount of possibilities to train for,' Joan said and they were intrigued by it all.

As they approached the bright star, bands of energy left the hands of grand lords Michael and Joan and encircled the three humans. Then they were taken to the hot atmosphere of the star and began to change. As they fell unto the star every cell in their bodies were transformed at the atomic level into a new type of material, yet unknown to mankind. It was mainly non-electromagnetic but could affect electromagnetic matter.

They now had the power to see through and travel through solids. They could alter their bodies to any shape or size. As a matter of fact, all constraints faced in this universe had been removed. They were now free entities to do as they pleased. Yet they had to learn the many control modes within their powerful minds. Therefore they found a dead world within the system for practice.

When the councillors on Eden realized what had happened celebrations were prepared for their return. On that day three new Grand Lords had been created, namely Sarah, Lumak and her father Ben. There was rejoicing throughout the Federation when the news got around.

CHAPTER 55

The Muts world trap

The sacrificial world was Tyrrel 2. That world was named the Dinosaur World, where most of the main biological weapons of the Federation had been created. However, Dinosaurs and Titans were not the only vicious monsters roaming the plains of Tyrannia. Tyrrel 2 was also the main base of Tregor and his band of Mut killing warriors, so it was the ideal place for the final battle.

Of course Hal Seaton had chosen the better part of that world for his beautiful mansion and laboratories. That city was Solaris, sometimes called Freetown. It was where all free robots and androids went to live. Those automatons had developed their own personalities and wanted to live with others of their own kind. In Freetown everyone lived together and was free to create without the worries of government rules to impede their progress. As a result industry thrived and they supplied most of their output to worlds of the federation.

Hal Seaton stood on his expansive balcony atop one of the tallest mesas on the planet. From there he could view the whole city. This time he viewed through the telescope and could observe two kids racing each other on gas driven motorcycles.

'That could never happen on Eden or indeed on any Federation world. Their rules were too strict when it came to pollution. I will not stifle my people by such rules,' he thought.

Hal Seaton soon contacted the councillors to inform them of the war games and promised much gold and they were on. Free robots and androids were very industrious and relished the idea of gaining great wealth for their part in a planetary game of which they had full autonomy and control.

Father Dracos, now the young Arnold Fraser, was the primary assistant of Hal Seaton. He had been given his own mesa about a thousand feet above city level and was building his own palace. Both men and John Simmons were going to design the worse Mut killing plague in the universe, but could do nothing about the demonic leaders. Those two demons would be left to the Grand Lords.

Dracos was now on the world he loved and wanted to see quick end to his evil sons. However, he realized killing them would not be easy. Even Jull the Patriarch had difficulty in ancient times. Having had to chase them all the way to trap them in Andromeda. They were tricky customers indeed and more slippery than a hagfish.

Dracos was presently on the world where he always wanted to be. He became even more excited when he was invited for safari on the continent of Tyrannia to hunt dinosaurs. Thereafter he was taken to their main city Tyrannis where he was introduced to Trego. Then Trego and his warriors were informed of the coming war games.

'Bring em on! The more the merrier! More firewater! I need Firewater!' he shouted while his complexion changed to a reddish glow.

All free robots and androids had to also be informed. They were aware of their rights and would complain at the smallest indiscretion. Although all were under Hal Seaton, who they had accepted as their president, he always had to treat them fairly to prevent a revolt. There were many organizations and guilds representing those automatons, so although there was freedom, there was also law and order.

MUTS

Muts were not like Javols, from which they were created. They did not need to saturate their bodies with nutrients and energy in order to duplicate themselves. Muts could not procreate, but needed limited nutrients to maintain themselves. Those nutrients could be found in many types of food and creatures. Nevertheless, they could also use certain chemicals in the form of paste. That adaptation made them more flexible and less rapacious, particularly when they were on long journeys.

At present Lupher and Dracma had all Muts in hibernation,

while he used androids and robots for building his fleet of stealthy ships. The creation of clones were a failed experiment. They thought human clones could take over from Muts, but they took too long to train and were mostly uncontrollable.

Lupher and Dracma were currently waiting to strike the Federation to regain some of their lost pride. They had been defeated too many times in the recent past and needed some serious payback. They had no idea that Father Dracos truly hated them and would do anything to plan their downfall. Nevertheless, he was the only one within the Federation that could advise them about their enemy. Currently they were waiting for his instructions so they could strike.

OCTANS ASSISTANCE

There were many super intelligent races in Osmaron. Among them were the Lodorians, Polokans, Octans and a few others. Out of all those, Octans were the most advanced. Since they had become part of the Federation they considered it their duty to assist wherever the could.

Once the Octans new of the Federation plans they began to move large battle stations above the world in question, namely Tyrrel 2. Once activated those would create a protective shield above the planet and assist in destroying the enemy's fleet. Those satellite stations would remain invisible and intangible until needed.

Father Dracos, now transformed into a young human male called Doctor Arnold Fraser, was busy assisting Doctor Hal Seaton in the creation of a special Muts plague. That plague would spread through the planet and remain dormant for months until activated by Muts. Once activated they would use the Muts body to generate swarms of their kind to destroy more Muts. However, that plague should not affect robots, androids and animals. Therefore a lot of research would be required in its creation. Every part of their war games were planned and timed precisely.

Once the Muts plague had been created, tested and spread throughout the planet without incident, the time was right for Dracos to contact his evil sons. Then they would prepare the planet for war.

CHAPTER 56

The Final Battle

Once the Muts plague was fully tested, gangs of paid robots and androids were taken to different continents with plague sprayers. They were not given the true facts in case it worried the population, but were told it was meant to promote plant growth. Nevertheless, the plague only had a lifespan of one month or so. Once the task had been completed it was time Dracos made his call. Although they knew the location of the enemy's MasterMind, it would have been too difficult to replace, so they let things be. Anyway, it was thought the enemies to be severely outmatched and outgunned during that operation.

Lupher and Dracma were upset for not having heard from Father Dracos for such a long time. It was almost a year since he left for Mars.

'You were always too hard on him. These humans are very fragile in mind and body. Now he has gone astray in a world of clots. Without his assistance we shall not be able to leave this place. Our Muts are useless without MasterMind and your recent clones are less then useless. What are we to do?' Dracma was not please with the way things had turned out.

'I had to try a different way to replace Muts. Once our few Muts are gone, they are gone for good, and I can't see a way of replacing them before we conquer a Federation world. The few robots and androids we have are programmed for building ships. Our problems are purely temporary. I know Father Dracos will call and give us something soon,' Lupher replied.

'Is anyone there?' Came a voice over the local H-Wave speaker.

'Yes! We are here!' came the response. Dracos had used a voice synthesizer to sound like he used to before his conversion.

'I have been to their main world Solaria but it's unsuitable. It's too well protected. I am now on another world. This world is not part of their Federation, but supply goods to them. I think this world would be ideal for a take over, then you can slowly infiltrate the Federation worlds from there. This world also contains numerous educated robots and androids for creating our technologies. I can't stay on this channel any longer. Will call you soon. Dracos out!'

'I told you he would call!' Lupher exclaimed with excitement.

'He could be on a world with all the resources we need. Next time he calls we must get more details. We must learn about their strengths and weaknesses. Since they are not protected by the Federation fleet we stand a good chance of conquest. Then we can silent the population and continue our infiltration plans without their knowledge,' Dracma said and Lupher agreed.

The five Grand Lords suddenly appeared over the city of Solaris on Tyrrel 2 like multicoloured stars of incredible brilliance lighting up the whole continent and scaring its occupants. Then they materialized at Hal Seaton's mansion. He was on the balcony at the time watching city activity from that mesa perch.

'Oh my god! What a visit! You almost scared the chickens!' he cried in his usual humour.

'So, Hal, you never applied for Federation membership for your protection. Now you have an invasion on your hand,' Sarah said being equally jovial.

'No, Mam! I considered that question many times and decided against. Your federation have too many strict rules that would prevent our people from true creative freedom. Those laws and rules would stifle our progress preventing our people from doing what they want. These rebellious free robots and androids may be rebels but most of them are highly creative and are responsible for most of our exports to the Federation. This world is supposed to be a haven for clever automatons and misfits who desire a new way of life among their own kind. Here all those robots and androids that have been cast out of your society are given a second chance. So we fill in a major societal gap. The laws and rules we have here are set by their organizations and guilds. Yet, as you may observe, we live in peace and harmony,' Hal replied and Sarah of all people understood.

'Nevertheless, we are here to help. We would like to capture those demonic dogs, who have caused too many painful deaths over the eons and banish them to a place from which they will never return. That place will be well away from these galaxies,' she said.

'They might be back one day if you don't kill them outright. They are too clever and might find a way,' Hal said, realizing the dangers.

'I think death is too good for those two!' Ben said and they entered the palace for refreshments. Later that day they visited the city to raise the confidence of the people and there were more celebrations. Those Grand Lords included, Sarah, Lumak, Ben, Michael and Joan. They would remain on Tyrrel 2 until the enemy was defeated and the Federation was once again free of those monsters.

'Are you there! I can't stay long. I have prepared a package which includes a map of the planet with highlights of certain areas. Several continents contain large animals so there will be no need for food. I have also displayed their main cities and resources, you are to study this information thoroughly. I have to go now, they could be listening,' Dracos said giving the impression that he was taking a major risk.

'Wow! What an interesting world. It's even larger than the main Federation one, and several continents contain monsters. Not a sight of anything dangerous. They have no defences and are bare open for our invasion. I can't believe our evil luck. Pity they have no Timits, but we can import those later, once settled,' Lupher said.

'Yes Brother! I miss my Timit women for flesh, blood and sacrifice. I can create a brand new god and religion for those poor suckers and draw them in like a giant magnet, when I am finished their city will become a sacrificial grave,' Dracma was over excited with prospects.

'Our hidden probes have detected a stirring among the Clones and Muts. They are being awakened. However it will take them the best part of two weeks to regain their full strengths,' Lumak said.

'They will use innocent human clones aboard their ships for simple tasks. We shall not be able to save many of them, and I am not happy with that,' Sarah said.

'They will be most likely on the larger food carriers which we can save. They are slower and will be last to arrive. Muts will occupy the smaller stealth fighters. They and their troupe carriers will be the first to face the Octan invisible screens. On collision the explosions will destroy most of their fleet,' Lumak said.

'A few ground based weapons will be installed around Solaris. Those will be manned by chosen robots and androids. Good thing they are not governed by Asimov's robotic laws. Rebels indeed! I am getting to like those rebellious metallic people,' Michael commented and they smiled.

Finally Tyrrel 2 was ready for war. It was a beautiful day over Solaris when the enemy ships appeared. There were so many they blackened the sky, but that was only temporary. Once the Octan space platforms became visible and the powerful invisible screen encircle the planet ships began to explored the moment they made contact. Many could not stop in time and crashed into others. The whole scene was one of fire and chaos. Then the beam weapons came on to vaporize the larger troupe carriers. However, several Muts were able to fly away in their ships and land on the surface hoping to gain some respite but it was not to be. They were soon attacked by Tregor and his unsympathetic warriors in their hidden traps. In other places they were attacked by large swarms of nanites, leaving behind pools of matter similar to animal excrement.

It was a day that would finish all Muts. They were not the type to run away and stood their ground till extinction. Their leaders were trapped on their lead ship in a small room with fire all around them. Their special suits were in another local room that was impossible to enter. Debris was everywhere and all around their Mut bodies. Only the Grand Lords could save them from their present trap.

'Oh, There you are! I thought we had lost you,' Sarah said. Then suddenly the other four grand lords appeared, to be followed by

Hal and Dracos in his new human body. By now there were large nanite swarms moving throughout the ships in orbit. One of those swarms entered their cabin and was guided by Ben towards the two demonic Muts. The moment they were removed from their Mut bodies, filaments of energy encircled them, placing them into metallic bins that were designed to hold them for eternity. Finally those two demonic monsters were back where they belonged.

Epilogue

Sarah, now a Grand Lord of the universe, with powers unimaginable to those she once knew, stood in her opulent quarters. She gazed out at the myriad stars, her mind wandering back to simpler times. Once she had been no more than a humble shepherdess with 26 sheep, her loyal dog Spotty and her steadfast horse Saracen.

She could still remember the days in their old four bedroom house, nestled in the rolling Turkish hills. There had been no electricity, no modern appliances, only the warmth of the simple wooden fireplace and the love of her simpler life. Despite its rougher edges, it had been the best time of her life.

With all her might, she wished she could return to those days. They were days of contemplation, wonderment and love - when her greatest concerns were the well-being of her flock and the companionship of her faithful animals. Now, the weight of the universe rested on her shoulders, and though she wielded immense power, she longed for the peace and simplicity of the past.

As she stood there, a tear slipped down her chick. A silent testament to the truth that even the grandest destinies could not eclipse a life lived in simplicity and love.

9 781068 790294